# THE COASTGUARD'S HOUSE DARLING ISLAND

POLLY BABBINGTON

# HELLO

Words, quilts, tea and old houses…

My words began many moons ago in a corner of England, in a tiny bedroom in an even tinier little house. There was a very distinct lack of scribbling, but rather beautifully formed writing and many, many lists recorded in pretty fabric-covered notebooks stacked up under a bed.

A few years went by, babies were born, university joined, white dresses worn, a lovely fluffy little dog, tears rolled down cheeks, house moves were made, big fat smiles up to ears, a trillion cups of tea, a decanter or six full of pink gin, many a long walk. All those little things called life neatly logged in those beautiful little books tucked up neatly under the bed.

And then, as the babies toddled off to school, as if by magic, along came an opportunity and the little stories flew out of the books, found themselves a home online, where they've been growing sweetly ever since.

I write all my books from start to finish tucked up in our lovely old Edwardian house by the sea. Surrounded by pretty bits and bobs, whimsical fabrics, umpteen stacks of books, a plethora of lovely old things, gingham linen, great big fat white sofas, and a big old helping of nostalgia. There I spend my days spinning stories and drinking rather a lot of tea.

From the days of the floral notebooks, and an old cottage locked away from my small children in a minuscule study logging onto the world wide web, I've now moved house and those stories have evolved and also found a new home.

There is now an itty-bitty team of gorgeous gals who help me with my graphics and editing. They scheme and plan from their laptops, in far-flung corners of the land, to get those words from those notebooks onto the page creating the magic of a Polly Bee book.

I really hope you enjoy getting lost in my world.

Love

Polly x

# 1

---

Lucie Peachtree peered out the kitchen window as a tractor slowly chugged down the lane. The lane where Rob had said they would get away and start afresh. The lane where he'd said it would be easier. The lane where he'd said they would hopefully start a little family in the country. Their children would have the same idyllic lifestyle he'd had. He'd said they would create memories there, grow old together there, drink bottles of sloe gin by a roaring fire there, and spend Sunday mornings snuggled up in bed.

Lucie had not been all in at the start; she hadn't wanted to live in a little village in the country, but Rob had talked her round. Life in the country had its challenges, but it would be amazing, he had said. They would live their life to the seasons; it would be pitch black in winter by mid-afternoon and the long summer evenings would be spent strolling hand in hand down the lanes. They'd grow vegetables, their little ones would potter around in wellie boots, they'd spend long hours exploring in the woods, and they'd stroll to the pub on Christmas Day.

Despite her misgivings, Lucie had decided that in the end, she didn't have a whole lot to lose. They'd been trying, unsuccessfully, for a baby for years, she could take or leave her job, and the housing market had rocketed, putting them in a very nice position to move wherever they fancied. It had never been a better time to sell, Rob had said. They would sell everything from their old life and rent a little place in a village while they looked around to buy.

Lucie had slowly come to quite like the country living idea and had thrown herself into it with gusto. She'd made up a Pinterest board on all things country, gathered books on growing vegetables, collected recipes for preserving, and had learnt the ins and outs of the best ways to keep bees. There'd been a brand new waxed jacket hanging in her wardrobe and she'd labelled one of the accounts in her savings with 'shed'.

And so, when a Grade II listed cottage came up for rent with a garden for bees, a coop for chickens and a log burner tucked in the sitting room, she had been there with church bells on. There was one small problem with the bells; as it had turned out in the end, Rob hadn't wanted a bar of them at all. He was, in actual fact, somewhere else ringing somebody else's bells altogether.

She hadn't known that then, though, and had thrown herself into it while Rob had told her he was at work; she'd refreshed their living room, styled every inch of their house, trimmed the hedges, painted the garage door, and jet washed the drive. She'd liaised with the estate agent, showed a couple around the house, and before she'd had time to think about it too much, they'd exchanged and were on their way to life in the country. It had all been perfect and idyllic and fabulous. Just. So. Lovely. Until it really wasn't, until it really wasn't at all.

Because what lovely Rob, who had been working all hours while she'd been boxing up their belongings and selling their house, had omitted to tell her about their idyllic new life in the country, was that actually, he wasn't going at all. And what she had technically done while she had been manically attaching brown tape to moving boxes was wrapping up their life. To make matters worse, on top of her facilitating the practicalities of concluding their years together, it had all ended with a note. A note and a baby. A baby who very much wasn't hers.

Lucie looked around at the cottage kitchen with its café curtains, the tiny table perched in the alcove by the window, a door you had to dip your head under to a minuscule utility room, a couple of steps up to a cosy living room, stairs coming right down into the middle of the house. Oh, how she had grieved in that living room. On that sofa. Long, gin-fuelled, binge eating sessions where she'd watched films, wished she'd had a happy ever after, grieved the miscarriages, stuck pins in pictures, and drowned her sorrows into her hairbrush. She'd cried and danced, screamed into cushions, eaten whole cakes in one sitting, and wondered if she would ever feel even half-normal again. Wondered if she would ever not feel sad.

The cottage and the little village with its solitary pub, many tractors, sweet old ladies with baskets, and Creepy Man on a bike had actually ended up being her saviour. She'd revelled in its solitude, battened down the hatches, cried a million tears, stalked Rob on social media, and felt all sorts of guilt about analysing the looks of a pregnant woman she didn't even know.

And then one night she'd arrived home from work, dropped her bag on the floor, got a bottle of wine from the fridge, heated up some onion bhajis, filled the funny little bath as full as it would go, stripped off her clothes, got in with her phone, and started viewing properties. Her rural country idyll was very much dead, but maybe there were other options still alive.

With the last third of the wine left in the bottle, the bath continuously being topped up with hot water, her hair washed and in a turban, she had looked at houses up and down the country. A flat in Edinburgh with a clock tower on the roof, what looked like not more than a cupboard in Notting Hill going for an extortionate amount, a farmhouse in South Wales with complimentary sheep, and a Georgian townhouse in Bath with a basement sauna. None of it had really done much to float her boat, and as she'd been about to put her phone on the side, finish her glass of wine, and pop in another bhaji, suddenly, something caught her eye. A post about a little place not far away on the coast.

*Imposing House by the Sea*

*This elegant and most impressive double-clad house is located in a historic part of Darling Island and boasts exquisite views over towards the historic Royal harbour and out to sea. Situated within walking distance of the iconic tram and Darling Street with its mix of local shops and cafés, it's the perfect location for relaxed coastal living.*

*With a whole host of original features on offer, this gorgeous house won't last long. Walking into the property, you are greeted by timber floors, old fireplaces, original fixtures and fittings, and from the third floor, stunning elevated sea views. Bedrooms are ready for you to put your stamp on, original bathrooms are in loved condition, and a third attic floor is just waiting for your personal touch.*

*Externally, a walled back garden with a sunny aspect offers a glorious place to sit and enjoy a coffee in the morning. A gate in the old fence offers a gently shelving slope down to the sea.*

*Darling is a quiet seaside town on Darling Island known for its fine architecture and olde worlde charm. Nestled on the beautiful hazy waters of Darling Estuary, Darling's sandy beaches and bustling community are a well-kept secret just off the coast.*

*You know you've arrived on Darling when you step off the Pride of Darling floating bridge and take a trip up the main street on the tram.*

*With its beautiful sea mists, flora and fauna, and the sound of the old foghorn in the distance, Darling will hold you in her grasp and never let you go.*

*Darling Island ~ just off the mainland, so very far from care.*

Lucie read through the listing again and took another sip of her winc. It sounded better than a cupboard in Notting Hill, of that she was certain. She knew a little bit about Darling Island; her friend Anais had a family holiday home there. They'd gone for weekends a few times over the years and as teenagers they'd spent weeks there lapping up the sun. It had always been one of those places not far from her doorstep and she'd always meant to go to more, but had never really got to it. Like Londoners and Big Ben.

Leaning over the bath, she drained the last of the wine, sat back in the water, and tapped on the pictures. Clicking the right arrow for the next image, as it appeared she laughed out loud, almost dropping her phone into the water. Imposing it most definitely was. Imposing and terrifying all wrapped into one. Needing some love was an understatement.

But as she tapped on the pictures and enlarged them with her finger and thumb, something stopped her from clicking the little white cross in the corner and forgetting the idea altogether. It was just the sort of place she and Rob had always talked about taking on. As she scrolled through and enlarged the pictures, it ticked all the boxes; something with a view, something with an attic, something with an out-building, a garden with scope, original features, somewhere near enough to walk to a few shops, not too remote, near the sea.

And for the next few days, she'd kept on going back to the images. On her break in the staffroom at work, she'd clicked on the link and read through the description. At lunch, she'd sat on a bench on her phone looking at images of the hazy blue waters of Darling Bay, and sitting in the tiny kitchen of the cottage alone, she'd enlarged the images and examined every single detail. She'd watched the online video tour so many times she knew it off by heart.

A week later, driving through the lanes on her way to work, she'd hit the button to call the estate agent to make an inquiry. A lovely woman, Emilia, answered the phone bustling with friendliness and had enthusiastically told Lucie a bit more about the house. Brimming with potential, she'd said, the first time it'd been offered for nearly a hundred years. The garden led out to the estuary. The rooms looked out to sea. The ferry was a mere hop, skip, and a jump and the tram was nearby. The Coastguard's House, Emilia had told her, was an integral part of Darling Island's history.

Lucie had nodded along, the pit of her stomach a flurry of excitement. As the green hedges faded to the start of the main road, the woman's tone had changed as if she needed to get off the phone. Anyway, she'd said, there had been two offers on it already and the vendor was going to decide that day.

Lucie had almost crashed the car, yelled out no, and as quick as a flash made a decision. Right there and then, as she'd indicated right to merge onto a dual-carriageway, she'd begun negotiations on a new start. Somewhere that would offer her some space from everything that had happened. An escape from all that had transpired with Rob, via an old coastguard's house by the sea. A house to heal a broken heart.

By the end of the day, Lucie Peachtree had very much sorted the new start she'd hoped for. She wasn't going to be trying for a baby, she wasn't going to be with Rob, she wasn't going to be strolling along lanes in a wax jacket with her babies, but she was going on a new adventure. Lucie Peachtree was escaping and Darling Island was calling her name.

## 2

———

Lucie turned off the fridge and, as instructed, left the door ajar and took one last walk around the cottage. It had most definitely been a good place to recover from a life breakdown. There had been a lot of crying and staring out the bay window into the lane. The cottage had offered a haven where long, sad weekends in old pyjamas, messy hair, too much cake, and lots of boxes of tissues had been at the fore. She'd spent whole swathes of time deeply mourning what she'd thought she'd had and barely venturing past the front door. She'd slothed around doing nothing but go to work, come back home, and sit on the sofa and eat. Her jeans could barely make it past her knees.

She smiled wryly at the little navy-blue sofa tucked under the low beams squeezed in opposite the fireplace. It had been the setting for long online video calls with her group of friends who had one by one pulled her out of the doldrums. Each in their own way, they'd helped her to think that life could turn on the up again. Five of them, friends since they were little, thirty-five odd years of friendship, a lot of water under the bridge, and all there on the end of a Wi-Fi signal ready to help.

At first, she hadn't told any of them what had happened. Shame, embarrassment, and malaise all wrapped into one bewildering package of doom. She wasn't sure why she'd been reluctant to tell anyone what had happened. It wasn't as if their little group hadn't seen it all over the years; love, marriage, dramas, births, lost babies, new houses, new husbands, divorce, accidents, death, highs, lows, and everything in between.

Through it all, there'd been one constant thing in all their lives; their friendship. All five of them had all but moved away from the tiny town they'd grown up in and circumstances had changed things, but they'd kept in touch through thick and thin.

Lucie, Anais, Tally, Libby, and Jane. The Hold Your Nerve girls. All with their own little nicknames, their own codes, in-jokes, and shared experiences going on for just shy of thirty-five years.

It had been Anais that Lucie had called first. She'd cried down the phone, snivelled and blubbed until she'd actually thought she didn't have a single tear left. The next day with huge puffy eyes, a red nose, and a swollen face, Lucie had woken to a message in the Hold Your Nerve WhatsApp group from Anais.

*Attention: Calling a Friday night CT. 8pm GMT. All required.*
*Anais x*

Lucie had cringed and breathed a sigh of relief at the same time. There hadn't been a Crisis Talk meeting for a long time. They'd all been busy getting on, or not in Lucie's case, with their lives. The last Crisis Talk had been regarding Libby, the one before that, Jane. Lucie hadn't been the centre of one since she'd had the last miscarriage.

On the Friday night, willing herself not to cry, she'd sat there in her pyjamas, a waiting bottle of wine, a family size bag of Maltesers, and a Coconut and Lime candle flickering on the side. The candle hadn't helped one little bit. Nor had the ginormous bag of Maltesers. The wine had brushed at her frazzled edges, but it was the Hold Your Nerve girls who had eased the pain. The friendship had scooped her up in its arms and helped to Sellotape together the dirty, great raggedy tear straight down the middle of her broken heart.

'The bastard!' Libby had yelled, shaking her fist in front of the screen.

'You poor, poor thing,' Tally had consoled.

'Ahh, I just simply cannot get my head around it,' Jane had said with a shaking of her head. 'What and why?'

'I could wring his neck,' Anais repeated a thousand times.

They'd cajoled and rallied and gone over and over what had happened until they'd been online for a long time. Coconut and lime had filled the air, the Maltesers were long gone, and as Lucie had got just past halfway through the wine, the video call had started to come to an end. Just as they'd all gone to go, Tally had been the one to say it.

'What would my mum say?' she asked with her wine glass held up towards the screen.

Lucie had laughed as they'd all waited. 'Hold. Your. Nerve.'

'Precisely! That's what we do, ladies. Until next time. Hold. Your. Nerve.'

Lucie had called the second of her Crisis Talk meetings after she'd bought the Coastguard's House sight unseen. There had been silence at first, and then Libby.

'Are you actually out of your mind?'

'I know.'

'Sorry, run this past me again. You've bought a house you haven't seen?' Tally had asked.

'I have.'

'How do you even do that?' Jane had queried.

'Loads of people do it.'

'Where did you do it if you weren't there?' Anais had asked with frowning eyes.

'I actually did it in the car on the way to work. That's not technically correct, but that's where it started.'

'You bought a flipping house you haven't seen on the way to work!' Libby had exclaimed.

Lucie nodded resignedly. 'Yes. I did.'

'You've lost it,' Tally had stated.

'What is it like?'

Lucie had put her wine down. 'Hang on, I'll put a link in the group.'

There had been a looking down at phones, frowns, scrunched up eyes, and not a word. Silence filled the air from all four screens.

Anais had piped up first. 'What the heck have you done?'

'Have you seen the kitchen?' Jane had yelled. 'There is green cladding everywhere!'

'I'm for once in my life, speechless,' Libby had said and then continued, 'Anais, why didn't you stop her?'

Anais looked back at the screen. 'Trust me, I would have if I had known. This is awful.'

'It says there's a garden with a gate to the sea! They call that a garden? You're going to be able to sue, somehow. You can't call that a garden. That's deception. And the moss everywhere. You'll be able to get them on a health hazard somehow.' Tally had frowned.

Jane mused. 'Why, oh why, would you have done this on a whim? You made all that equity from the house. Rob may be a cheating scumbag, but he washed his hands of the house and left you with all that money, and you've bought that. I cannot, repeat cannot, believe it!'

Lucie had chuckled. 'I take it by your responses you're not going to wish me luck on my new adventure, then?'

There had been blank faces in response. Anais had piped up, 'I'm going to call Dad.'

And then Libby, 'Hold. Your. Nerve.'

# 3

All sorts of regret rushed through Lucie's mind as she drove past the now-familiar tall hedges along the lane out of the village. The village she was meant to have lived in until she was grey and old with Rob. She'd become quite attached to the hedgerows on her commutes. They'd cosseted her somehow in thinking time as she drove to and from work. She may or may not have spoken to them a few times through tears and sniffles. Now, it was as if they were another friend raising their eyebrows and asking her if she really thought what she was doing was a good idea.

Tapping the steering wheel nervously, she had no idea if what she was doing was good or not, but she was pleased that she was going to try. It was as if her whole body had let out a huge sigh of relief at the anticipation of what Darling Island and the Coastguard's House were going to bring. It was about time to stop the pity party, pull her socks up, put her head down and get on with her so-called life.

She wriggled and attempted to adjust her seatbelt where it cut into her now very plump middle. She'd put on a tonne of weight while she'd lived alone in the country cottage. She'd sought refuge in calories, diving headfirst into anything and everything that had taken her fancy. Greasy foods, cream cakes, bags of crisps by the dozen, and chocolate bars for lunch. Wasted calories on alcohol, hoping it would put a stop to tears, somehow numb her from her new normal. It hadn't worked in the slightest.

Sighing, she shifted in her seat. She could feel the weight gain everywhere. Her jeans were so tight the waist button was undone, the zip dug into her stomach, and she could feel the denim fabric stretching over her bottom at the back. Extra weight spilled over her bra at the front and she could feel a heaviness in her upper arms. She was still far from obese, but she was very uncomfortable.

"Puppy fat on a tiny petite frame," her mum had always said, with an intending-to-be-kind smile. Lucie had done her darndest to watch that puppy fat over the years. Always being careful, leaving the treats for the weekends, forcing herself to go to the gym, eating dressing-free salad for lunch. And then boom, when she was left in a cottage in the country on her own, overindulging every night had become her new best friend.

She sighed as she drove along and pressed the large black button in the centre of the console. Turning it, she flicked through the menu on her apps. In a fit of enthusiasm a couple of nights before, she'd subscribed to an all-singing, all-dancing motivation app, parting with her PayPal balance for a new way to lose weight.

As part of the same enthusiastic burst, she'd also considered what was little more than a fancy exercise bike with a very fancy price tag. The bike came with the added benefit of a monthly subscription and a screen. According to the website, if she committed she would be able to connect, via its cutting edge streaming facility, to exercise classes around the world. Here she would be able to remotely pedal like a loon with other sweaty out of condition people around the globe in the comfort of her own home. Yeah, nah.

She nodded her head in gratitude that she'd decided to sleep on the exercise bike and had seen sense. She abhorred the gym and had only ever dragged herself in there once a week to stop herself from feeling guilty. Doing it at home on a stationary bike almost made her want to gag.

She flicked through the motivation and meditation app promising everything from bone deep sleep to yoga on the beach. As it connected, soft twinkly music filled the car and Motivation Medleys began to play. A strong, not very happy sounding voice spoke to her from the speakers filling the air with its monotonous tone.

'I am motivated. I can have the life I want. I am filled with power.' It instructed.

Lucie made a funny face and answered in her head.

*I am unmotivated. I wanted a lovely little life and a baby. I am not powerful.*

'I am full of energy. I believe in myself. I am confident that I can achieve my goals.'

*I'm tired. I do not believe in myself. I do not have any goals.*

'I am ready to take action. I get things done.'

*I don't know what to do first. I am fat.*

'I can do this. I have the ability to make my dreams come true.'

Lucie chortled out loud at the last one.

*I cannot do this. I do not have any dreams. They went out the window with my partner and his baby.*

On and on the monotonous voice went. 'I am strong. I am able. I can do this.'

*I don't know if I can do this.*

'I believe in my power. I'm excited about my future.'

Lucie hit the button to stop the woman's voice from droning on and on any further. Life-affirming and motivating it was most certainly not. Gripping the steering wheel harder, she wanted to scream.

*I've bought a house without seeing it, in a place I don't know. I'm on my own, I have hardly any money left, and my life is going nowhere fast.*

She flicked the app to the next track. All sorts of things were promised. A night as calm as sleeping under the stars, a healing motivation to bathe with, and it even instructed her that finding Zen and serenity was within reach. A body scan would help her to calm anxiety, and a mindful tea or coffee break was accessible for anyone, anywhere. All were but a click away.

Lucie nodded to herself and spoke to the little screen beside the steering wheel, 'Yes to healing, yes to a calming body scan, yes to mindful coffee! All of it. Give me it all.'

As she got closer and closer to the coast, the motivation app was toast, as she got more and more apprehensive. She had no idea what she was doing or how it was going to turn out. Part of her, though she only admitted it to herself, was also very scared. She'd only really ever lived with Rob and now being on her own felt massive and all sorts of wrong.

Loads of things had gone through her mind as she'd thought about moving in, from DIY to security. Most of all, on top of paying bills and navigating her new life, she was worried about living on her own in the house. She was freaked about being alone at night and apprehensive about the house backing onto the beach.

Plus, on top of that, there was the Darling fog. That spooked her a bit too. She'd read all sorts about it; how romantic it was, how it blurred the edges of the ride across the estuary, how Darling residents knew by the hazy blue water and the lifting fog that they were home. But a detached house on the beach in swirling fog had suddenly not seemed quite as attractive as the romantic movie-like notion as reality got closer and closer.

Lucie didn't like the sound of any of it now. Regret reverberated through her body, thrumming through her veins as she drove along. The initial buzz perpetuated by the enthusiasm of the estate agent had all but dwindled away. Rather than the oh-so-exciting anticipation of a new house and new place to live, she was feeling unloved, unhealthy, and unmotivated. And most of all, very, very alone.

Pulling into a lay-by, she put the car in park, switched off the engine, and checked the map. According to its information, she had ten minutes to go until she came to the infamous Darling floating bridge. She'd googled it a few days before, learning that it ran continuously throughout the day and could just rock up whenever she wanted. At least there was that; no tickets and planning, just turning up and tears.

After taking a wrong turn, about fifteen minutes later, she drove slowly and carefully past the signs for Darling Island. Following the instructions, she pulled up behind a shiny car with a huge spare wheel attached to the back door. A woman head to toe in sparkles, a designer bag, and immaculate dark hair got out. She was joined from the back by another woman who looked the same, only older. This one, with a distinct lack of glitter, stood by the car in a pink fluffy jumper, huge gold headphones, thick socks, and sliders. Lucie wondered where they were off to and smiled as the glittery one nodded in greeting.

Looking out, she gazed over the estuary and squinted. The house was somewhere there on the right but directions never being one of her strong points, she couldn't be certain. The distinctive blue water she'd read about rippled in the distance and she wasn't quite sure if she was imagining it, but somehow under the blue sky, there also seemed to be a hint of the famous fog. She pressed her window down, stuck her head out and inhaled deeply as she watched the ferry make its way over the estuary. The air was good, she had to give it that.

Her eyes roved to the left, settling on a queue of foot passengers standing behind a barrier, most of them not interested in the comings and goings of the Pride of Darling, instead looking down at their phones. She watched as a man in a white polo shirt with blue epaulettes and thick navy-blue trousers with a reflective strip on the bottom, stood at the front of the ferry peering off the end. He started shouting, addressing the people sitting bumper to bumper in their cars, 'Darling for the bay! Foot passengers on the left! Darling Island only!'

Lucie's eyes moved from the man to a large sign on the right.

*Darling Floating Bridge is a vehicular chain ferry crossing over to Darling Island, nestled just off the dazzling blue waters of the south coast.*
*Family-owned, wholly operated, and still privately run by The Darling Floating Bridge Company, it is one of the few remaining chain ferries in operation today.*
*First established in 1871, some of the original ferries can still be seen at our boatyard. The Darling floating bridges remain the only way to cross to Darling Island. The Pride of Darling crosses the narrowest point to Darling East with the best views of the estuary by far.*
*7 days a week. 365 days a year.*
*First ferry runs continuously from Darling East 5.30am. Last ferry 12.55pm.*

Lucie looked over towards the floating bridge and wondered what happened if you needed to get to the island in the middle of the night and then remembered the ferry at the other end ran through twenty-four hours a day. She watched the man in the uniform hold his hand up in front of him in a stop sign and with his other hand indicated for the foot passengers to walk on. People held their phones out, tapping a little gadget he'd taken from an old tan leather satchel slung across his body. Once everyone was on, he moved back towards a gate, opened a door to a small cupboard, pushed a button, and indicated for the cars to move forward. A few minutes later, with bumpers nearly touching, they were loaded on board. The man smiled and waved and stopped to chat to the man in a Toyota beside her. He approached her window next.

'Morning, my lover.'

Lucie attempted a smile at his friendly greeting. 'Morning.'

'Day out to Darling? Return? Nice day for it now the fog's lifted. It's going to be unusually warm for this time of year. Be nice there on the bay this afternoon. Careful though, there's a storm rolling in later.'

'No, not a return, thanks. A single.'

The man frowned, and his deeply tanned skin wrinkled further. 'Rightio,' he said, looking down at the machine. 'You're not coming back, then? Staying for a few days?'

Lucie nodded. 'You could say that, yes.'

The man's head shot up at the inflection in Lucie's voice. 'Resident?'

'Am I a resident?' Lucie asked back, a hint of surprise in her voice.

The man smiled a cheery smile. 'Sorry, love, I have to ask. I'm not some creepy old man. It's the law, see. Darling Island has its own laws. Even though I know you're not a resident, I have to ask.'

Lucie squinted and tried to work out what he was saying. She stopped herself from sighing. She was a resident now, she supposed, not that she was going to be informing any old Tom, Dick, and Harry that every five minutes. She was scared enough about the whole thing as it was. But she'd tell this one. He seemed okay.

'Resident? Yes, yes I am.'

The man's whole demeanour completely changed, and his eyebrows shot up to the top of his forehead settling his skin into deep seafaring lines. 'You're a Darling resident? Is that what you're saying?'

'I am,' Lucie confirmed with a nod, her face serious.

'I see. Then you won't be needing any of this then,' he said, wiggling the machine in front of her.

Lucie didn't know what else to say as he paused. She ventured, 'Thank you. I'm not sure what you mean, though.'

'You're moving to Darling?' he asked with a question in his voice.

Lucie's eyes widened. 'Yes. I am. Today, in fact.'

'There you are then. Residents have a travel permit, but I'll take your word for it. Welcome, my lover. I hope she treats you well.'

Lucie wasn't sure who he was talking about but smiled anyway. 'Thank you.'

The man didn't move onto the next fare but continued, 'Where would that be, then?'

Lucie answered with a frown.

'Where would you be moving, my lover? Over the back there behind the bay? I see old Davenport's house sold and there was one in the mews they said went for a pretty packet.'

Lucie wasn't sure what to reply, but he continued anyway, so she needn't have worried, 'Can't be the Coastguard's, not a young lass like you and a place like that. We've all been waiting to see who would take it on.'

Lucie nodded, and the man's eyes widened in surprise. He tried to hide his shock but failed. 'Well, there you go.' He tapped on the door frame and smiled. 'Good luck with that, then. You're going to need it.'

# 4

Lucie attempted to appear confident and sure of herself as she gave the ticket man an optimistic little wave as she drove off the ferry. Inside she felt far from confident, and optimistic had gone out the window with the look on the man's face when he'd wished her good luck. His look had been a combination of disbelief, shock, and surprise.

Pulling slowly off the ferry ramp and up the slipway, she followed the signpost pointing to the right towards Darling Bay. As she got going, her phone suddenly connected and clicked through to the motivation app and the same droning voice was in the car with her again. A long bell chiming sound went off as if it was inside the speakers and a low chanting began.

'I am a part of something wholly bigger than myself.'

*Much, much bigger. A house clad in green with an overgrown garden and no working toilet.*

'I choose now to show up in my life and make the best of any opportunity presented to me.'

*I don't have a choice. My partner left me for a much better offer.*

'I tend to what needs to be done in my life with spirit and grace.'

Stabbing at the control, Lucie turned off the affirmations and a few minutes later was pulling down a narrow side road to double-check the address. And then in no time she had indicated and pulled onto the road. Her heart sank as she peered through the windscreen. Putting her head in her hands, the voice from the app went over in her head.

*I am a part of something much bigger than myself.*

She looked over at the house. The estate agent's description had been, at best, hopeful, at worst, completely and utterly disingenuous. The Coastguard's House sat in a row of similar detached shiplap clad houses; only all the others were pristine. Each one of the others wore a bright, glaringly white coat of paint, apart from one odd one about two-thirds of the way down, which was blue. Sighing heavily, she brought up the pictures on her phone. She could see that the photo of the front of the house had been taken from about halfway down the path. Now she knew why. A combination of dumped building materials and broken garden furniture suffocated under knee-high weeds. Cladding hung off above the window to the left and a thick layer of green moss covered the whole of the right side of the roof. She couldn't believe her eyes. It wasn't just a bit on the rundown side. It was more than terrible.

About the only thing making it obvious that the house was the same one as the one in the pictures were the three porthole windows on the third floor. Lucie put the heels of her hands into her brow bone, elbows on the steering wheel, and moved her hands round and around. When she looked back up, nothing had improved. She didn't know what to do, so she just sat there staring. A full fifteen minutes went past with her staring out the window, not a clue what to do. Not a single car drove past her and there was no movement from the other houses. It was as if as driving off the floating bridge or whatever they were calling it, she had driven away from life and left civilisation behind.

Not knowing whether to laugh, or cry, or what to do, she just continued to stare out the window as an old ripped flag on the top of the house flapped around in the wind. A seagull landed near the front door and took a few steps. It moved its head around as if to say no thanks and quickly took off, swooping down in front of the car and then flying off out towards the estuary.

'What have I done? I will not cry,' Lucie said to herself as she braced to get out of the car.

Undoing her seatbelt, she felt the unfastened button on her jeans and wanted to cry about the weight she had put on, too. Heaving herself out, she approached the house and pushed the mossy green gate in the middle of the fence. Daunted by the weeds, she leant down, pulled her socks over the ankles of her jeans, and gingerly picked her way up what she could just make out was a stepping-stone path. Finally arriving at the top of the path, she just stood there with her hands hanging by her side. She didn't even want to go in. A lone, thorny climbing rose with some kind of mottled disease snaked its way up from a broken pot by the front door. A dirty laminated sign reading 'The Coastguard's House' with a slash of ripped brown tape at the top sat beside a threadbare doormat.

She couldn't even stand to go in and instead pulled her phone out of her bag where four WhatsApp messages had arrived.

*Hope you arrived safely.* From Tally.

*Send us some pics!* Jane had added with a love heart.

*I hope it goes well today x.* Anais had typed.

*Good luck. Love, Libs.* Was Libby's message.

Lucie swallowed a lump in her throat. Her four friends, as usual, were there for her. She went to take a photo of the battered front door, the pile in the garden covered in weeds, the mossy roof, and post it with a message that she was having massive regret. Buyer's remorse looked scary when it was regarding a house. The exercise bike would have been much easier to send back. But, just as she took the last picture of the mossy roof, she changed her mind about posting photos in the group. Instead she took a huge breath and pulled out the keys. It was time to face the music. Stop the tears, stop the pity party, stop the woe is me. It was time to pull on the big girl pants. Possibly in the next size up.

The door dropped from its hinges a little bit as it opened and Lucie stepped in. The musty air hit her like a tonne of bricks. The unaired, dank, lifeless smell, still and depressing. Faced with a square hallway with a couple of little steps up to a staircase and another few down to another small lobby area, she raised her eyebrows. It wasn't too bad, but the photos had definitely shown it in its best light. The clad walls had a coat of green paint Lucie couldn't believe anyone had actually put on out of choice, but it was at least all in one piece. A filthy mottled grey fitted carpet, cleverly left out of the pictures, had come away at the steps, and one of the doors was off its hinges and leaned up against a nearby wall.

As Lucie walked around, her initial hopefulness in the hallway dissipated as quickly as it had arrived. Opening doors and going up and down steps, things got a lot, lot worse. She walked around from one room to the next with little shakes of her head and focused on trying to keep her face from crumbling into tears.

After a conversation with the estate agent and the fact that the owner didn't want to pay for house clearance, a scattering of furniture had been left. A deep burgundy leather wingback chair sat in a front sitting room butted up next to an exposed brick fireplace. The door to a wood-burning stove rested by its side. Waist-high statues of the Three Wise Men, one with his left hand missing, were perched in the corner and beside them an armoire in petrol blue, the inset of the doors hand-painted in dark red and bright yellow.

A tiny second sitting room showcased an electric bar fire sitting directly on the hearth of an old fireplace where a hand-painted green mermaid on a gigantic canvas smiled down on the occupants. Everywhere she looked, green paint greeted her except for the kitchen, where old timber cupboards wore the same burgundy red paint as the armoire at the front. On top of the worktops, open shelving in a glossy dark grey held various discarded bits and bobs. A row of well-used copper saucepans, a space for a fridge, thin mean-looking dark grey carpet tiles on the floor. An immersion heater with its copper pipes on display had somehow been squeezed into the corner beside a small Belfast sink.

Lucie looked into a mirror balancing on top of the mantel-piece in the kitchen and spoke out loud.

'I choose now to show up in my life and make the best of any opportunity presented to me.'

A small corridor led to further rooms off another hallway. She opened a small doorway to what she assumed, due to her scrutinisation of the online plans, housed a narrow set of timber back stairs. Peering her head around, she slammed her hand over her mouth. Cobwebs made an intricate pattern up to the top. Each step of the stairs was wearing a layer of droppings from more than a few mice. A row of hooks at the foot was rammed with old fishing nets, oilcloth coats, ropes, and a black plastic bucket underneath was full of mouldy fishing umbrellas. A huge greasy, grimy oblong plastic tub with a lid stood next to the bucket. Lucie kicked the lid with her foot and as it fell to the floor, gagged as a putrid smell hit her nostrils and maggots wriggled around inside. She slammed the door behind her, made her way back through the house to the two-level hallway, and went to see what was on the first floor. No doubt there would be more delights to be had up there.

Upstairs, the bedrooms weren't presenting her with many opportunities. A timber bed frame in a box room sat without a mattress, and a gabled window to the back looked out to sea. In a large bedroom, a door led out to a small inset deck perched on the jutting out floor below. Old mossy timber looked back at her like a death trap stopping her from stepping outside. A decorative tin ceiling in an ensuite bathroom was entirely painted in dark grey; the feature wall at the end mustard yellow. Lucie turned the tap on the freestanding bath and a trickle of water pooled in the bottom.

Just as she'd had enough and was gripping onto the thick, nautical rope handrail on the stairs on her way down, she heard an engine out the front. Hoping it was one of the many things she'd ordered to arrive on the first few days, and with any luck, the arrival of the fridge, she made her way down. Peering out the window, she saw a man, possibly in a uniform, emerging from a white four-wheel drive. He jumped cleanly over the picket fence and made his way up the path. He didn't look like a delivery driver. He did look rather nice. A minute later, there was a rapping on the door. She opened it to be greeted by a huge grin, a very nice tanned forearm, and a thatch of dark hair. A broad Australian accent followed the grin.

'Hey. I'm the neighbour, Leo. How are ya?'

Lucie swallowed. 'I'm very well, thank you. How are you?'

Leo chuckled and jerked his thumb. 'Glad to hear it. I live next door, next door but one if we're being pedantic. Holler if you need any help.'

Lucie had never quite had an offer like that before. She suddenly wanted to laugh. An extremely attractive man, without a wedding ring it had to be said, with sparkly eyes, and a uniform was standing in front of her surrounded by broken furniture and weeds, asking her if she needed any help. *Might be nice. I could be persuaded.*

The droning voice from the meditation app went through her mind. *I make the best of any opportunity presented to me.*

'I'm fine, but thanks for the offer.'

'Where are you staying?'

Lucie frowned. 'Where am I staying?'

'Yeah. I mean where are you staying while you fix this place up?'

Lucie let out a funny little laugh. 'I'm staying right here.'

The Australian frowned. 'You're a joker, rightio. Love someone with a sense of humour. She'll be right.'

'I wish I was joking,' Lucie said, not sure who he was referring to, and assuming it was the house, she looked behind her. 'I'm going to be living in it from now on.'

'Oh. I see. Your other half is following with the van, is he?'

Lucie smiled, noting the gold signet ring on the little finger of his left hand. 'There is no other half.'

'Oops, bit rude of me. Well, nice to meet you. Let me know if you want anything.'

'Same. Nice to meet a neighbour, Leo.'

'There's a storm coming through this evening. You'll want to, umm, stay safe. I'm on duty, but old Peggy and John will be able to give you a hand if you need anything. They're in between us. Bit, how can I say, eccentric.'

'Thanks. I'm sure I'll be fine. The house must have stood up to a few storms over the years.'

'I should say so. You'll know about it when it's coming when the horn goes off.' Leo chuckled at the frown on Lucie's face. 'Don't tell me you don't know about the Darling foghorn?'

'Well, yes, I've heard of it.'

'I thought legally they had to put it on the details…' Leo trailed off.

'Why would they need to do that?'

Leo looked at her as if she was not quite right. 'It's just a bit noisy. A dirty great foghorn goes off just down there. One of the last three still in operation in the country.'

'Well, that gives me something to get acquainted with.'

Leo backed down the path with a big smile and looked up at the house. 'Oh, you'll know about it alright.'

'Okay, well thanks for stopping in, Leo.'

'My pleasure. Don't worry. She'll be right.'

Lucie followed his gaze, doubting very much whether she or the house were going to be right, as he put it, but she liked his enthusiasm. At that moment things were feeling all sorts of wrong, but this neighbour had ever-so-slightly taken the edge off things. Rob and his baby? Who were they again?

# 5

On a fold-up chair with a battered old leather seat, Lucie gazed out the kitchen window. After looking around a bit more, feeling thoroughly disheartened, and speaking to Leo on the doorstep, she'd walked back in, plonked herself down, and hadn't had the energy to venture any further.

On shows she'd watched on starting a new life in the country or escaping to the sun, they must have cut the bit where reality hit. They'd clearly axed the frames where the new abode so full of potential and promise in the run-up hadn't quite lived up to its expectation. The bit where the person on their own sat on a chair in a quite frankly horrendous kitchen, wanted to cry, and didn't know where to start with anything, let alone a new life. That person couldn't even have a cup of tea.

She opened her emails and checked on the notification from the appliances company. That afternoon, if the tracking notification was correct, she would have a French door fridge taking pride of place in the abysmal kitchen, a smart kettle would be attached to an app on her phone, she would be able to vacuum with a new Dyson, and there would be a dishwasher in the gap in the worktop. At the sight of the utility room, where moss grew on the inside of the walls and the floor, and cupboards looked as if they had been used to store engine parts, she'd had second thoughts on where the new washing machine was actually going to live.

The following day, the few things she still had from life with Rob would arrive. A small part of her mammoth collection of fabrics, her second sewing machine, the odd few bits of furniture that hadn't been sold. All of it ready to live with her in this new place.

Swiping up on her phone, she scrolled right, tapped the blue Facebook button, and clicked on Rob's profile. Looking through what he was up to had become like some sort of horrible, dirty little addiction she couldn't quite resist. An addiction with the worst comedown ever. She'd wondered why he hadn't blocked her, but she was still able to see him living his best life with Serena from his work. Twenty-four-year-old Serena. The one with the model figure and huge baby-blue eyes.

A sudden memory blasted into Lucie's mind as she sat on the funny leather chair. Lying on a hospital bed being told by the sonographer that there was no heartbeat. Another failure. Another big, deep well of grief. Another round of trying. Now Rob didn't need to try anymore. Didn't need the grief, or the failure. Didn't need her. Rob had two new heartbeats to see him through.

She sighed, snapping the cover shut on her phone, and opened the back door. Light and fresh sea air flooded through the kitchen; at least the air wasn't mossy. As she gazed out, she still couldn't muster the energy to actually step outside. More or less certain that the old outbuilding, supposedly a 'granny flat', would hold more junk and the shed down the back would present another opportunity for tears.

Right down the end of the garden, the sun glowed above the haze at the bottom of the sky and by the fence next to the old brick wall, she could see the sea. In and out it moved, rhythmically soothing as she stood by the door thinking, gazing, determined not to cry. She looked up at the sun and wondered where this storm Leo had warned her about was going to appear from. Right now it was a beautiful day, with sunshine beating down onto the surface of the sea.

By around lunchtime, the kitchen held a French door fridge, a flashing kettle was on the side, and a new washing machine was plumbed in. That was about the only bit of hope the place held. Realising she had no food, no milk, and an impending sense of doom, Lucie picked up her bag and car keys, trudged through the weeds in the front, and went to get in the car. Changing her mind as she clicked the alarm, she turned on her heel, and started on what the house details had told her was the short walk to the tram.

Ten minutes or so later, Lucie was approaching the tram stop. She could remember the tram from the holidays with Anais. All five of them as teenagers riding up and down laughing and giggling. There weren't that many things she did remember from those days, but as the tram trundled along with its bell ringing, she could see little had changed about the tram itself.

Walking to the Victorian timber shelter, she looked up at a small digital sign and joined a short queue of two. The flashing sign juxtaposed against the old-fashioned craftsmanship of the shelter and beautiful old benches. The sign flickered, informing her a Bay tram would arrive in two minutes, a Darling Main shortly after, and a Castle tram in fourteen.

As the tram arrived and she waited for the passengers to get off, she watched as a pretty woman in a white polo shirt with blue epaulettes on the shoulders, navy-blue trousers, and waistcoat bustled around.

'Darling Bay!' she called out. 'All stops Darling Bay.'

Lucie got on behind an old man with a shopping trolley and

too big sloppy shoes. The woman spoke to him, her face breaking into a smile.

'Hello, Mr Cooke. How are you?'

'Not too bad, thanks, Shelly.'

'Where've you been this morning, then?' she asked, looking pointedly at his trolley. 'Down by the horn collecting, have you? Find anything nice down there?'

Mr Cooke opened the lid on his basket and held out two what looked to Lucie like pebbles. She watched as this woman, Shelly, peered down. 'Nice. Very nice. Better watch out later, storm's on the way in.'

'Off home now, Shelly. You know me. I won't be out and about in a Darling storm. I'm tucking up and watching the fishing online. Who would be out later, I ask you?'

'Not me, I'll be clocking off from here and getting home way before the fog drops in.' The woman laughed and then turned to Lucie. 'Hello.'

'Hi. I'm not actually sure where I'm going.'

'Well, you're on your way to Darling Bay if you stay on here, my lover.'

'Right, I just tap, do I?' Lucie smiled.

Shelly held out a machine and just as Lucie went to tap her card, she looked up. 'Sorry, I completely forgot to ask. Resident?' The end of her sentence lilted up in a question.

Lucie smiled. There it was again. The weird resident question. 'Yep.'

Shelly, who was looking down briefly at her phone, snapped her head back to the conversation.

'I meant, do you live here? You're a resident here on Darling Island?'

'I am as of today, yes,' Lucie replied as she looked around the relatively empty tram. Highly-polished timber seats gleamed, a bell with a long braided rope sat in the middle at the top, and sea air blew through from open sliding windows.

Shelly lifted her chin and widened her eyes. 'Today? What, you've moved in today?'

'Yes, I have,' Lucie replied. Here was another person speaking to her as if her business was openly discussed.

'Free for you then,' Shelly said, a slight frown on her face. 'You'll need to apply for a permit, but go on with you. Welcome.'

'Thanks. Where do I apply for one of those?'

'The town hall, though I think you might be able to get them online too, depending on your documents.'

'Right, thank you,' Lucie replied and went to step forward.

'Coastguard's House. Yes? Wow.'

Lucie frowned. 'How do you know that?'

Shelly started laughing. 'Ahh, I put two and two together. I'm not psychic. My parents live a few doors down. You won't have met them yet as they're in Spain, but they said you'd be moving in this week. I'd completely forgotten about it.'

'Ahh, right, yes. I met another neighbour.'

Shelly's face changed. 'Australian?'

Lucie felt a tinge of blush on her cheeks. 'Yes.'

'Pretty easy on the eye, that one. My sort of neighbour,' Shelly chuckled. 'Lucky you.'

Lucie didn't say that great minds think alike. 'Mmm.'

'Take a pew then.' Shelly gestured to the seats at the front and moved towards the back of the tram.

Lucie watched as Shelly then walked back past and took a few steps towards a huge old bell. 'I don't suppose you can recommend a café at all? Somewhere to get a bite to eat,' Lucie asked.

'I can indeed. You'll be needing Darlings.'

'Darlings? Where will I find it?'

'I'll give you a shout when you need to get off and point out the way to go. The stop before the bay there. It's a bit off the beaten track. Tell them Shelly sent you, and they'll let you in.'

Shelly laughed. 'Joking, the food is amazing. It's hidden away. You have to be in the know, as it were.'

'Thanks. It sounds just what I'm looking for.'

Shelly lowered her voice. 'Ask for a Darling basket.'

Lucie nodded, and as the tram moved away from its stop, she peered out the window and then watched Shelly going about her job.

'First stop Darling Fire Station, Town Hall, then all stops Darling Bay!'

As the tram glided along, Lucie was surprised to feel a small smile not just at the sides of her mouth but somewhere inside too. The tram trundled past an old church surrounded by hydrangea bushes, it then made its way past more rows of white houses. A white building set back with a sign 'Doctors on Darling' over the door was nestled in a row of old buildings and a pub on a corner looked like somewhere to stop for a drink. As the tram continued on its way along Darling Street, Lucie got glimpses of the blue of the water in between the buildings. An old fire station loomed up ahead, a Temperance Hall sat back beside a mini-roundabout, and a butcher with a striped awning and a sign announcing to the passing eyes of the tram, 'DJ's Quality Meats.'

At least one thing was for certain; Darling Island, the neighbour, the tram, and her first trip out weren't half bad.

## 6

Lucie followed Shelly from the tram's instructions to walk away from Darling Street, through an alleyway, down a cobbled road with mews houses and to take the bend at the end. She did exactly as directed until she smiled as she came to a little row of shops and the café sitting at the end of them.

Darlings was just as Shelly had described. A tiny little white bow-fronted shop front completely covered in climbing flowers. Along the sill at the front, window boxes spilled over with plants. Coach lights hung on either side of a bow fronted door, and a little panel of blue announced 'Darlings' to passers-by. Two small café tables with billowing tablecloths and little plant pots were squeezed in outside by the window, another one by the door.

An old Pashley bike sat underneath the window boxes and a row of bikes was wedged into a little bicycle rack to the left. Signwritten onto the glass in a panel above the window 'Darlings' was engraved. Vintage lace café curtains hid the bustling from inside, and a cluster of pots in a little cage hung from the wall, filling the air with the scent of herbs. A small timber glass-fronted box showcased a handwritten menu and an old doormat flattened by time and feet hugged a half step at the front.

Pushing open the door, a bell tinkled from overhead and Lucie had to stop herself from gasping. What Shelly hadn't told her was that the tiny place would be rammed with people, and that it was absolutely stunning. An assortment of pots filled with plants jumbled together on all and every surface. Tiny bistro tables were squashed into every available space and the whole place was lined with floor to ceiling shelving.

Lucie stood by the door, taken by surprise for a moment. Darlings was packed and she presumed she had not a hope of getting a table. She went to turn around and then, as if by magic, a child-sized woman with long glossy hair scooped up in a clip at the back appeared and smiled. Creamy golden skin and eyes almost the same colour worked with the smile to make Lucie feel welcome.

'Hello. Err, I was hoping to sit down, but it looks like you're full.'

The woman whisked a bottle of water from a table and raised her eyebrows. 'Table for one. I've got one tucked over there.' She pointed over to the other side of the room.

Lucie followed the woman's eyes to a small table squeezed in on the right. 'Perfect. I'm fine anywhere.'

As if she had wheels in her white tennis shoes, the woman zipped in between the tables, plumped a little blue gingham cushion on the chair, and from the large pocket on her butcher's apron took out a small menu.

'There you go. Can I get you something while you're deciding? You look like you might be in need of a cup of tea. Possibly a pot of tea.' Kind, friendly eyes sparkled as Lucie sat down.

'Ahh, yes, it's been a long day already. Thank you.'

'Oh, right. What brings you to Darling then? Not on a jaunt to the bay for the day?'

A little half-roll tipped Lucie's eyes. 'I wish.'

The woman called out cheerio to a customer and flicked her eyes back to Lucie. 'Sounds like you might actually be in need of a caffeine shot. I can bring you a nice coffee if you like.'

'Actually, yes. I'm out to buy tea bags and milk for later, so I'll have a coffee now. That would be lovely, thanks.'

'Certainly. You can have a little look at the menu and I'll be back.'

With a whoosh, the woman was gone and Lucie was left with the menu. Putting it down on the table, she took a breath and gazed around. Floor to ceiling shelving held layers and layers of fluted cake moulds and hundreds of little bowls. Enormous glass jars were filled with bags of coffee and a whole stacked up section groaned in an assortment of teapots.

Lucie looked to the end where suspended shelving over an old-fashioned counter displayed masses of bottles and kitchen paraphernalia. Looking down at the menu, she was surprised at what was on offer. A couple of set breakfasts, pastries, orange and apple juice, sandwiches. Frowning, she looked for what the conductor Shelly had told her to ask for and saw nothing about a basket. Putting the menu back down, she sat gazing around at the goings-on. The intermittent whirr of the coffee machine accompanied her thoughts as she sat tucked up by the wall. The coffee machine hissed and whirred, spoons clinked against saucers and a faint hum of chatter reverberated around in a busy swirl.

A movement caught her eye outside, and she watched as a woman in a swimming costume with a hoodie over the top, goggles around her neck, wet hair, and Birkenstocks leant a bike on the wall and pushed open the door. The woman who had served Lucie met her in the centre of the café, kissed her on both cheeks, and held up a small basket. Lucie couldn't hear what was being said, but there were smiles, a quick chat, and the transferring of the little basket. Two minutes later, the woman was back out the door. She popped the basket into the front of her bike, hopped on, and rode off over the cobbles.

In a flash, coffee suddenly appeared on the table. It had arrived in a small fluted bowl. The woman smiled. 'There you go. Let me know if you want a mug. It's a Darling thing, I thought you might want to try it.'

Lucie's mind suddenly zoomed back years, and she remembered the little bowls thing. When she'd been to Darling all those years ago with Anais, the house had always been filled with them. At night they'd had hot chocolate in little bowls with the family name painted on the side. Lucie smiled, not sure about the bowl, but there was no way she was going to be asking for a mug. 'Thanks. Umm, I was told to ask for a basket, but now I'm thinking I might have heard that wrong.'

The woman whipped her head up from the iPad she was popping numbers into, the surprise evident in her voice as she spoke. 'Oh, are you a resident?'

Lucie nodded and preempted what she presumed would be a question about the house. 'I moved in today, actually. The Coastguard's House.'

There was a widening of the silky tawny-brown eyes. 'Welcome! Yes, I should have realised. Leo told me he'd met you.'

Lucie frowned for a second, remembering her neighbour from what felt like a lifetime ago. 'Ahh, yes, we met this morning.'

'He comes in for a flask of coffee and a basket before his shifts,' the woman explained. 'I'm Evie, by the way. Nice to meet you.'

Lucie smiled. 'Lucie.'

'Good old Leo. He told you about the baskets, did he?'

'Actually no, it was on the tram.'

'Shelly? Goodness, she must have liked the look of you, then.'

'Yes. She was the one who told me to come here. I don't

think I would have found it otherwise. In and out of the lanes and alleyways.'

'Nope. Probably not. We're quite hidden back here, just the way we like it. A few roads back from Darling Street and it's like a different place. Okay, then. Welcome to Darling. One basket coming up.'

Lucie didn't have time to ask about what was in this basket as she watched Evie zoom off towards the back. What seemed like only a few seconds later, a small white basket appeared on the table. Lucie gazed at it and then around the café suddenly seeing them everywhere. In a wicker basket, a blue and white gingham napkin was knotted at the top. She undid the knot, unfolded the fabric, and peered inside. Tucked in were two tiny fluted doughnuts, a small baguette sliced in half, a little glass jar with a ceramic lid with what looked like jam.

Evie smiled. 'There are a few types of baskets, sometimes an evening one if we're up to it. This was the last one for today.'

'Lovely, thank you.'

'You can order the lunch baskets and pick them up. They change every day depending on what we have. We do them for school and work lunches and all that. Leo has his own version made up nowadays. Enjoy.'

Lucie took a sip from the bowl and watched as an old man beside her took one of the little fluted doughnuts out of his basket, dipped it into his bowl of coffee and popped it into his mouth. She followed suit. As the delicious flavours hit her taste buds, she smiled. So far in Darling, so good.

## 7

After hopping on the tram to make her way back home, lost in a world of her own, Lucie then found herself walking along the road back towards the house. It stood out on the end, appearing to keep watch out over the estuary. Swallowing a tiny little gulp, she tried to quell the feeling that what she had done was not only stupid but scary too. She was alone in a huge house whose security looked at best dubious and at worst dangerous. Not only that, she'd spent a lot of money bar her savings and she was alone. It did not feel good.

Holding her head up to the sky, she tried not to worry and convince herself that something had driven the crazy feeling to buy a house on the internet. She'd always told herself she believed in the universe doing its thing; now it was time to hold onto that premise for dear life.

She'd always believed in silly little superstitions and that she could read vibes. In light of what had happened with Rob, how wrong that had been. She'd missed quite a big vibe right there under her nose, a rather large occurrence she'd not seen coming. A vibe she most certainly had not picked up in any shape or form. One where, rather than the sweet village and cosy little country life with her, Rob had found himself a whole new world. Somewhere with a twenty-four-year-old blonde with big blue eyes in situ, who was just about ready to very conveniently have his baby.

She felt sick even thinking about it and vowed as she got back to the house that she wasn't going to stalk his social media later on. That she wasn't going to look at Serena's photos online. She wouldn't expand on the images of Serena and her friends all smiling and giggling into the camera. Serena with a baby bump, Serena with her mum balancing a cup of tea on the top of the bump, beaming Serena holding up an impossibly tiny pink Babygro.

As she got to the Coastguard's House, she put her hand on the gate and looked at the long grass. She had no idea where to start. She didn't even own a lawnmower and knew even less how to operate one. The old ripped flag at the top flapped in the wind, and she shuddered as she looked at the three porthole windows at the top. On the internet, the portholes had looked lovely and unusual; now they looked downright creepy. The house wasn't smiling as far as she was concerned, and she wasn't looking forward to the storm or the long night ahead.

Her phone began to vibrate in her pocket. She wasn't in the mood to speak to anyone as more and more feelings of doom and gloom descended as she approached the front door. Her friend Tally's name flashed across her phone. Feeling too guilty to ignore the call, she pressed the green button.

'Hi.'

'Hey, how are you getting on? I just thought I'd touch base.'

Lucie stuttered and then, out of nowhere, felt a huge lump in her throat and tears pricking the corner of her eyes.

'Luce? Are you okay?' Tally asked.

The only words Lucie could manage to get out were, 'Hang on a sec.'

She put her phone in her left hand, inserted the key in the

front door, walked through the hallway, made her way through the house, and slumped down in the kitchen. The lump in her throat was still there, but she'd managed to stop it from turning into full-blown ugly crying. 'Sorry. I was just getting back from the shops.'

'You sound upset.'

'I am a bit.'

'Has something happened?' Tally asked, her voice laden with concern.

'What, apart from buying a house sight unseen on an island I know next to nothing about, not knowing a single soul, and being on my own?'

'Yikes. You are in a bad way.'

'What on earth was I thinking?' Lucie asked. 'I must have had some sort of grief induced madness.'

'I don't know. You always say the universe works in its own way. It must be that.'

'Yeah, precisely, and you always tell me that's poppycock,' Lucie shot back.

'I do. I just wished you'd run it past the group beforehand. We would have made you see sense, or at least tried to.'

'Hmm. I wanted to just do it, you know? All four of you would have advised me against it. Look what happened when Anais said she wasn't happy.'

'True. Anais is Anais, though.'

'What about when Libby was going to put her money into that multi-level marketing thing with the aromatherapy oils? We all came down on her like a tonne of bricks.'

'Precisely my point! Thank goodness she put that in the group. Remember those articles Jane found about it?'

Lucie poured water in the new kettle, poured it down the sink, refilled it and switched it on. 'I do. At least I have a house out of it, I suppose. There is that to fall back on out of this mess, and at least I don't have to live in the same area as my ex-partner and his new baby.'

'I can come whenever you like. When is Anais coming? Three pairs of hands are a lot better than one.'

'She's getting back to me once she sorts a few things. I thought you'd be too busy. What about the girls?'

'I'm always busy. Luce, I have a partner and a nanny, so the girls will be more than fine.'

'The place is a mess. You won't want to be staying here. It's awful.'

'You know me, I don't care about stuff like that. Look, let me know.'

'At least I'll have decent beds soon, I suppose. I now have a fridge and a washing machine so I can have a cup of tea. The thing is, Tally, I just don't even know where to start.' Lucie felt the same lump make acquaintance with the back of her throat again. A small sob came out. 'I've been with Rob since I was sixteen. He might be a you know what, but he always did all this sort of thing.'

'I know. Although he let you get on with selling the other place on your own well enough. You'll be okay. It will just take a bit of time. Good things are around the corner.'

'I don't think I will be okay, that's the problem. Now I'm here, I feel much worse. The reality is making everything even more horrible, not better. I just feel so pathetic. What a loser I am.'

'I get you. It must be awful. You will improve, though. Moving is stressful enough as it is. Throw in what's happened and if you felt okay then I'd be very worried. It's understandable that you feel as you do.'

'I suppose so. I just can't stop thinking about him and her. It's like constantly there in my head. They seem so cosy and together and it was all going on right under my nose. She's so pregnant too.'

'Try not to do it to yourself. You're torturing yourself.'

'She's all over the internet with her bump and her blue eyes, and I'm sitting in a kitchen with green walls, a ginormous frigging mermaid smiling down, and lifesize statues of the Three Wise Men in the sitting room. And, to top it off, I'm the size of a house.'

Tally burst out laughing. 'Sorry, but that is absolutely hilarious! I couldn't believe those statues in the pictures in the group. Where does someone get things like that?'

'I don't even want to know. Everything is so creepy. There's a huge laminate and gold bar too, complete with optics and velvet-covered stools. I couldn't even stomach taking a picture of that.'

Tally chuckled. 'Don't knock it. I think you might be needing it by the sound of it.'

Lucie rummaged around in a box to find the teapot, rinsed it out, took the tea bags from her bag and opened the box. 'At least there's a funny side to it.'

'There's always a funny side. How long have you got off work?'

'A few weeks. I've got loads of holiday built up because of, well, you know why, because we thought we'd save it for when I got pregnant.' Lucie sighed.

'That gives you plenty of time to get on with it. All you need to do is get the house in some sort of order, and you'll be fine.'

'You won't say that when you see it in real life. It's awful. I must have been stark raving mad to do this! What was I thinking?' Lucie asked with a sigh.

'You'd be surprised. I'm very good with a pair of rubber gloves.'

Lucie stopped another sob from emerging. 'I don't even know where to start.'

Tally joked, 'You need a hazmat suit and a bottle of gin.'

'Can you bring both when you come?'

'I have PPE at my disposal from work if I need it.' Tally chuckled.

'I'm dreading this evening. I haven't even got the mattress from the back of the car yet. Right now sleeping in the car looks a whole lot more attractive than being anywhere in this house. At least the toilet works, I guess, I'd presumed it was going to be a problem. I don't have to dig a hole in the garden.'

'You'll get used to it. It can't be that bad.'

'I've not been on my own since I was sixteen,' Lucie replied flatly.

'Well, I have and I am here to tell you that you will survive. You are more than capable of this, Luce. You're a big grown up, and you are going to smash this.'

'I don't feel like it. I keep getting tearful. It's pathetic. *I am pathetic.*'

'No, you are not. Look, I'm going to have to go. What do we say?'

Lucie's response was more than feeble and barely audible. 'Hold. Your. Nerve.'

# 8

Clicking the fob for her car, Lucie thanked her lucky stars for the vacuum-packed mattress slotted in the boot. Heaving it out, she dragged it across the weeds and leant it up beside the front door as she struggled with the key. Feeling her jeans digging into the extra weight in her middle, tears streamed down her face as she dragged the mattress up the stairs, pushing the bedroom door open with her foot.

Collapsing on an old chair by a marble mantlepiece, she looked up at the high ceilings and windows out towards the sea. If she squeezed her eyes to a slit to hide the decor and looked out the window over the garden, the view was the best thing about the place. Blue water rippled in and out, and sun streamed down through an odd few puffy clouds in the sky.

Finally wedging the mattress up by the far wall, Lucie plonked herself down, dropped her head into her hands and the tears changed from a few running down the sides of her cheeks to real crying. After a few minutes letting it all out, a wiping away of the tears, and trying to pull herself together, she sat glumly trying to decide what to do first to make the room a tad more comfortable.

Thick dust sat on every surface, the green cladding surrounded the room, and now the bed frame, which she'd thought would be good enough to tide her over, looked worse than terrible. An old laundry basket lay on its side by a door to an ensuite, and thick blue-green swag and tail curtains with gold writing on them in French clung onto curtain tracks at the window.

Gritting her teeth, a few minutes later, she'd gone downstairs and was back with the vacuum. She flung the door to the tiny balcony open and heaved up the double-hung sash windows. A gust of wind came in, the first indication she'd seen all day of the impending storm. Bending down to plug in the vacuum cleaner, she stopped at a loud sound. It was the first time she'd heard it. The infamous Darling foghorn. One of the last places in the country, according to Leo, using both satellite navigation and a horn to warn of fog. Stopping what she was doing, Lucie put her head out the window and listened. Unable to see any fog, she couldn't stop herself from smiling as her brain registered things from the past. The sound harked back to just about remembered days in Darling with Anais. It all came flooding back to her. She adored the romantic sound, as if it was speaking to her from the past.

A few more blasts and it stopped. She switched on the vacuum, pushing it back and forth around the room, and in a short time the canister was full. Three canisters later and she was beginning to lose the will to live, at the same time as saying silent prayers that she wasn't dealing with carpet.

Another half an hour and the curtains with the gold writing had been ripped down and dumped out the window, the room was free of most of the dust, and a mouldy shower curtain in the ensuite had joined the curtains in the garden.

Left with a dust-free room, she'd mopped and mopped again, sprayed the skirting boards, wiped down the window ledges, and disinfected the doors. Semi-pleased with her efforts and at least knowing it was cleaner than when she'd started, she set to work on the bed frame. Many buckets of water later, three cloths, and a lot of elbow grease and even the bed frame was looking up. Rapidly losing the ability to move any part of her body without it hurting, she heaved the mattress onto the bed, went back out to the car, pulled out the holdall with clean linen and her duvet, and made up the bed.

At least she had the bed made up. A few moves in the past had taught her that importance when moving into a new house. Little had she known that in the not too distant future, she would be doing it on her own.

~

Later on that evening, exhausted, Lucie cupped her hands around a mug and sipped on a cup of tea. The fancy night time tea bag specially blended with all sorts of things wasn't doing its job. The wind now howled around outside, the sea sounded angry, and a door somewhere out the back banged incessantly over and over again in the wind.

Lucie laughed to herself at her earlier brave words that tonight she would start a new alcohol-free diet regime. One thing was certain as she listened to the storm getting louder and louder, this was no time for sweeping plans on dieting new starts. With the dark, scary, uncomfortable night looking in at her, and nothing but the banging door for company, she dumped the herbal tea down the sink and poured herself a glass of wine, hoping it would take the edge off everything.

Getting up with the wine in her hand, she gazed out the window, feeling the fraught wind whip in through the gaps in the woodwork. She could see lights over on the other side of the water and hear the foghorn sounding again. With the wind howling, she stood in the funny little burgundy kitchen in the light of the fridge, deciding what might make her feel even the teensiest bit better. She'd bought a few bits and bobs to tide her over with the half-hearted notion of healthy eating in mind, but in a little deli halfway up Darling Street, she'd decided supplies were needed just in case.

In a package of greaseproof paper, she unwrapped fresh pasta, and put a pan of heavily salted water on. From a small cardboard moving box labelled 'kitchen dry supplies' she poured some olive oil into a pan, sliced in a couple of crushed garlic cloves, sprinkled in a few shakes of dried chilli, and added a chopped bunch of freeze-dried parsley. Draining the pasta, she squeezed in a healthy dose of fresh lemon juice and salt, piled it into a bowl, and plonked herself down at the kitchen table.

The sound of the foghorn in the distance went again as she sat with the pasta and the small glass of wine. The wind whistled through the gaps in the windows and she could hear the flag on the top of the house flapping around, sounding as if its days were numbered.

A loud bang went from somewhere in the garden, and she could have sworn she heard the latch on the front door rattle. Flicking her phone on, she turned on the meditation app and pressed play. The same monotonous, droning voice came from her phone.

'I can do this. I have the ability to make my dreams come true.'

Pah! She flicked back to the search window and scrolled down and read through the topics; self-confidence, wellness, happiness, gratitude, compassion, manifestation, whatever that was, and right at the bottom, forgiveness, that would be a whole other load of affirmations for another day. Clicking on manifestation and reading the blurb that meditating with manifestation in mind would bring about positive changes in life, she clicked to be enlightened.

'Get in a comfortable cross-legged position, your hands in

prayer pose, make sure your shoulders are down and relaxed, your jaw loose, your chin tucked in, your lips softly touching together.'

Lucie continued to eat her pasta and sip on her wine. Her jaw was far from loose, her tense shoulders so tight she felt as if a wire had pulled them up and tied them to her ears. Running water sound came from her phone, the formulaic voice droning on.

'Let go of any distractions or outside noises, just simply let them go. I want you to visualise in your mind, how you want your life to look. How do your relationships look? How do you feel? Visualise your home environment. How does that look? How does it feel in that environment?'

Taking another forkful of the pasta, Lucie raised her eyebrows and looked around at a broken pane in the window and burgundy red kitchen cabinets. *Yeah, not looking that great at the moment. Relationship? Currently at a zero. Home environment? Absolutely dreadful.*

The voice continued on getting softer and slower. 'Now, consider, how is your health? How does your wellness look? Do you want to feel strong, fit?'

Lucie glugged the wine. *Ho. Ho. Ho. Being able to do my jeans up would be great.*

'Put your hand on your heart and imagine there are no fears in your life. Imagine waves of calm transcending through your body. All the way down they go, rooting you to the inner workings of the earth.'

Bang!

Lucie dropped her fork into her bowl as the lights went out. She sat frozen to the chair, her eyes enveloped in black. Just as they began to adjust, the lights flickered again and were back on as quickly as they'd gone off. A fizzing and it happened again. They turned on again and the room lit up. She felt as if there was a face staring in the window.

She pulled over her laptop, typing 'storm in Darling Bay' into the search bar. A post on the Darling community Facebook came up. Shelly, the woman from the tram she presumed, had written a post.

*Stay safe in Darling tonight. The storm will peak in the early hours. Let's hope the electricity stays on. Make sure your sandbags are in place.*

A wave of fear went through Lucie. She tried to tell herself that the house had been standing guard to storms for a very long time and that it was more than capable of staying upright, but fear coursed through her veins. She rushed to put her phone and computer on charge. Simple. If she was in danger, she would just call the emergency services. How hard could that be? Someone would be there to help, surely.

Opening the under the sink cupboard, she saw nothing even remotely resembling an emergency candle. She'd have to rely on the torch on her phone if she needed a light in the middle of the night.

Her phone buzzed with a WhatsApp message in the Hold Your Nerve group.

*How are you getting on?*

*Not too bad.*

*How's the weather? The whole coast is having storms according to the Beeb.*

*Yes, a storm has come in here. It's a bit scary, if I'm honest. I'll send you a pic.*

Lucie slowly made her way up the stairs. As she opened the door to the rooftop deck and stood there in the howling wind, she held up her phone, went to take a photo, changed her mind, held the button down and panned around along the horizon. She pressed send and added a message.

*It's blowing a gale and the electricity flashed off for a second.*

Anais was the first to respond, *Ahh, there's nothing like a Darling storm.*

The little dots flashed to show that Tally was typing a message.

*Looks wild out there, Luce.*

*It is. I'm questioning everything.*

*You'll be fine.*

*I don't feel fine.*

*It's not surprising.*

Lucie closed the door behind her. *Anyway, enough of me. How is everyone else?*

Tally added an eye roll emoticon. *Oh, you know, same old same old. I've spent all day stuck in an air-conditioned room examining people.*

*Ahh, you must be looking forward to a bit of time off.* Lucie added.

*I definitely am.*

*Are you sure you want to be spending your time helping me do something to make this place more habitable? It doesn't sound like much of a holiday to me.*

*Will you be providing me with lots of friend therapy and nice food?* Tally asked.

*That I can do. I'm not sure what else I can offer you, though. It really is a lot worse than I thought here.*

*A weekend in the sea air will be good for me with what's going on in my head. We'll have a giggle like we used to when we were teenagers, I'm sure. Trundling up and down Darling Street and sitting on the bay.*

*I hope so. Right now, I'm feeling as if everything is wrong.*

*Hopefully, you'll feel better when you wake up in the morning. Hold. Your. Nerve.*

Ten minutes later, Lucie peeled off her clothes and stood under the shower in the main bathroom. At least that worked. It had looked as if there was little hope of hot water coming out of the old copper pipework and goose neck head but it gushed out as she stood on the tiled floor and let it wash over her. It didn't wash away her brain full of thoughts. As she stood there, she couldn't get the image of Serena out of her head. So pretty and young and pregnant. It was as if she glowed with fertility, accentuating every single failure of Lucie's own.

Trying not to think about Serena and Rob and their baby nor the howling storm outside, she soaped every part of her body, rinsed it off, did it again, and then pushed the lever in and wrapped herself in a towel. Sitting forlornly on the edge of the bathtub, with her wet hair in a turban, she waited for the water to evaporate from her skin as wind whistled in through the window and pellets of rain banged on the panes. Getting more and more disillusioned and anxious at the looming night at the mercy of the storm, she tried to think of the words from the meditation app that morning.

*You are powerful. You can do it.*

But she did not feel powerful. She did not even want to be powerful. She wanted to curl up in a ball, close her eyes, shut out her new reality, and pretend that none of it was happening at all.

Lucie woke with a start, her eyelids flying open, but she didn't move a muscle. If there was someone in the room, she would play dead. Her ears strained, a banging outside, a howling, a whistling and whooshing. The sky seemed to grumble overhead and a loud clap of thunder was accompanied by a flash of lightning in the room. She clamped her eyes shut, listened further, and then opened them again.

Slowly reaching under the duvet for the cord on the lamp, she flicked the switch, ready to be faced by the intruder in her head. Nothing happened, the room remained in darkness and she froze. The predicted power cut had clearly occurred at some point since she'd forced herself to get into bed and attempt sleep.

She lay there thinking about the night. All thoughts she'd had that she would be lulled off to sleep by the gentle lapping of waves had evaporated as soon as it had begun to get dark and real fear had taken their place. Everything in the house was alien and unknown. Every squeak and sound made her mind tick and skin crawl. The walls and windows seemed to rock and jolt, almost as if the old house itself was in the sea. She told herself that her imagination was working overtime, but she was sure she could feel the house move in and out in time with the crashing waves at the end of the garden.

As she lay there, three short mournful blasts sounded on the foghorn as she wondered if she had the gumption to make it to the tiny ensuite bathroom. The foghorn and the wind alongside the imaginary intruder in her head had been the only things in the room through the already long night. Swiping up on her phone, she pressed the torch and its bright beam shone around the room. No intruder, just billowing curtains she'd put up just before she'd collapsed into bed, a rattling sash window, and the old pendant light in the middle of the ceiling eerily moving back and forth in the wind.

Lying there for ages, Lucie tried to decide what to do. A few more flicks of the switch told her the power cut was still happening and she thanked her lucky stars she'd put her laptop, iPad, and phone on charge just after dinner. Rob had always been in charge in times of storms and things. 'Plug in your devices,' he'd always said. He'd just taken care of things she didn't even think about. Like what to do in a storm. And now she had no Rob to plug in her devices. No Rob for anything. Now it was just her, alone with a dirty great foghorn and a creaking old coastguard's house for company.

Putting her phone back on the side, she squeezed her eyes

shut, willing herself not to cry, pulled the duvet over her head, and hoped it wouldn't be too long until she dropped off to sleep.

As she lay there with her eyes forced together, she decided that first thing in the morning she'd head for the floating bridge and call her time in Darling a day.

# 9

The next morning, Lucie had been elated to wake up still alive. With bare feet, and wearing pyjama bottoms and an old t-shirt, she stood with a steaming cup of tea in her hand looking out to a foggy sea. The Darling mist stood to attention behind the fallen down fence and weeds threatened to choke everything. The foghorn sounded again in warning, but as far as she could see, the eye of the storm had gone.

As she stood there, her eyes couldn't quite get a message to her brain to decipher whether the mess in the garden had been worsened by the storm. Two weathered Lutyens benches covered in lichen were strewn on their backs by an old brick wall, the little door on the old coal shed hung disillusioned on its side and a brick outbuilding's roof sported a faded blue tarpaulin held down with a row of broken bricks. Little puddles of gloom all around illustrated the driving rain that had hammered down on the old house during the night and a barking dog somewhere added to the feeling of doom.

Lucie stood there for ages, sipping on her tea, taking it all in and watching as the misty fog almost seemed to lift before her eyes. As if by magic, the same hazy Darling blue from the day before began to peep out underneath the rising fog. Pushing down a feeling she'd never really known before, a cross between fear and sheer panic, she decided as the sun gained back some space over the mist that the back garden was the last of her worries.

Walking back into the house, she went through the kitchen stopping to top up her tea, down the step to the back hallway, back up the two little steps to the entrance hallway, and sat on the bottom step of the stairs cradling her tea. If she wasn't going to take off as she had said she would in the night, she had to have some sort of plan of attack. Moping around and crying was going to get her nowhere.

There was no other thing for it than to formulate a schedule and get stuck into it. The clock was ticking and fast. She didn't have long until she had to be on the Darling punt every morning for work, no budget as such, and certainly no one willing or able to help. The green cladding stared back at her and she could see the bell cord swinging around by the front door. She looked up at a red mirror in the shape of a telephone box nailed beside the front door and shuddered.

Sitting there on the bottom step, scrolling through the Darling community page, she could see that, compared to a few other people on Darling, including one whose roof had completely slid off into the garden, she'd got off lightly. With the electricity flickering back on just as she'd been in the bathroom after she'd first got up, she realised that it could all be a whole lot worse.

At the sound of the front gate, she jumped up and poked her head around the gold velour curtains in the sitting room. The Australian was on his way down the path. Mortified that he'd seen her, she waved back at his smile and jaunty little salute. Braless, make-up free, in saggy old pyjama bottoms, and a bird's nest for hair, greeting a neighbour was not what she was wanting to do.

She opened the front door, arms folded over the old t-shirt, and tried to smile through her discomfort. *Hello, you are really rather nice.*

Leo grinned. 'How are ya?'

'I'm good, thanks. How are you?'

Leo chuckled. 'Survived your first Darling storm, I see.'

'Yes. Just.'

'I thought as much. We lost power in the night. I wasn't sure whether you were okay or not. So I thought I'd check on my way to work.'

Lucie swallowed. She didn't mind too much that this hunk of an Australian was checking up on her, that she knew for a fact. 'Thanks for thinking of me. I've been better, but I'm okay. It was quite the way to get acquainted with Darling and the house.'

'What's cooking then?' Leo asked, jerking his thumb towards the house.

'What, for today you mean?'

'Yeah. You've got your hands full with all this.'

Lucie grimaced. 'I have to try and make a start on it all somehow. I'm just not sure how much I can get done.'

'Ah, she'll be right.'

'I hope so,' Lucie said, gazing at the little pile of white wicker baskets in the crook of Leo's arm.

She nodded down towards them. 'Where are you off to with those?'

Leo followed Lucie's gaze to the baskets. 'Darlings, it's a café over by the mews.'

'Yes. I went there yesterday.'

A frown crossed Leo's handsome tanned forehead. 'Right you are. I didn't think you'd have come across it yet. I meant to mention it to you, but it totally slipped my mind.'

Lucie nodded. 'The woman on the tram told me.'

'There you are then. Getting your information from Shelly

right from the start. You won't go wrong there. She must have liked the look of you to tell you about Darlings.'

'I guess so. Yes, it was lovely in there.'

Leo held up the little stack of baskets. 'These baskets save my life. You'll see them all over the place.'

'Hmm. Actually, yes, I had one yesterday. It was delicious.'

Leo smiled. 'Ahh, you are in already. They're not just a Darlings café thing. If anyone offers you a basket, you say yes. Got it?'

'I do?'

'Learn from my mistakes.' Leo grinned again. 'It's an old Darling superstition and a peace offering in one. You'll probably have a few left on the doorstep before the end of the day.'

'Will I? Oh, right, okay.'

'Yeah. They're like currency around here.' Leo chuckled. 'I had to raise my game, as it were, on the basket front. I nearly didn't make it back from that mistake. Not much a trainee doctor can put in a basket. I said no to one and ouch.' Leo sucked air in through his teeth and winked.

'Good to know.'

'Right, well, if there's nothing you want me to help with, I'll be seeing ya.'

Lucie raised her eyebrows. She could think of many things she could ask Leo to help her with. Not all of them were house and DIY related. 'Thanks, Leo. I might need a favour in the garden with lifting a few things. It really is like a jungle out there.'

'Yeah.' Leo nodded and then waved his hand around. 'Best view in Darling though right here in front of your eyes if you ask me and I've seen a few on my travels around the world. Just look at that water and that sky, it never ends on a nice day.'

'Yes, at least I have the view to comfort me.'

'You'll have this place shipshape in no time. Bit of paint and a whole lot of clearing up. The thing is most people can't see it at first glance because of all the crap everywhere, but this here is one mighty old house.'

Lucie, forgetting her braless, unkempt state for a moment, stepped out onto the terrace and followed Leo's gaze to the flagpole at the top of the house. 'There is a lovely old house in here somewhere. There must be. I'm holding onto hope.'

'Just waiting to come out,' Leo replied kindly. 'Give us a shout then if you want anything. If I'm in, I'll help.'

Lucie watched and smiled as Leo walked down the path. *Don't, actually, mind if I do.*

After showering, tying her hair in a ponytail and putting on jeans and an old t-shirt, Lucie made herself some coffee and took another slower walk around the house. Nothing had improved overnight in terms of the sheer amount of work she had to take on, but as she noted things down and nodded here and there, she remembered why she'd been attracted to the place in the first place The old fireplaces, timber floors under revolting carpet, the high ceilings, the antique cladding, the little steps up and down to small hidden rooms, the rooftop decks and the view; all things she valued in a house. All the things she and Rob had always vowed they would have in their next place.

With one hand on her hip and the other around a mug, she looked around the kitchen. She couldn't fathom who had painted it burgundy and edged it in charcoal grey. It was as if someone had purposely set out to make it dark, depressing, and gloomy. On closer inspection, the open shelving only needed paint, the Belfast sink was in good condition, and the cooker would do for a bit. It was surprisingly okay compared to the rest of the house and just about bearable to live with at first. She decided as she pushed up the window to let in some fresh air that she'd spend the morning clearing and cleaning the kitchen and the afternoon she'd set to work on the study to set up her sewing bits. At least that would give her a start, and she would be able to start pottering with her sewing again.

Sighing as she walked out towards the study, she was just resigning herself to days of cleaning ahead but pleased to have a plan, when she heard a sharp rapping on the door. She opened it to see a man standing with a large version of the white basket she'd seen in Darlings in his arms. He smiled a friendly greeting. 'Hello. How are you after the storm? I'm Otis Smith.'

'Hi. Can I help you?'

He held up the basket. 'I come bearing gifts.' He laughed.

Lucie didn't really know what to think, but smiled remembering what Leo had told her, took the basket, and peered in. Little greaseproof packages tied up in butcher's string looked back at her.

Otis continued. 'Some of my mum's cake. Have you had any other baskets yet?'

'No. Should I have?'

'Oh, no, but yes, you will once word gets around. I was just asking to see if you know what they are. It's a Darling thing. You get them arriving for everything. You'll get used to it - birthdays, Christmas, new house, funerals, babies. All sorts. They multiply on the doorstep.'

'Yes, I just realised what this is, thank you. Leo down the road here told me.'

'I bet he did. Rookie mistake from him to say no to the first one when he arrived. It went around like wildfire. Shelly was not impressed. She said something about antipodeans. My Dad, of course, had to mention the cricket. We did laugh.'

Lucie chuckled and stepped back a tiny bit. 'Thanks, then.'

'Oh, no, it's not just that. I'm not some weirdo turning up on your doorstep with a basket,' he said, pointing back to the van and sticking his hand in the pocket of his shorts and pulling out his phone. 'Hang on,' he said as he scrolled down with a frown. 'Yeah, here it is.' He looked back up with a quizzical look on his face. 'What was it? The Hold Your Nerve girls or something. Does that mean anything to you at all?'

It was Lucie's turn to frown. 'Err, yep, it does. Sorry, did you get an email from someone?'

'Yeah, yeah. I've been booked in for this for a few weeks,' he said, looking down towards the van.

'Booked in for what? Sorry, I'm not with you.'

'You name it, my lover. Bit of a play it by ear job.'

A flutter of irritation ruffled through Lucie's stomach. 'Sorry to be rude, I don't have the foggiest what you are talking about.'

'Otis & Co are here to help. We mainly do painting and decorating, but I've been speaking to Tally, and we're down for a bit of garden clearance too.'

'Oh my goodness! Are you kidding me?' Lucie squealed.

'I'm not at all. I thought it was going to be a much bigger job of clearing up after last night, but looks like you got off lightly.'

'They've booked you to come and give me a hand? As a surprise! Oh my!'

'They certainly have,' he said, looking at his email again. 'Tally, that's who I've been talking to. She said you've had a bit of a rough time and will be needing as much help as you can get. You're looking at that help right here, right now.'

'Ahh. Yes, well, she's not wrong there, and I definitely need all the help I can get.'

'You've got me and my lads at your disposal. I'll go and sort out the van. I take it there's a tea going.'

Lucie wanted to jump off the step, throw her arms around this man in the polo shirt, and scream, instead she smiled and nodded. 'Coming right up.'

Standing in the burgundy red and charcoal grey kitchen waiting for the tea to brew, Lucie opened the WhatsApp group.

*I can't believe you've done this for me! Thank you all SO MUCH.*

Jane was first to respond. *Ahh, they've arrived. You're so worth it. We love you, Lucie Peachtree.*

61

Tally's reply was next. *Scumbag Rob can stick it in his pipe.*

As Lucie typed out a message, one came in from Libby. *Can't wait to see how it looks once they get on it.*

Lucie shook her head and typed again. *You shouldn't have done this but thank you. It must have cost a fortune!*

Anais sent a message with a blowing kiss emoji. *You're worth it.*

*Hahahaha, I am!* Lucie messaged back. *I'm just making them tea now.*

Libby chimed in. *It was an arm and a leg like everything when Anais is involved.* She added a load of winking emoticons at the end.

*There's a skip arriving and a man with a van on standby to do a run to the dump if you need it.*

*I'll definitely need it. I can't thank you all enough.*

*How was the storm last night in the end?* Tally asked.

*Scary. I hid under the duvet for most of it, including when the electricity went off.*

*Ahh! I hate that feeling!* Jane added.

*I know.*

*Much damage?* Jane asked.

*Nothing worse than what's already here.*

*Good.*

*At least it will be a bit easier with the help. Thank you. I feel like I could cry all over again.*

*Yeah. Don't worry, Luce. There is a plan. We're going to have you plastered all over Facebook in your gorgeous new house with your new life. There may or not be a professional photographer involved,* Libby added.

*Will I have a pregnant partner over ten years younger than me?* Lucie joked.

*Not sure we can rustle that up. I did hear there was a rather tasty Australian a few doors along though.*

Lucie laughed to herself in the kitchen and typed back. *Don't be ridiculous! I'm not going anywhere near a man for a very long time.*

*How are you going to get that babba then? Sperm donor?*

Lucie smiled at the banter. A question like that from anyone else would not have been well received but from her girls, it was funny. Just.

*Might be a better bet than the last one I tried.*

*That's not hard after what he did.*

*The Hold Your Nerve girls have him in their sights.*

The little dots by Jane's name flashed. *Hahaha. Oh yes. Rob McKintock. Mate, you are so going down.*

Lucie watched as the men picked up a large, plastic, very ugly garden storage cube and lifted it across the garden as if it was light as a feather. They'd only been going for a few hours or so, and the garden was looking better already. Two of them were going around clearing stuff for the skip, one had a strimmer, and the other was sucking up debris from the terrace with a leaf blower.

In the house, the wingback chairs, old ladder, and an assortment of mismatched furniture were now in the dining room at the back and the sitting room was ready for some work. The Three Wise Men were perched in a little alcove by the front door.

In white overalls, Otis had made short work of an assortment of holes and chipped paint on the clad walls. Now instead of the holes, filler looked back and the tall skirting boards and windows were already rubbed down.

Lucie exclaimed as she looked around. 'I can't believe how quickly you've got to work. Just having the junk gone makes it look better.'

Otis rubbed his chin. 'We don't mess around. I've seen a lot worse than this. Not a bit of Artex in sight and a whole lot of beautiful old workmanship. Clear out the crap and get down to the bones of it as it were. We did the same in my place though that was pillar box red not green.'

'Oh really?'

'Yep. Snowdrop White now joins me for the football at night.' He laughed.

'Too funny.'

Otis nodded. 'Trust me. This old bird is going to scrub up well.'

'I hope so, I really do.' Lucie sighed.

'Tough time of it?' Otis asked with a kind look in his eyes.

'Just a bit.'

'Good job you found your way to Darling then. You won't look back.'

'I hope so. I used to believe in the power of the universe before... Before what happened to me.'

'Yeah, don't know about that. Looks like old Lady Darling-down was calling for you, though. That's the old wives' tale for newcomers. Not that I'd know. I've been here all my life, but that's what my old nanna used to say. I wouldn't have it any other way than living here. Who wouldn't want to live so very far from care?' Otis winked.

Lucie followed his gaze out the window and though she felt a long way from not caring, something somewhere inside did seem to agree.

## 10

---

S itting on the tram, Lucie resisted the urge to sit with her head bent to her phone. She stopped herself from scrolling through what would no doubt be a whole load of new images from Serena's fabulous weekend full of things done by pregnant people. Instead of making herself feel sick at how Serena had replaced her, she watched as Shelly rang the bell and the little blue and white tram started to make its way along Darling Street.

'Morning, Lucie. How are you getting on?'

Lucie couldn't believe Shelly had remembered her name. 'Yes, good, thank you.'

'The lads are doing a good job, are they?'

A little part of the old Lucie, the Lucie who lived in a busy town, wanted to tell Shelly to mind her own beeswax. However, Darling Lucie smiled. 'They are. I've been cleaning and scrubbing for hours. Just popping out for a breath of fresh air while they went home for a break.'

'I don't envy you the job of cleaning up that old place. It'll be worth it in the end though, as long as you are not shy of a bit of work. It's a lot to take on and even once it's done, the maintenance on the place down there in the sea air will be a lot. What a place to live though!'

Lucie couldn't have said it better herself. 'Yes, it is. My first-day nerves seem to have worn off a bit, thank goodness. I had begun to ask myself what I had done. In the storm, I was ready to do a runner.'

'Not surprised, that storm was a killer. That old house has a lot of fond memories for the folk of Darling though, so you'll have that on your side.'

'I just hope I eventually do it justice.'

'Ach, sure you will. So where are you off to?'

'I thought I might pop into Darlings for a basket and then pop to sit by the bay.'

'Not a bad spot, I'd say. Walk around to the left, past the old bandstand, around to the end, and look around the bay from there. You'll see the horseshoe if you're lucky.'

'The horseshoe?'

'It's an old Darling thing. The bay is said to be shaped like Lady Darlingdown's horse's shoe. That's what they say, anyway.'

'Right. Wow, I'm learning a lot of things about the ways of Darling.'

'Many more where that one comes from.' Shelly winked. 'They say if you can see the horseshoe, you're good to go, if not, well, yeah, we won't talk about that.'

'What happens if you can't?'

Shelly shook her head. 'Let's just hope you can.'

Lucie smiled and, a few minutes later, made her way off the old tram. Shelly waved as she got off and she looked down the length of Darling Street. A shop with a double bay front and blue and white tessellated tiles was being painted in front of her and a woman stood talking to a workman by the window. She wondered what the shop was being fitted out for and frowned at the sign for 'Brisket and Beer' being removed from the top.

Five minutes later, she was outside Darlings. As before, she could make out from the front the packed tables inside. She recognised the woman she'd seen in the swimming costume and Birkenstocks sitting talking into her phone at a table adjacent to the window, and a tiny little dog was under the table next door nestled up to a leg.

Pushing open the door, as last time she was surprised at how many people were squeezed into the tiny place. The heaving shelves full of bowls, jars and cake moulds looked as if they might all suddenly topple onto the floor and the same waitress, Evie, with the big tawny brown eyes, appeared to be scooting around on wheels. Evie shot her eyes over towards Lucie and raised her eyebrows at the same time.

Lucie lifted her hand and pointed out the window as if to say that she wanted a takeaway. 'I was hoping you might have a basket.'

There was a small frown and then a smile. 'Of course. We've sold out of the made-up ones. I'll get you one sorted if you can hang on for a bit.'

Lucie opened her mouth to say something and promptly closed it again. Clearly, you got what you were given where the baskets were concerned. She hadn't even said that she was supposedly on a diet and would prefer something light. 'Yes. I can wait. Thank you.'

Standing by the window, feeling a bit like a spare part, she watched as the little café did its thing; another waitress in the corner stood on a ladder on wheels taking down little coffee bowls, an older woman behind the tiny counter was busying around making food and in the corner, a group of ladies were playing cards.

Not long after, Evie came back with a basket in her hands and held it out. A blue and white gingham napkin tied up at the top hid what was inside. Lucie looked up with an expectant look on her face and indicated that she'd pay with her phone.

'Oh, no, no.' Evie pushed the phone for Lucie to put it away.

'I'll chalk you up and you can pay at the end of the month. Depending on what you're offering. Simple.'

'Sorry to be a bit thick. I don't pay now? Is that what you're saying?'

'Correct. You'll work it out.'

'How will you remember?'

The silky brown eyes showed a hint of humour. 'We're a bit special on Darling. We don't forget anything. Joking! I don't really know. I just remember.'

'So how will you let me know what I owe?'

'If you bring me something, then you get it for less. Like the old days, you know?'

Lucie didn't really understand but pretended she did. She'd have to ask Leo, he'd probably know. 'Okay. Thank you.'

'You're welcome. See you next time. If we're a bit quieter, hopefully we can have a sit and a bit of a chat.'

Lucie was surprised at the friendliness. 'Oh, yes, thank you, that would be nice.'

Lucie made her way to the door clutching the basket, resisting the urge to undo the knotted gingham linen and peer inside. Instead, she made her way down the cobbled street to what she thought would be the road to the bay. Weaving her way in and out, little glimpses of the Darling colours greeted her everywhere. An old door painted in hazy blue tucked under a staircase, a bunch of vintage buoys tied up with blue nautical rope, a tiny set of stairs going to nowhere. Three little pitched roof windows, a whole long line of pots filled with lavender, a pale blue bench offering a seat.

Lucie had flashes of teenage years as she could feel and hear that she was getting closer to the bay. Making her way through another few roads jumbled with an assortment of white and pale blue houses, she stopped as the bay came into sight at the end. The hazy blue sea was doing a very good job of making the night's storm a figment of her imagination. It looked strangely still and calm after what had gone on. The sun peeped down onto the sand, and Lucie looked down at her map. Shelly on the tram had told her to head to the end and look back. She did as instructed, passing a row of buildings with pale blue scalloped awnings on every window. Sun bleached blue mooring buoys bobbed about in the water and a boat chugged out towards the estuary.

Making her way back to the end, Lucie put her hand on her forehead and squinted back. Looked like she was out of luck. She could see the shape of the bay, but no horseshoe was making itself known to her. She hoped that wasn't a bad omen.

Sitting down on a bench, she put the basket on her lap and opened the gingham linen. Inside was a similar version to the previous basket she'd had. A small rustic baguette sliced in half, a little package of greaseproof paper, a jam jar with a blue gingham lid, a tiny glass pot and bottle, and a small insulated fabric bag. Tucked down the side were a faded napkin, a little pot of sea salt, and a small cheese knife. All Lucie's ideas of a fat-free salad with as little calories as possible went into the bay as she unwrapped the greaseproof paper. Inside was a rustic cacciatore sausage sliced into pieces. In the pot, a tiny label tied to the front read homemade relish and in the insulated fabric envelope, slices of cheese had been wrapped in paper.

Lucie laid a blue and white napkin on the bench, perched the pot, baguette, and bottle full of cordial on top and tucked in. She sat overlooking the water wondering if she had arrived in foodie heaven and decided that Darlings would not be included in her diet plans ever. It was just too good.

Just after she watched a boat go by and a seagull swoop in and land nearby clearly hoping for a tidbit, she suddenly stopped, nearly dropping the baguette in her lap. It was all of a sudden there, right in front of her. Her eyes made out the horseshoe shape as if it had been there all along. The buildings marked the little holes in the shoe, the road, the curve, and the trees behind the houses a tie at the top.

She smiled to herself. Darling Bay was looking better by the minute; maybe she wasn't going to be running off back to the mainland after all.

By the time Lucie made her way back to the tram, Darling had begun to settle in her bones. She wasn't sure if she was imagining it or not, but she felt a smidgeon of hope on the horizon. Somewhere inside, she felt a teeny bit better. The relentless and constant urge to break down into a big blubbery sobbing mess had eased just that little bit as she walked along by the bay and then headed to the tram. Maybe things would look up.

As she got off the tram and made her way along the road and the house came into view, her enthusiasm waned and her heart began to sink. She may have had a lovely sit on the beach, seen the infamous horseshoe form in front of her eyes, sampled a Darling basket in all its glory, and had a lovely ride on the tram back home, but none of it made the state of the house any better. In lieu of all that, it actually now appeared worse.

If she could manage to ignore the scattered debris and junk, there were a few semi-encouraging signs as she made her way to the front door. The weeds and grass had been mown and you could now actually see the lower floor of the house. The whole area needed more than a smattering of care, but the garden now looked a tad better.

Walking down the path and arriving on the doorstep, a little basket was propped to the left of the door. Lucie pulled off the wrapping to find a fancy hand cream and matching soap. She read a small card tucked into the side of the basket.

*Best wishes as you settle into Darling life. Come along and say hello.*
*From all at Darling Sailing Club.*

Lucie smiled as she walked into the hallway. The Darling Island basket thing was doing its job; it felt lovely to be welcomed. Turning left into the sitting room she raised her eyebrows at its improvement. The green paint was but a distant memory hinting just a little bit of its existence under the primer. From the top of a ladder Otis smiled, took out his headphones, and climbed down.

'How'd you get on?'

'Yes, lovely. I got a basket and then went to sit by the bay.'

'Lucky you. They must like the look of you.'

'At least I've got something going for me.' Lucie laughed.

'I bet that was tasty. Darlings never disappoints.'

'Out of this world. Bang goes the diet. Little slices of some sort of meat. Do you know what that is?'

'I do indeed. That would be a Royal Darling sausage.'

'Hah. Hah. Are you having me on?'

'Nope. I'm not. We survive on it over here. There's another once a year sausage too. You'll get to know about that at some point.'

'Ooh. Sounds umm interesting.'

'I'm surprised you haven't seen them hanging up all over the show. They're everywhere.'

Lucie thought about it for a second and realised she had seen sausages in quite a few places; behind the counter in Darlings, in the small supermarket and in a couple of shops as she was getting off the tram. 'They keep us going over here when the weather gets tough, or that's what happened in the old days.'

'Very nice too. I could get used to that kind of lunch every day of the week.'

Otis laughed. 'I do have that lunch every day of the week and I have done since I was at school. Me and all the other Darling kids on the ferry had more or less the same in our lunchboxes in those days.'

'Good memories, eh?'

'Ach, yes and no. You know what it's like.'

Lucie nodded. She guessed she did. Many, many of her memories though, in fact nearly all of them, included Rob. Now he was making memories with somebody else.

'I'll be doing the old Darling punt commute soon,' Lucie noted.

'There are worse ways to get to work. Still family owned and run. Actually, the family owned a lot of places on the bay, back in the day. Not that there are many of them around these days. The family, that is.'

'That's nice to hear it's a local business.'

'Mmm. Yes. You'll be needing to get yourself a permit for all things Darling, especially if you're going to be going back and forth every day.'

'It's on the list.'

Otis smiled and went to climb back up the ladder. 'Okay, back to it then.'

'Yep, thanks again.'

'It's looking better already, isn't it?' he said as he pointed up to the old pressed tin ceiling.

'I should say so. I'm going to get stuck into the utility room and by the end of the day, at least I'll know that the kitchen and that room are clean. Burgundy and grey but clean.'

Otis waved his hand in front of his face and started to dab a paintbrush into a tray. 'Don't you worry about that kitchen. I had a look at those cabinets while I was making a cup of tea. They might be old and an atrocious colour, but nothing one of these won't make a tidy job of,' he said, waggling the paintbrush around. 'You mark my words. They call them handcrafted boutique Shaker style kitchens in the fancy bespoke kitchen shops. Ask me how I know.'

Lucie raised her eyebrows. 'Not seeing it right now, but I'm willing to take your word for it.'

'By the way, what did you see at the bay?'

Lucie put her head on the side and frowned. She contemplated and then replied, 'Yes, I saw it.'

Otis nodded. 'I thought you might. You're okay then. You can stay.'

A few hours later, Lucie nibbled on her lip as she leant into the old clawfoot bathtub with a green spiky scourer. Her mind moved methodically with the scourer going back and forth over everything that had happened. As years of grime lifted from the enamel on the bottom of the tub, she realised that she was now referring to the thing with Rob as a trauma. Was that overly dramatic? To her, it was not. Flashbacks to the day she'd found out would come back to her as she was going about her business. Snippets of the first time she'd realised that it wasn't just another woman but that there was also a baby involved.

Rinsing the bath, watching the stained water swirl down the plug and then sprinkling a fine layer of powder on the bottom and starting the whole process again, she thought about the situation. It was like it had its own rhythm; at first a raw unbelievable hurt she thought she would never ever get over, then denial, then anger mutating to something resembling acceptance. Apparently, these were stages, but it didn't seem to be working in that way for her. Rather than moving sequentially between stages, she flitted like a rocket between an overwhelming plethora of emotions rendering her a lot of the time exhausted.

*Scrub, Scrub. Scrub. Not pregnant. Not pregnant. Not pregnant. Scrub. Scrub. Scrub. Alone. Alone. Alone.*

Lost in her own world, she thought about being on Darling, about her lovely girls who'd kicked the wheel of friendship into action just as they'd always done, and about the fact that at least she had come out of it with a house.

Bum up in the air, head down by the plug, she continued to scrub as if the bathtub was Rob and Serena trying to make them vanish from her mind. Finally feeling as if she'd made headway, she stood up and looked out the window to the water. As a boat sailed past in the distance and she could hear the sound of the waves she hoped that eventually, like the grime in the tub, the whole sorry mess would wash away. She hoped that Darling and its hazy blue would help to heal the rip in her broken heart.

# 11

---

**P**ulling her earphones out of their small white plastic case, Lucie put them in her ears and tied on her trainers. As she sat on the bottom of the stairs, she could feel the extra weight spilling over the top of her daggiest old jogging bottoms. She hated the way it made her feel in every sense of the word. Rob had never liked it when she'd put on weight. Not that he had ever said anything. He'd told her the opposite, in fact. He'd said he'd loved her just as she was. That old chestnut. There was one small problem with the whole thing; he had loved someone else just as they were, a little bit more.

She'd decided the night before that she needed to do something about the creeping weight before it became another too-big-to-overcome problem rearing its ugly head in her life. After she'd finished tidying up the house stuff the evening before, and barely able to keep her eyes open, she had made dinner and then Googled 'how to easily lose weight and get fit'.

Of course, if anyone had known the answer to that question, first of all, they wouldn't be plastering it all over the world wide web for any old bod to peruse the answer, and secondly, they most definitely wouldn't be offering it for free. The initial search deposited her swiftly down a wide and long rabbit hole whose depths she didn't emerge from for a long time. She'd read all sorts; articles on why you might have put on weight after a relationship breakup to healthy choices for the new you after a divorce. None of them grabbed her by the balls.

She'd had another look at the bike with the inbuilt media and perused the website of a woman from Dartford who now lived in Bali, exalting the holistic secret to shedding weight. For a very tidy amount, Dawn from Dartford, who now went by the name of Moonstone, would beam herself back home to Blighty via Zoom, and teach you how to sculpt your body into a whole new holistic plant-based existence. And it was only a hundred and fifty pounds a month.

By the end of the mammoth vortex of Googling, Lucie had felt like she needed a brain cleanse, let alone a diet. The many choices had made the job of even thinking about getting fit and losing the piles of unhealthy choices sitting around her middle, a mountain to climb.

In the end, she'd decided that she definitely didn't have the money to plough into the lack of leanness in her body, and certainly did not possess the motivation for plant-based experiences from Bali. So, she'd closed her laptop, stuffed in another spoonful of buttery pasta, and decided that Darling would be her motivation. Who needed a stationary bike as expensive as a holiday? Who needed to eat a diet of just plants? She would start simple and small. She would combine the expulsion of the extra pounds on her body with exploring the island she now called home.

Closing the front door behind her, she made her way to the beach, gazing up at the old foghorn and lighthouse in the distance. As she plodded along, everything wobbled. She was the walking, talking version of a blancmange. She chuckled and shuddered to herself at the same time as the pale pink jelly-like afters from the school canteen appeared in her mind. She was right: she jiggled just like a blancmange. She thought about it as one foot stepped in front of the other. She so wanted to be more sparkly champagne jelly, less Pepto Bismol scrambled blancmange, and her way to achieve it was going to be long bracing walks by the sea until all signs of the overeating on the cottage sofa were long gone.

Heading along by the water, she thought more about the school blancmange and she was suddenly back in the school canteen. Tally stood beside her, their slightly musty, definitely grotty, grey-green trays pushing along the railing to the dinner ladies behind the dusty plastic roller hatch. The blancmange stood in front of the ladies with the netted hair, and then a long-handled spoon was plonked in and a pink pile of wobbly gelatinous dessert was slopped onto their plates.

Another image danced in front of her eyes. She stopped as she felt the now all too familiar lump in her throat. Rob was in the picture in the canteen. Just like he always had been for as long as she could remember. There she was next to Tally, and then a nudge and a smile as Rob queued up behind them. A connection of eyes. A fluttering of lashes.

She pushed away the image and continued on her plodding walk; her kneecap persisting in poking out of the hole in her jogging bottoms at the knee. She had to constantly keep hiking the stretched elastic in the waistband back over her waist. The crotch sagged to her knees and her muffin top spilled over at the top.

Taking in huge lungfuls of sea air and feeling the breeze on her cheeks, she could smell all sorts of things from the coast. It was sweet and somehow fresh at the same time. Passing a couple on a bench with a flask of tea between them looking out over the water, she smiled. She watched as two men in bare feet and half wetsuits carried windsurfers down towards the shore. Music from an old VW van with a cream crocheted dreamcatcher hanging from the window, its back door open, tinkled across the path. A girl with white-blonde hair and deeply tanned skin sat cross-legged by the van hugging a mug of steaming tea. She raised her eyebrows in a friendly greeting as Lucie passed.

Walking further and further away from the Coastguard's House and the main part of Darling, the feel of everything began to slowly change. She'd read that the other side of the island attracted walkers, nature enthusiasts, and those really looking to get away from it all. Things felt more remote, the sky now appeared endless, the sea stretching out a long way until it met the sky at the end. Everywhere she looked, Mother Nature was quietly getting on with her thing and it worked its magic on the shoulders so tightly wound up near her ears.

A swoop of birds flew high above, a sound she couldn't quite put her finger on came from the trees, waves lapped in and out, tumbling down onto the beach. Even the clouds seemed to be different on this side. Tinged with the Darling blue, she thought, and then thinking that she was imagining things, she whipped her head to the left and right. It must be the tiredness. Things were not tinged with the Darling blue. It was just a cloud.

Her mind started to whir again as she jiggled along. It tumbled over everything she had done and everything she had to do. Thank goodness for Otis and Co. She checked her calendar and closed her eyes for a second. She was quickly running out of time. The day when she had to go back to work loomed and time was moving at an alarming rate of knots. She'd be lucky if the house was liveable by the time the men had finished. What they had done had been more than impressive, but as the enormity of the task and the size of the house became more and more evident, she had realised that she was looking at years to get the house anywhere to what she would have liked.

The slow and steady walking on the pavement by the sea had helped her shoulders, but wasn't doing a whole lot to calm her mind. As the path got rougher and rougher, it eventually tapered off until she was walking along on a grassy, sandy verge hugging the coast, a narrow road to her left. Failing to shut off her mind, she stopped, plonked herself down on the grass, peered down at her stomach to see if it had gone down, and disappointed that it was very much still there, she took out her phone and put the earphones in place.

Navigating to the meditation app, a few minutes later, she was up again and listening to affirmations. As she walked along, she passed an old faded sign. She could just about make out that it said the road, slipway, and jetties were private, but assuming it meant for boat owners, she continued on, spying a place to stop, rest for a bit and continue with the remainder of the meditation. It started to play in her ears.

'You are able to make your own choices in life.'

*No doubt of that, I didn't have a whole lot of say in the matter.* She thought as she pulled her joggers back up.

'You can connect with your real self.'

*Who even is that?*

'You own your own pain.'

*I'm well aware of that, thanks.*

'Your suffering connects you to your heart.'

*Pah!*

'You have the power to do whatever you want.'

She spoke out towards the sea, her voice high and shrill. 'Sorry, not feeling that way right now.'

Tutting at an oversized German car parked right where she had been intending to cross over, she manoeuvred her way around it, stepped over a weird little low timber boom gate, veered off down a rough bitumen road, and stood looking down towards the shore.

'Breathing in, breathing out. Feel the power of the breath. Stomach is lifted and full of pure, undiluted air. Stomach is empty, air is taking away the pain. Cleansing light is flooding every single cell of your body.'

Lucie didn't know about being cleansed or lifted, all she could feel was the gluttony of grief slapped all over her petite frame.

'Slowly put your hands into prayer pose, feel the beating beauty of your heart right underneath your hands.'

Having no idea what prayer pose was, Lucie joined her palms together and stuck them on her chest above the extra weight spilling out over the top of her bra.

'Close your eyes. Look deep within. Retract into the real you. Connect to the darkness at the back of your eyelids. Make your way to the centre of your body. *Feeeeeel* the roots of the centre of this wonderful full woman we call Earth.'

Opening the corner of her right eye, Lucie watched a seagull toddle past, examine a piece of grass, peer up at her, and then move swiftly on. A boat sailed past in the distance, its sail billowing in the wind. The jogging bottoms had ridden down again, but she let them hang there, going with the flow, not bothering to yank them up.

'Inhale, pushing your stomach out, now raise your centre to the sun. Salute the planet, raising your hands over your head and letting divine air flood through your body.'

Doing as instructed, Lucie felt the waistband of her jogging bottoms drop down under her bum and with her throat facing up to the sky, she inhaled, and left them where they were. Following the commanding voice, she wooshed out the air and then nearly jumped out of her skin as a voice interrupted her in full flow just as her hands had clasped tightly overhead. Unused to saluting the sun or posing in prayer, she stumbled back at the voice, regained her composure, and stood gaping in front of her.

A hard tanned set of abs under an extremely taut chest stood in front of her in a wetsuit with the top rolled down. There was a surfboard, at least that's what she thought it was, under the arm. The feet were bare, tanned. There was not even a glimpse of a smile. A just visible bump on an otherwise perfect nose. An ever-so-handsome face. A crinkle of age around soft green eyes. Eyelashes. Gosh were there eyelashes.

'Err, did you not see the sign? Would you mind moving?'

Lucie went to smile and then didn't. A hint of irritation touched at the middle of her eyebrows. How dare this god ask her to move? Like, who did he think he was? Yes, he might walk the land in a different zone to mere mortals by way of his extra-ordinarily good looks, but that didn't mean he could tell her what to do. She'd had enough of that.

Lucie, lovely, polite, most-of-the-time-happy-before-she'd-been-dumped, Lucie looked up at the unsmiling eyes. Aston-ished at the sound that came out of her mouth, she realised that the app had not done anything to relieve her pain, but it had worked on her power or assertion or whatever they were calling it. 'No, sorry,' she attempted to bark. Power Lucie had arrived.

She quickly yanked her jogging bottoms back over her bum, pushed the earphone in a bit tighter, flicked her eyes away, rearranged her hands back into the prayer position in the centre of her chest and lifted her chin just a little bit. The man said something else, but she completely ignored him. She wouldn't even waste what little energy she did have on him. It had depleted enough of her reserves just in the effort of drinking in his very fine form.

He didn't move and waved his hand in front of her, rolling his eyes as he did so. She pulled out one of the earphones.

'Yeah, you're going to need to move. I need to back my car down here.'

Lucie felt her ribs rise a little bit. Being Power Lucie felt quite nice. 'The last time I checked it was a free country and unless you are working for Her Majesty, you can't tell me where to stand or, for that matter, what to do.' Lucie couldn't even believe her own voice. The last time she had heard it had been just before she had started going out with Rob.

The man's eyes travelled down to where the saggy crotch of Lucie's bottoms was nearly down at her knees. She wasn't sure if she was imagining it but a hint of pity may have crossed his face.

'The last time I checked you were standing on my slipway, on my land, leading down to my boat, which I need to put on the trailer on the back of my car.' He jerked his thumb to the car she had passed parked behind them.

Lucie spluttered. 'I didn't know I was on private land.'

'That's why I asked if you'd seen the sign.'

'I see.'

'I don't mind anyone walking along here. Darling's offerings over this side are the best, but when you're standing in the way...'

'Right. There's no need to be rude about it.'

'I wasn't rude.'

Power Lucie appeared somewhere again and did a cross between a snigger and a snort. 'You don't think it would be agreeable to address someone in a bit more of a friendly tone?'

The man put his head to the side as if he was considering Lucie's question. He definitely looked at her saggy crotch again. 'Nup. Not really. I wasn't trying to be your friend, enquiring about your health, or wondering how your day was going. I was just asking if you wouldn't mind moving out of my way.'

Dropping her hands, where they had been anchored in prayer pose just on top of her boobs, Lucie took a few steps to her left. She was now standing on the grass. 'Will that do?'

'Thanks,' he said and with a rapid wave of his hand, still no smile, and a quick flick up of his eyebrows, he dismissed her, put his head down, and headed to his car.

Lucie put her hands back into prayer, pretended to be

unperturbed and to continue with her posing. She raised her hands above her head and did her best attempt at saluting the sun. Ascertaining that he'd moved far enough away, she took a sneaky look as he walked over towards his car. The rolled down wetsuit, the bottom, the long legs, the broad tanned shoulders.

All of it quite frankly delicious and even better from the back.

## 12

Enveloped in the murky green cladding, Lucie dragged her way up the stairs to peel off her sweaty Power Lucie clothes and get into the shower. Even with a day of cleaning and painting ahead, she was not in a fit state to be seen by anyone. It had been a shame the man with the abs and eyelashes had witnessed her saggy knees and drab attire. Not that he would be looking at her. He, like the rest of the world, would most probably be hooked up with the Darling version of a Serena. This version would likely be all cutie pregnant too. Though by the looks of him and his age, he would possibly already have a couple of perfectly turned out children along with a highly educated, exquisitely finished, lean and powerful, plant-based partner.

After standing in the shower rinsing off all the thoughts that had accompanied her on her walk, she made her way downstairs, made a cup of tea, opened the fridge, decided against a slab of chocolate, grabbed her laptop, and sat down on a once bottle-green, now sun-bleached and sad looking outdoor chair. Pressing the cross to open a new tab, she typed in 'leggings for walking' working on the basis that there was no way she wanted anyone, let alone the man with the surfboard, to see her in her baggy trackies and dropped crotch ever again.

She read through an article going deep into the technology of the production of leggings. It informed her that whether or not she was going for walks in the park, extended treks through forests, hikes in muddy woods, or going up the shops for a bottle of wine, the best leggings were comfortable, flexible, sweat-wicking, and a dream to both wash and wear. The right legging, according to Tallulah Brown from Woking, would see you through any adventure.

After flicking around on too many websites and gaping at the one hundred and fifty pound price tag for a pair of leggings promising to sculpt and tone as she walked, she settled on Lululemon. This brand being the one whose best-selling legging, loved, adored, and cherished by the masses would allow her to go out and about on Darling weightless, encased in buttery soft fabric and ready for her practice. The legging reviews noted that they may also sculpt and be comfy at the same time, too. If only that were true. A few minutes later, her tea was finished and an email told her that the buttery goodness and a new way of stretching was on its way.

Going back in to top up her tea and choosing to slice an apple instead of giving into the tempting delights of a chocolate Hobnob, Lucie picked her way over the weeds to the small, shed-like cottage down at the end. The online listing had referred to it as a granny flat. There was no way anyone would put a granny in the building in front of her.

A narrow, sandy semblance of a driveway led down from the side of the house and the small pitched roof building was sporting the same blue tarpaulin on the roof as the coal shed on the other side. 'Subject to council approval,' the details had said the granny flat could be utilised for rental income. Lucie actually laughed out loud as she pulled open the door. What she quickly worked out was this building was not fit for anyone, let alone a granny. Bat poo layered the floor, an old canoe was tied up to the left, and a wood burning stove from the dark ages leant precariously on its side due to a missing leg.

The old floorboards creaked and grumbled at her as she gingerly stepped through the sitting room, a door led to a strange little hallway in the middle of the place, and a steep stairway led to a mezzanine floor. Sticky, congealed poo covered everything. A patch of thick moss grew through the middle of the walls and a slimy circle of mould sat by a window looking over towards the house next door.

She tried, and failed, to push up the window and stood looking out across the estuary. At the end, she could just make out the Pride of Darling floating bridge and looking the other way, she could see the jetties she'd seen that morning on her walk. Out a grotty back door, a small deck straddled right up next to the fence. A washing line had been fixed to the back of the building but had long since given up the ghost and looked on forlornly towards the water.

Up the stairs to the mezzanine, stacks and stacks of old newspapers were dumped in the corner. A waist-high statue of Mary matching the Three Wise Men in the house was lying sideways on an old tartan blanket. She picked up a newspaper and read the date across the top. July 1976. To the right, a small door led to a corridor where two doors opened to the back of the building. In one, a shower over a bath, a toilet without a seat or lid, a tap hanging from the wall. A red spotty dirty old shower curtain swayed eerily in the wind.

As she picked her way back through and down the narrow corridor, she opened the other door to another tiny room. It was just big enough to fit a small single bed, possibly a cot. She tried to swallow down the feeling before it had arrived but didn't manage it in time. Oh, how many cots she'd looked at. How many nurseries she'd decorated in her head. How many pretty little pictures of the ABC's she'd perused in frames. Her heart felt heavy as she made her way back down the stairs. No partner, definitely no baby, what felt like no hope and a copious amount of bat poo in a granny flat not fit for human life. A new life by the sea like on the shows on the telly, this most certainly was not.

She looked up as she heard Otis and Co arriving and sighed. Things needed to look up in Darling, and soon.

L ater on that day after more cleaning, a full skip, lots of paint, and further clearing of suffocating weeds, Lucie was on her way to collect the much praised Darling resident permit. Just about everyone she had spoken to had told her about this elusive thing. It had started out in life as a paper document at the turn of the century, morphed into a circular pass similar to an old-fashioned tax disk with the Darling foghorn emblem watermarked on the front, but was now in digital form and worked beautifully via an app on your phone.

Alighting from the tram at Town Hall, Lucie looked over at the imposing building. It was hardly like the seventies brutalism of the council offices where she'd lived with Rob. On the left a Victorian clock tower, on the right a green dome, high up overhead a plaque informing patrons it was built in 1898. A sign read 'Municipality of Darling.'

Pleased for the first time to be presentable and not covered in primer or dirt or both, she adjusted her hair, smoothed down her jacket and gripped her bag over her shoulder and headed in. Inside, a hush descended, and the air took on a cool, deep scent. Lucie immediately felt as if she had done something wrong. A woman in a tight skirt, red hair, and matching lipstick made a small nod and smaller smile with no invitation to break the hush.

Walking down a long, wide corridor, oak panelling ran

down either side. The hush seemed to increase as she made her way into the depths of the building. It was bizarrely quiet and, apart from the woman with the red hair, skirt and lipstick, she hadn't seen or heard a single soul. At the end of the corridor, three arched windows topped with timber Venetian blinds sat under elegant high ceilings and looked out towards a garden. On the left, a huge room was piled with conference chairs. She turned again and then saw a sign for the council. Another long corridor and by the time she'd arrived, she'd worked out that she'd have been better off going around and in a side entrance.

In contrast to the hush of the rest of the building, the council waiting area was busy. A winding snake of nylon belts led to a bank of windows. A laminated sign instructed her to use the QR code to scan in and go from there. Twenty minutes later, which had flown by as she'd waited in line observing the goings-on of Darling residents doing their thing, she was in possession of a Darling Resident's Permit right on the end window of her phone.

Making her way back along Darling Street, she decided that she'd walk to Darlings. There she'd get a cup of tea, and considering the size of her stomach and imminent arrival of the buttery leggings, she would resist a chocolate croissant or afternoon basket if there was such a thing, and then make her way back to the house for an evening of painting. As she got to Darlings, she was surprised to see it only half full. Feeling bold, she made her way to a small table by the window. A different waitress came up, offered her a coffee and deciding she'd prefer it over tea, it arrived in a bowl with a small cake on the side. Her phone buzzed as she kidded herself that the size of the little icing covered sponge meant it would have little to no calories and popped it into her mouth.

*Hey, Luce. How have you got on with everything?* the text from Tally asked.

*No change, really. There's a lot less junk though, and the walls are less green. How are you? How are the girls? I'll whip them up something later.*

*Don't be silly! You don't have time for that! Shouldn't complain. Work is busy. Life is busy.*

*That's what happens when you go and get yourself twins and a full-on career.*

*I know. I just feel like I'm juggling all the balls at the moment. I don't have time for anything really apart from work and small children.*

*And a husband, career, house.*

*Oh, yes, of course.*

*Look, please don't worry about coming to help. I'm fine. The workmen have been great. It's really helped. I'll be grand.*

*Gosh, no! That's not why I'm texting. I've already packed a bag. The girls are going to my mum's. I'd love a couple of nights with you.*

*What's up? You seem flat.*

*I knew you'd pick up on it. Things aren't great here. I didn't want to burden you with it after everything you've been through.*

*Right. I see. Don't tell Anais or she'll call a meeting.*

*I know I won't, I'm not at crisis point yet, but it's not far away.*

*Good, well not good, we'll talk it through. Okay, well, I'll get things ready and we'll walk to the pub or something and have an easy weekend.*

*Sounds like just what I need. I just don't know what to do and I feel so ungrateful.*

*You are entitled to feel however you want to feel. You have the power to change whatever you like.*

*Blimey! Where'd that come from?* Tally asked, adding a laughing emoticon.

*Hahahahahaha. From this meditation thingy I've subscribed to. You have someone new to meet. Her name is Power Lucie.*

*Goodness!!!! Can't wait to get acquainted.*

*You're going to love her. She's fab.*

*I will. We're going to get her back on the right track and shove her under Rob McKintock's nose.*

Back at home, Lucie smiled at the conversation with Tally. She'd always suspected Tally had never loved Rob. She'd never said anything as such, but there had always been something there. A hesitance, a look sometimes. Lucie had often wondered if Tally had known something about Rob that she hadn't. Something from someone at school. If Tally had suspected anything from the beginning, she had clearly been right all along.

Lucie made her way up the little steps in the hallway and then down again to the room at the back she'd labelled in her head as her sewing room. Just a few days earlier it had been doused in green, the floor had sported a nylon grey carpet, and yellow and white chevron curtains with water damage had hung limply at the windows. Now, bar the fireplace in the middle, fitted cupboards on either side, and one wall entirely made up of pine shelving, it was empty and dust free. Though still only wearing a coat of primer, she could now just about visualise the room for her sewing supplies. A room she could escape to and fiddle and craft to her heart's content. Somewhere she could get lost and not think about Rob.

She'd always pottered with sewing here and there from when she was a youngster. Until Tally had given birth to the twins, she'd dabbled mostly in bits and bobs for the home. She'd made quilts for her mum, made tablecloths and napkins for the local hospice's Christmas appeal, sewn patchwork cot bumpers for a few girls she'd worked with, and made book bags and beach totes for everyone under the sun. But it was the arrival of Tally's girls that had really sparked something in her. It had all started with tiny little bloomers in the softest vintage silk fabric covered in the sweetest ditsy flowers. Tally had cried when she'd presented them to her and it had only spurred Lucie on more. A plethora of things had followed.

Lucie stood in the middle of the little room at the back of the house and looked at the stacked up boxes full of her most prized fabric. She had another load of them in a lock-up storage unit back near her house with Rob. Not being able to face going anywhere near the area once she had been exposed to the truth, she'd left her collection of fabrics where they were. She'd put them in a box at the back of her head and had decided that it was something that really didn't need action until she was more inclined to face the music.

Lucie had been collecting fabric and making things for years, and the move to the country cottage had included her small portable sewing machine and odd few favourite fabrics. She'd realised once she'd found out she was alone, how crucial her sewing and crafting was. The little machine had been a lifesaver. She'd bought it on a whim while wandering around John Lewis with Anais, and it had slowly taken over her main machine and happily moved into the tiny utility room in the country for six months. What she hadn't known then was her trusty machine and boxes of fabric would be moving with her to a little island just off the coast.

She scanned down the boxes, each one carefully packed and meticulously labelled with its contents. The boxes of her favourite Liberty ditsy cotton, her vintage florals from a closing down fabric shop in Hull, which had listed its stock on eBay, and her favourite very valuable vintage collection from Laura Ashley.

Flicking open the top of the Liberty box, she pulled out two pretty pink and blue coordinating florals and walked over to where she'd set up her portable sewing machine. Placing the fabric on the makeshift cutting table, a breeze coming in off the water fluttered around the room. Working swiftly, she soon had pieces for the tiny little billowy puffy skirts for Tally's girls she had seen in her head. They would be edged in a frill and maybe topped with some ribbon. A thick waistband had been cut where a button would sit at the back.

Flicking the switch on the machine, she felt herself automatically take in a deep breath and start to relax. Her shoulders dropped as she clicked the foot up and threaded the fabric underneath. She might have paid to subscribe to a meditation app, but as soon as she was lost in making things, her mind went into its own little meditative zone. As the needle on the machine zipped along, it was almost as if she had been hypnotised. Back and forth it went. Turning the pieces she'd cut out into little items of clothing. Hemming the skirts, adding the frills, attaching the waistbands.

Not long after, she held the two identical skirts up in front of her, more than pleased with her creations. They were gorgeous, and she knew Tally and her girls would adore them. Examining the neat stitching, she smiled at how quickly they had come together. She hadn't needed a pattern; she always worked completely by eye. Her mum had always told her it was a talent, a gift she should explore. She'd never really felt the pull, content in her little world, and had not gone much further with it other than making clothes for the people around her having babies. Wishing and hoping that one day it would be her.

She'd deliver little things beautifully in tissue paper and ribbon and sit back as the oohs and ahhs came. Then there were her favourite things she'd whip up for the home; gorgeous pillows, quilts, tablecloths and napkins, pillowslips and bedding. All carefully selected and meticulously put together with her vast collection of one-off vintage fabrics and normally topped with her signature ruffles, scallops, and frills.

Gazing out at Darling through the window, she thought how much she would have liked to spend hours at her machine rather than try to get the house up to scratch. She could quite happily spend the whole day lost in a world of her own, healing her heart, and creating a quilt for her new bedroom, the one she would sleep in alone, make a Lucie Peachtree version of a picnic blanket for afternoons out at Darling Bay. Maybe a picnic rug crafted with fabric from the seventies. Cushions for the sitting room and little café curtains for the kitchen.

Instead, she had the battle of the tiny back stairs to conquer. She'd had another peek into it the night before and decided it wasn't the most important job in the house, but the most horrid. She could easily close it up until it was the last job on the list, but something was urging her to spruce the stairs up and make them smile again.

Placing the skirts neatly back on the cutting table, she switched off the machine and walked into the kitchen. With a cup of tea in hand, she made her way to the back stairs. In the light of day, they were still daunting. She didn't even want to use the vacuum, and she was more than tempted to slam the door behind her and never open it again.

Big girl pants time went through her head and ten minutes later, with her mug on the little windowsill and holding the hoover arm over her head, she methodically went back and forth, back and forth. The cyclonic machine was doing well at its part of the bargain. She watched as it sucked up years and years of cobwebs layered with dust from time gone by. Dead flies and what looked like ants with wings joined the party and before long, she was clicking the button on the barrel and on her way out to the skip. Shaking the barrel over the skip, a gunky grey pile of grime billowed around her. Jumping back instinctively, it almost felt good to watch it land back down on top of the old junk. More dirt evicted from her new abode.

As she went to walk back in, she waved as she saw Leo striding down the road, clearly late and hustling for the ferry. He waved, called out hello, and tipped his hand to his head. She swallowed and raised her eyebrows as she turned away. She'd had worse neighbours in life. Stepping back over the threshold, she took a break sitting on the bottom step of the stairs, opening her phone to see if Tally had replied about the skirts. Navigating to her emails, she saw an offer from a homewares boutique in her old town who were having a fifty per cent off sale, and tutted at yet another intrusion to her inbox from the bike company informing her in the subject line that it was never too late in life to get fit. Seeing an email from the HR woman at work, she frowned and tapped. She went cold as she read down as the message in the email came crashing down around her ears.

The email informed her that she was going to be made redundant. It had been on the cards for a while, but in all honesty, the problems the company was going through because of supply chain issues with China had not been at the front of her mind since what had happened with Rob. It had been as if she had been at work in body, but not fully in mind. She'd gone through the motions, ticked the boxes, turned up on time, and done the minimum. Now, it was no longer to be.

Leaning back on the stairs, she didn't know what to do or think. All she felt was numb. Was there anything else she could lose? Was this what it felt like to feel as if you had zero control over your life? In the space of not long at all, she'd lost her partner, her house, her rainbow babies, her dad, and now her job. She felt as if someone was playing a cruel joke and that she had lost her whole existence.

Her phone buzzed with a video call from Tally. She clicked the button and waited for it to connect. Beautiful Tally with her deeply golden skin, caramel hair, deep brown eyes, and pretty pink smile, was sitting in her office at work.

'Thank you for the skirts. The pictures are amazing.'

Lucie smiled back in response. 'You're welcome. It was good to get back to it. I really enjoyed making them. I saw a little girl in the village a while ago in something similar.'

Tally shook her head. 'Don't tell me, you knocked them up in ten minutes or something.'

'Not quite, but no, they didn't take me long at all.' Lucie chuckled and batted her hand in front of her face.

'You really need to get going on this shop thing and selling your stuff.'

'Looks like I'm going to have to now.'

Tally frowned. 'What do you mean?'

'I've just been made redundant. I won't be going back to work, I'll be going to get my things.'

'What? Oh no!'

'It was on the cards, as you know. I had that formal meeting and everything. I don't know, I just didn't think it would actually happen. To be frank, I took it all with a pinch of salt. What an idiot.'

'Oh, dear, oh, dear. Now what?'

Lucie rolled her eyes. 'I am officially up the creek without a paddle.'

'I can't believe it. When it rains, it pours.'

'Yep. I'm screwed, more or less. Although at least it actually isn't currently raining because if it was, this place would be even worse.'

'There's no mortgage on it though, right?'

'No, but that means nothing. There's no way I can stay here without a job. The upkeep alone would cripple me, that's even if it's fully habitable. I'll have to put it back on the market.'

'Don't be ridiculous! You are not doing that.'

'I don't know what I'm going to do. At least I won't lose money, actually, I will. The cost of moving and the tax and everything have been massive.'

'What about your dad's money? Is there any of that left?' Tally asked.

'Not really. It all went into the other house. I presume that's why Rob gave most of it to me and wiped his hands of it.'

Tally did a little sniff. 'Pah! I suppose at least he had the decency to do that. I told you about that nurse here who got that huge payout from her uncle, who was that international motorcycle star, remember? She paid for a house with her boyfriend, he stayed around for the minimum, and then bang, took half of everything without a look back.'

'I guess I should be grateful for that. Though Rob is going to get his mum's house when she finally goes, and you know how much that's worth. It's hardly like he's going to be a pauper. Half of me thinks the timing was very good on his part where that is concerned. Even half of that would have been a fortune.'

'Hmm. He's no fool. Crikey, what are you going to do?'

'I literally have no idea. No idea at all.'

'Dare I say it, but you don't seem too upset.'

'I guess not. I feel numb. I don't know, maybe it's a good thing? Draw a line under the whole lot, as it were. Force me to do something else.'

'Perhaps. A bit crap though, to have to deal with this too. Look, I can lend you money, you know that.'

'Yeah. Thanks. I won't need it I don't think as long as I get my act together. I'll have to look for a job.'

'What about the fabrics and stuff? I can put you in touch with the woman at the girls' nursery who is the buyer for that department store. She's always all over it when the girls wear your stuff. She was only gushing the other day over their little day bags with the frill.'

'I guess there wouldn't be any harm,' Lucie mused, shaking her head.

'And you should get stuff online. How many times have people told you that?'

'Ha! Too many.'

'There you are then.'

'The fabric things will never pay the bills, Tally. It's just a hobby. I'll have a look for a job. Get my CV going.'

'Good idea. Okay, well thanks for the skirts. I can't wait to see them in the flesh. Look, sorry, I have to go, my next patient is waiting. I'll see you soon anyway. Chin up.'

'Thanks.'

Lucie watched as the image of Tally disappeared, and she walked into the kitchen. Opening the fridge, she took out a packet of Hobnobs, made a cup of tea, went out to the garden, dragged the horrid old plastic chair right down towards the back, flopped in the chair, opened the biscuits, and proceeded to eat the lot. By the end of the cup of tea and with the empty wrapper beside her, she stared out to the water. The strangest thing about the latest news was that she wasn't upset. Was it at all possible to be completely cried out? Or had something changed?

It was similar to what had happened with the man in the wetsuit. Somewhere deep down inside, there was a smidgeon of resolve. Something was telling her that she would be fine. Power Lucie had arrived. And to all intents and purposes, it felt very, very good.

She smiled to herself and then spoke out towards the water. 'Lucie Peachtree. Hold. Your. Nerve.'

## 13

Lucie spent way too long finding a parking space on Darling Street, doubling back and ending up in a side road behind the town hall. Realising her mistake, she admitted that the tram was always going to be a better option if the parking was like this all the time. Darling might be good at a lot of things, but as far as she could see, parking in the tiny cobbled streets was not one of them. Locking her car, she made her way along the pavement. The afternoon had turned overcast, and there was a threat of rain in the clouds above. She hoped it would hold off.

Strolling along, she peered into the window of a children's shop. Gorgeous little knitted garments hung from wooden pegs on a string washing line running from left to right. Little rag dolls were propped in a vintage children's chair and a Scandi-style cot sat in the corner with a fabric mobile twirling over the top. She peeked further in the window and felt a wave of sadness wash over her. It was just the sort of shop she'd dreamed about mooching around in while pregnant. She'd even gone over it in her head. How she would ponder and potter around looking at little bits and bobs, buy a little stuffed toy, hold up tiny clothes. Now, via the magic of technology, she was witness to Serena doing exactly that. She'd seen her on her Insta stories, all creamy golden skin and blue eyes gazing into the camera, clutching tiny little outfits and teddies, and displaying the biggest, happiest smile.

Lucie continued to walk and window-shop and smiled at a man etching signwriting onto the window of a double fronted shop. Outside a florist completely painted in the Darling blue, its window frames a very pale oyster pink, a woman in a long apron stood chatting with a man holding a bike. Lucie looked past Darling Street to the jumble of houses behind. Every one bar the odd few painted in white. Little cottages with tiny windows. Doors down to basements straight off the pavement. And everywhere she looked, the fluttering blue and white bunting seemed to make things smile. Just as she was about to head to Darlings, she bumped into Shelly, the tram conductor, coming out of a small deli.

'Oh, hello! How the devil are you? How are you getting on at the house?'

Lucie, feeling ridiculously pleased to be recognised, smiled. 'Hi! Phew! Hard work, but I'm getting there. It's going to be a long road. To be honest, I think I might have bitten off more than I can chew. When I was looking for something, I had a list of wants, but now I'm on my own, those wants have changed to home comforts and things that actually work. Oh, and no weeds! That would be a bonus too.'

Shelly nodded. 'Ahh. Yes. That wasn't an easy place to take on.'

'I'm learning that and fast.'

Shelly puffed her ponytail up behind her. 'It'll be grand once you've broken the back of it. I did the same with my place. The day I got the keys, I sat out the front and sobbed. I refused to even go in! I went to my mum's. Too funny. I remember that like it was yesterday.'

'Ha. I think I'm in the same boat.'

'You'll be fine. I walked past it yesterday actually and it looks better already just having some life in there.'

'Oh, right, that's good to know then. The skip's filling up fast, that's for sure.'

'Yeah, I saw that. Otis is a grafter. You'll be fine there.'

'My friends did it as a surprise. I wouldn't have had the budget for it otherwise. It's been brilliant.'

'Wow, that's some group of friends you've got. What, they paid for Otis and Co to come in for you?'

'Yes. I know. We've known each other since we were little. One of them came into quite a bit of money. I guess it was her who paid for it, really.'

Shelly chuckled. 'My kind of friend.'

'Yes.' Lucie looked at the little basket with the blue gingham cloth Shelly was holding. 'Ooh, something nice in there? I'm on my way there now.'

'Yep. A lunch special. Not sure what will be in it today. You'll be lucky to get a seat in there today. It was packed to the rafters when I picked this up.'

'It has been every time I've been in there. I'd better shove off then. Nice bumping into you. Pop in if you're passing again,' Lucie said.

Shelly smiled. 'Will do.'

Lucie sat down in Darlings and, not fancying a coffee, ordered a tea. Suddenly realising that she had no job, she changed her mind on the basket and sat at the last available table in the place, people watching. Her mind went over and over what she was going to do about work. Part of her was pleased, but she couldn't put her finger on why. Her job was her old life, her life with Rob. Her life where she'd thought she had known where it was going. Where she would live in a little country village, bake bread, sew lovely things and spend her days looking after her babies. She'd keep her job part-time and everything would be tickety-boo. That was all but a pipedream in another life.

She looked up and over towards the door as the bell tinkled and a man walked in with a stunning woman. As she looked more closely, she realised it was the man with the wetsuit and no smile. She watched as they got to the counter and joked and laughed with the waitress. The waitress passed over two white baskets and there were more smiles. The woman pointed outside and did a little shake of her head.

Lucie's face turned down at the scene playing out in front of her. The beautiful people with their gorgeous clothes, little baskets, happy smiles. They probably had little ones at school, a lovely, clean house with a distinct lack of cobwebs and statues of the Three Wise Men for company. No wonder whatever his name was hadn't smiled at her in her saggy crotch tracksuit, sweaty armpits, and rolls of fat. His wife looked like a supermodel. A posh supermodel. Lucie couldn't quite remember but the woman looked familiar; she was someone who had done a line of underwear for one of the big high street stores. Marks and Spencer or Debenhams or someone like that. Yes! It was definitely one of those. Flipping heck. An underwear model. Marvellous. And there she had been pretending that her mind hadn't taken a little wander to running her hands over the man's magnificent abs.

She sighed, turned her back so she couldn't see, and sipped on her tea and continued to think about what had happened to her life. No point crying over spilt milk, wasn't that the saying? No, she was going to work her bum off and turn her life around. She pulled the tiny little notebook she kept in her handbag and took the lid off her pen.

Five minutes later, she had a mind map. In the centre was a

bubble divided into three. In each section, three different parts of this thing she was now calling the start of her new life. The sections stared back at her; house, job, and health. Bubbles swirled away from each of the sections. From 'house' she listed all the rooms and underneath each heading added what needed to be done. It wasn't for the workshy. Next to 'job', she listed ideas, including registering her details online, setting up a job search, and looking at the local community pages. Under 'health', the only thing she could stomach listing was walking and stop eating crap.

Putting her teacup down and picking up her pen again, she doodled all the way up and down the margin. Her mind flitted back to the conversation with Tally. Tally was correct; she had always said she was going to do something about her little hobby, but never had. There had always been something more pressing on the horizon and starting a business had always seemed like too much bother. She'd always just liked the stability of a nice monthly salary. The little deposit in her bank account on a certain day of the month with all the tax and insurance and all that stuff done for her. She quite liked buzzing along to work with a milky coffee and being part of a structure. Chatting to the other girls in the office once in a while, going out for a stroll into town at lunchtime. Wandering around the shops. Popping out to meet Rob for drinks on a Friday. Working for herself had never really offered her that.

She thought about her fabrics and making things; there certainly wouldn't be many costs to get her up and running. She had more fabric than she knew what to do with, machines, and now even a dedicated workspace. Maybe this was the universe again trying to tell her something? Lose a partner and a house, gain a few pounds and a small business.

Tally and the girls had always been adamant that she was seriously missing out on a lot of money on the table by not selling her creations. But Lucie had never wanted it enough.

Her mind had always been on something else. She loved her little hobby, her little room stashed with fabrics, making things for her friends, the odd Christmas market stall here and there, but that was always as far as it went.

She gazed out the window onto the street and then circled the small business idea. Her mind went around and around along with the pen. Where would she even start? What would she call it? Would she need insurance and banking stuff and all that? How would she sort it all out on her own?

On the list she wrote down that she would talk to Jane for a bit of advice. She flicked her phone on and scrolled to Etsy and then browsed a website making platform. By the looks of it, she could be up and running fairly soon even with her limited knowledge of all things tech.

By the time Lucie Peachtree had walked out of Darlings, her new business had been born.

## 14

Feeling a lot more hopeful about everything with the lightbulb moment about selling her handmade things, Lucie followed her steps back to her car. Just as she was walking along Darling Street, a few drops of rain fell onto the back of her neck. Picking up her pace, it began to pour, she made her way along the street, past the Town Hall, to the side road a few down and got to her car.

As the heavens opened, she clicked the door and hopped in. Sitting watching the rain lashing down onto the windscreen, she wondered what would happen in the house. Would the rain bring more things to repair? At least there wasn't a storm to contend with, or at least not one that she knew of.

Mulling it over and with thoughts rushing through her brain, she indicated, pulled out onto the road, turned the blower up, and flicked the windscreen wipers on to full. Making her way back through Darling, she watched as she sat at a red light. People ran along under umbrellas and dodged under shop awnings out of the rain. Tapping her fingers on the steering wheel and waiting, as the lights changed and no one moved, the rain seemed to get even harder. Hammering down on the glass, visibility changed and she started to wish she wasn't in the car. Rivers of water rushed down the gutters and a van in front of her showered a woman on the pavement in an arc of rain.

And then suddenly waiting to cross another light, as quickly as it had started, the rain stopped just like that. As fast as it had come down, it was gone again. As if someone had been sitting in a cloud, got a bit bored, and decided to have a bit of fun for the afternoon. They'd looked down on Darling Island, turned on a tap, watched as chaos ensued, and then decided everyone was wet enough and turned it back the other way.

Lucie looked in front as the car she had been sitting behind moved across the junction, water splashing up from the tyres, the tarmac now a dark glistening grey. She'd been staring at the back of the same car for a long time waiting in the queue of lights in the rain and now it finally indicated to turn left and she moved along the little road to head back home. Coming to the end of the narrow road, just for a second, she was disorientated by a glimpse of the blue and white tram somewhere in her peripheral vision. She flicked her eyes to the right, taking them off the road for an instant. She hadn't seen the car before it was way, way too late. The car which clearly had right of way. She was stunned as she jolted forward a little bit and then stopped. She didn't move and just sat in the middle of the junction, not knowing what to do. This was another Rob moment. He would have known what to do.

The bang and crash had been loud enough to tell her there was damage. A woman opposite with a scarf tied under her chin and beige mac was shouting on the pavement. Lucie blinked a few times and then put her hand on her seatbelt. But as she watched things unfolding in front of her, she was unable to move, even though nothing hurt. As far as she could tell, there was no glass anywhere, but there was a lot of noise. A horn honked from behind. One, two, three loud beeps and then another one. Someone shouted. Her door yanked open.

'Are you alright? What the actual hell do you think you were doing? You sailed on through! Unbelievable! It's a good job I saw it coming. I could tell you weren't going to stop!'

The voice continued when Lucie said nothing.

'Hello!'

The voice continued talking to someone else, 'I think she might be hurt.'

And a woman's voice.

'You hardly even touched her. She's probably just in shock.'

Lucie looked to her right. The perfect arm of the underwear model from Darlings leaned into her car. A flash of pert breast in a strappy top. Lucie thought about the fat spilling over her bra as the underwear model peered in.

Lucie still hadn't said anything. What was the procedure when you'd gone straight over a Stop sign causing a man, his gorgeous, slim, leggy, perfectly turned-out wife and fancy car to bang straight into you?

Resisting the urge to either burst into tears or do a runner, Lucie turned to her right at the same time as attempting to undo her seatbelt. As she got out of the car, the woman on the corner, who, seeing that it was just a traffic incident, had lost interest and moved on. Underwear Model was now looking down at her phone and the man previously in a wetsuit was standing looking at the bumper of her car. She blinked a few times as she looked up at him.

His face registered recognition. 'Oh, you again. Not saluting the sun today?'

'No, I was on my way home.'

Lucie stared. Normally in life, she was fairly compos mentis in most situations that were thrown at her. Mostly she had the ability to converse like an adult, behave in a polite and overall personable manner in whatever situation she found herself in. However, it appeared that this man with his eyelashes, abs, and soft green eyes, rendered her unable to do any of the above. She was shocked to hear the tone of her voice as she replied. As it had done before, when she had been standing in her old joggers, she bristled.

'What do you want to do about it?'

His eyes widened incredulously at her attitude. 'Right, so, let me get this straight. You just sailed through a Stop sign, causing me to do an emergency manoeuvre when it was my right of way. You could have caused a very serious accident, and you are asking me what I want to do about it? Is that what I'm hearing?'

Lucie could barely register what he had said. She was much too busy imagining running her hands over the abs, getting lost in the eyelashes, having a long conversation about where he had been all her life. 'I'll get my insurance details.'

'Sorry, did I hear you apologise?'

The blancmange gracing her outside now moved swiftly around her entire being. Lucie felt as if everything was wobbling and not because of the accident. Most definitely not because of that. What it even was, she had no idea. It had never made an appearance while she'd been with Rob, but it was causing her to tremble all over.

As she stood there, she was still preoccupied by things other than insurance but made all the motions that she was serious and capable whilst inside she jiggled. She looked down at her phone and flicked through her files, praying what she needed would be there. After opening a few duds, including a recipe for beef stew with red wine, she finally got to a copy of her car's insurance policy. She pressed the arrow button in the corner and looked up.

'AirDrop?'

He sighed. 'Hold on. I'll turn it on.'

Lucie looked back down at her phone and his tan leather, I'm-from-Surrey-or-possibly-Oxfordshire-maybe-the-Cotswolds boat shoes, and waited for his phone to appear on hers. Under 'Devices' someone called 'Sue Hooper's Mac' appeared and under 'iPhones' a Matilda Huntington-Jones appeared. Of course. Of course, Underwear Model's name was Matilda Huntington-Jones.

And then there it was: George D. *George D? Hmm.*

Lucie pressed the grey button and waited for his phone to ding. 'Right there you are, then. I'll be in touch. Or will you be in touch?' As she registered the reality of dealing with insurance companies, she felt a little shiver of sadness at the prospect of her new partner-less life. Rob had always done stuff like insurance. He'd loved spreadsheets and numbers and shopping around for deals as if they were going out of fashion. In her old life, he would have been there to just deal with something like this. In fact, he would have positively relished it. He might have done what he did, but for the boring old practicalities of boring old life, he'd always been the person you wanted on your team. Now he'd turned coat and was playing for the other side.

George's face clouded a touch. 'There's some damage to mine. I can't quite work out how, seeing as I was going so slowly, thank goodness. It's more than a small dent, though.'

'That's why they're called bumpers, isn't it?'

George just looked at her and didn't reply to her question. 'Okay, are you sure you're okay?' He jerked his thumb towards her car.

'I'm fine.'

He then shook his head as if changing his mind. 'Do you want to call someone to drive you home or something?'

'No, I don't.'

'At the end of the day you might have a bit of whiplash or something like that.'

'I feel perfectly fine, thanks. You seem okay too.'

'Okay, well if you're sure. How far have you got to go? Are you heading to the ferry?'

Lucie frowned. 'What ferry?'

'Sorry, I assumed you were on your way to the ferry. You said you were going home.'

'I am, but not via the ferry. I live just down the road there.'

'Ahh, okay. Where are you staying, then?'

Lucie sighed. She was now over the whole thing and being watched by Underwear Model, who was now sitting on the bonnet of their car and admiring her legs, wasn't helping.

'I said I live here. I live down by the water over there.'

'Over the other side of the punt?'

'Yes. So, what are we doing about the insurance then? I have no idea if my car is damaged or not. Not really my department. I have no idea about cars and even less interest.'

George looked back at her. 'Looks like quite the nice little Audi to me for someone who has little to no interest in cars,' he replied, holding his fingers up as air quotes around "little to no interest."

'As I said. Not my department. My partner, I mean, ex-partner, and something to do with a limited edition that would actually go up in valuation. No idea. The paint colour or something. It just looks dark blue to me. I really couldn't care less.'

'Makes sense.'

'Okay, well, sorry about that.'

'How about I follow you home, then? I'm a bit concerned now.'

Lucie looked over at Underwear Model, thinking she'd rather curl up in a ball than let these two see the Coastguard's House. 'Nice of you to offer, but no, I'm good.'

'I think I will anyway, if you don't mind,' George replied without smiling.

Lucie sighed. Clearly, this George thought he owned the place. First asking her to move when she'd been out on her walk, and now acting all the concerned citizen. 'If it would really make you feel better.'

'It's nothing to do with feeling better. I do not want it on my conscience or around Darling that some woman, who possibly shouldn't be on the road at all, caused an accident which I was, unfortunately, part of, crashed into someone else on the way home, or worse, knocked over a child or something.'

Lucie felt on the tad alarmed at his change in tone and backed right down. 'Okay,' she replied as she opened her door. 'Just follow me.'

Driving carefully along with his car following behind her, Lucie navigated through the narrow back roads of Darling until she came to the junction where most people turned for the floating bridge. As her indicator ticked, she felt her neck. Was it stiff? What even was whiplash? She had no clue. Flicking her eyes to her wing mirror, she was secretly pleased George D had followed her. He was absolutely right. The last thing she needed was another accident. She'd been more than lucky that she'd got away with a dent in her bumper. She was grateful that he wasn't going to sue her for her house, albeit a house clad with murky green and covered in moss.

She drove along, taking a few forks in the road and then indicated to turn down towards the Coastguard's House and then pulled into the road. Pulling up to the house, she parked on the lane and got out of the car. The Otis and Co van was on the drive and as she stepped up onto the pavement, Otis came out from the back and waved.

At the same time, George D got out of the car and before Lucie could say anything, he'd lifted his chin to Otis, and raised his eyebrows in acknowledgement.

Otis called over from the skip. 'Alright, George? I haven't seen you out there for a while.'

'I've been away again.'

'Water temp's been a beaut.'

'I know. I was out yesterday.'

'Ahh, yeah, I went out last night. Got a quick one in after work.'

George turned to Lucie. 'Are you feeling okay now?'

'Yes. Fine, thanks.'

Otis frowned. 'What's been happening?'

The first smile crossed George's lips. 'Not that I knew it at the time, but our new neighbour here decided she quite liked the feel of my bumper.'

Lucie swallowed and thought about feeling the abs.

Otis laughed. 'You can't keep out of trouble, can you?' he said, looking at George.

'Tell me about it,' George replied and raised his eyebrows.

Lucie opened the gate. 'Thank you for escorting me back home. That was nice of you to be concerned.'

'No problem. It's what we do here.'

Lucie nodded. 'I pinged you my number too if you need to change your mind on the insurance or anything.'

George went to walk back to his car. 'Don't worry about it. Should be fine,' he said as he got in.

Lucie made her way back to the front door, and Otis stood on the drive. 'You okay?'

'Yes, I thought I was fine before, but now I feel a bit shaken; it was quite a bump. I'll go and make a cup of tea and bring you a cup out and have a sit down.'

'Best offer I've had all day,' Otis joked.

Ten minutes later, Lucie was sitting in the manky old white plastic chair out the back with Otis beside her.

'Not your best start to your time in a new town.'

'Nope. I guess it could have been a whole lot worse.'

'You sure did pick someone to bump into,' Otis mused.

'I know. Blimey. What, is he the local superstar with resident model wife or something? Don't tell me, they live in a huge modern house with all the bells and whistles and have four gorgeous children and a nanny.'

'Ha! Not quite.'

Lucie wanted to grip onto Otis's shoulders and grill him

about George D, extracting every little bit of information about him she could. She attempted, however, to remain nonchalant and sipped on her tea and asked, 'They live locally too then, do they?'

Otis pointed down towards the water in the same direction that she'd been on her walks. 'He lives in a big white house down there. If you haven't seen it already, you definitely will.'

'Right, yes, I think so. Sort of curved at the front?'

'That'd be the one.'

'Ah, well. I probably could have picked a better way to meet the neighbours.'

'Yeah. He's alright, though. Can't knock him after what he's been through.' Just as Otis was about to continue, his phone rang. He slipped it out of his pocket and grimaced. 'I have to take this or I might not make it through the night alive.'

Lucie chuckled and went to pick up the mugs. As she walked into the house, she thought about George D and whether or not she would bump into him again. By the way she felt, she was really rather hoping that she would.

# 15

Balancing a cup of tea in one hand and gripping the back of the horrid old plastic chair with the other, Lucie dragged it further over the garden. After the earlier downpour, the sun had started to dip in and out through a honeycomb of clouds, allowing the Darling blue underneath to show its face, and Lucie had decided to have a break and sit in the warmth of the sun. Getting to the back fence, she bumped the chair up over the section where the fence was lying on the ground and pulled the chair over towards the water. If she was going to be living by the sea, she might as well make the most of it. She couldn't quite believe, by the lack of outdoor seating areas, that the previous occupants had clearly not been interested in the garden and its view.

Old fishing buoys littered the narrow section of shore, a smattering of seaweed washed in and out, an oar leant up against a pile of wood, and a huge plastic fishing box was wearing the same moss as the roof of the house. Putting her mug of tea down, she pulled her jogging bottoms up to her knees, dragged the chair into the water, picked the tea up, and sat watching the gentle waves lapping at her feet. Needed improvement, but not a bad place to sit with a cup of tea.

As she watched a little group of birds potter around in the sand and wondered if fish could swim this close, she thought further about her job, the insurance thing with her car and the house. All in all, she had no clue what to do about anything. Part of her wanted to just hibernate and forget about her life. She would stay under her duvet and spend every night eating and eating until she was so fat someone would need to come in with a crane to lift her and deposit her on the loo. Apparently, there had been a study at a university in Stockholm on women who used food to take them out of a situation. The study had gone on to refer to the phenomenon as 'emotional eating.' She hadn't needed a lecturer from Sweden to educate her on that.

The meditation app dinged, asking her if she had practised the art of keeping her mind healthy today. She laughed to herself. Did sitting in an old plastic chair with a cup of tea constitute as keeping her mind healthy? She thought not.

She mused it all further; other people clearly had an exponential crisis and emerged from it setting themselves shiny, admirable goals. She was crawling her way out of it, wondering how in the name of goodness she was going to survive life without her crutch of the post-grief cheeseboard. She sat there with the tea, the water, and the birds, pondering it all for a while, and then took out her phone. After replying to a text from Jane, she messaged Anais to see if she was able to chat. Anais responded with a video call.

'Hi! How are you? And where are you? Looks nice! Ahh, I miss Darling.'

'I'm good, well, as good as someone who owns a mossy house and has no job can be.'

'No job! What?'

'I am officially being made redundant.'

'Nooooooo!'

'Yes. It was on the cards, remember I told you?'

'Yeah, you need that now like a hole in the head, though.'

'I know.'

'You don't seem too perturbed.'

'Hmm. I know. Strange. I guess I'm not.'

'What are you going to do?'

'I don't really know. Look for a job, I guess. Tally said about doing the homewares and sewing stuff. I've made a lot of notes and have a bit of a plan.'

'Excellent. We've all been telling you that for long enough.'

'I know.'

'Maybe it's the universe moving things around for you to finally get going on it properly.'

'I would have preferred it if the universe had been a little less dramatic. The addition of a twenty-four-year-old and a baby was a bit harsh.'

'At least you can joke about it,' Anais admitted.

'I don't have a lot of choice.'

'I guess not.'

'Don't say anything, but I don't know, I've got used to it. I almost, dare I say it, have a little bit of me, who is, I don't know what the word is, relieved, is it that? Yes, I think it is.'

'Relieved? I'm not with you.'

'Oh, I don't know. I'm probably talking rubbish, but I was with Rob when I was sixteen, did all the things, bought a house, went on holiday, worked the same old nine to five, tried to have a baby. Blah, blah, bah. I've never done anything but follow that line. You know? It's sort of boring and predictable. The trajectory of my whole life was mapped out. Or so I thought.'

'Mmm. I don't think it was as bad as all that, but I get where you are coming from.'

'Anais, I haven't even had sex with anyone other than Rob.'

'Well, that's not all it's cracked up to be! That I can tell you.'

'You know what I mean, though.'

'Maybe there are things around the corner for you that you thought were never going to be.' Anais laughed and rolled her eyes. 'Sex with all sorts is coming for you by way of the universe and Darling.'

'Goodness! Who would want me anyway? I've put on a tonne of weight, and I can't even remember the last time I was wearing proper clothes and didn't look like I'd just come through a hedge backwards.'

'I bet you don't. How's the house going?'

'Better, but still loads to do. Not helped by the fact that I had an altercation with a car.'

'Oh, what sort of an altercation?'

'One involving an up himself, very good-looking I do have to admit, local, his stunning wife, and their extortionately expensive car.'

'Yikes. What happened?'

'Just a bump in the end. It was my fault.'

'Blimey. A new house, you've lost your job, had a car accident. Makes you wonder if there's anything else on the cards. So much for things coming in threes. You've had loads more than that.'

'Yes, yes, it does. I wonder what is going to happen next?'

'I'm not actually sure if you want to know.'

## 16

A few days later, Lucie sat at the table in the kitchen with a cup of tea and her open laptop by her side. She rebuked herself for even letting the thought of looking at Rob's Facebook page enter her head. Instead, she navigated straight to Groups and looked through the Darling community page.

There was a very rare allotment available after the sad passing away of Percival Firth, the renovation of one of the old trams was going well, and the library was going to be closed for a whole morning for deep cleaning. Lucie scrolled further down. The jobs were few and far between. A housekeeper for a large house plus a boat and boat shed, an assistant for a new bakery opening on Darling, and an admin assistant for a tile company in Darling Main.

With nothing taking her fancy, she clicked on to her emails. Six new emails in her box, none of them particularly interesting. One from HR giving her copious amounts of details about her redundancy, including a pdf attachment full of all sorts of legal things, whereby the words seemed to actually jump off the page and dance in front of her eyes. There was also an email from Tally. When they'd chatted and Lucie had sent her pictures of the skirts, Tally had said she'd mention it to the buyer at the nursery if she bumped into her. Now, Tally had forwarded an email from the woman noting that if Lucie wanted, she'd be more than happy to have a Zoom meeting, and maybe Lucie could send through a few samples.

Lucie read through the email. It seemed way too good to be true. The cut from the shop was probably going to be massive and it wouldn't be worth her while in the long run. She'd heard about people who tried to turn their crafting hobby into a business working for more or less nothing or what was termed in other parts of the planet as slave labour. So far, the turns in her life had been far from good, and why would this be any different? This was probably going to be nothing more than a goose chase, but what did she really have to lose?

Pouring herself what she reckoned was her fifty-seventh cup of the tea of the day, she thought about the little skirts she'd made. They'd taken her no time at all and completely been conjured up out of her brain. She'd first made tiny little bloomer versions when Tally had had the twins and she'd gone out shopping with Anais for pretty little things. In shop after shop, bland, overpriced, unisex baby clothes with grey elephants and muted tans had stared back at them. Anais had winced at some of the things and by that evening, Lucie had raided her fabric stash and in fabric covered in ever-so-pale daisies and little pink leaves, Tally's twins had the most beautiful bloomers with little matching crowns and bibs.

Oh, how they'd laughed at the crowns. Lucie had realised how little she knew about babies when they'd tried to ram them on their heads. The next time she made anything, she'd added a sweet little floral headband and left it at that.

Sitting at her laptop, she mentally went over how many little items of baby clothes she'd need to make in an hour to make any money. With her notepad out, she soon worked out that actually, it was not a lot. Staring at the screen, she wondered what to reply to Monica, Tally's friend from the nursery. Did she really want to bother? She assumed it wouldn't take her too long to get another job and did she really want the stress of having her own business? She would always be wondering where the money would be coming from. It just hadn't ever been anything that was going to be her scene. An entrepreneur, she was not.

After walking into the sewing room, she rummaged through the top box. There was more than enough fabric there to make a few things up. If she could stomach it, she could even drive over to her storage unit and get some things she'd already made. Deciding, in the end, that she had nothing to lose, she replied to the email.

*Dear Monica,*

*Thank you so much for chatting with Tally. I am really glad you've always liked the little things I've made for her girls. As Tally said, I currently don't have a website or anything like that (all of my ideas and creations are one-offs and straight out of my head), but I would love to have a chat with you. I'll make up a few bits and bobs and put them in the post if you like - your daughter sounds like a sweetheart.*

*Kind Regards,*

*Lucie Peachtree.*

Reading it through again, Lucie thought that honesty was the best policy. Monica had asked if she had an online presence and had used a few buzzy industry words, projections, and stuff like that. The only thing Lucie knew for sure about what she created was that she was never, ever going to run out of ideas. Before she changed her mind, she hit send, made another cup of tea, took out two biscuits, and dunked them in the tea.

Back in her inbox, an email slid in at the top. After a world-wide delay, Lululemon had outdone themselves and a pair of buttery loveliness would be winging its way over to Darling Island the next morning. She chuckled. Sculpted, entrepreneur, buttery clad Power Lucie was on her way.

Lucie had woken up and momentarily forgotten where she was. There was something outside letting her know quickly enough though as the Darling foghorn sounded. Opening her eyes, she stared directly up at the ceiling. Even though she was darned if she would admit it, she was still feeling weird about waking up in bed on her own. It was strange, really, because she'd always loved the times when Rob was away. Looked forward to a few quiet nights doing her own thing. What she hadn't known then was that Rob himself wasn't quite as alone as she'd thought he was.

Sitting up and walking across the bedroom, she pulled back the curtains and glanced outside. Sure enough, the foghorn was definitely correct. A thick layer of fog sat down by the sea. At the very top, it faded away showing a narrow line of Darling blue. She smiled to herself as she looked at the horizon. Either she was imagining it or her overall mood and outlook on life had lifted just a little bit. She was hardly jumping around celebrating that her partner had decided on a whole new family unit with someone else, but as she looked out across the estuary, she felt a little bit brighter.

Thinking about it on the way down the stairs to make a cup of tea, going past the green clad walls and the statue of the Three Wise Men now standing in the hall, she thought it was something to do with the redundancy. Instead of making her crumple into a ball and give up, it had almost made her bounce back. Yeah. She could and would survive.

As she stood by the kitchen cabinets waiting for the kettle to boil, she scrolled down the meditation app and looked for something that might be a good start to her day. Next, instead of half a packet of Hobnobs, chopped up some fruit, added a dollop of homemade yoghurt she'd bought from the deli and topped it with a sprinkling of coconut.

Tucked in beside the table, she sat with the fruit and the yoghurt, ridiculously pleased with herself for her healthy choice, but still positive that she preferred a Hobnob smothered in milk chocolate rather than an apple covered in a cheat's version of cream.

Looking out towards the water, she wondered why the gradual change in mood. Her whole outlook felt different. She was enjoying the days in the new house and not minding the perpetual access to the fridge. Just as she was thinking about another cup of tea, the bell went at the front. She squeezed herself away from the table and opened the front door.

'Ahh, there she is. I thought it was about time I had a parcel to deliver. Postman Paul here.' A wide grin accompanied the friendly greeting.

'Hello, Postman Paul.' Lucie laughed.

'Nice to meet you, finally. I heard you'd moved in. How are you getting on?'

'Not too bad, thanks. As you can see, I've got a lot of work on my hands.'

A small basket was hooked over Paul's left arm. He held it out. 'This is for you from all of us at Darling Post Office.'

Lucie took the small, rectangular basket and peeked inside. Under white tissue paper sat a beautiful mug, a tin of loose leaf tea, and a packet of artisan biscuits. 'Ooh, delicious, thank you so much. I can't wait to tuck into these. I certainly need many tea breaks in this place.'

'You're welcome. Yes, I can see you've got a lot on your hands. It'll be worth it in the long run.'

'I hope so.'

Paul held out a postal satchel. 'Right you are then, and here's your actual post. Lulu something or other.'

'Oh yes! Lululemon. My leggings have arrived. Thank you. These are going to transform my walks, apparently.'

'Really? There you are then, my lover.'

Lucie laughed. 'I think I have to put my side of the bargain in too to see the results I want.'

Paul nodded. 'Fog's up this morning. Careful what you get up to if you're on the water.'

'Oh, no, no. I won't be on the water, Paul.'

Paul looked up at the sky. 'It'll have lifted in not too long by my reckoning and then we're going to have a real Darling day.' He turned around and pointed along by the sea where Lucie had walked before. 'The blue'll be fantastic down there later. Mark my words.'

'Right. Thanks for the tip,' Lucie replied, holding up the satchel. 'With these arriving, I've got no excuse.'

'Yeah, lovely day to sit up there. Make your way all the way to the end and let yourself take it all in. I've lived here all my life and there's nothing like it. Well, our place in Greece comes a close second, but not quite.'

'Thanks, Paul. I'm sure I'll see you again.'

'Oh, yes. I'm Darling's only postie. You'll be seeing me again for sure.'

An affirmation of self-love was playing on Lucie's phone as she took the leggings out of the packet and held them up in front of her. She'd read so many reviews on leggings that in the end she'd actually forgotten which ones she'd ordered. All she could remember was that firstly, she was sceptical, and secondly, that they promised to be buttery and comfortable which she doubted. She did, though, hope that they would perform all sorts of magic and give her the impetus to get out there and walk off the months of sitting on the navy-blue sofa in the tiny cottage, eating away her sorrows. A humble pair of leggings, an island full of fresh sea air, and a lot of walking were also going to wash Rob McKintock right out of her hair. Or so she hoped.

She peered inside the leggings at the label and then ran her hands over the fabric. It was definitely buttery, she'd give them that. The voice from her phone filled the room with its soft dulcet tones and accompanying background music.

'I adore my body. I am constantly amazed by the way it moves, the way it breathes. It provides me with a loving home.'

'At least someone has a loving home,' Lucie said to herself as she pulled the soft material up over her legs. The waistband sat beautifully, and the fabric felt amazing. She felt as if it was an illusion. For someone who knew a little bit about fabric, she'd just watched a miracle occur on her legs. Frowning as she looked down, she was pleasantly surprised.

The image greeting her now, courtesy of a rather on the expensive side pair of leggings, was vastly improved to the woman who had left the house for her walks before. Then, in her saggy old joggers with the crotch down to the knees and seat resembling a nappy, she'd appeared as she had felt since Rob had left; the epitome of grotty. Now encased in the miracle leggings, she felt a little bit better.

Running her hands over the leggings, she thought that perhaps they were another message from the universe that there was a glimmer of hope on the horizon. That she was going to survive. She still had to tuck in the blancmange wobbles in the top, but overall the leggings were not bad. Not bad at all. Not twenty-four, blonde, blue-eyed, and pregnant, but not quite given up the ghost yet.

'When I move my body, my cells tingle and I am creating my own life force all about wonderful me. I am a vision of how I want my life to be,' the voice informed her.

'Goodness. Am I? Almost frightening, actually.' She chuckled into the mirror.

Looking down at the leggings, they skimmed her ankles just

as the many reviews had said they would. Indeed, had her legs lengthened a smidgeon? She looked back in the mirror, closed her eyes, opened them again, and decided to test out the way the leggings apparently moved seamlessly with one's body.

Attempting ten jumping jacks, everything from her upper arms to her wrists wobbled, she nearly keeled over due to the effort, and collapsed on the floor breathing heavily and laughing. She looked into the mirror as the voice droned on in the background. Ignoring the monotony of the voice, she laughed and spoke to herself, 'Okay. Going hard, people, going hard. Leggings in situ, trainers to be ordered, next stop: the world. Power Lucie is on a mission. A mission to find herself.'

Walking right down by the water, Lucie held both her trainers in her hands and let her toes sink into the cool sand. Tied up boats bobbed around on their moorings and whatever was happening to her inside when she walked by the sea, was happening again. The coastal air and water were working their magic. She gazed down at large clumps of green-brown seaweed, hopped over a pile of weathered driftwood, and bent down to examine a few shells. As she wandered in and out, lulled by the tide lapping back and forth, her mind gradually began to relax and decompress. Looking around at the hazy fog, as Paul had said, it was just starting to lift. Thick, sweet sea air brushed against her face and the sounds of the tide soothed her as she walked along.

She'd turned the other way when she'd come out of the house, walked along the road, back down to the water, and was heading towards the Pride of Darling punt. She could see the tram station in the far distance and people here and there as the fog began to lift.

As she got closer and closer to the floating bridge, she

watched it gliding its way over the rippling water. Stopping, she leant against a railing, the smell of seaweed and a salty brininess filling her nostrils. A colony of seagulls swarmed over the top of the ferry, appearing to drag it along underneath them. A short line of cars waited on the slipway to load onto the floating ferry and coming the other way, school kids in uniform and backpacks stood to the side leaning over the railing looking down into the water.

Lucie spotted the same ferry man in charge as when she'd first arrived on Darling Island. As he stood waiting for the ferry to slip into shore, he smiled and waved to passengers waiting and bent down to talk to a child in a pram. Lucie looked at the old ferry and let out a little sigh. She'd not been here very long but already it felt comforting as she watched it going about its business. There was something about the white and blue paint, the taut wires slipping in and out of the sea, the coming and going back and forth all day long. It felt solid and comforting and reliable. Rather the opposite to her ex.

As she watched the goings on, she thought about a video she'd watched while stuck down the legging vortex. Your core and your mental health, according to a woman from New Zealand on the app, were an integral part of the feminine psyche. The video had claimed that ten minutes a day working on your core would help in so many ways. Do it anywhere, it had said; standing in a queue for the bus, in your lunch hour at work, while making a cup of tea. She'd quite liked the idea of doing exercise for just ten minutes a day and so had watched as the woman in a crop top, long French plaits, a tan, and bare feet demonstrated all sorts of exercises to do in just ten minutes a day.

Recalling one of the videos, she used the railing to steady herself and began to lift her right knee up and down. Three sets of eight later, she wondered if the burn coming from both of her legs was normal and switched legs. Just as she had done three sets of rising up and down onto her toes, and was feeling as if someone had stood behind her with a match and set fire to her calves, she stopped and squinted. George D. George D standing on the ferry. George D and Matilda whatever-it-was, whatever-it-was were on the ferry coming back.

Matilda was sporting a red boho dress with a handkerchief bottom, puffy cuffed arms, and a tie on the centre panel. A clutch bag was tucked neatly under her arm and a fedora with a red ribbon topped it all off. Lucie sighed: it was the sort of outfit that shouted, I'm fun, I'm free, I'm rich, I love sitting around for long days in the sun, I often flit off to the South of France for a few days, I take my fedora with me everywhere. It was the sort of outfit Lucie, with her petite frame, would resemble a sack of potatoes in. In addition, the fedora would be squashed and the red would have sucked all the colour out of her skin.

She watched as George D strolled off the ferry beside Matilda in the flowy red dress. She wondered where they'd been. Matilda looked up at him and smiled; he didn't seem to smile back. *Probably on the way back from the school,* she thought and was almost immediately struck by a pang of sadness. The little scenario, minus the ferry and the boho dress, was how she thought it was going to be for her and Rob. She would be clad in a cosy Fair Isle jumper and they'd flit about in the countryside with their little family and everything would be tickety-boo. There would be wax jackets, welly boots, happy smiles, and country hats. Only there wasn't.

She lifted her right leg to the side for three sets of eight and watched as George D and Matilda strolled along the slipway. They weren't holding hands and weren't doing that tight little side-by-side walk that hopelessly in love couples did, in fact they weren't close at all, but they were ticking all the other happy couple boxes right there in front of her eyes.

Not wanting to witness the perfect little scenario any longer, she turned around and worked on her other leg. Five minutes later, her legs now wobbling not only like blancmange but also topped with jelly, she continued her walk. Most people, including George D and Matilda, were long gone; the ferry had unloaded, the snake of cars waiting was now bumper to bumper on the ferry, and it was preparing to go the other way. A few straggling passengers headed to the tram and a man in a white Land Rover was leaning out of the window chatting to a woman in a suit. As she got to the end, she saw Leo, the Australian, in his work uniform and a leather satchel over his shoulder. Spying Lucie, he broke into a huge smile.

'Hey, how ya going?'

Lucie smiled, thinking how lush he was. Everything about him seemed to be burnished bronze and taut. 'I'm good. Much better than when you last saw me.'

'Good. I heard you had an initiation into all things Darling with a bit of a bang.' Leo winked.

Lucie frowned. 'What do you mean?'

'A bump with a big car.'

Lucie chuckled. 'Oh, yes! Gosh, not one of my better moves, that. How the heck do you know?'

'Remember, you can't do anything around here without everyone knowing. See that ferry there? It's like an old school newspaper gossip column. Everything gets talked about on there. You've certainly made it known you're here, that's for sure.'

'Yikes. It was the tram. It totally threw me. It was a very good job neither of us was going fast or it would have been a different matter altogether.'

'Of all the people to get in a traffic accident with!' Leo raised his eyebrows. 'By the way. I'm having a barbie if you want to come along. Saturday night.'

Lucie wanted to ask what he'd meant by the first comment, but the moment had passed. She certainly wasn't going to say no to a barbecue. She'd had worse invites in her life.

'I'd love to. I'll have my friend Tally here.'

'More the merrier,' Leo replied.

'Lovely. Thank you. What shall I bring?'

Leo considered for a second. 'Salad would be good.'

'Excellent. See you for a few sausages then.'

Leo laughed. 'Yeah, nah, this is a proper barbie. There won't be a sausage in sight. Not even a speciality Darling sausage.'

'Rightio. I like the sound of it.'

'There'll be a few Residents invited.' Leo winked. 'Now you're officially a Resident permit holder, I'll let you in. You still need to be on your best behaviour, though.'

'Appreciate it. Lovely. I'll bring a salad, drinks, and my very gorgeous friend. I think you'll like her.'

Leo smiled. 'See you. We'll start your initiation process then.'

## 17

The next day, Lucie wondered what had happened to her legs and then realised. The ten minutes of tiny little movements the day before had somehow resulted in someone pouring molten lead into her calves. Now she was finding it very tricky to move said legs in any direction at all. Wincing as she took the few steps up in the hallway, she pushed the door open to the sitting room and looked around. It was faring better without the friendly faces of the Three Wise Men by the fireplace, and light now actually came in from the window. Things were looking up. According to Otis, who knew everything about paint, its application, and the whys and wherefores of the drying process, the walls were two top coats and the same in days away from the murky green that had greeted her when she'd first arrived, from being but a distant memory.

Dragging the ladder over, she sat on the bottom step and stared at the jumble of paint accessories. Suddenly, she was back, way back, standing in denim overalls and laughing. Rob was just in his boxers, jumping about, wielding a paintbrush and messing around. They'd laughed and joked and mucked about as they'd painted the tiny box room earmarked for the nursery.

A few months later, that same nursery door had been ceremoniously closed with more than a few tears.

She scraped the huge industrial tin of paint towards her, tilted it back so she could read the instructions, and sighed. Being in charge of a can of paint, apart from a touch-up on the garage door at her old house, was a new experience for Lucie. Not that she'd ever thought that she couldn't do it, more that it had always been something that was mostly done by Rob.

Now she had more than a few rooms to practise her painting technique on. Over a cup of tea, Otis had been an excellent help in the conundrum of what and how she was ever going to get the house even half livable. He'd divided up the time he and his lads had available, ascertained the jobs she wouldn't be able to do on her own, and instructed her on what to do after they had gone. He'd told her that they would be better off spending their time on clearing the crap, as he had called it, fixing things, preparing surfaces, priming, and getting things working again and that anyone could learn how to use a paintbrush. With mugs of tea in their hands, they'd gone around the garden noting down jobs and stood in the granny flat where Otis had shaken his head and spent a lot of time with his eyebrows at the top of his forehead.

With what Otis had done, the Coastguard's House was clear and cleaner but now a shell. Every piece of dirty old junk had been removed, the garden before more wasteland now had blades of grass, and the front path was clear. The granny flat, while not clean or painted, had been removed of its more undesirable items, and the third floor in the house with the portholes was a little less on the house of horror's side.

Wedging a screwdriver under the paint lid, Lucie gritted her teeth and levered. Not budging, she put her weight behind it and jimmied it all the way around. As it finally flicked off, it felt like she'd climbed a mountain. Stirring the paint, she watched as it swirled. It wasn't just the paint swirling, her whole life was swirling too. But now, with her new reality, she was determined to get stuck into the Coastguard's House and shed the despondency and sadness of the past few months. The pure white paint felt like a clean slate - soothing to her jagged, cried-out edges, and as she poured it into the tray, she decided that surely there were better things than being with the person that Rob had turned out to be.

A few minutes later, she was standing at the tongue and groove clad wall with the paintbrush. She tried to remember what Otis had told her. He'd mentioned all sorts when talking to her about DIY; ocular sander, working horizontally, easing the paint in, allowing a minimum of drying time, watching for runs. She started painting back and forth. The brush smoothed over the primer and after a while, she almost gave herself a side-eye. Who knew she would quite enjoy painting? Perhaps not three floors or a granny flat's worth, but so far, so good.

By the time Otis and Co had arrived to jet wash and undercoat the outside weatherboarding, she'd already completed one wall. As she saw them pull up and climbed down off the ladder, she popped back to the kitchen, flicked on the kettle, and went to open the front door. On the now clear front step was a basket. Gathering it up into her arms, she waved to Otis and took the basket in. After putting water in the teapot, she pulled off the tissue paper from the basket and looked inside. A white candle with the Municipality of Darling sticker on the side filled the air with the scent of lavender. In beautiful white calligraphy, an old-fashioned luggage label had the council's foghorn label printed on the front.

*Welcome to Darling. We hope you love it here. From all at the council.*

Lucie put the candle down and leant against the sink and gazed out the window. A golden arc of sunshine speckled through the clouds bouncing off the water at the far end of the garden. With her middle fingers, Lucie pulled her eyelids down to squeeze away even the thought of a prick of tears. There was no way tears were happening again. Big girls in old houses did not cry. But the basket with the candle had jolted something inside. It somehow embodied the huge journey she was on. Solidified that she'd made it to this little island on her own and that other people were willing her to do well.

Pouring the tea, she distributed it to Otis and Co and abandoning her paintbrush, picked up the little basket Otis had brought with him on the first day. Crooking it in her arm, she walked over the damp grass, past the granny flat on the right and the old gnarly apple tree on the left. Steadfastly ignoring the piece of tarpaulin flapping in the wind, and the state of the wonky old shed, she stepped over the fallen down fence towards the water. Still in the same place as she'd left it, the chair was sitting in the shallow water, gentle waves lapping at its plastic legs. Rolling her jeans up to her knees, pulling off her socks, and paddling to the water with her tea, she plonked herself down in the chair. With the basket on her lap, she took out the cake and observed the sunshine dance through the clouds onto the sea.

Sipping on her tea, she bit into the cake and looked out to sea as flashes of things went through her head. She hadn't thought she would ever be sitting on a grubby old plastic chair with a basket full of cake, a mug of tea, and her feet in the sea. She'd thought her life was going in a certain direction. Presumed that she was in the driving seat. But with Rob's announcement, all her hopes and dreams had crashed and burned. It was as if he had waved a wand like a magician in charge of her fate and poof, everything had gone. All that she had thought defined the rest of her life was no longer with her. Not her house, not the lost babies, not her childhood sweetheart love. All vanished in the flick of a black, white tipped stick. As she sat there cradling the tea, she felt so strangely alone, but at the same time, free. The defining thing about what had gone on with Rob wasn't just about what he had done, or the existence of Serena, it was that in doing what he'd done, he'd swept Lucie's whole life since she was sixteen under the carpet. Now she stood very much on the other side of that carpet, watching him family up with someone else while she stood there on her Jack Jones. It had been unexpected and not nice at all.

She sat there trying not to dwell on being alone and willed herself to think about instructions on the affirmation app. These told her to let thoughts go, to watch them float away. She attempted to release them and, with her feet in the water, she let all errant thoughts of diets and pregnancies and paint and leggings wing their way over the clouds.

She watched a swallow swoop and a boat sail past in the distance and came to the conclusion that she wasn't in all that bad of a place. The black hole of despair that had joined her in the little village cottage and followed her to Darling had finally closed, and something in the very back of Lucie's mind was telling her that she'd come home.

## 18

After crossing on the Pride of Darling and driving to park near her old job, Lucie sat in the car watching a gaggle of workmen beside a building site. Big clumpy boots, huge floppy tubes, high vis vests. The drum on the concrete mixer lorry swirled around and around. The orange signage revolving over and over again. The driver sat with his elbows on the steering wheel, eyes glued to his phone, his hazard lights blinking as the whole road queued to manoeuvre around him. As Lucie observed, noise surrounded her, a multitude of machines whirring and screeching for one single shop driveway. She sat there listening and watching as equipment knocked and clattered up to a crescendo, then hissed as the decibels went down again.

Sighing, she watched the minutes on the clock on her dashboard tick by slowly amidst the bustle outside. It had been much quicker than she'd calculated to get off the island and back to her old office, and now she had little choice but to wait and prolong the agony. She pushed the button on the steering wheel to drown out the noise from the cement mixer and played the meditation app.

'I am happy with my body. I do not have to define myself with how I appear to the outside world.'

Tutting, she pressed stop, not in the mood for the droning voice or observations on her body and thought about having to go back into her office. It strangely held no pull for her. She didn't even want to see anyone. She really could take it or leave it. A few of the girls she considered acquaintances but not actual friends. They were just people she'd known at work. She'd always saved her social diary for her four girlfriends and what she did with Rob. Plus, when she'd failed to get pregnant or married and her life had stalled, her work friends moved on. Most of them had begun to have families, plan weddings, and have lots of other things in their life anyway. When Lucie had not been able to get pregnant, she'd found she'd drifted away from the conversations in the tea room more and more and eventually didn't talk to too many of them at all other than the regular casual conversations of what was for dinner.

After gazing out the window as the wet concrete streamed down the tubes glugging onto the driveway, she finally got out of her car and strolled the short walk to her old office. Priscilla, the woman in HR, had been just about cordial as she'd tapped away on her computer, clearly finding the whole thing a blip in her busy day and awkward at the same time. The woman had not been designed for dealing with people.

Lucie had tried to make the whole thing more pleasant for both of them by asking niceties, but it hadn't seemed to work. Priscilla wasn't going to be drawn away from her script, which did not include being nice. Lucie had sat quietly waiting to be dismissed and gazed at Priscilla over the laminate desk. Priscilla's cheap dark-blue top stretched over her ample chest and plastic charm bracelets lodged on the pudgy creases of her wrists. Finally, Priscilla tapped the paperwork on the desk and pushed her keyboard away from her, laced her hands into a bridge and leant forward, looking at Lucie through her greasy, overgrown, salt and pepper fringe.

'So, what are your plans?' Priscilla asked, her voice portraying little emotion.

Lucie sighed inside. She had no inclination to share anything even remotely personal with Priscilla. No one had liked Priscilla in the office since the day she'd started the job in HR and installed out-of-touch processes with barely any relation to the actual job in hand. Priscilla had billowed around in voluminous skirts clutching an iPad and told anyone who would listen that what she was implementing came directly from the bosses in America.

'My plans?' Lucie replied, barely able to keep her voice interested.

'Yes. Will you be looking locally for a new job? You'll need to put in a formal request for references through me.'

Lucie pasted a smile on her lips. 'I've got a bit of leeway, actually.'

Priscilla nodded and pushed a clump of greasy hair away from her eyes. 'Mmm. Let me get straight to the point.'

Lucie couldn't stand it when people said that. They never got straight to the point. She always felt as if it precluded a lecture. She wasn't wrong this time, either. The cheap charms jingled on Priscilla's wrist as she began to speak. 'Leeway doesn't pay the bills, does it? In my vast experience in HR, it's best to strike while the iron's hot. Don't let yourself not have a job. It doesn't ever look good on paper to have gaps. Gaps are not looked on favourably by employers.'

Lucie took in Priscilla's slightly shiny, definitely smug, rotund face. 'I don't think a gap will be too much of a problem in my case.'

'That's what they all say! Yes, yes, no doubt you've got a few savings behind you. Don't be so sure. We all have bills to pay at the end of the day, and before you know it, the redundancy payment will not look quite as healthy when you have the big one to pay.'

Lucie gathered her bag, making indications to leave. 'The big one?' She frowned.

'The mortgage payment,' Priscilla said with a smug smile and ran her eyes up and down Lucie's green midi dress. Lucie put her bag on her shoulder and looked around the dark little room. A pair of Minnie Mouse ears were propped over the top of Priscilla's computer screen and a line of nodding cats bobbed up and down beside her desk phone. Lucie couldn't resist interjecting satisfaction into her voice as she stood up and pushed her chair in.

'It wouldn't really make much difference to me.'

Priscilla snorted and then followed it up with a smirk. 'Oh, that's not what the research says. The thing is, when I did the training in America for redundancy handovers, it was flagged as the main thing to mention. Not wanting people to lose their houses, obviously. We did a lot of role-play on it.'

Lucie widened her eyes. Clearly, Priscilla had not passed the roleplay module if her handling of the past half an hour was anything to go by. 'Yes. But that doesn't matter to me.'

Priscilla frowned. 'Really, why not? I thought, you know, in lieu of your recent, umm, situation, you'd be anxious about how the future's going to go.'

Lucie couldn't be bothered with any dallying around the topic and wanted to go. 'I don't have a mortgage,' Lucie said bluntly and watched as Priscilla's jaw dropped.

'Oh, right. I presumed with what happened with you and your partner. You being left…' She trailed off and didn't finish the sentence.

'Well, you presumed wrong, and for the record, I wasn't left. See you, Priscilla,' Lucie said and under her breath added, 'Wouldn't want to be you.'

When Lucie made it back to the car, the concreting guys were still standing watching the wet grey cement pour onto the drive. Why it took seven of them to supervise the pour, Lucie couldn't fathom. She messaged Tally as she stood by her car.

*It didn't take long. Just heading there now. Message me when you're on your way.*

*Okay. Will do. xxx*

Lucie strolled to the small coffee shop she'd often met Tally in when she was at work. Tally's surgery was a ten or so minute walk in the other direction, and they'd often meet for a quick sandwich for lunch. Opening the door, the busy place bustled around her. Bright lights above, white walls, a pink fluorescent light with the word 'coffee' in scrawling handwritten font hanging on the wall. Little fake green succulent plants stood on laminated tables and black salt and pepper pots stood to attention. It was so far from the ambience of Darlings that Lucie was shocked. She'd never noticed how stark and uncomfortable the coffee shop was before, but now she was comparing it to Darlings. Darlings wrapped you up in cosy, pulling you in and cosseting you from the outside world. The hundreds of little vintage bowls stacked on the shelves, the tiny tables packed into every available inch. The stacks of baskets behind the counter and the friendly smiles. All so very different from this generic, trendy place.

Lucie ordered a pot of tea for two, took a menu from the slot by the cabinet, and went and sat down at a table by the window. As she gazed outside, she realised that the place reminded her of Rob. He also worked not too far away and sometimes she'd walk past the coffee shop to meet him in the park in the summer after long, hot days in the office. With her chin on her hand, she watched the goings-on outside in the street. A bus stopped and a few people rushed off, a man in a Mazda reverse parked and very nearly bumped a big grey car, and people on their lunch hours hustled towards the town.

Tally breezed in five or so minutes later, and Lucie smiled as she watched her beautiful friend shimmy in and out between the tables. Tally, as ever, completely oblivious to the fact that she was turning heads. Tally kissed her on the cheek.

'Hey, darling. How are you?' Tally asked, stood back and looked Lucie up and down. 'What have you done? You look better than the last time I saw you. Much better.'

'Do I?' Lucie exclaimed. 'I don't feel it. I feel like a blob.'

'No, something's definitely different,' Tally said as she sat down.

'No idea. It must be the sea air or the Darling air, ha!'

'Whatever it is, it's agreeing with you. You look better than you have for a long time. A very long time.'

'That's probably because the last time I saw you I had been crying for about three days and hadn't washed my hair for a week.'

Tally nodded. 'There is that.'

'How are you?' Lucie asked.

Tally glanced out the window as she sat down. 'I've been better.'

'I can tell. Things haven't improved?'

'No. Nothing's changed. If anything, they are worse.'

Lucie looked glum and shook her head. 'I don't know what to say. I really don't.'

'There's nothing you can say. What do you say to someone like me? From the outside, it looks like I've got it all, but I'm just so unhappy. I should never have married him in the first place. I feel so mean saying that.'

'Hmm. It's been going on a while now, Tal.'

'I know. I feel like I should just put up with it. Shut up and put up. I have a nice enough husband, twins, a thriving practice, a nice house, stuff me, even a holiday home. I should be happy, right?'

Lucie shook her head. 'I don't think I'm very qualified on happiness at the moment.'

'I just look back to, what, thirteen odd years and know that I never loved Alec, not truly deep down. Not like I see other people love their partners. Like I love him, but I'm not in love, I think that's what I mean. I feel like such an awful person.'

Lucie nodded and listened. They'd been here before. Quite a few times.

'I was swept up in it all. The big surgeon with the fancy family. Me from a comprehensive school and a single mum. Their big houses and staff. My mum said it to me when we were talking about getting engaged. She said that I had been given a choice not to end up like her. A choice to marry a highly successful doctor and be part of a family like that. She said I would never get the chance again and that it would open so many doors. I suppose she was right. She told me not to end up like her.'

Lucie nodded as Tally continued, 'The worst thing is that Alec hasn't done anything wrong, not really. On the whole, he's a nice guy, right?'

'Yeah, that's questionable. He hasn't done anything wrong because you do everything. Literally everything. You work, sort the childcare, do all the domestic stuff, and do everything for him in every department. It all just works for Alec, doesn't it?'

Tally sighed. 'I know. All he does is go to work and sometimes he'll read the girls a story. Even work is organised by his secretary. Plus, there is a lot of schmoozing that goes on in his day.'

'And what about the other thing?'

'The sex thing? Yeah, no change there. Just like everything else in his life. It's facilitated for him whenever he wants it.'

'Just say no, Tal. Honestly, he can't just have it whenever he wants it.'

'I can't be bothered with the sulking and the drama. Maybe I'm just dead inside.' Tally sighed. 'It's just easier to get it over and done with.'

'It's not right to feel like that, sorry, Tally, it's just not. I told you this last time.'

'I know. I of all people should know that. I'm a GP for goodness sake!'

'Have you thought anything else about leaving?' Lucie asked.

A cloud went over Tally's face. 'All the time, like all the time. I just feel too guilty. It'll break up the family. The girls. His mum will be devastated.'

'You have to do what you have to do. The only person who is important in all of this is you. Ask me how I know that.'

'I know.' Tally shook her head and put her cup of tea down on the table. 'Let's not talk about it. Enough of that. What are your plans?'

'That's the second time today that I have been asked that question. I don't have any.' Lucie laughed. 'It feels quite nice. I've had plans for so long that now it's like I'm in freefall. Rob pushed me out of a plane and I'm waiting for the parachute to open. It's quite nice floating around in no man's land.'

Tally raised her eyebrows. 'The parachute being Darling Island. I still can't quite believe you've done it, Luce.'

'Nup, me either. I'm liking it and I never thought I would say that about the situation I'm in.'

'You're going to have to get a job at some point.'

'I'm alright for a bit, but yes I will have to.'

'Have you applied for anything?' Tally asked.

Lucie shook her head. 'No. I haven't had it in me. I've just been informed by Priscilla in HR that the mortgage is the biggest payment and I don't have that. So, yeah, I don't know. Something will come up, I hope.'

'There are worse ways to come out of a relationship.'

'I suppose there are.'

'What about Monica from the nursery?'

'Yes, hopefully something will come out of that.'

'Have you made up some bits and bobs or did you already have some stuff done?' Tally asked.

'I've done some of the bloomers like the ones I originally made for the girls, bags, cot stuff. I'm going to whip up a few quilts.'

Tally sat back and put her teacup down. 'What did the documents say with her email? I feel a bit bad that I've never really talked to her properly about what she does.'

'It's a much bigger deal than I first thought, so I guess it won't go anywhere. I haven't got big expectations. She's the buyer for a chain of lifestyle boutiques with a department on things for babies, which makes up a large proportion of their business.'

'Right, so what, they buy stuff wholesale?'

Lucie sighed. 'I don't have a clue if I'm honest. I just sew stuff. I'm not good at all that.'

'You better brush up on it then. Work out how much you need to make and all that. This could be just the opportunity you are looking for. You know how lovely your bits are. Everyone gushes over them.'

'I should. You're right. Yeah, I'm going to do my homework before the call. I know I can do the production side of it, the rest of it, I don't have a clue. I can learn, though.'

'It can't be that hard. I remember the first day she saw the baby bag and the bloomers at the nursery. She was salivating. I think it's your eye, Luce. You seem to team together the most beautiful fabrics and then add the ruffle or the frill and whatnot. Imagine me trying to do that! I can barely put that iron-on hem stuff on and get it right.' Tally laughed, waving her hand in front of her face.

Lucie chuckled. 'Honestly, it's a lot easier than it looks.'

'No, you're just saying that. You don't even use a pattern!' Tally exclaimed. 'You just look at stuff and say that you can make it better and what's more, you always do.'

'Ha! I do. At least I was given some talent in life, I guess.'

'Oh, yeah! Just a bit. You've always had it, you were just preoccupied with other things for the past few years.'

'Like trying to have a baby with a cheater. My biological clock was ticking so hard, it drowned out everything else in life. Look where that got me.' Lucie sighed.

'You'll be fine,' Tally said confidently. 'Look how well you're holding up so far.'

'I hope so. Anyway, enough of that. I can't wait to see you at the house when you come to stay.'

'I'm really looking forward to it, even though I feel a little bit guilty about the girls. What have you got lined up for me? Hoovering cobwebs and suchlike? On my hands and knees scrubbing floorboards and painting kitchen cabinets? At least I'll get a break from home.'

'Okay. Brace yourself.'

Tally laughed. 'You haven't said that for so long.'

'Yes, I have got all the above lined up for you but, also, we are going to a barbecue.'

'Blimey, it didn't take you long to get your feet under the table. Where?'

'At the house of one quite tasty Australian going by the name of Leo.'

Tally scrunched up her face. 'Ooh.'

'I know. Obviously, I'm joking about him, though he's defo tasty.' Lucie chuckled.

Tally quipped. 'Yeah, it's nice to dream sometimes though. I do it often.'

Lucie put her cup to her lips and took a sip of her tea. A car on the opposite side of the road in a little parking lay-by caught her eye. She squinted at the number plate and went cold as she realised it was Rob's car.

Tally saw her face drop and followed her gaze. 'What? What's wrong?'

Lucie pointed. 'That's Rob's car. I do not want to see him. I knew I should have just gone straight back to the island.'

Tally squinted. 'Did you see him get out?'

'No. I can't make out who is in the car with the sun coming down like that. Oh goodness! I really don't want to see him. What if he comes in here!'

Tally raised her eyebrows. 'Don't worry, we'll just leave or I'll be telling him to leave. Whatever you want.'

Lucie peered through the glass as the car door opened and then closed her eyes. Tally shifted in her seat and peered around the blind. 'Oh no. Ahh. Sorry.'

Lucie opened her eyes and stared as Serena, who she'd examined in so many pictures online, got out of Rob's car. In a skin-tight beige ribbed dress, from behind she didn't even look pregnant at all. Her perfectly curled blonde hair fell down her back and as she turned, her huge bump protruded in front of her. Little beige ankle boots, a tight cream cropped cardigan, and a crossbody bag with a chunky gold chain completed the picture. She was the epitome of happily pregnant, her glow emanating from every orifice.

Tally put her hand on Lucie's, her eyes full of concern. 'Are you okay?'

Lucie nodded. 'Actually, I am. She looks so young! It almost seems ridiculous.'

They watched as Serena, with a woman who was most probably her mum, stood waiting to cross the road. Lucie looked away, and a strange sound came out. 'She looks like an advertisement for a pregnancy supplement or something. How does she even manage to pull that off? How very ironic!'

Tally didn't laugh but tutted. 'Because she's in cloud cuckoo land. She's hardly juggling a marriage, a house, other kids, and a career from what I've learnt. Her most pressing thing to worry about at the moment is her blow dry. And we all know how that will go.'

Lucie sighed. 'I suppose so. I guess it's not her fault, at the end of the day.'

'Hmm. Not her fault! It takes two to tango - she knew the score.'

'True.'

'Shall we leave?' Tally asked as they watched Serena laugh and smile with her mum as they crossed the road.

'It looks like they're going the other way. No, I'm fine.'

'It's so horrible for you after what you've been through. I'm sorry you had to witness that.'

'Yeah, I know. Maybe it's good that it happened now, I don't know. Better than a few years in if I'd ever fallen pregnant and then there would have been children involved.'

'Like me, you mean?' Tally asked with a sad look on her face.

Lucie squeezed her eyes together and grimaced. 'Oh, gosh, sorry. I didn't mean…'

'It's fine. You're right, though. It is better that it happened now. I'm surprised you're okay though, it must feel like crap.'

Lucie laughed. 'I told you this is Power Lucie you're witnessing. She wears buttery leggings and listens to apps on living her best life.'

Tally laughed. 'I think I'd better subscribe to this thing.'

'All joking aside, I think it's the move too. Maybe deep down, like really deep down, I wasn't happy either. I don't know. Moving seems to have drawn a line under everything. Maybe all along I was needing a fresh start.'

'Well, there's no doubt about the fact that you got that. You have it in spades. Complete with moss, junk, mould, and foghorns. Oh, and a rather tasty Australian neighbour.'

'Yes, yes, I most certainly do.'

## 19

Looking down at the route Lucie had plotted for herself, she suddenly realised she was actually looking forward to her walk. In her old life, she dreaded exercising and going to the gym. She had suffered its sweaty smell and horrible intimidating machines to keep the puppy fat her mum had always told her she held onto off her petite frame. Those days of dragging herself to the gym were long gone, and on Darling, walking by the sea, taking in nature, and revelling in the fresh air didn't even feel like exercise at all.

The foghorn went off in the distance, making her smile as she pulled on the buttery leggings and then stood in front of the mirror, squinted, and looked closer. Either the leggings had actually performed miracles, or there was just a tiny little bit of a sign that the physical work on the house and the miles she was walking were beginning to work. She had a very long way to go, but it seemed as if there might be a little bit of progress.

She wound her long, chestnut brown hair with its natural golden highlights up into a bun on the top of her head, pulled on a hoodie, put her earphones in her pocket, and made her way down the stairs.

As she pounded along past the floating bridge, the fog close to the ground and the early-morning commuters lining up, a fine misty drizzle filled the air. It brushed around her face and filled her mouth with salty grains when she licked her lips. The voice on the app began to play.

'I focus my energy on pushing myself out of my comfort zone.'

Lucie couldn't believe it when she heard herself repeat the affirmation in her head. Was it finally working? *I focus my energy on pushing myself out of my comfort zone.*

Three times it instructed her to repeat the words and she did. Mind-boggling. The voice then moved on.

'I have an abundance of inner strength.'

*I have an abundance of inner strength.*

Stopping at a bench after repeating the affirmations, Lucie thought it must be a blip that she'd found herself not only repeating but nodding along with the affirmations too. Pulling her phone out of her pocket, she tapped on the YouTube app and opened a video 'Ten minutes to Ripped Abs.'

She watched as the girl on the video looking all of twelve instructed her to lift her legs in a myriad of ways. Gripping onto the back of the bench for dear life, she followed along. Ten minutes and twenty seconds later, she'd collapsed on the bench. Her abs felt far from ripped, whatever that even was. They felt more as if someone had taken each side of them, twisted them into a knot, and added a squeeze for extra pleasure.

Not long after, she'd double backed and was walking down Darling Street as it came to life. The trams trundled back and forth, their bells ringing, the cafés set back from the tramline were busy with people, and the clock on the town hall clock tower struck as she went past.

Walking along, Lucie peered into shop windows; she took in the Darling sausages hanging in the deli, gazed at a boutique homewares store filled with pretty things, and sniffed outside Candles on Darling, its scent filling the air outside. Lucie walked into a greengrocer with hessian covered stalls outside and as she browsed, she smiled as a lady with a blue apron, white shirt and glossy dark hair came out from the back.

'Hello, Bella,' the woman said, greeting her with a friendly smile.

Lucie smiled. 'Err, hello. I'm just here to say thank you for the basket. It was left on my doorstep.'

The woman nodded. 'Coastguard's House?'

'Yes,' Lucie replied, by now used to the fact that she stuck out on the small island like a sore thumb.

'How are you getting on, Bella?' the woman asked, a hint of an Italian accent lingering somewhere.

Lucie chuckled. 'Slowly. Very slowly. I'm Lucie. Nice to meet you.'

'Sofia. Welcome to Darling.'

'This shop is amazing. I haven't been in a greengrocer for years.'

'Thank you. We don't just sell fruit and veg, we have a lot of pasta and bits and bobs from all over the place, too.' Sofia laughed.

'I'm in luck then. I love pasta with a passion.' Lucie replied.

'We do lots of odds and sods and stuff for the baskets in Darlings. Well, my mum does when she's feeling like it.'

'Oh, right, I had a lunch one last week.'

'Sausage?'

'Yes.'

'My mum's. Best cured sausage in the land.'

Lucie nodded. 'I think you could be right.'

'You wait until you try the vegetarian lasagne. It's mind-blowing!'

'Sounds like I better get back to my walk. Living on Darling comes with a few calories,' Lucie joked.

'It does indeed, and we have loads of foodie events. You'll have to get an invite to Dinner on Darling, if there are any left.'

'Oh, right, what's that then?'

Sofia waved her hand towards the door. 'Down on Darling Bay there. It's an old traditional thing every year, it was something to do with the horses and the good weather back in the day. It's residents only and everyone gets all dressed up and does a traditional Darling dinner. A bit like a street party, I suppose.'

'Sounds interesting,' Lucie replied, thinking that it was early days for her to be going to a Darling event as the odd one out newcomer and that she would give it a miss.

'Well, nice to meet you then, Lucie. I'm glad the basket arrived safely. I hear you had a little altercation on the street with your car. Maybe don't do that again.' Sofia's eyes twinkled.

'I don't intend to.' Lucie laughed.

'You went and bumped your car into Mister D. Too funny. We all had to laugh at that,' Sofia said and then looked down at Lucie's trainers. 'Where are you off to bright and early?'

'I'm on a walk around the island. I'm heading for the marshes and to do a bit of rock pooling. If there's much to see around that side.'

'Oh yes, there are loads of lovely things to while away some time over there. It's lovely on that side. You won't see many folk over there at this time of day. It'll be nice and quiet.'

'Hmm. Good. It'll give me a chance to get some headspace. Then I'm going to walk back towards the house and get going on painting again. I was hoping to get some more done in the garden today, but the weather might change that.'

Sofia looked at her smartwatch and tapped a few times. 'It says we're in for a downpour this morning. Have you got a raincoat with you?'

'No, I haven't. I thought I would chance it,' Lucie replied. 'Now, I'm wondering if that was a mistake.'

'Ah well, good luck with that then, maybe it'll hold off if you're lucky. It's lovely over on that side, even in the rain. There's nothing better than some Darling fresh sea air to start your day. Nice meeting you, Lucie. You'll have to pop to the pub one evening for a drink.'

'Oh right, yes, thank you, what pub do you go to? What's the best pub in Darling?'

Sofia shook her head a couple of times. 'That's debatable, there are a few contenders. The best one, in my opinion, is The Darling Inn.'

'Oh yes, where's that again?'

'Not far from Darlings café. Go directly from there heading for the water down towards the bay and you'll see it sitting back just off the road there. A long line of white buildings with the pub right in the middle.'

'Oh, yes, I did see it,' Lucie replied. 'The one with the blue tile?'

'Yes, that would be the one. They have the most amazing food. Plus, we have our own little micro brewery on Darling. Delicious, though very potent.'

Lucie laughed. 'Sounds like my cup of tea. I'll make a beeline for it.'

'Absolutely. See you then, Lucie, enjoy your walk.'

# 20

Watching a tram rattle away, Lucie couldn't stop herself from smiling. There might be rain in the air, but there was something about this island that was improving her mood. She kept wondering when she was going to come crashing back down to earth with a bump. Considering life had bashed her around for the past six months, she had no job, no partner, and no plan, she was surprisingly sprightly of step.

Taking it all in as she walked down towards the bay, it looked as if Sofia and her forecast might be wrong as little tiny patches of blue broke through the misty sky. Lucie stood looking down at the row of white buildings. Higgledy-piggledy roofs made their way behind the water in the bay. A row of pale blue striped umbrellas jostled for space outside a few shops and The Darling Inn sat plump in the middle of it all, the whole of its front tiled in aqua pale-blue vintage tiles.

As she walked closer, she stopped to amble beside the cottages lining the approach to The Darling Inn. A jumble of terracotta pots spilling with plants sat on windowsills, a rusty old anchor was perched behind a white outdoor chair, and a tiny pale blue door with a latch led to a basement. Lucie peered over the other side of the road and down into the bay at low tide. An old weathered rowing boat perched precariously on the dark sand, a carpet of seaweed held a plethora of sea life, and a row of small fishing boats wore faded orange buoys along their sides. A family with toddlers sat on a set of old stone steps going down onto the sand, and a group of pensioners sat on a bench with ice creams nearly as big as their heads.

Lucie got closer to The Darling Inn and peered up at the tile and the three chimneys jutting out from the top. A sign dangling by rope on the front door announced the freshest seafood dishes at the oldest pub on Darling, and two coach lights hung over a gigantic blackboard with a scrawly menu handwritten in chalk. Whipping her phone out of her pocket, Lucie held it up to the chalkboard, took a photo, and sent it to Tally. At least she had one thing straight, she now knew where there was a nice pub.

Fifteen minutes or so later, Lucie had left the bustle of the bay behind and was back to walking by the sea. The weather had changed again, the patches of blue taken up by fast-moving white and grey clouds. She wasn't sure how she knew it, but she had the distinct feeling that the fog was coming in. White-capped waves broke out to sea in the far distance, and the pale greens and yellows of the seagrass swayed in front of her eyes as she gazed towards the horizon. Her phone buzzed, and she glanced down to see a call coming in from Jane.

'Hi, Jane. How are you?'

'Hi, lovely. Just a quick call to see how you are getting on? I thought I'd have a word rather than send a message. I haven't spoken to you for a bit, sorry, I've been really busy. You know how it is.'

'I'm good, actually. Surprisingly good.'

'Oh, right, yes, you sound it. How come?'

Lucie sighed. 'Good question.'

'The sea air or something?' Jane laughed.

'I'm not sure, but if you had told me at the end of last year that Rob would be having a baby with someone else and I would be living in a huge old house on my own, I would have lost the plot.'

'Yeah, tell me about it. You were with him since the year dot, that alone must be really hard to get used to. Are you really okay? Or are you just saying it so I don't worry?'

'I'm not saying I'm running around celebrating, but I don't feel too bad. I don't know, maybe I'm just over the hump, the worst of it, as it were. Something has definitely shifted. There have been enough tears, Janey.'

Jane sighed. 'Hopefully, that's the last of them. I heard about what happened when you went in about the redundancy.'

'Oh, what, from Tally?'

'Yeah, she said it was horrible. That she looked really young.'

'Mmm. She did. I don't know, but somehow it was good for me in a way to see her in the flesh, as it were.'

'Gosh, that just must have been like a stab through the heart though, what with what you've been through.'

'It wasn't pleasant, that I do know.'

'You poor thing. You should have called me.'

'In a way, I just didn't want to talk about it. You know? Poor old Lucie, boo blooming hoo. I'm sort of sick of my own pity party.'

'You definitely sound a bit brighter. What's happened to you? Not that I'm knocking it!'

Lucie started chuckling. 'There's a new me. Her name is Power Lucie.'

'What? What on earth?' Jane laughed.

'Yeah, she was born from an affirmation meditation thingy I subscribed to one night in a fit of self-pity. Thank goodness I didn't plump for the fancy exercise bike too.'

'Ha! You're hilarious. So what is this? What, like a course or something?'

'No, it's an app.'

'I see.'

'There are thousands, and I mean thousands, of things on there to listen to to improve your life.'

'Blimey, I think I need some of that. Where do I sign up?' Jane laughed.

'Some of them are ridiculous, but others are quite good.'

'They're clearly doing something by the sounds of you.'

'Maybe, or maybe I'm just getting used to everything that's happened and getting on with it.'

'Or a combination of the two. Whatever it is, I'm liking the sound of Power Lucie.'

'Yeah, me too,' Lucie agreed.

'So, you've got Tally staying?'

'I have. I've told her what to expect with the place. It's not quite up to Tally standards.'

'Who can live up to those standards, Luce?' Jane asked.

'Good point.'

Jane's tone got more serious. 'How did she seem to you when you met the other day?'

Lucie paused. 'Yeah, not in a good way. No better, possibly worse. What has she said to you?'

'Just more of the same. I don't think it's good in that household.'

Lucie sighed. 'The thing is, she's been saying this for a couple of years now. I'm at a loss as to what to suggest.'

'Yep, exactly. The longer she continues to do everything and never get a break, the more it will go on. Why would you change, right? When there's someone running around serving you left, right and centre? It just won't happen.'

'Hmm. She told me she never really loved him in the first place and that her mum had said she would never get a chance like it again in life.'

'I know, and that she didn't want to end up having the same

life as her mum, that marrying into that family would be her way out.'

'She said the same to me ages ago,' Lucie agreed.

'Did you say she should leave?' Jane asked.

'Not in so many words, but it's on the cards, I think. He's still not lifting a finger.'

'I know. Why would he, though, if he knows no different? He's literally had a woman doing something for him for the whole of his life. First his mum and his nanny, then a secretary at work, and then Tally stepped in for his social life, and she ticked all the boxes on wife and family. She even looks the part.'

'Yeah, plus on top of that, she's got a demanding job. I don't know how she does it. I could just about keep on top of my monthly cycle and fertility appointments.'

Jane sighed. 'She's always been like that though, remember when we were teenagers? Always studying and working two jobs, looking after her mum and somehow doing it all whilst looking like she'd just stepped out of a Timotei ad.'

Lucie burst out laughing. 'I can barely remember what one of those is, but I remember someone running through meadows with her hair swishing and we always had it on the side of the bath.'

'My point precisely. Tally is always swishing around looking fabulous with zero effort while the rest of us mere mortals have to work at it.'

'Always been the same, Janey. She's an alpha - seriously intelligent, beautiful and nice. It hardly seems fair that one can be so gifted.' Lucie laughed.

'I know.' Jane sighed. 'I hope you enjoy having her over. Hopefully, a break will do her good.'

'Hope so.'

'I'll be there to help when I can. How's it all looking now?'

'Much better. To be quite honest with you, I don't know if I would have stayed if it hadn't been for the help you girls got me in, especially once I got the redundancy news. It really wasn't pleasant.'

'It was that bad, was it?'

'Yeah, that first night when there was the storm, I was scared and lonely and had so much regret. Now, because of what they've done, it's bearable. Just. It's amazing what a bit of time can do.'

'It sounds grim, but at least you're on the way up now. I have good feelings about this, Luce.'

'I need them and I can't get much lower than I felt in that cottage!' Lucie laughed.

'Where are you, anyway, it sounds windy?'

'I'm just out on a walk. I've been walking since I've been here. It's what I've been looking for all my life; walking by the sea is my kind of exercise. Who even am I saying that? I had to drag myself to the gym, as you know.'

'Sounds like my kind of exercise too.'

'Janey, I've even bought leggings! It's astonishing and I'm actually wearing them as we speak.'

'Nooooo! You're kidding me. You're wearing exercise gear! Blow me down with a feather.'

'Yeah, I'd hardly call them exercise gear; they are buttery leggings from Lululemon. Have you heard of them?'

'Can't say that I have.'

'They're meant to make you feel as if you have nothing on while you are exercising.'

'Interesting. Send me the link. What made you order them, then?'

Lucie thought about when she was standing saluting the sun in her baggy crotch joggers and laughed. 'I had my oldest jogging bottoms on and I was out in public, and the back fell down while I was listening to that same app and a bloke was asking me to move off his driveway or something. It wasn't one of my better moments.'

The frown in Jane's voice was palpable. 'Wait, what? Whose drive were you standing on saluting the sun? I can't even believe I said that. You, Lucie Peachtree, were doing yoga? Am I hearing that correctly?'

'Doing yoga would be vastly stretching the truth. I was out on a walk with the affirmation app going. I was wearing my oldest joggers and this guy I now know is called George asked me to move from the slipway down by the water, not his driveway to his house.'

'Right. I see.'

'Yeah. Apparently, he lives in some big house down here and is in possession of a model wife. Like an underwear model. You'd recognise her. Ahh, what was the name again? I can't recall it now. Matilda something-something.'

'No idea, but sounds like you need to give her a wide berth. No one needs an underwear model as their neighbour when their late thirties are looming in the distance.'

'Oh, gosh, don't remind me. My biological clock is burnt out, it's ticked so much.'

'Ha! At least you can joke about it. Millions cannot.'

'Only with you girls,' Lucie replied more solemnly.

'How are you feeling about that?'

'About to start looking up sperm donors online,' Lucie quipped. 'Or I'm going to have a one-night stand on Darling and hope for the best.'

'I don't recommend that in your case, Luce.'

'What? What is that supposed to mean? I am more than capable of doing that.'

'Really! You've been with Rob since you were sixteen, unless there is something you're not telling me. I would not advise dabbling with a one-night stand at this stage of your recovery process. I do not think that would go down at all well.'

Lucie laughed. 'I'm not ruling out anything.'

'Oh, dear. I can see another crisis meeting on the horizon,' Jane predicted.

'Nah. I'll be fine.'

'Okay, look, I'll love you and leave you. I'm glad you're okay. I'll catch up with you later. Hold. Your. Nerve.'

'Sweet. Thanks for calling, Janey. Speak soon.'

Lucie had made good progress with her walk and was more than pleased with both her step count and the performance of her leggings. She chuckled to herself as she made the loop around beside the beach and was facing the boats not far from where she had first stood saluting the sun.

Holding onto the fence, she began to go through a standing leg exercise video and just as it was about to end, she touched the screen on her phone and it clattered to the ground, slid across the floor, and slipped down through the storm gutter. Lucie wanted to scream.

'Noooooooo! Don't do this to me,' she said as she crouched down in the gutter and cursed the broken part on the grill. She could see her phone face down on top of a faded old crisp packet and a pile of leaves. She sat crouched, looking at it for ages, wondering what to do. Walking back over to the beach, she foraged around until she found a stick, went back to the drain and after poking it in and around a bit, quickly ascertained that the stick would do nothing other than potentially push the phone further out of reach.

Reaching down, she stretched her fingers as far as they would go, but the phone was just that bit out of reach. As she stood there wondering how to rectify the situation, she saw a few cars at the sailing club and thought about walking down there to ask for some help. As a light drizzle started, she knelt down again, stretched her arm as far as it would go, and then laid down flat in the gutter with her left arm squeezed through the grill and poked in the drain. Stretching and fiddling with her fingers, her shoulder felt as if it was going to come out of its socket as she inched her arm further in. Her cheek was stuck to the tarmac with little bits of grit poking into her cheekbone when she heard a car pull up and then a voice.

'Hello? Err, hello down there!'

She heard footsteps, but didn't move her arm as her fingers brushed the edge of the phone. She was so close she didn't want to move an inch in case she disturbed it further. All she could see was tarmac, gravel, and grit, and the very nice boat shoes she'd seen when she'd bumped into the owner's car.

'I thought it was you!' she heard George exclaim. 'What the heck are you doing? You're lying in the gutter? What the?'

Lucie's mouth was scrunched up next to the ground. She blurted out, 'Phone.'

'What?'

'Can't move. Dropped my phone,' she said as the broken drain grill tugged on the skin on her shoulder.

'Are you some kind of stark raving idiot? You're lying in the gutter with your arm down a drain. Anything could be down there.'

Power Lucie suddenly appeared and was not in the mood. She hissed, 'Mind your own beeswax.'

'Huh! You expect me to leave you lying there? Really! Oh yeah, great, that will look charming when something happens to you and I'm standing in court. Oh yes, officer, yes, I was standing there watching the woman with her arm in the drain. No, I did not think about my duty of care and my debt to society to do the right thing. No, not at all.' He sighed and tutted.

Power Lucie heard herself swear and tell George to get lost. George, however, completely ignored her and crouched down by the drain. 'Can you feel it?'

'Yes, of course I can blimming well feel it! Do you think I'm face down on the road for fun?'

'I have no idea, but my arm is undoubtedly longer than yours, so I am assuming if I shove my arm in the same place, I can retrieve it for you and then you can be on your merry way.'

Power Lucie was at the fore. 'I can do it well enough on my own, thank you very much, Mr D.'

George rolled his eyes. 'Just pull your arm out.'

Lucie stopped herself from yelping as she pushed her arm in further and her fingers brushed the top of her phone. As she laid there with the gravel pressing into the side of her cheek, she thought that he was probably right. His arm would be able to reach it. She weighed up what to do and decided to relent. Pushing herself up with her right hand on the ground, she went to pull her left arm out. It was stuck on the jagged edge of the drain. She yelped.

George crouched lower down. 'It's stuck. I can't believe you forced your arm down that broken gap.'

Power Lucie swore under her breath. 'I know that, funnily enough.'

George got on his hands and knees and peered at her shoulder. 'I just can't understand how anyone in their right mind would have done this. All you needed to do was get a hook or something.'

Lucie felt far from in her right mind. Not only was she lying on the side of the road with her arm in a drain, she was staring at the very tight abs and nether regions of a man who was making her pulse more than race. He smelt good too. Just out of the shower, some kind of aftershave. Ahh. She rested her head back down and felt woozy.

'I'll be fine in a sec. I'll just need to wiggle it out bit by bit.'

George put his hand on the grill, his upper arm brushing the top of Lucie's head. 'Keep still. If I lever this a bit, you should be able to release it.'

Lucie gasped as he pulled and lifted the grill the tiniest bit, as it dislodged it ripped at her top and skin. Wincing in pain, she squeezed her eyes together, jolted, and knocked the phone. They both heard the sound of it clattering further and further away. She felt warm blood oozing down the top of her arm as she wriggled her shoulder to pull it out and the grill scratched further into her skin. As her arm finally came free, her thin t-shirt ripped away at the sleeve.

George moved around as she sat back on the kerb and looked at the top of her arm. 'Looks nasty.'

Lucie couldn't speak. Her arm felt numb, and she wasn't keen on blood at the best of times.

'Lucie?'

She still didn't say anything as she felt blood rush to her head and her face flush as she put her head down in between her knees.

'It looks nasty. I'll get you in my car,' George commanded.

Lucie held her hand up in a stop sign. 'No, I'll be okay.'

George gently touched her arm and then pulled the fabric at the top of her shoulder away. She was sure plump flesh was spilling out all over the place by her bra. 'You need to get this cleaned up at least.'

'I'll be okay.'

George looked around. 'Where's your car?'

Lucie looked at her arm and gasped at the blood. 'I don't have my car. I was on a walk.'

'Okay. I'm having none of this! Get up, I'm getting you in my car. You can't walk home like this. Honestly, there's blood pouring down your arm. Don't be ridiculous.'

Lucie didn't move, and George went to lift her arm. 'I'll help you.'

Blood pumped around Lucie's head, making her woozy, but she pretended she was okay. 'I'll just sit here for a minute and catch my breath.'

Ignoring her, George put her arm around his shoulder and she held on and hoisted herself up. Before she could say anything, he'd thrown his other arm under her legs and was carrying her across the tarmac, over the grassy sandy edge of the beach, and towards his car. Power Lucie was long gone as she leant her head back and she felt more and more strange that she'd succumbed.

Putting her in the front seat, George then pulled around the seatbelt, hopped in the driver's side, and turned on the engine. Lucie felt her head flop back against the headrest. 'I'll be fine once I get home. I'll get straight in the shower and put some Savlon on it.'

George did not smile. 'You're not going anywhere other than my house.' He added a swear word at the end as he put his left arm behind the passenger seat and reversed the car. 'You have a cut in your arm and you looked like you were about to pass out.'

Lucie didn't have the energy to say anything else and a few minutes later George indicated off the road and proceeded up a steep drive to a huge white house. The car squelched over gravel, turned down the side of the house and parked at the end. He came around to the passenger side and helped her out. Opening a side door into a boot room where wellies were lined up neatly under a coat hook holding riding hats and coats, Lucie went through as George held open an inner door and instructed her to sit down. Doing as she was told, she sat down at a large table in the kitchen and examined the top of her arm.

George opened a door to the side of the kitchen units and came back with a large plastic first aid box. He placed it on the table, filled the kettle with water and then peered at Lucie's shoulder. The bleeding had mostly stopped, the scratches on her upper arm to her elbow had turned into thick red welts and her once white t-shirt was now ripped at the shoulder and covered in dirt and blood.

'Hmm. It doesn't look as bad as I thought, now it's stopped bleeding. Have you had a tetanus lately?' George asked.

Lucie swallowed. It was about all she could do to stop herself from drooling. She couldn't care less about a tetanus. The eyelashes, the green eyes, the everything.

It was about all she could manage to stutter, 'No idea.'

George swore. 'You have no idea when your last tetanus injection was?'

'No. As a rule, I don't throw myself around near drains and cut up my arm whilst out on a walk by the sea.'

'Funny that, because I've run into you three times and each of those times you've either been falling over, causing a traffic accident, or putting yourself in danger. Therefore, I assumed you'd possibly know when you last had a tetanus.'

There wasn't much Lucie could respond, so she just nodded. George prodded the side of her shoulder and she winced. 'Do you think anything could be broken?' he asked. 'There's no swelling from what I can see.'

'I have no idea. One of my best friends is a GP.'

'How is that going to help you?'

'I don't know. I could FaceTime her or something.'

George frowned and shook his head. 'Look, you know what? I think as you said before, the best thing you can do is to have a shower and you can assess it then.'

Lucie went to push her chair out. 'Yes, yes, I'll call a taxi.'

Rolling his eyes, George rooted around in the first aid box. 'And how are you going to do that when your phone is currently on its way out to sea via a drain down the end of the road?'

Lucie looked up. 'Hmm, good point. Would you mind calling me a taxi or dropping me home then, as I said in the first place?'

George made an irritated sound. 'You'll be lucky getting a taxi on Darling at this time of the day. I meant have a shower here. I'll make a cup of tea while you go up and use the bathroom. I'll get you a clean t-shirt or something, and then we can decide if you need to get a couple of stitches. I don't think so, but I'm no doctor, obviously.'

Lucie didn't know what it was, but she seemed to have lost the ability to think straight around this man. She shook her head and then nodded, trying to decipher what he had just said.

George looked at her with a question written all over his face. 'What do you want to do, then? I'm happy to take you home now or you can get cleaned up here and we can assess it from there.'

Lucie blinked back to reality and turned to look at her shoulder. It was a sticky mess and throbbing, but she was fairly sure she wouldn't be needing stitches or to see a doctor. She could quite easily go home, but she liked, rather loved, the idea of staying with him for a bit. An excuse to get to know him.

Then she remembered Underwear Model and thought how ridiculous she was being. He was clearly irritated by her. She went to say no and then she looked over and was astonished to hear the completely opposite words coming out of her mouth. 'Yes. I think I will have a shower here, if you're sure you don't mind?'

'I wouldn't have offered if I minded,' George replied. 'I'll show you the way to the bathroom. Hang on, I'll get a t-shirt.'

Lucie stepped along the landing and, following instructions, opened a door at the end. A huge bathroom with a large window looked out over the garden and she could see glimpses of the sea in the distance. A large double walk-in shower with oversized marble tiles, a little step up to an egg-shaped standalone bath. She ran her finger along an exquisitely clean vanity and then gasped as she looked in the mirror. The fine drizzle and escapade with the drain had done nothing for her appearance. Her normally crowning-glory hair had fallen from the bun in places, there was grit in her cheek, a dirt mark on her temple and her bra, very much on the side of granny and grey, was poking out the side of the ripped t-shirt. She rolled her eyes and picked up a bottle of fancy soap. What was she even thinking? No doubt Underwear Model would turn up shortly and make her feel even worse about herself than she already did.

*I possess the power to be in control of how I feel.* She heard the app voice say in her head.

Sneaking open the vanity doors, she peered inside. Nothing really very interesting. None of Matilda's products, in fact no girly stuff at all. She frowned: not even any children's toiletries. She was clearly in some fancy guest bathroom. Of course she was. These Beautiful People had guest bathrooms and wings, she had vermin-ridden granny flats and life-size statues of the Three Wise Men.

Taking a towel from a stack of clean ones and letting her clothes drop to the floor, she stepped into the marble shower stall and pulled a matte black lever. Piping hot water gushed from a gigantic black square rain shower head. She sighed and then winced as the water touched the skin on her shoulder. Standing there easing her upper arm under the water, the blood began to wash away. Once the dirt and dried blood was gone, there was a fairly deep cut, plenty of angry looking scratches, welts, and the beginnings of a bruise, but overall it was fine.

She sighed to herself as she pushed the lever to turn off the shower, wrapped herself in the towel, and wound her hair back up into a bun on the top of her head. What was she even thinking, having a shower here? The shock had rendered her momentarily crazy. She'd go downstairs and make a speedy exit as soon as she could. She'd embarrassed herself enough for one day.

With the clean t-shirt over her leggings, she made her way back across the landing, down the wide stairs, and through the hallway to the kitchen. The house of course was lovely. Modern but classic at the same time. She spied two large linen Chesterfields as she went past the sitting room and large ginger jar lamps on side tables. Definitely no life-sized statues of things from a nativity play. Pushing the door to the kitchen, she was relieved not to see anyone else. George was sitting with two mugs of steaming tea in front of him.

'How is it?' he asked as he looked up. There seemed to be genuine concern in his face, or was he just doing that to get rid of her as quickly as he possibly could?

Lucie lifted up the arm of George's t-shirt. 'Yeah, not too bad. I'll live.'

George made a funny face, frowned, got up, moved around the table, and peered more closely at Lucie's upper arm. She swallowed as he touched her skin. 'Not too bad? Looks pretty bad to me.'

'No, I'm fine.'

He walked back around the table and passed over one of the mugs of tea. 'Biscuit?'

'I'd love one,' Lucie replied.

He took a biscuit tin out of the cupboard, pulled off the lid, and passed it over. Lucie peered in, took out a Garibaldi and looked back up at him. 'Thanks for this. I would have been fine to go home, but it was nice to have a decent shower.'

'You're welcome. You've not got a decent shower at your place?'

'Pah! I'm lucky there's running water. The shower is, umm, decrepit, but at least it works and is hot. The whole house is a mess mostly.'

George nodded. 'It's a lovely spot.'

'How long have you lived on Darling?' Lucie asked.

'On and off for years. I'm more or less here full-time now. I like being out on the water.'

Lucie nodded. 'Yeah, I can see why. I've already got used to my walks by the sea. There's something about it.'

'That's what they say.'

'So, where were you before?'

George didn't seem to want to be drawn on the subject. 'Over the other side. What about you? Where do you work?'

'Good question,' Lucie said, and George raised his eyebrows. 'I've just been made redundant.'

'Oh, right.'

'I'm pleased in a way. It's drawn a line under a few things, as it were.'

'I see. So, you're job hunting, are you?'

Lucie scrunched up her nose and chuckled a little bit. 'I guess I should be, but I haven't had the oomph yet, what with the house and everything. There's no mortgage on it so I'm okay for the minute.'

George nodded. 'Right, whole different ball game then. Not a bad boat to be in.'

'Yeah, I'm lucky.' She then shook her head. 'Actually, it's nothing to do with luck. We worked really hard to get to where we were and my dad left me some money when he passed away.'

'Sorry to hear that.'

Lucie batted her hand in front of her face. 'Oh, sorry, you don't want to be hearing my life story!' She finished her tea and put her mug down. 'Thanks for this again.'

'No worries.'

'I'll be fine to walk back now.'

'No, I'll drop you. You've got no phone and all.'

Lucie shook her head and blinked. 'Ahh, I forgot about that! Another headache to sort out. I can't believe it slipped down like that. Of all the luck.'

George frowned. 'I've got a spare phone somewhere. You can have it.'

'Oh, goodness, that would be lovely.'

'I'm not sure where it is. If it's not in here, it will be in the office,' George said and walked into a room off the kitchen. A few minutes later, he was back. 'I remembered I did take it into work.'

'Thanks for the offer, anyway.'

'I can pop it over later, if you like. Might get you out of a spot of bother temporarily. It's such a pain sorting out phones and things like that.'

'Yes, I know. It would really help me out if you don't mind.'

'All good,' George replied, and looked at his watch. 'Right, I'll get you home.'

Five or so minutes later, George's car pulled up outside the Coastguard's House. He looked over. 'It's looking more lived in, at least.'

'Yes, I have a long way to go, though. Getting the roof clean and that flag repaired is next on my list.'

'That will make the world of difference. Sorting out all the junk and doing the grass has spruced it up. Otis and his lads are diamonds.'

'They are. I was really lucky to get them.'

'Right, well, I hope you're okay. I'll pop you that phone over later.'

'Lovely. Thank you. That's really kind of you.'

'Are you sure you're going to be okay?'

Lucie wanted to reply that she was more than okay if she was going to be seeing him again later, but she just nodded as she got out of the car and closed the door. She waved as he pulled away and smiled to herself as she walked towards the house. She chuckled as an affirmation she had listened to that morning sidled on into her thoughts.

*I embrace new situations and I am ready to let someone into my life.*

## 21

L ucie closed the front door behind her and looked around
the hall. The Three Wise Men were staring at her from
the corner, and the hallway window squeaked in the wind
coming in off the sea. The funny little place seemed as if it was
welcoming her home; even the Wise Men appeared to be
pleased to see her. She shook her head: the incident must be
turning her funny.

Stepping slowly up the stairs, she pulled off the leggings and
changed into her work jeans, took off the t-shirt belonging to
George, and pulled on a painting shirt. She rolled her shoulder
around and pulled down the sleeve, looking in the mirror. It
was fine, but sore, and a bruise under the skin was already
starting to come out. Most likely someone like Tally would tell
her to sit down and rest, the burgundy and dark grey kitchen
was telling her another story.

Ten minutes later, she had a coffee, a piece of toasted banana
bread and was starting to clear out the kitchen. Otis had loaned
her a hand sander and a pack of sandpaper disks, a tin of primer
for wood, clear instructions and told her precisely what to do.
She'd listened carefully to what he had said and hoped that he

was going to be correct that the finished cupboards would be less scary than what she was currently faced with. The burgundy and grey was not only dreary and unappealing, she felt when she'd made dinner there that it was a health hazard too. It wasn't a nice feeling, at all.

With Radio 2 playing and the window and back door open, by lunchtime the top of her arm was throbbing, but the contents of the kitchen were in the room where her sewing machine was, and the few cupboards had been blasted with the hand sander. As Otis had said, burgundy dust was everywhere, and she had been grateful for the face mask. Zipping around with the Dyson, she then washed her hands and face, made herself a sandwich, and went down to the chair in the water. As before, she rolled up her jeans and paddled to the chair with the sandwich and a drink, her iPad and sat watching the seagulls and boats. Not a bad setting for a spot of lunch.

She flicked through her iPad, scrolled through the Darling community page hoping to see a job, sighed that there was nothing, and looked through the email from Tally's friend from the nursery. She clicked on the link to the website and explored the pages. She could see why they would be interested in her stuff. The baby section was high-end, boutique bits and bobs you would most definitely not find on the high street. Lucie was shocked at some of the prices. Were there really people out there who paid that much for a handmade tassel garland? By the number of gushing reviews, clearly there were.

She sat there with her feet in the water and throbbing arm and went through in her mind what she could charge for her stuff if this was the league she was going to play in. It was mind-boggling to her that people would be prepared to part with good money for the things that came out of her head. The girls had all told her more than a few times that she was crazy not to turn her hobby into a business, so maybe this was the time.

Leaving the chair where it was, she made her way back

across the garden, past the granny flat and old coal shed, and into the kitchen. The paint job now seemed daunting again; it was yet another moment in the journey when she realised she didn't have Rob or, in fact, anyone at all. She half wanted to call it a day, strip off her painting clothes, get a piece of cake, and amble into the back room and spend the afternoon with her sewing. Sewing and creating would make her feel better. Horrid kitchens put paid to that. Standing looking down at her iPad, she made a bargain with herself for three more hours of work, then she'd clean up, walk to the tram, head to Darlings for some afternoon tea, and be back in time for the phone drop off from George.

Three hours later, right on the minute, the small burgundy kitchen was no more. Whilst she'd worked, she'd flitted from apps, to the radio, to a podcast on the life and loves of Elizabeth Taylor. She'd listened while she'd leaned into the corner cupboard whilst holding her breath and balanced on the top of a ladder to reach the plinth on the cupboards. Letting out a huge sigh when she'd finished, she stood with her hands on her hips, the affirmation app playing on the side.

'I create the life I want to lead. I am in control of the forces around me.'

Lucie smiled. Was part of what she was hearing true? Was it good to be grabbing this new normal of hers by the curlies and pulling on her big girl pants and giving it a go? Was it better to be taking charge than sitting on a sofa and eating away her worries? Had she shed enough tears and was now ready to welcome the new Lucie into her life? She couldn't answer: all she did know was that with the burgundy cupboards now a distant memory, she would at least be able to enter the kitchen without feeling as if she was going to be struck down salmonella.

With the bruise on her upper arm clearly coming out, she had her third shower of the day, blasted her hair, put on some make-up, a flowy top, spritzed herself with Calvin Klein, and pulled on what she called her 'nice jeans.' As she managed to do up the top button, she looked in the mirror and smoothed her hands over the front of the jeans. The ten minutes of standing ab workouts, walking and Darling air must be doing something. Miracles were occurring in front of her eyes.

Fifteen minutes later, she made her way past the Darling punt. It was about halfway over the water, all signs of the earlier rain were long gone and the sun glinted off the sea. She stopped for a minute and gazed down in the water; a few tiny fish swam around near the chain for the ferry and the tide lapped against the shore. Making her way to the tram, she smiled as one came into her vision from further down Darling Street. Its blue and white livery caught her eye and the tinkle of the bell chimed through the air. As she arrived at the tram shelter, she recognised a man she had seen around a few times. He was in a raincoat, too big business shoes, and was leaning on his shopping trolley.

'Good day,' he said and tipped his hand to his forehead.

'Hello.' Lucie smiled.

'How are you?' he asked with kind, twinkly eyes.

'I'm fine, thanks, you?'

'Perfectly well, thank you. I should introduce myself. Mr Cooke.'

'Oh, yes, hello. I'm Lucie.'

'Yes, I know that. Coastguard's,' he said and lifted his chin an inch.

Lucie was now more acquainted with the people of this small island already knowing where she lived. 'Yes.'

'I live just over there,' Mr Cooke said, pointing a gnarly old arthritic finger to a row of three-storey white houses not far away.

'Ooh, nice spot there looking over the estuary.'

'Yes, indeed, but I spend a lot of time down near the water over that side.' He pointed way over Lucie's head.

'Not a bad way to spend your time.'

Mr Cooke rummaged around in his trolley and then held out his palm and moved it in Lucie's direction. Three flat grey pebbles were next to a tiny feather and a shell. She narrowed her eyes and looked a bit closer. 'Oh, yes, what lovely finds.'

Mr Cooke looked very pleased with himself and pointed to the feather. 'Haven't seen one of these for a while. I'll be the talk of the group later. I think I'm on a winning streak at the moment.'

'The group, right, what group's that then?' Lucie asked.

'Darling Flora and Fauna Appreciation Society, splinter group to the one just over the other side on the mainland.'

'That sounds interesting.'

'I'll upload these later and wait for the comments to come in,' Mr Cooke said, clearly very satisfied with himself.

'Excellent. The group's online, is it?'

Mr Cooke nodded. 'It is now. My grandson bought me one of these,' he said and wiggled an iPhone in the air. 'Best thing since sliced bread. My wife would have loved these things. There we are.'

'Yes, what would we do without them?' Lucie asked and suddenly went cold. She didn't have hers. 'Ahh, I've just realised I dropped mine earlier!' She rummaged in her bag, glad to see her iPad at least. 'Good job I've got my credit card here.'

'How did you lose it?' Mr Cooke asked.

'That's a very long story. I was out on a walk down the end there this morning and I knocked it. It slid and slipped into an old drain. I couldn't believe it. Just my blooming luck at the moment.'

'That's not good.'

'Luckily, I've got a spare one coming later.'

'You are lucky. They don't come cheap.'

Lucie nodded. 'No, they don't.'

'Though for what they give you, they are cheap, I suppose,' Mr Cooke noted.

'True.'

'I'll send you a pdf if you like?' he said, looking back down at his palm and then up at Lucie again as the tram pulled in.

Lucie frowned. 'A pdf?'

'On the flora and fauna.'

'Right. Okay yes.'

'You said you walk? I think you might like it.'

'I've started to walk, yes. I'm really enjoying it.'

Mr Cooke smiled broadly. 'It gives you something to look out for whilst you're walking, like searching for treasure.'

'Thank you, Mr Cooke. You know, actually, I think I'd quite like that.'

'You most certainly will. I can tell.'

They both stepped on the tram where Shelly the conductor in her tram waistcoat was standing. 'Morning, Mr Cooke. Any good finds today?'

'Loads of them,' Mr Cooke replied. 'I've just been filling in the new resident of the Coastguard's House here. I'm going to send her a pdf.'

'Sounds good to me.' Shelly laughed as she rang the bell and the tram rumbled off down Darling Street.

Strolling along Darling, Lucie was astonished when Sofia from the greengrocer waved as she walked past. She ambled along, trying to ignore the pain in her upper left arm and instead looked up at the pretty white and blue bunting and stopped to look in the window of the florists. She pottered along further and then stood by the door of a tiny Chinese restaurant called China Darling. Cupping her hands around her eyes, she stood with her nose against the glass. It looked like the prettiest Chinese restaurant she'd ever seen. The whole of the inside was decked out in the Darling blue and white. White walls plastered with lovely vintage Chinese silk pictures. From the ceiling rows and rows of vintage upside-down paper umbrellas in an array of blues and golds, little garland strands of fabric were tied to each one. Lucie's fabric antenna started to twitch, and she made a mental note to come back one day for dinner.

A few minutes later, she'd veered off Darling Street and was strolling over the cobbles towards Darlings. A couple on matching bikes rode by, and a woman with a dog stopped as the dog said hello. Lucie smiled as she approached Darlings. Today, the billowing tablecloths on the tables out the front were the same as the little napkins in the baskets, a pale blue gingham. On each table a china floral teapot was stuffed full of flowers, a little love heart chalkboard was swaying back and forth in the wind, and a birdcage planted with flowers was perched by the door.

A lovely old labrador lay asleep beside the downtrodden doormat and just as Lucie was about to open the door, a woman came bursting out a stack of baskets in her arms. Apologising and standing back to wait, Lucie stood to the side and peered in the window. A little blackboard caught her eye wedged onto the windowsill inside.

*Help Wanted. Apply Within.*

Lucie walked in, and as before, sighed at it all. A waitress was at the top of the ladder on wheels gathering a stack of fluted copper cake tins and Evie was leaning over a table with a bottle of spray and a cloth. Evie flicked her eyes towards a table about halfway down and raised her eyes. 'There you go. Coffee?'

'Yes, please,' Lucie replied. 'And a basket if you have one.'

Evie nodded, and as if by magic, was gone. In a flash, she was putting a little bowl of coffee and a basket on the table. 'How are you faring down there at the house?' she asked.

'Not too bad, thanks.'

'Leo said you've got loads done already.'

'I have, yes. It doesn't feel that way when I'm there, but when I walk back in, it's definitely improved. I got started on the kitchen today, so that's good. I'd had enough of it, and time is marching on.'

'Sounds like you're busy.'

'Yes,' Lucie said, looking down at the little bowl full of milky coffee. 'I'm glad to have a bit of a break to come in here, to be honest.'

'I wish I could say the same. We've had one of our lovely girls go into hospital. Left me right up the creek.'

Lucie nodded. 'I saw the sign in the window.'

'Yep.'

Lucie surprised herself at the words coming out of her mouth. 'I could give you a hand if you like, while you're looking for someone.'

'You're good in the kitchen, are you? Have you got any experience?' Evie asked.

Lucie contemplated the question for a second. 'I worked in a coffee shop many moons ago, but I know my way around a kitchen and I can serve a customer. I was just offering, sorry, didn't mean to put you on the spot. No worries.'

Evie smiled. 'All good. You know what? It would really help me out. I was wondering how I was going to cope next week.'

'Suits me. I'm in between jobs at the moment.'

'Yes, I heard that.' Evie laughed. 'You can't move around here, you'll get used to it. You look like you could scoot around tables, serve a few coffees in bowls, make up some baskets.'

'I think I could just about manage it.' Lucie laughed. 'Beats spending ten hours a day painting a house.'

'Well, thank you. How about you come in when we're closed and I'll show you around?'

'Sure.'

'Thanks, Lucie. You've got yourself a deal.'

Lucie smiled and watched as Evie zipped around the little shop. She could see why Evie needed help; she was trying to do everything at once and just about keeping her head above water. Taking out her iPad, she connected to the Wi-Fi and the iPad buzzed with a message from Tally on Messenger.

*How's it feeling now?* Tally asked, referring to Lucie's shoulder. Lucie had sent her a picture of her arm on Messenger and relayed to her what had happened.

*It's fine. Just as you said, the bruise is coming out and it's throbbing.*

*Yeah, that's a good sign. Any redness or swelling?*

*Not really.*

*Just keep an eye on it.*

*Will do. How are you?*

*Knackered and over it.*

*Ouch. You need friend therapy.*

*I do. Good job I've got you and I've just been talking to Libby.*

*What you really need is a lazy afternoon with Radio 4 and a long, never-ending pot of tea. From there you need to move swiftly on to comfort food and box sets, preferably on the BBC.*

*Hahaha fat chance of that in my life right now.* Tally added the eye roll emoticon.

*I think I'll call a stop to the working bee weekend and we'll do just that. The house is just about up to it.*

*Suits me. Xxx*

*Oh, and guess what?*

*What?????*

*I've got a temporary job.*

~

Opening the front door, Lucie patted one of the Three Wise Men on the head, stepped up the little steps and down again and opened the door to the kitchen. Coughing as paint fumes engulfed her, she pushed up the sash windows and propped open the back door and looked around. It was small and old-fashioned, but Otis was right. It looked so different without its coat of burgundy and grey. The open shelving now seemed happy enough to display a few of her things, the corner cupboard didn't feel as scary, she would actually be able to store her china in it, and the door to the pantry in the corner now almost asked to be open. Examining the cupboards, she could see that Otis had also been correct on his estimation on topcoats and that she still had a long way to go. Rome, clearly, wasn't built in a day.

She went upstairs to the loo, touched up her make-up, went back down and into the sewing room. The kitchen stuff was stashed all over the place, but the cutting table was clear. A nearly finished quilt in Liberty fabric was waiting to be edged with a frill and a baby blanket's seams were waiting to be pressed. She ran her fingers over the soft fabric and picked up the quilt's frill. Threading the fabric through and pressing the pedal with her foot, she was lost in a world of her own as she zipped her way along.

An hour or so later, she jumped at the sound of the bell at the front of the house and looked at the time. As always happened when she was lost in fabric, it had flown by. Patting the back of her hair, she smoothed her top and walked through the hallway to the front door. George, in dark blue jeans and a blue casual shirt, was standing on the path with a phone in his hand.

His eyebrows shot up as he looked at Lucie. 'Blimey. You look a bit better than earlier. You were white as a sheet when we were having that tea.'

Lucie laughed. 'That's not really hard. The last time you saw me, my face was in the gutter.'

George's face broke into a smile. A previous tension in him had eased somewhat. He looked up at the house. 'They've done a good job. Makes the world of difference when you're up close. It's not easy doing this cladding.'

'I know. I'm so grateful.'

George held out the phone. 'Here you go.'

Lucie gestured to the hallway. 'Do you want to come in for a tea?'

George hesitated and shoved one of his hands in his pockets and looked up at the flagpole on the top of the house. He then looked at his watch. 'I'd love a quick one and a nose around at what you've done.'

Lucie opened the door and waved him in, pointing to the Three Wise Men. 'You have to say hello to these three to be allowed past.'

'Goodness. What in the world are they?'

'I know. Mary's in the building out the back.'

George burst out laughing. 'I've seen it all now. They'll certainly keep you company when the fog rolls in.'

Lucie led him into the kitchen. 'Don't jest, I think I might have started talking to them. Here we go. You'll have to perch yourself there for a bit. I've been painting today.'

George sat down and Lucie ran the kettle under the tap and plugged it in in the utility room away from the paint. Once the boiling water was in the pot, she smiled. 'Okay, guided tour.'

Opening the door to the back stairs, Lucie held it open and George peered up the steep stairs. Lucie chuckled. 'I'm not sure what happened in here, but there were maggots and loads of old fishing gear and more cobwebs than I've ever seen in my life.'

She led him into the sitting room. The cladding was now wearing a neutral shade of Farrow and Ball. 'Otis and his lads did all the prep on this and I did the rest bit by bit. I was stuck on a ladder for a long time.'

George ran his finger over the cladding and looked up at the pressed tin ceiling. He then pointed over to the exposed brick fireplace. 'It's come up well. What about that, does that work?'

'I think so, but I'll need to get it checked. The hearth here was home to the Three Wise Men when I first arrived.'

George laughed. 'Are you keeping them?'

Lucie joked, 'They're the only friends I've got at the moment.'

'When's your furniture arriving?'

Lucie stopped and flicked her eyes out towards the window. 'Umm, I'm not sure, really. It's a bit complicated.'

'Right.'

'I'm just making do at the moment.'

'You'll get there,' George replied as she opened the door to her sewing room. 'I've got the kitchen stuff in here at the moment, but this is going to be my sewing room. I love making things.'

George looked around. 'Yep, this is nice too. The place is going to be lovely when you've done it all. You can't beat that sound either, can you?' he said, peering out the window and down to the sea.

'Nope. I'm loving it. Even the foghorn. I've got used to it already. The first time I heard it, I almost jumped out of my skin,' Lucie said as they walked back, went into the kitchen, she poured the tea, and they stepped out into the back garden. George made a face at the tarpaulin on the granny flat roof. 'What are you going to do with that?'

'Goodness knows! I'll cross that bridge when I come to it. There's a lot of bat poo in there at the moment. I can't even stomach it. It's going on the list for someone else to sort.'

'You've certainly got a lot on your plate.'

'I'm quite enjoying keeping busy, as it were.'

'The house is a fresh start?' George's eyes were kind as he asked.

'You could say that. Let's just call it a new start on my own. I was with someone since I was at school and now I'm not. I'll leave it at that.'

'Doesn't sound pleasant. Darling will help. It was good for me.'

'It has already. I've found a love for walking by the sea.'

'And lying in the gutter,' George joked.

'Mostly I'm upright.'

'Or saluting the sun.'

Lucie shook her head. 'Ha. I must look like a right nutter to you.'

'I think we're all a bit crazy in our own way,' George said as he finished his tea. 'I'd better be off.'

They made their way around the side of the house.

'See you then, Lucie.'

'Thanks for the phone.'

'You're welcome. Don't worry about getting it back to me. Whenever you're ready. It's been sitting in a drawer for ages anyway.'

'That's so kind of you.'

'My number is in there just in case you need assistance in getting your arm out of a drain in the future,' George joked.

Lucie tried to sound light hearted and casual as she replied. Really, she wanted to shout at him as he made his way to his car that she'd quite happily stick her hand down another drain if it meant he would swoop down and pull it out for her.

## 22

Lucie walked along by the ferry, approaching it from the far side as it clanged onto the slipway. She looked up at the white hexagonal tower with the flashes of blue, and the ferry master waved and smiled. She stopped herself from turning around to see if he was waving at someone else, put on a big smile, and waved back. As she carried on along the pavement, she felt a happy little glow at the cheeriness. Darling was most definitely doing its thing, and Lucie Peachtree was more than welcome to oblige.

Hazy, foggy mist was lifting from the water, the blue she'd got used to seeing when the sun poked through was making an appearance and white was slowly moving up and away across the sky. Lucie looked up and watched, wondering what the weather would bring. She'd already got used to its changeable nature and how the infamous Darling fog would lift in the morning to reveal sunshine on the water and at certain times descend as if out of nowhere. A few people had told her, including Shelly on the tram, that the weather could be forecast by the colour of the water. Of that, Lucie was dubious. She would obviously have to live on Darling for a long time to be anywhere close to being able to recognise that.

Veering off from her usual route, she took a slightly different way home. She walked along a road lined with a long row of white cottages, their gardens sitting squarely in front of them. Jumbled together, each one wore hanging baskets, one housed a flagpole in the garden, another completely covered in ivy, its paned windows open to let in fresh air. One with a stable door painted in the Darling blue was surrounded by pretty flowers and a cat sitting on a windowsill keeping guard.

She stopped and leant on a picket fence with her feet in what a YouTube video had told her was 'first position' and slowly pushed herself up and down. As she counted through the sets of eight, trying to ignore the burn in her calves, core, and bum, she gazed at the cottage in front of her. Vintage shutters with cut-out anchor shapes embraced each of the tiny windows, two huge sandy coloured pots stood either side of the front door underneath a thatched roof. Lucie took it all in, half-wishing to sit down and stay for a while and just gaze at the little dome kettle barbecue tucked in the corner, a couple of blue and white striped deckchairs on a cobbled patio, an outdoor coffee table sitting low topped with lanterns. She closed her eyes as she lifted her legs and tried to imagine the Coastguard's House looking like a lovely welcoming home.

'Hello,' a woman in a floaty white dress, gigantic floppy sun hat pushing a bike and smiling said.

'Oh, sorry. Hello,' Lucie replied. 'I was using your fence to aid in the rebirth of my legs.'

The woman chuckled. 'Be my guest. I could do with some of that, too.'

'I was admiring your cottage. It's so pretty. I love the shutters.'

'Thank you.'

'I'm Lucie. I live just over there. I bought the Coastguard's House.'

'Ahh! Hello. I've been meaning to drop by with a basket. I'm Hennie, nice to meet you.'

Lucie didn't say how at first she'd thought the basket dropping thing a bit odd, she wasn't sure if she did think it was weird now she was getting used to it. Actually, it was rather nice. 'I've had some beautiful ones.'

'I bet.'

'It's a lovely tradition when you move somewhere new. It made me feel a lot better about what I'd done. I'm loving being part of Darling already.'

Hennie laughed and pulled off her sun hat and dropped it in her bike basket. 'It all stems from the Darlingdowns. Superstition and all that. It's meant to bring good luck.'

'Right. I see. I've heard those Darlingdowns have a lot to answer to.'

'Indeed they do! How are you getting on with the house?'

Lucie rolled her eyes. 'On the first night I didn't think I was going to make it at all, so I've moved on from that. That was ages ago now, though.'

Hennie frowned. 'Was that the storm night we had a while ago?'

'Yes. If I'm honest, I was quite worried in there on my own.'

'Euuh, yeah, not a good day to move in. Did you have any damage?'

'Nope, luckily nothing. My mental health took a knock, though.' Lucie chuckled. 'I was scared out of my wits.'

Hennie laughed. 'I bet! There are some strange old creaks and noises in old houses when you're not used to them.'

'Yes! How about you? Did you have any damage?'

'I didn't, not really. I have some holiday cottages around the island and I lost some guttering in one of them. That was about it.'

'Oh right. What, you rent places out, do you?'

'Yes. It keeps me busy. You'll have to get on it with that place at the back you've got there. And doesn't the little wing on the side have private access?'

Lucie batted her hand in front of her face. 'Ha! You're joking. They're barely habitable. That's a long, long way away and I'm not sure I'd be much good at it.'

Hennie waved her hand around to the cottage. 'This place was falling down. And when I say falling down, I mean it had no roof.'

Lucie's eyes went huge. 'Wow! You'd never know!'

'Yep. Next time we bump into each other, I'll show you the before and afters. It's been quite the journey,' Hennie replied.

Lucie looked at the Pashley bike. 'Nice bicycle. I was only thinking the other day it might be a good idea to get myself one. The parking isn't great here.'

Hennie's face broke into a smile. 'Yes, I got one because I was having problems with my back and I thought it would help my core. I've not looked back. I hardly use my car nowadays only when I go over the water.'

Lucie chuckled. 'Mmm, I need core work.'

Hennie squinted her eyes and looked up and then back again. 'I have a bike, actually, it needs a new tyre. I have them for my holiday places. You can have it if you like. In lieu of a basket.' Hennie laughed.

'Gosh, that would be so kind of you. How much are you asking?'

'Oh, no, nothing. It's very old. It's how we do it over here.' Hennie laughed. 'You'll get used to it.'

'I think I am already.'

Hennie parked her bike up against the fence. 'I'll get a new tyre put on and I'll drop it over one day.'

'That would be lovely. You're sure I won't owe you?'

Hennie shook her head. 'Get away with you. There'll be something you can offer me once you get yourself settled in.'

Lucie laughed. 'About the only thing I can do is make quilts and cushions!'

Hennie raised her eyebrows. 'There you are then. Music to my ears. As a woman with holiday cottage lets, that sounds quite good to me.'

'Right, well, when you pop over, I'll show you some of my stuff.'

'Look forward to it, Lucie. Nice to meet you.'

'Likewise. See you,' Lucie replied and as she walked away, a little bit of Darling warmth was right in her centre along with burning in her legs.

Lucie made her way back to the Coastguard's House full of optimism. If places like the beautiful chocolate box cottage she'd just seen could be turned around, maybe there was hope for her yet. She smiled at the friendliness of Hennie and couldn't quite believe that she'd offered her a bike. Hennie'd said it was old and needed a bit of sprucing up, but still.

Smiling at the Three Wise Men, she went into the kitchen, put the kettle on, and got ready to spend the rest of her morning getting a website and social media set up for her sewing bits and preparing for the meeting with Tally's friend from the nursery.

With a cup of tea in hand, she put her laptop on the cutting table, opened a browser, and navigated her way to a website builder. Libby had recommended one and said she would be up and running in no time. Lucie was more than dubious and had visions of herself still sitting there at midnight with her head spinning. As she signed up for a free account and made some graphics on an online design tool, it was much easier than she thought. Not long after, she had a two page website and Fleur & Follie, her new little business had a digital presence in place.

As she clicked here and there, an affirmation went through her head; *I am capable of creating my own wealth. I am powerful and in charge.* She looked at the white web pages and the pretty peach flower design and calligraphy handwriting font; it had all been so quick and so easy. Shaking her head, she chastised herself. Why had it taken her so long? So many people had told her so many times. Now she was the proud owner of a web address, a website, an Instagram page and an Etsy shop. All of them perfectly coordinated. All of them with Lucie's style all over them.

More than pleased with herself, she walked around downstairs, looking at walls for somewhere to set up a background for the Zoom call with Monica. She needed a spot that made her look less bag lady in a moss-covered abode, more bright, airy, capable woman who could deliver. With not a lot to choose from, rooms primed but not yet painted and a couple still sporting the hideous green, she settled on the main sitting room to the front. The cladding had turned out better than she could have hoped and she'd painted a beautifully crafted shelf in the same paint. Dragging a fold-up table into the sitting room, she pushed moving boxes across the hallway and set them on top of the table to balance her laptop. After much faffing and fiddling, finally the webcam lined up with the shelf.

After ten minutes of searching, she found a box with some of her homewares and placed a white enamel jug, an oversized candle, and one of her little baskets with a frill on the shelf. Finding a vase, she filled it with water and made her way around the garden, hoping she'd find something passable. There wasn't much on offer; a few sprigs from the old apple tree, some seagrass from down by the water, in one of the beds she found an abundance of mint growing away to itself and salvaged some lavender from a bush at the front. Plonking the whole lot in the vase, she placed it on the shelf, wiggled the camera, sat down at the table and got her face in line. What appeared on the screen looked exactly as she had hoped. The Three Wise Men were safely hidden from sight, the once green walls were nothing but a figment of her imagination, and the bat poo from the granny flat did not appear to belong in the creamy white herb-filled scene she'd created.

After making a sandwich and leaving her laptop exactly where it was, she went out through the back garden, over the broken fence and sat with her feet in the water in the old plastic chair.

She thought about the meeting, attempting to preempt questions, and tried to squash her nerves. Tally had told her she'd be fine, but it was okay for Tally; Tally breezed through everything in life. Then she thought about what had happened since she'd learnt Rob's news. How the whole trajectory of her life had been ripped apart at the seams. As she watched a stray fish in the water and a dragonfly land, she thought that really it couldn't get a lot worse. At the end of the day, she had nothing to lose.

Closing the lid on her laptop, Lucie put her elbows on the table, head in her hands, and stretched the skin back and forth on her forehead. The meeting had turned into an hour and a half chat. Monica from Tally's nursery had spent a lot of time gushing and when Lucie had offered to make a four layer frilled sundress with ruching to the top, vintage fabric and pretty ribbon ties for Monica's daughter for their holiday, Monica had almost been beside herself with anticipation. The meeting had ended with Monica saying she would be in touch with a wholesale order for scalloped ruffle cushions, drawstring bags, bunting and pram blankets. She had her first order for her creations, and she couldn't quite get her head around that it had all fallen into place.

She looked around the sitting room in its new coat of Farrow and Ball white, the staged shelf behind her set up as if she was in command of her life, and the view out the side window with the glimpses of the sea. Pushing her chair out, she nodded to herself, and thought that perhaps she was more in control of this life than she had first thought.

*I command my destiny. I choose to make choices that show me the way.*

## 23

On her hands and knees with the sander in her hands, Lucie wriggled out from under the bath. The carpet glue on top of the floorboards in the ensuite bathroom was coming off beautifully. The revolting wee stained carpet had been removed and chucked in the skip more or less as soon as it arrived. Otis had recommended that a quick sand, seal, and a bath mat would do until she had the money for a new bathroom and now she was giving it a go. She'd had a good old look on Pinterest at timber floors in bathrooms and ascertained that it was worth a try. With her shoulder pounding, she stood up, adjusted her mask, folded back the shutters, and went over them too.

Everything was slowly coming together. Her early efforts on the bath, the removal of the carpet, and a new shower curtain meant that she could now at least get clean without feeling worse than when she started. Finishing up with the sander, vacuuming and clearing up, she went downstairs, made a cup of tea, picked up her laptop, and went into the back room. Nearly all the kitchen boxes had now been put away, and she felt more on top of things than she had since she'd first found out about Rob, Serena, and their baby.

She pressed on her iPad and video called Anais. Anais appeared on the screen with her hair up and a cup of tea in her hand.

'Hello. I was just talking about you earlier. I was on the phone to Tal, she said you've done something to your arm and you've lost your phone.'

'Yeah, I had a bit of a run in with a drain.'

'Nightmare.'

'Yeah, I'm doing well, though.'

'Tally said you were looking much brighter; she was right. That sea air must be doing something to you, Luce. You look so much happier.'

Lucie fiddled with her earring. 'I guess that's because I am happier. If you'd asked me that when it first happened, I would never have thought I would say that. But woohoo, look at me - I'm doing okay and I've got a new job and a new business.'

Anais frowned. 'What? Tal didn't tell me you had a job.'

Lucie laughed. 'Joking. I'm filling in at that local café, Darlings. You said you remembered it. I have no recollection of it from back in the day at all.'

'Ahh, yes, yes. Of course! Everyone knows Darlings. It's the local meeting place.'

'Yeah, that place.'

'Sorry, how did you get a job? What from Evie, that's her name if I remember rightly?'

'Yes, I didn't realise you knew her.'

Anais smiled. 'My parents have a house on Darling. Evie is from one of the oldest families there. I don't really know her as such, I know of her.'

'She seems to know everyone and everything.'

'She's lovely. She turned that place around back in the day. I always remember Mum talking about it.'

'It's dreamy in there. I want to live in there, Tal. I don't know how she does it if she's the one doing it all, but it works for me, that's all I can say.'

'A lot of work went into it, I do know that. There's one up in town now and a couple along the new train line. I'm not sure if they do the bowl thing there, though.'

'I've never heard of them. She didn't mention that.'

'She wouldn't.'

'Why not?'

'Another weird Darling thing. No bragging.'

'Right.'

'I bet she was all over you,' Anais noted.

'What do you mean by that?'

'Come on, Luce, do I need to spell it out for you? We've all been telling you for years, it was just Rob who didn't. You have a brain, and you're bouncy and funny and pretty, and a bit weird, good weird. And all your pretty fabric-y bits. You're Darlings to a tee. Everything in there is all part of Evie's branding, including who works there right down to the dog and all the pots and the flowers and whatnot. Surely you must have noticed how it's all just so.'

'Of course I have.'

'So, you're right on the money.'

'Don't be ridiculous! What does all that matter, to how I can do a job? It's not about what you look like.'

'It's the way of the world, Luce. Anyway, whatever. Maybe you'll end up staying there for a bit. There are a lot worse places to make a living.'

'Like you'd know, Anais!' Lucie joked. 'I'll see how I get on. I might hate it.'

'Yeah, maybe, maybe not. Perhaps it's just what you need. I can tell you one thing. It's most definitely a way to get to know your way around Darling.'

'Hmm, good point.'

'What else has been happening?' Anais asked.

'Nothing much. I have been flat out making stuff and painting. What else do you know about Darling?' Lucie asked. What she really wanted to say was how much do you know about George, but there was no way she was admitting anything to anyone, and least of all to one of the group. She would never live it down.

'As you know, I haven't been for a very long time.'

'Because you're always jetting all over the world.'

'Something like that. I hear Tally's coming over,' Anais replied.

'Yep. I think I'm going to be the one giving the counselling this time. And here I was feeling all sorry for myself.'

'Hmm. It's not great, from what I can gather. She needs to just call it a day.'

Lucie nodded. 'According to the front page of the paper, there are plenty of people in marriages of convenience.'

'Gosh, that sounds dire.'

'I know. I'm glad I'm out of the game when you hear things like that.'

Anais laughed. 'Not for long, girlfriend, not for long. I'm setting you up an online dating account.'

'Ha! Over my dead body. I would rather be alone and scared in this creaky old house than sitting in a pub swiping right.'

'Never say never, Ms Peachtree.'

'I suppose you are right. Anyway, there was a point to my call. I was wanting to show you my new website.'

'I can't believe you've finally done it! So proud of you. What's it called?'

'I'll send you the link,' Lucie replied, sent Anais the link, and waited as Anais copied and pasted.

'Yes, love it. Simple and chic with the lovely pastel frill. Just like your stuff. So, now what?'

'Now I'm going to start taking some pictures of my things

and putting them online. The site has a shopping cart thingy. It looks simple even for someone with my limited abilities in this area.'

'It's going to be great.'

'There's one problem. A lot of my stuff is in the storage unit. All my collections of my gorgeous vintage fabrics. It means I will have to go over that way. I don't want to go anywhere near my old life after the Serena sighting.'

'I don't blame you.'

'Seeing Serena wasn't too bad, but once was enough, and I do not want to bump into Rob. I mean, I probably wouldn't, but do you know what I mean? I don't want to even chance it.'

'Totally! He's the last person you want to see. Could you get the whole lot posted to you?'

'I guess so. It will probably cost an arm and a leg.'

'I'm paying if it does. Nothing is worth you having to see Rob.' Anais sighed. 'The next time we all see him, he's going down.'

'You have to stop saying that.'

'It will happen. Trust me. He doesn't know what he's lost, or for that matter what he's got coming when the lovely Serena has the baby and everything hits the fan.'

'Ahh, good luck to them. I don't care. And how good does it feel to say that?'

'You go girl.'

'Ha! You're nuts, Anais. Okay, I'm going to go, I have a multi-million pound fabric empire to work on.'

'I'll leave you to it. Next stop, the moon. Hold. Your. Nerve.'

Lucie pressed the red button on her iPad and walked out into the hallway. The Three Wise Men looked up at her. It certainly didn't look like the surroundings for a successful business, or a successful anything, but something had shifted again; she had moved on and it felt fab.

Looking at her watch, Lucie made another cup of tea and planned her next route around the island. She remembered Mr Cooke and his pdf, opened her laptop and emails, and navigated to his message. She'd sent a reply in thanks, but hadn't really got much further than a brief scan of the flora and fauna to be found all over Darling, Darling Bay and its surroundings.

As she waited for the tea to brew, she read through all sorts of things. There were rare birds, amazing shells, fascinating sea life, sea glass to collect, and a plethora of stones and pebbles washed up from all over the show.

Scanning her way to the end of the first document, Lucie was surprised at how right Mr Cooke was. Maybe he had seen something in her she hadn't even known was there. The document had piqued her interest. Opening a map of Darling in another tab, she plotted a rough route, hoping that it wouldn't involve losing anything. Instead, she intended it would aid in the further enhancement of Power Lucie and the loss of the extra tyre currently still hanging on for dear life around her middle.

She grabbed the new leggings from the airer in the utility room, picked up George's phone, made her way across the hallway, and opened the front door to get her trainers from the porch.

As she opened the door and looked at the front step, she stopped in her tracks. Another basket was sitting there just to the right. Otis had told her they would arrive bit-by-bit, but she hadn't really thought it would be true. She'd already had more since the first few; one from the off-licence with four mini bottles of wine, and the florist had sent a little plant, which was sitting by the front door.

Picking up her trainers and the basket, she put it on the floor in the hallway, sat on the bottom step and opened it. A small hardback book with 'Walks on Darling Island' on the front was nestled in beside a baseball cap in navy-blue with the Darling badge on the front. A little envelope held a small piece of paper with a few words.

*Welcome to Darling. For your walks.*
*Try not to do anything that involves the emergency services.*
*George.*

Lucie blinked and held the piece of paper up to the light. That was a turn up for the books! How strange this little place was. Sending people you didn't even know baskets. She actually wondered what would be arriving on her doorstep next.

She flicked through the book. It was actually quite appropriate. It was probably sent with some sarcasm from what she'd seen of him so far, maybe not. He'd seemed a little bit softer when he'd stopped for the cup of tea, and he'd done a nice thing with the phone. He'd hardly been polite and welcoming the first time she'd met him, though. Then again, she'd been more than on the rude side. She grimaced at the thought, now somewhat embarrassed. She'd been far from polite and she'd told him when her phone was down the drain to mind his own business. Turning the card over and over and flicking through the book, she tried to make out what to think about the delivery. She wondered about whatever her name was, Underwear Model. Why wasn't she on the card?

As she gave one of the Three Wise Men a stroke on her way out, she suddenly realised it was another one of Darling's things. As Anais had said on the phone, Darling had its own funny little ways. As a neighbour, George was obviously bound by something to at least show a modicum of welcome. Of course, that was it! That was why he'd done the phone thing too. He was clearly suspicious and was hedging his bets. Helping with the phone first, making her the cup of tea, dropping off the phone and then following up with the basket just like everybody else. George had stacked himself up a few credits with the Darling fairies just like the good resident that he was.

Putting the book, the cap, and the card back in the basket, she re-tied the laces on one of her trainers. Whatever, no point wasting any energy whatsoever on it. She would concentrate on walking and affirmations and a little bit of bolstering for the new girl in town; Power Lucie was evolving and ready to go out to play.

## 24

A few days or so later, Lucie fiddled with her bracelet as she stood on the side by the water, looking over at the ferry making its way across the estuary. A hazy early morning greeted the passengers, and the foghorn sounded in the distance. She blinked a few times as the Pride of Darling got closer, and she could just make out Tally standing looking over the side down into the water.

She observed as it arrived on the slipway, clanging and banging, and she waved as Tally looked over and followed the other foot passengers off. Tally breezed along looking a million dollars; slim and somehow casual and smart at the same time, she always looked pulled together. Lucie, in her midi dresses, frilly tops, and big tote bags made with Liberty material had always felt a bit of a ragbag when Tally was around. Tally had always said she could never pull off Lucie's style and loved all the frills and ruffles, but Lucie had never really believed her.

Tally put her arm around Lucie and squeezed. The hug was loaded, just that little bit too tight, as if it carried something with it. Lucie stood back. 'You okay?'

'Yeah, yeah, I'm fine. I'm glad to be here. I needed to get away.'

'Has anything happened?'

'No, not at all. That's the whole point. I couldn't wait to get away, and he didn't even notice. He barely looked up from his breakfast.'

'Oh dear.'

'Anyway, I don't want to talk about it.' Tally looked around. 'Hello Darling!'

'You're funny.'

'Gosh, it's a bit different from the last time I was here. I was trying to work out when that was.'

'How do you mean different?'

'Maybe I'm imagining it. It's like some secret world. The getting on the ferry, the water, the hazy, misty fog. We thought it was a right pain when we came here with Anais, now it feels like you're leaving all the crap behind. It's probably because I'm older and wiser.'

'Hmm. It is like that. The saying is correct; it is so very far from care.'

'In my case, I am literally doing that; leaving things behind, I mean. I'm not including the girls, obviously.'

'How are they?'

Tally nodded. 'Yeah, really excited to be with my mum.'

'That's good then.'

'I think she'll be exhausted by the end of the weekend. They don't stop.'

They got to Lucie's car, and she opened the boot. 'I wasn't sure whether or not you'd want to walk, but it's just down the road here.'

Tally peered out the window as they made their way towards the Coastguard's House and turned into the road. The house came fully into view and Tally pressed her window down. 'Oh. My. Goodness! Luce! Waaaaah! It's flipping amazing!'

Lucie giggled as she parked the car. 'Are you looking at the same house as me? This one on the end.'

'Yes, I am! And I'm looking at all the others and can clearly see that this one has taken the best spot. I thought you had lost the plot when you said you'd bought this.'

'Wow, you're making me feel a lot better about the whole thing,' Lucie replied, tapping the steering wheel happily.

'It's a lot, lot, lot better than the photos you put in the group.'

'Really? I thought it was a lot, lot worse.'

'Nah. This is gold. I'm jealous of the sea, the fog, the flagpole.'

'You won't be when you get inside; there are Three Wise Men in the hall, a creepy granny flat down by the water, and the main bathroom has a hole in the floor. That's just for starters.'

'I don't care. Ooh, I can just imagine it with all your pretty quilts and fabrics. Cushions, little baskets and liners. Flowers by the door, a hammock, all your books and stuff. Mmm.'

'I did not expect this reaction from you, Tally. Who are you again? You never gush.'

'I know, I am an ever-so-serious boring old GP with a husband I don't think I'm in love with, a lot on my plate, and I'm in serious need of some much-needed downtime.'

'I'm your girl. I'm even going to take you on a nature trail.'

They walked through into the hallway and Tally collapsed into fits of giggles at the Three Wise Men. 'What on earth! Firstly, who would have them in their house and secondly, err, why are you keeping them? Would they not have been the first thing to land in the skip?'

'I don't know. I've sort of got attached to them.'

'No, I draw the line at that. They are exceedingly creepy. They can't stay.'

'You should have been here on that first night in the storm. It was awful, really awful. I was scared out of my wits. Those three were the last of my worries.'

Tally put her bag down and poked her head around the

sitting room door and clapped her hands over her mouth. 'Ooooh. Fabulous! What happened to the green?'

'I told you I've been painting all hours of the day and night. Farrow and Ball came up trumps.'

'They did indeed. Ahh, the cladding. The exposed brick and the fire. You couldn't make this up. I love it. Rob McKintock can shove this where the sun doesn't shine.'

'What's he got to do with it?' Lucie giggled.

'He has nothing on this, and he doesn't have lovely old you, that's what he's got to do with it.'

'Yeah, he traded me in for a younger, prettier, more pregnant model.'

'Nup. You've won. I know that already. I am so, so, so proud of you. You downplayed how hard you've been working. You must have worked day and night.'

'Tal, I had the men you all paid for, and they did a lot of it. Without them, it would have been a whole different ball game. I've just continued on from where they left off.'

'I know, but it's much better than I thought. I honestly thought you were going to have to take a knock on it and try and get rid of it at a loss.' Tally spun her head around. 'Sorry, did you feel that?'

Lucie giggled. 'I did. It feels like it moves, but it doesn't. According to everyone and Leo, the neighbour, it's the timber in the wind. Wood breathes, apparently. Who even knew that? Not me.'

'Right,' Tally said as she took the steps up through the hallway and then down the other side, following Lucie into the kitchen. Tally nodded over and over again. 'Yeah. Sweet. You've outdone yourself on this too. Gosh, that picture you sent me of the burgundy paint was horrendous. I have to admit, I wasn't looking forward to eating out of this kitchen. Now look at it.'

'I don't know what to say. I can't believe your reaction. I

thought you were going to be the opposite. I had visions of you forcing me to come home with you.'

'Nope. I love it. Even with that monstrosity out there,' Tally said, pointing to the granny flat with the bright blue tarpaulin, the bricks holding it down, the moss, and the weedy garden all around it.

'Yeah, that's going to take a bit of time. I'll get to it eventually. But it's come up pretty well overall. I knew right from the minute I viewed the images online. The reality was just a little bit different when I got here. The bones are here.'

'I hope I'm not rostered down to work on that,' Tally joked, peering further at the granny flat.

'You're not rostered to do anything. I've cracked on with it all. The bathroom is even good enough to have a decent wash in, and I've got all new towels edged, of course, with a vintage fabric ruffle.'

'I knew it. I knew you'd get your groove back.' Tally gave Lucie a huge hug. 'Well done you, Luce. Well done you.'

'Ahh, thank you. I'm a bit blown away by your reaction.'

'No, this is brilliant. I can feel it in the air, in my bones, in the water, whatever. Lucie Peachtree, my friend of a trillion years, you are going to thrive here. Something very good is around the corner.'

# 25

'How the heck did you do that?' Lucie asked as Tally walked out of the bathroom.

'Do what?'

'You know what I'm going to say.'

Tally laughed. 'Something about me scrubbing up well.'

'Yeah. You have a shower and shove your hair up on top of your head and put on white trousers and a black top and look gorgeous.'

'You, my friend, need to back yourself a bit more.'

'Maybe.'

'What's the plan?'

'I'm going to hop in the shower, dry my hair, and then we'll make the salads, stroll over to the tram, go to the off-licence and head to Leo's house. He said it was casual regarding the time to arrive.'

'It'll be lovely on an evening like this. I presume it will be in the back garden by the water. We'll need a jumper for later. I'm looking forward to a barbecue; I can't even remember the last time I had a sausage.'

Lucie laughed. 'Let me fill you in on something.' Tally raised her eyebrows and listened. 'This is apparently a proper barbecue. There will be no sausages.'

'What? I thought the Darling sausage was famous!'

'That's the cured one, and there's one for an annual dinner or something, but there are not any sausages tonight. He made a thing about it.'

'Ooh fancy. I thought the whole point of a barbecue was a sausage,' Tally joked.

'Nope. So yes, I've had to raise my salad game. I'll be turning up at my first Darling gathering well prepared.'

Strolling along Darling Street, Lucie and Tally stopped to look in shop windows and watched the trams go past. Tally gazed in at the children's boutique and pointed to a little girls' sundress. 'You see, this is what I mean, that dress you've made for Monica is leaps and bounds above that. I bet it's made in China too.' Tally squinted in and turned her head to look at the price tag. 'Eeek, I need a mortgage to get two of those for the girls.'

Lucie nodded. 'You're standing next to an expert now. I did a lot of research before that meeting with Monica. It's a crazy world. Though there are a few sticking points for regulations and labelling and stuff like that, it's high entry price points. She was all over it with the red tape side of it and pointed me in the right direction to one of their suppliers who deals with all that.'

'You want to get in this place too.' Tally nodded towards the shop.

'One step at a time I think.'

Two minutes later, they were standing outside Bottles on Darling. Tally laughed. 'Not quite the supermarket wine aisle. My goodness, even the off-licence is quaint. Show me the way.'

They giggled and laughed as they fell in the door and Tally

stopped as they walked in and gazed around. It was like an old-fashioned apothecary shop. Deep vintage green almost black shelving lined panelled walls. Under each bottle, handwritten labels taped with washi tape described the contents. Soft jazz music played and behind a panelled counter, a line of scented candles filled the air with a combination of incense and a woody, spicy amber.

Tally whispered, 'I've just died and gone to off-licence heaven. Why isn't there a Bottles on Darling where I live? I want to be able to potter along the road, pop in, grab myself a bottle of bubbles, and potter off again.'

In the corner, a few black café tables with Bentwood chairs were squeezed in between rows and rows of French wine. Little tasting glasses were laid out beside them and a couple were sitting chatting.

Tally whispered again and pointed to a small doorway. 'What's through there?' More candles flickered as they got closer and Tally turned, her eyes as big as saucers. 'Blimey, Luce. It's a gin room! Come to Mama.'

Lucie and Tally weaved their way around the room. Gins squeezed in from all over the place greeted them. Gorgeous bottles, fancy labels, and the same soft lighting and jazz music as the front of the shop. The light flickered and caught the cut glass all around them.

'Mind blowing.' Tally giggled.

Lucie started to read from the back of a bottle of gin in a faux posh accent; she held her right hand up as if she was on the stage, and gesticulated towards the shelf.

'This one is from Pretty Beach. Distilled with wild strawberries from Strawberry Hill in Pretty Beach with hints of hedgerow botanicals and sounds of the sea... Oh how divine, darling,' Lucie drawled the words in the Queen's English and then stopped as she heard someone come in behind them.

Embarrassed and realising the person was closer, she turned around.

'Oh, hello!' she exclaimed and felt Tally turn beside her.

George was standing with a six-pack of craft beers in his hand. 'That sounds nice. Strawberries from Pretty Beach.' He raised his eyebrows at her silly voice.

Lucie coughed and put the bottle of gin back on the shelf. A funny look passed over George's face. 'Good to see you upright this evening.'

Tally side-eyed, Lucie laughed and gestured to Tally. 'This is my friend, Tally. The GP I was telling you about. This is George, my, well, I suppose George, you are my neighbour. The one who helped me with the, umm, phone situation.'

George held out his hand. 'Nice to meet you, Tally. Good to see Lucie will be in capable hands for the evening. At least we know she'll be safe.'

Lucie chuckled. 'You really do have the wrong impression of me, I think. Most of the time I'm accident-free on the whole. As a general rule, I keep myself out of trouble.'

Tally smiled. 'We've been exploring the delights of this wonderful shop.'

'I heard.' George smiled.

Lucie screwed her face up. 'Sorry, private joke.'

'Be my guest. I was just after one of these,' George said as he reached over and picked up a bottle from the shelf behind Lucie.

'Off somewhere nice?' Tally asked, having moved swiftly into a combination of her schmoozing voice and doctor's voice.

'Actually, no. I'm home alone, but I had a huge clear out today and realised I was out of gin and sometimes a nice gin and tonic on a warm evening is the way to watch the sun go down.'

'I should say so. Nice to meet you then,' Tally said. 'Enjoy your evening.'

'Will do. Have fun, ladies.'

Lucie felt her eyelashes fluttering. What on earth was happening to her? 'Oh, we will. See you, George.' She gazed after him as he walked away.

'Luce!' Tally swore. 'Who in the name of whoever was that?'

'The one who helped me try to save my phone.'

'Hang on. Is he the same one whose car you bumped? The one with Underwear Model?'

'The very one.'

'You didn't tell me that bit of it!'

Lucie screwed up her nose. 'What?'

'My goodness. He is, I don't even have a word. You might have to resuscitate me after that and I am a respectfully, though not fully happily I must add, married woman.'

Lucie batted her hand. 'Don't be ridiculous!'

'And how much does he fancy you? Wow!'

'Me? You really are a comedian, Tal.'

'Of course, I am. Reaching over, brushing your shoulder, giving you the eye.'

'Not at all! You are imagining it.'

'I am not. All the eyes between the pair of you. Plus, it was like I was invisible.'

Lucie screwed up her face and shook her head. 'No way. You're being weird.'

'I cannot wait to put this in the group chat. Goodbye, Rob McKintock. Goodbye.'

'You are doing nothing of the sort!'

'Ha! Yep. This is sooooo good.' Tally giggled and rubbed her hands together.

'He's with that model Matilda whatshername-whatshername. He literally wouldn't look at me if I was on fire. Not that I want anyone looking at me anyway. I told you, was it you or Janey? I'm doing a sperm donor as my next relationship. Much less chance of him running off with the Serenas of this world.'

'No, no. There was something there. I witnessed it with my very own, very highly educated eyes.'

'There was not. The first time he clapped eyes on me, I was wearing my oldest joggers and the bum fell down. That was not a good look. He thinks I'm weird, live in a dirtbox of a house, and feels sorry for me. Nothing more, nothing less. I am telling you that now for a fact.'

'Oh no, Luce. Oh no, oh no, oh no. That was a thing that just occurred right there and I am going to sit back and get ready to watch the show. Ding blimming dong.'

Lucie pulled the dish out of the fridge and put it on the kitchen table. Tally peered in through the clingfilm and sipped on her wine.

'Looks fancy enough to me.'

'I hope so. Okay. I'll just go and get a basket.'

A few minutes later, Lucie was back with an oval lidded wicker basket. One of her scalloped edged liners in a pretty floral fabric hung out over the top.

Tally nodded, touched the frill, and put her wine glass down. 'See, this is what I mean.'

Lucie frowned. 'What?'

'Most people have a cool bag from Sainsbury's, Waitrose if we're being fancy. You have a wicker basket with a lid. Not only that it's lined with a frill. You are an expert in dining al fresco.'

Lucie giggled. 'You may have a point.'

'I bet you have matching napkins and picnic blankets for this too,' Tally said, touching the frill on the basket.

'Guilty. I might have to mention the tablecloth, too.'

'You don't need to tell me. We've all witnessed it over the years.'

'It's nothing,' Lucie replied as she lifted the lid, popped the salad in, and put in a bottle of gin.

Tally let out a gigantic sigh with a whoosh. 'Gosh, I'm having a lovely time. It is so nice, and I mean so nice, not having to be the one doing all the thinking all the time. Bless my mum for looking after the girls. It was just what I needed coming here.'

'Glad me and my Wise Men could be of service.' Lucie laughed as she picked up the basket and handed Tally a bottle of wine. 'Okay, down that drink and let's go.'

W alking up the path to Leo's house, they could hear the faint sound of chatting and music from the back garden. They rang the doorbell and waited. With no response, they walked down the side of the house and Lucie called out. 'Helloooo. Hi!'

Two seconds later, Leo appeared. He broke into a huge smile. 'You made it. How are ya?'

Lucie felt Tally beside her tense and stand a bit straighter as she stepped forward and kissed Leo on the cheek. 'We're good thanks, Leo. How are you?' Lucie asked.

'Great.' Leo turned to Tally and held out his hand. 'Leo.'

Tally took his hand. 'I'm Nathalie.'

Lucie snapped her head to the right. Tally only ever used her full name when she was trying to impress. It hadn't been out to play for a very long time. Lucie widened her eyes as Tally smiled at Leo and he put his other arm on her elbow. 'How are ya, Nathalie?'

Tally's voice moved from its usual schmoozing doctor combo to something altogether new. A voice Lucie didn't think she'd heard since they were at school. She sort of purred. 'I'm good. Nice to meet you.'

Lucie stood beside them. 'Yes, Leo's in the same field, not that I know anything. He's at the new hospital out at Newport.'

Tally let out a girly, giggly sound. Lucie frowned and stared at Tally. Tally looked up at Leo. 'Ahh, right. Okay. I'm a GP.'

Leo smiled. 'Good luck to ya with that. Hope they're paying you well.'

'Not enough, not enough.'

They followed Leo to the back. A massive barbecue was nestled in the corner of a block paved terrace. Plump outdoor cushions lined expensive-looking outdoor sofas. Shelly from the tram was sitting with a glass of wine, and a few people were standing down by the fence at the back near the water.

Lucie observed as Tally conversed with Leo. He got her a glass of wine and Tally passed over the basket with the salad and the gin. Lucie shook her head as she took it all in. This was a turn up for the books. In all the years since Tally had been married, said she was unhappy and had gone back and forth about what she was going to do, there had never been even a sniff or mention of anyone else. Lucie was gobsmacked to admit that from what she could see, Leo was clearly changing that. It was like something was lit between them and it was running in torrents back and forth.

A few hours later, the evening had been lovely, but the damp, foggy air had dropped in. Leo had brought out tartan blankets, lit a big chiminea in the corner, and poured everyone another drink. A couple of people had gone home and Lucie was left sitting next to Shelly whilst Tally and Leo discussed his work and training through the system.

Shelly sipped her gin. 'Loving Darling so far?'

Lucie nodded. 'I really am. The last week or so a few things have slotted into place. I have to admit when I first arrived, I didn't think I was going to stay.'

'Mmm. It grows on you.'

'The house was such a mess, but in the long run, I think it

will do me the world of good.'

'Yes, it's a lovely place to live.'

'Did you hear I'm helping out temporarily at Darlings? You were the one who first told me about it that day. Remember? That seems like ages ago now.'

'I did hear when I was in there yesterday. You won't go wrong with Evie. Mind you, she takes no slackers.'

'I'm not work-shy.'

'I can see that. What's next on the house?'

'Day by day or I should say month by month. I don't have an agenda. I'm going to find my feet with it.'

'Good idea. You wouldn't be interested in a microwave, would you?'

Lucie nodded. 'I don't have one, actually. Why? Are you selling one?'

'I'm not, you might not have met her yet, my friend just got a free mini microwave with a washing machine and tumble drier. Anyway, long story short, she gave it to me but it doesn't fit my plates. Would you like it?'

'I'd love it.'

'Leo said he thought you might. What's your number?'

Lucie took out the loaned phone. 'Oh, err, I'm not sure.'

Shelly frowned. 'You don't know your number? What?'

'I lost my phone, and this is a replacement. I need to see if I can get my number back. I haven't had a chance. This is George's phone, you know George?'

Shelly's eyes nearly fell out of her head. 'I do know George. We all know George.'

*Tell me more. Tell me more.* Lucie thought. 'He helped me out.'

'You're honoured. That I do know.'

'I am? What do you mean by that?'

Shelly leant forward to the coffee table, sliced off a piece of cheese on a cheeseboard, and popped it into her mouth. 'Oh nothing.'

*No, no, you cannot leave me hanging,* Lucie thought and decided to take the plunge and do some digging. 'His wife is a bit of a stunner. Talk about make you feel a bit shabby.' Lucie trilled out a fake little laugh.

'Yeah, she'd like to be his wife. He doesn't have a wife. You must mean that Matilda, do you?'

'Oh, right. I assumed...' Lucie let the rest of her sentence hang in the air, hoping for some more information.

'You assumed wrong.' Shelly took another piece of cheese and a sip of wine. 'Very, very sad situation. Awful.'

Lucie didn't say anything and just waited.

'Do you know what happened?' Shelly asked.

'No, I don't know what you're talking about.'

Shelly sighed and shook her head and lowered her voice. 'It's best you know, really, because it's a bit tricky. George's daughter had a terrible accident. Yes,' Shelly stopped talking and nodded. 'It was awful.'

'Oh! I had no idea.'

'No. You wouldn't. He never talks about it. He's a bit grumpy, really, most of the time because of it. Not that I'm judging, that's why I was surprised about the phone.'

Lucie frowned. 'What happened?'

Shelly looked away. 'An accident at a children's party. His daughter was in one of those fairy costumes, and it caught fire.' Shelly lowered her voice. 'His ex partner was with her when it happened. There were many, many surgeries. They weren't together by that point, anyway, the ex couldn't deal with it. She ended up, you know, being admitted.'

'Right, sounds awful. The daughter? She's okay now?'

'Hmm. Yes and no, she has to have a lot of therapy still.'

'What happened to the partner?' Lucie asked.

'She's with someone else now, and they had a couple of other children, but I think she's still up and down from what I've heard.'

'Oh, I see. Wow, complicated. And George?' Lucie couldn't resist asking.

'Well, now you're asking. He didn't do anything at all when he was first back here. Someone, I can't remember who, Evie maybe or, hmm, might have been Mr Cooke persuaded him to go to the dinner, and that was all we saw of him for like a year or so.'

'The dinner?'

'Sorry, I keep forgetting you've only just moved over. It's a yearly invite-only dinner thing. Dinner on Darling. George goes to that but other than that, and things at the sailing club, he keeps himself to himself more or less.'

Lucie wanted to jump down Shelly's throat. *How do I get an invitation to Dinner on Darlings? I'll pay anything.* She pretended it was the first she had heard of it and frowned. 'Dinner on Darling?'

'Yes, you'll have to come.'

*Pleeeaaaaaase.*

'I haven't been invited.'

'You just were.'

'Pardon?'

'I'm the Chairwoman. I just invited you.'

'What? Really?'

Shelly chuckled. 'Perks of the job. Can you make mashed potatoes?'

Lucie nodded solemnly. 'I'm up there with Nigella.'

'There you are then. You're in.'

Lucie felt inordinately pleased with herself but desperately wanted to get the conversation back to George. 'So, yes, George was great about the phone,' she said, tapping it. 'He's on his own now, is he, since all that happened?'

'Hmm. There have been a couple of women on the scene now and then. You know what Darling's like. It goes around like wildfire. He was only part-time here then, but he moved over a while ago. You'll see Darcy when she's here. Lovely little girl. Such a shame.'

Lucie wanted to know more about Underwear Model. 'And what about the one I thought was his wife?'

Shelly batted her hand in front of her face. 'Pah! He entertained her for a bit because her father is something to do with George's business interests - I'm not sure about the full story. Darling was not keen on her. I can tell you that for nothing.'

'Right.' Lucie felt mildly alarmed at Shelly's change in tone.

Shelly narrowed her eyes. 'You see, we check you out on the punt. They text me on the tram with a photo and then I do a recce on anyone coming up on the tram too. By the time we've sent anyone to Darlings or in her case not, you are either very much in or you're out.'

Lucie's eyes widened in alarm, and Shelly burst out laughing. 'Joking! I got you.'

'Oh, I was really worried then! Oh my! It's like some sort of cult. I was wondering what I'd let myself in for.'

'No, but all joking aside, she was rude to the crew on the ferry and then she stalked onto the tram announcing that she wasn't keen on public transport and looked down her nose at me. Then a few days later, she found herself in Darlings and demanded that Evie clear a table for her when the place was packed to the rafters with residents.'

'Right, I see.'

'I imagine from what I have seen, and I have to admit, heard, about you so far, that you will realise how that all went down. Red floaty dress and fedora or not.'

Lucie burst out laughing. 'Don't make me laugh, Shelly! I thought the same about the blooming hat.'

'Stuff like that does not bode well here. No time for it, you see. No time for it and not enough people.'

'No. I mean, yes, I do see that.'

'There you are. So old George there. Takes no prisoners.'

Lucie gulped a ginormous mouthful of wine, digesting what Shelly had just said. Not that she'd mind being a prisoner of George. So there was that.

Woken up to a gentle breeze, Lucie could tell that the fog that had come down at the barbecue had already lifted. She didn't know how she knew that by the sound around the room, but she did. Mr Cooke had told her on the tram that it was something to do with the fog changing the density of the air. Or something like that. Maybe she had that bit wrong.

She turned over in the handmade Liberty sheets and sighed. Her mind went over the evening before. Tally had knocked back the wine like it was going out of fashion and spent the vast majority of the evening talking to Leo. No doubt Tally, even with the enormous quantities of alcohol she had consumed, would still emerge from her room looking beautiful without a sore head in sight.

Lucie said a silent thank you that the glasses of wine she'd poured had been small, that she'd downed tumblers of water in between, and that she had passed on the gin. She'd only gulped on the wine at the end when Shelly had informed her further on the private life of George and that Underwear Model was not his wife.

She turned all the information over in her mind deliciously, and then coming to her senses, squeezed her eyes together and asked herself what she was doing, even contemplating it all. The marital status, or lack thereof, of George was of no interest to her whatsoever, she tried to kid herself as she wriggled her feet around on the bare floorboards to locate her slippers.

When she passed the Three Wise Men in the hallway and arrived in the kitchen, Tally was sitting there looking down at her phone. The Baccarat coffee pot was on the hob and it looked like the kettle had just boiled.

'I just topped the pot up. I thought I heard you get up. I've moved onto coffee.'

'How in the name of goodness are you not hungover? How do you look like that?'

Tally frowned. 'Why would I be hungover? I didn't drink much at all.'

'Yeah, right! You were drinking like a fish. You really packed it away!'

'Nah. I was pacing myself,' Tally replied, shaking her head.

Lucie poured out a cup of tea and took milk from the fridge. As she poured it in, she concentrated on her mug without looking at Tally. 'How was Leo?'

She heard Tally's voice move ever-so-slightly to her GP voice. 'Yeah, yeah. He seems nice enough.'

*Right, so this is how we're going to play it.* Lucie thought. 'Uh-huh. What did you talk about? You were chatting for ages.'

'Were we?'

'Yes, you were. No one could get a word in edgeways.'

'Oh, I dunno. Stuff. Boring old medical stuff.'

'Didn't look boring from where I was standing.'

'Yeah, it was. Totally boring. Hang on, Luce. I'm just sending a text to Mum to see how the girls were in the night.'

*Changing the subject, are we?* Lucie thought. It was so Tally. Lucie had seen it long ago when they were young; the nonchalant attitude, the ignoring of the subject, brushing the whole thing off. This was serious.

Tally looked up from her phone with raised eyebrows. 'How are you feeling? Sore head?'

'Goodness no! No way I was up for a sore head today. I had a lot of water breaks and was watching my measures.'

'Right. It was nice, wasn't it?' Tally noted.

'Yeah. I enjoyed myself.'

'I needed to let my hair down a bit.'

'You did.'

'What were you chatting about with Shelly? She seems nice.'

It was Lucie's turn to be nonchalant. Lucie batted her hand in front of her face as she waited for slices of toast to pop out of the toaster. 'Oh, you know, this and that. Bits about life on Darling, gossip, stuff about the library and the Town Hall.'

Tally took the toast and started to slather on butter. 'What sort of gossip?'

Lucie tried to keep her voice on an even keel. 'It turns out that George is not with Underwear Model at all'.

'I knew it! I told you. So he's not all coupled-up. Wow, in you go, Luce. In you go. Peachtree's going in.'

Lucie laughed. 'Don't be daft. Things don't happen like that at our age. It's not like when we were young.'

Tally sighed. 'I know. I was just being hopeful. It's a shame we're old and boring.'

'Yep. Old, boring, and past it.'

'I can't even remember what it's like to go out on a date and, I don't know, have fun with someone,' Tally said wistfully.

'I know.'

'I know we don't talk about you know who, but at least you had date night once in a blue moon.'

'Yeah, problem was he was also having date night with someone else!' Lucie chuckled. 'I cannot believe I can even joke about it. How things change.'

Tally sighed. 'I don't even know the last time I went out without first having to arrange it, then organise the childcare, then sort out Alec's clothes, then book the Uber or whatever, and have to pay. Even if we do go out, it's normally something to do with his career or the club and by the time I've worked all day and got there, I'm shattered anyway.'

Lucie nodded. 'Maybe it's time to stop doing it.'

Tally looked out the window. 'Maybe it is.'

Lucie picked up her tea. 'Come on. I'll take you to my secret spa. It's where all my most important decisions have been made lately.'

'Ooh, you didn't say there was a hot tub.'

Lucie giggled and led Tally over the messy garden to the fallen down fence. Tally frowned and wrinkled up her nose. 'Where is it?'

Lucie moved her arm from left to right, pointing to the horizon. 'This is it. This is my spa.' She grabbed the other drab old plastic outdoor chair and dragged it to the edge of the water. Leaning down, she pulled up her pyjama bottoms. 'Come on.'

Tally squealed. 'This is the funniest looking spa I've ever seen.'

'It's magic, Tal. Come on.'

Tally pulled her pyjamas up to her knees and paddled out to the two chairs. They both plonked themselves down and sat beside each other facing the horizon with their feet in the water. 'Sometimes all you need is your feet in the water, a cup of tea, and a slice of Marmite on toast with a good friend, Luce.'

'The butter has to be salted and just melting. And thick. Has to be.'

Tally wooshed out a sigh. 'Wow, it *is* nice here. You're so right.'

'Something happens to your shoulders out here. The tension goes.'

'Pah! If it wasn't happening to me, I would say that you were cray-cray, but you're right. It's like someone wrapped you up in a hazy blue thing and everything went soft.'

'Tell me about it.'

Tally sipped her tea and sighed again. 'People would pay good money for this. Good money.'

'I know. It's a Darling thing.'

'Yeah.'

'Just off the mainland... so very far from care.'

# 26

With the meditation app playing on what she was now calling 'her' phone, Lucie stared at the sample diet plan she'd somehow come across when she'd been trawling the internet looking for leggings. The diet plan instructed a few things on top of what to eat; to wake at 4.30a.m., to start the day with sound healing bowls, to cleanse the body with daily turmeric, to slowly and calmly chant as the sun rose, to celebrate the fullness of life with cacao sessions, and to add phytonutrients to everything entering one's being.

Lucie squeezed her eyes together, trying to read the tiny words on the back of a packet of frozen summer fruits from the freezer and then scanned the diet plan again.

*On waking: fenugreek seeds soaked in distilled spring water*
*Breakfast: 4 almonds whisked into 1 whole egg white*
*Snack: 1 cup of black coffee*
*Lunch: a cup of steamed veggies with half a grilled fish*
*Snack: 1 green tea with a handful of gooseberries*
*Supper: clear organic vegetable soup*
*Snack: 1 cup almond milk with a pinch of psyllium husk*

She read through it again and gazed out at the water and spoke to herself, 'What even are fenugreek seeds? Half a fish! Something or other husk. Gooseberries? Who has gooseberries?' Running her finger down to what was being suggested for the second half of the day, she laughed. 'They call that a snack? Crikey, no wonder I'm plump. This is what is referred to as starvation.'

Letting out a massive sigh, she shook the frozen fruits into the blender, added a carton of juice, dumped in some yoghurt, and whizzed. Stuff fenugreek seeds at four-thirty in the morning for a game of soldiers. She'd rather suffer the plumpness of her upper arms than subject herself to that. Life had been hard enough since the note from Rob, she didn't need punishment by way of fenugreek and psyllium too.

Pouring her effort at a smoothie into an old French jam jar, she snatched it up and opened the back door. She had no healing sound bowls or cacao at her disposal, but she was more than happy with her own version of a morning ceremony as she looked out at the water. Enveloped in the Darling morning air, she would experience her very own Coastguard's House spa experience. With her iPad tucked under her arm, she made the now familiar walk to the back of the garden. The chair was in its same spot and with the fruit smoothie, she sat there with a spoon and the silence and waited. Sure enough, as she took long slow breaths in and out, the spa worked its magic. She felt her shoulders drop and circled her left arm. It was still sore but had healed well.

She let her eyes rove around the horizon for a while, drinking in the hazy blue, and then suddenly, before she knew what she was doing, she was on social media looking at Rob's profile. *I just need to have a quick look,* she told herself. *It won't do any harm. I'm fine now. I really am.*

It did a lot of harm. But she couldn't stop scrolling. *Ahh!* She thought Rob hated social media! He had always rolled his eyes and said that no one cared and it was all so fake. His thoughts on that had clearly done an about turn. As she scrolled through at him posting all sorts, it turned her stomach. And Serena. There she was. So pretty. So, so young. So, so pregnant. She felt sick to her stomach as she read through Rob's bio. A little icon at the top showed a man and woman and a baby and then written underneath.

*Figuring out the family thing one step at a time.*
*Babymoon booked.*
*Soon to be dad.*
*Living my best life.*
*Days with Serena.*

Lucie plopped a spoonful of raspberry red yoghurt-y slop in her mouth and didn't know whether to roll around laughing, throw up, or break down into big, ugly, sucky, snotty tears.

'Living my actual best life? Really!' she shouted out to sea, disturbing a seagull who squawked, looked around in alarm, and flew off low over the water.

Putting her head back and looking up at the sky, thoughts went through her head about her and Rob and what they'd had. *What was she then? Clearly, she was his worst life.* As she studied his tiles more, there was no way she was going to cry, or be sick for that matter. It was actually more than comical - both the declarations plastered all over social media and the complete lack of sensitivity to her. Soon to be a dad? Pah!

Whatever she tried to think, though, a little part of her was unbelievably sad. It hit her like a bus even though she was pretending to laugh. The little corner of her heart with the rainbow babies, the nursery with the closed door, the navy-blue sofa in the cottage stained with her tears, the plump roll of fat attached to her inner thighs. All of it topped with a big old helping of sorrow and no fenugreek seeds in sight.

Splashing around in the water, she looked down at her feet. She'd been doing so well too. Why had she caved and looked? She'd actually started to believe the app that she, in fact, was beginning to live her version of her best life. Now she felt abandoned and left for dead.

The more she thought about it, the more she realised a lot of what she was sad about wasn't actually Rob. It was the other stuff. Being in a relationship, planning with someone, thinking that everything was sorted in her life, navigating things as part of a unit. It was almost as if the actual Rob bit wasn't the bit that made her sad. The making a family thing and growing old with someone was what she was grieving. Was it that and not some loss of a love that underneath it all wasn't really there?

She analysed it over and over and then thought about something she had seen in Tally when she'd introduced herself as Nathalie to Leo. That was it. That sparkle in Tally's eye. That whole change in Tally's being. Lucie realised that with Rob it had once been there, but that it had withered away long ago. Left possibly back in the school canteen with the dinner ladies and the blancmange.

Wiggling her toes around in the hazy blue water, she watched the waves go in and out and took a deep breath in. She had to pull herself together. In the cold reality of the position she found herself in, she had no time for Sad Lucie. Sad Lucie needed to whip out her big girl pants, pull them up over her hopefully shrinking middle, and place Power Lucie to the fore.

She thought about her upcoming week and realised that, at least, she had zero time for moping. It was more than a blessing that it was her first day at Darlings and she was darned if she was going to let Rob and his figuring out how to be a family mar her day. Pushing herself up from her chair, she nodded. She was going to do her utmost to have an okay day. She'd give it her best shot, but actually living her best life? Probably not.

Sitting on the tram, Lucie watched Darling Street go past the window. She wondered what the day was going to bring. When she'd been in to have a chat and look around, Evie had been lovely, business-like but friendly, and quick, so, so quick. She'd flitted around from this to that, showing Lucie one thing with one hand and talking about something else at the same time. She'd also simultaneously instructed the cleaner, taken a call, and directed a delivery all whilst showing Lucie around.

Lucie had taken it all in. Everything was more or less easy to follow. Evie had the working of the place down pat. It was hard to see with half a brain cell how you could get it wrong. However, according to Evie, many many people had got it very wrong. Some hadn't even lasted an hour, they had been unable to get their head around the basket thing, not stacked the dishwasher quickly enough, and had not put on what Evie had called a "Darlings Smile" when serving tables.

Lucie was more than sure she could muster the ability to slap a 'Darlings Smile' on her face and trying to push all thoughts of Rob and his booked babymoon out of her mind she strolled away from the tram stop and let her eyes wander down the street. Darling was waking up. The bunting fluttered above a scene of quiet bustling, and as she was crossing over the mews, she bumped straight into Hennie from the cottage with the yellow shutters.

'Oh hello! You're up and about bright and early,' Lucie said.

Hennie smiled. 'I've been for a swim down at the bay. I've got a huge day ahead and I always find it goes better if I have a dip.'

'Can't be bad. I'll have to put that next on my list of things to enjoy in Darling. Not quite sure about my swimming skills though. Not my, umm, area of expertise, as it were.'

'Ahh, yes, I hear you. I just float most of the time, but even that is good for me. You'd be amazed.'

'I'll have to try it.'

Hennie looked at Lucie's basket and touched the frill liner. 'Ooh, I love that! Where did you get it?'

Lucie smiled. She was used to people asking about the things she had made. 'The basket is vintage. I have a huge collection of them. I made the liner.'

'Ooh, you made it, wow it's gorgeous!'

'I'll make you one if you like. A swap for a bike.'

'Done.' Hennie chuckled. 'I see you're already getting in on the Darling bartering.'

'I'm learning,' Lucie replied.

'Anyway, where are you off to?'

'I'm helping out in Darlings, actually.'

'Are you now?'

Lucie widened her eyes and joked. 'Yes. I hope I survive. I've heard it's a war zone in there.'

'You'll know soon enough with Evie.'

'I hope I do okay.'

'You'll be fine. You look the part anyway.'

'You're not the first to say that!'

'I bet I'm not. We all know Evie's tricks. Rightio. I need to get on. Have a good day.' Hennie smiled and went to move away. 'Oh, yes, are you coming to the dinner?'

Lucie frowned for a quick half second, wondering what Hennie was talking about. Then she realised the annual dinner. How could she forget? 'I am. I've had an invite.'

'I've heard, but wasn't sure if you'd confirmed or not.'

'Right.'

Hennie smiled. 'Shelly. I swim with her.'

'I see.'

Hennie chuckled. 'You're good at mashed potato then?'

'I think so. We'll soon find out.'

'It's a huge, funny old tradition. The dinner is all about the Darling sausage.'

'Right. And I got mash. Blimey, the bar is quite high for me to perform.'

'Yeah, no pressure or anything. If you get it wrong, you'll be asked to leave the island. We'll push you over a rope bridge like that show in the jungle.'

Lucie's eyes widened. 'How many people will be there?'

Hennie sucked air in with a little whooshing sound. 'Depends on Shelly. It's mostly residents and then anyone else she asks.'

'Okay, so I'm lucky to be invited. Is that the long and the short of it?'

'Eek, pretty much.'

'Great. I'm very honoured.'

Hennie gripped the handlebars on her bike. 'Yes. See you then, Lucie. Have a lovely day. Hope you survive.'

## 27

Arriving around the back of Darlings, Lucie smiled as she walked through the walled yard. Fairy lights were strung in garlands overhead, a little set of timber tables and chairs was tucked into the corner next to a jumble of terracotta pots filled with herbs and geraniums. The smell of coffee filled the air via the back door propped open with an old anchor as a doorstop.

In a small back kitchen, shelving was crammed with vintage café au lait bowls, two industrial dishwashers were whirring away to themselves, a long Butcher's block counter was stacked with piles and piles of plates and glass water bottles were lined up on trays. Evie came in from a tiny stable door on the left with a pile of linens in her arms. Lucie followed her into the front kitchen where a young girl was surrounded by half baguettes and little jars of jam.

'Morning, Lucie!' Evie smiled, passing Lucie a white shirt with blue on the collar and a blue apron. 'Ready for the craziness of Darlings?'

'I sure am. I've been practising the smile.'

Evie chuckled. 'This is Piper. She's an all-around diamond. Thank goodness we have her.'

Lucie smiled at Piper and immediately felt four hundred years old. Piper glowed in the prettiness of youth; her lightly tanned creamy skin loving the white polo shirt. Ribbons in the Darling blue were tied at the bottom of her hair. 'Lovely to meet you,' Lucie said.

'Hi.' Piper smiled whilst her hands were submerged in a huge industrial sink full of bubbles. 'Welcome to the madhouse.'

Evie's eyes flicked around to the front as the little bell over the door tinkled. The café was already busy, the tables outside were all occupied, and a man came through the door with a large tray of croissants covered in tea towels.

Five minutes later, after getting changed in a small bathroom on the first floor, Lucie was in the kitchen, Evie was zipping around front of house, Piper was pressing buttons on an iPad getting orders made and putting them on top once done. There wasn't a lot of time for chat or niceties. Lucie plastered on the smile, put her head down, and got on with it. She went along the line, methodically filling the little baskets; blue and white linen napkins laid in first, fresh out of the oven half baguettes, tiny pots of handmade apricot jam. She then filled some baskets with an egg and some with a croissant, the knot in the top indicating which was which.

Watching what went on as Lucie worked through the huge pile of baskets, she could soon see where the gaps were from the missing staff member. Tables were only just getting cleared in time, the line for the baskets was just that one too long, and the dishwashing process was backing up. With Piper running from clearing outside tables to making coffee and Evie serving baskets, Lucie had to work on her own initiative.

Finishing the baskets, she went through to the back kitchen and quickly unloaded the first dishwasher packed with jam jars and glasses, stacking them on a dumb waiter by the front counter. Gathering dirty glasses from the worktop and front kitchen, she reloaded, put in a tablet, and not having a clue which button did what, pressed one which she thought might make it start. It whirred and she could hear the water filling up. Filling the sink with hot water, she started rinsing plates, sprayed down the sides, swept the floor, and pulled the lever on the dishwasher. As it opened, a billow of steam puffed up in her face just as Evie scooted into the back.

'Ahh! Thank you. Sorry, it's been so busy this morning. I've just left you to fend for yourself! Are you okay?'

'I'm fine. I wasn't sure where everything went, but I presumed the glasses went over there. I've made a start on the plates and the baskets are done.'

'Lifesaver! Thank you. Blimey, what a breath of fresh air not having to instruct someone what to do all the time. I knew you'd be fine.'

'You did? How?' Lucie smiled.

'You get to know after years of it. It comes with the job.' Evie chuckled as a voice called out from the backyard. 'That'll be Otis with the egg delivery.' She glanced out to the front and then flicked her eyes back again. 'Do you mind bringing them in? I need to get back out there.'

'Of course not,' Lucie replied. 'Leave me to it.'

Lucie went out towards the yard where Otis was coming through the gate with a large tray of eggs in his arms. He frowned as he saw her. 'Oh, got yourself a job, have you?' His eyebrows shot up in question.

'I have. I bet you didn't think you'd see me here.'

'Hope your stamina's good.' He laughed. 'You look the part though. Okay, here you go. These are apparently the best eggs in the land from my mum's chickens. You can't get fresher or better, according to her.'

'Ahh, I wondered how even the eggs tasted amazing when I had a lunch basket the other day.'

'Well, now you know. My mum is a woman of many talents.

She has her own chicken raising secrets that no one is allowed in on.'

'Too funny,' Lucie said as she took the large cardboard tray.

'How are you getting on at the house?' Otis asked.

'Not too bad. The kitchen is brilliant. Sorry, I meant to send you some pictures. I followed your instructions to the letter, and it came up so well.'

'Yeah, I knew it would brush up nicely. You get a feel for it when you're in my game.'

'It did! I have to say I half didn't believe you.'

Otis rolled his eyes. 'Story of my life.'

Lucie laughed as Otis turned to go. 'I need to get going. By the way, how is the shoulder? I hear you had a bit of an argument with a drain.'

Frowning, Lucie shook her head. 'How do you know that?'

'It was broadcast on the ferry the next morning and then Shelly put a Facebook post up about it. Joking. I surf with George. He said you'd had a run of it.'

'I have. I don't think I can get any further bad luck if I try.'

'Nah, and now you're working in Darlings for your sins.'

'Ha!'

'Okay, I'm off. I'm working on the new bakery down on Darling Street there. Do you know it?'

'Nope.'

'Just off the tram stop in the middle. They're from Pretty Beach, the people who've bought it. Supposedly the bread is amazing and something about a bun. I know there'll be some happy people in Darling to have a bakery back on the island.'

'I bet. I'll keep a lookout for it when I walk home.'

'Walk home? Evie'll have you working until midnight,' Otis joked.

By lunchtime, Lucie was well in the swing of Darlings and already feeling it in her left arm. The systems were simple, the coffee in bowls quick to serve, and the baskets, once made up, were easy to deliver. Lucie had spent her time re-filling baskets, boiling eggs in the back kitchen, loading and reloading the dish-washer, and clearing tables. Just as a few tables had left and the rush had seemed to ease off a bit, she was spraying a table when the door opened for the millionth time with more customers. She looked up and felt her stomach flip.

George walked in with three Darlings baskets in his arms and frowned. 'Oh, hello.'

'Hi.' Lucie beamed. 'How are you?'

'I'm good.'

Before George could say anything, Lucie spoke, 'I'm helping Evie out of a spot.'

George lifted his chin. 'I see. How's that on your shoulder? It was quite the bruise you had on the way.'

Lucie was surprised that his face showed genuine concern. 'It's fine.' She pulled the sleeve of her polo shirt up and turned her left arm around to show him.

'Ouch! Is that what you call fine? Looks pretty nasty to me.'

Lucie looked at the bruise. He was right, it was still black and blue. 'It looks a lot worse than it is.'

'Right.'

Just as Lucie moved the salt and pepper pots to spray the table, Evie came in from the front. 'Hey, George. How are you?'

'Very well, thanks.'

'How do you like our new member of staff?' Evie joked.

George put the stack of baskets on the table and Lucie could have sworn she saw a twinkle in his eye. 'Looks good to me.'

After her shift at Darlings had finally ended, Lucie had not been shocked to see the step counter on her phone. She'd not stopped from the moment she'd stepped in the door and nor had the steady flow of customers. Evie and Piper had both worked at the same speed, and Lucie had shaken her head as she'd left amazed at how Evie did it.

More than pleased with her forethought at a picnic blanket, hat and a book with a free, if late, lunch in her basket, she made her way to the bay. The Darling blue greeted her and a hazy sunshine fell onto the water lapping onto the beach. She walked along, looked back, and waited. There it was, the horseshoe shape right before her eyes. Looking back at the bay with her hand over her eyes, she tried to decide on the best place to sit. Evie and Piper had told her if she sat on the far right side of the beach as it swept around, she'd catch the warmth of the sun trapped by the tidal wall.

Making her way around, she could see that they were right. The little sandy beach felt warm as she placed down her blanket and basket. Taking the weight off her feet, she slipped on her sunglasses, put her head up to the sun, and let out a huge sigh. What a day so far and she still had admin to sort out for Fleur & Follie and was hoping to start on the utility room painting. As she unknotted the gingham linen napkin in the Darlings basket and laid it on her blanket, she smiled at the little lunch. It was no wonder it was so popular. Fabulous Darling sausage, a boiled egg she now learnt was from just up the road, a pot of home-made relish of which she'd seen huge vats in the back kitchen, and in a small brown paper packet a lemon shortbread biscuit.

Feeling her whole body decompress, Lucie thought about her old job. Her lunch hours there consisted of a walk into town, a sandwich from Boots, and a mooch around the shops. Sometimes on the odd occasion she'd meet Rob in the park or Tally in the coffee shop. As she watched a boat go by, she shook her head. None of it was quite like this. Lunch hours, or rather, late afternoon lunch hours, on Darling were in a whole other premier league. One she was quite enjoying playing in.

She smiled at the six messages on her phone. She felt so grateful, as usual, for her little group of friends. Every single one of them had texted her to either wish her luck or see how she'd got on in Darlings. She read and replied to Tally first.

*How are you getting on? Hope you're having a good day? Xxx*

*It was actually really good!*

She watched as the little dots flashed. Tally had probably finished at the surgery and was waiting to pick up the girls.

*What?!! Excellent. I've been wondering how you were getting on. Did you like it?*

*It was so busy I didn't have a lot of choice.*

*Good busy, I hope?*

*Yes. I met loads more people too.*

*Of course. I hadn't thought about that side of it. A good way to get to know everyone.*

*Yeah.*

*At the BBQ, Leo said he goes there every morning. Did you see him?*

Lucie raised her eyebrows. Interesting. Very interesting. Tally was turning the conversation around to Leo.

*I didn't. He'd been in really early when it was just opening.*

*Oh right. Who else did you see? What about that Shelly we met?*

*No. There was a really nice young girl who works there part-time while she's at uni. Her name is Piper. Oh and George came in for a basket.*

*Ooooooooooooooh!*

*Hahahahah. It's nothing anyway.*

*Right you are. Millions would believe you.*

Lucie sent two eye roll emoticons and waited for the next message to arrive.

*You are forgetting that I witnessed what happened in the nicest off-licence in the country.*

Lucie wanted to massage back that she wasn't the only one witnessing things. She had it noted that Tally had introduced herself as 'Nathalie' to Leo, but she didn't.

*No. You're imagining it.*

*I'm not. Whatever.*

*Anyway, I've got a little idea for the girls in my head.*

*Yes. My favourite thing to hear you say!*

*Linen dresses buttoned all the way up the back with tiny buttons. A ruffle on the bottom and the sleeve. Edged in Liberty fabric on the ruffle.*

*Yes, yes, and yes.*

*Won't the buttons be a pain?*

*Yes and no. I'm all for the cuteness hahahahaha.*

*I thought you might be lol xxx I'll get them made up. I was thinking bags, too.*

*Lovely. How do you have time?*

*I'll fit it in between painting the utility room!*

*Are you back at the coffee shop tomorrow?*

*Yes, I'm there all week.*

*Do you think she'll offer you a job?*

*No idea.*

*Would you take it if she did?*

*I'd have to think about it, but it could get me out of a stitch.*

*Yes. Right, I need to go and get the girls. Speak to you later. Well done today. Xx*

*I'll send you some pics when I cut them out.*

*Lovely x*

Lucie sat there with her legs stretched out in front of her looking out to sea. She wondered what she would say if Evie offered her a job. She'd never seen herself working in a kitchen, but she'd quite enjoyed the frantic pace, the smiling locals, and the day-long banter. It had certainly flown by, which her mum had always told her was the sort of job you wanted.

As the waves lapped onto the shore, she thought about how working for Evie could actually be just what she was looking for. She would have enough money to get by, she could spend time on Fleur & Follie, and the rest of the time she could slowly but surely get through doing up the rest of the house.

L ucie looked around as she sat at the tram station. A woman with a checked tote bag on the bench beside her was lost in a world of her own as she circled words on a word search. A man in a running vest and blue mirrored sunglasses jogged past, and a little boy trailed along after his dad, whinging about the fact that his legs hurt. She listened to the low hum of the tram in the distance and as it pulled up, smiled at a couple of women getting off. One in head to toe sparkles, the whole of her glittered. The other with gigantic gold headphones nearly as big as her, a fluffy purple jumper and bright pink plastic sliders. The younger woman was smiling while chatting with Shelly as the tram came to a full stop. She heard Shelly say goodbye to them and then turn and speak to the woman with the checked bag.

'Afternoon,' Shelly said as she rang the bell and then she smiled at Lucie. 'How was it?'

'Great. I really enjoyed it.'

'I bet you're feeling it now?'

'I should say so. My legs are like lead.'

'Epsom salt bath will do you good. I have them after a double shift here.'

'I'll have to get some.'

'Yeah. By the way, I'll have that microwave for you soon. If you're not there, I'll just leave it down the side, shall I?'

'Yes please, in the shed would be great. Thank you so much. Everyone has been so kind and welcoming.'

'Not a problem.'

Lucie sat on the hard timber tram seat, recovering from the physical tiredness and mental exhaustion of learning so many things. She gazed at Darling Street going past the window and turned around to look at the packed tram; at school-run time it was the busiest she'd seen it. The bell then dinged, and it slowed down to a stop; an old lady got on with a shopping trolley and Lucie stood up to give her her seat. The tram trundled off again and Lucie moved to the back for the breeze and so she could look out at the view. At the next stop, she watched as school children stood in their groups with their backpacks waiting for the tram and the odd business person in a suit looked down at their phone. The tram pulled to a halt outside Darling Town Hall as Lucie held onto the overhead rail, looking out over the other side.

'Hello.' She heard a voice say and presuming it wasn't her the voice was talking to, she didn't turn around. She felt a gentle touch on her right elbow. 'Hello again.' Turning, her eyes fell on George. She couldn't decide which was better: George in a wetsuit with the top rolled down or George in a button-down shirt, smart trousers and chestnut Chelsea boots.

She immediately felt a mess and touched the back of her hair. She supposed that it was better than how she had looked in the baggy bottoms saluting the sun, so that was a bonus.

'Hi.'

'How did it go?' George asked.

'Darlings?'

George nodded, and Lucie couldn't help staring at his eyelashes and green eyes. 'Yep.'

'Yes, it was good. I actually enjoyed it.'

'And what about your injury? How's that feeling?'

There was no way that Lucie was going to admit that since she'd unloaded her third dishwasher of the day, her arm from her wrist to her neck had been throbbing in pain. The bruise now seemed to hurt every time she moved it too.

'It's fine. Thanks for asking.'

George just smiled.

Lucie raised her eyebrows in interest. 'How was your day?'

'Backwards and forwards with meetings all over the place. I've been on the ferry twice.'

'Goodness, you'll be ready to get home and make a cup of tea, then.'

'That I will.'

'Shelly has just informed me of the therapeutic powers of an Epsom salts bath and I think it would be right up my street after scooting around Darlings all day.'

George followed Lucie's gaze along the tram to Shelly. 'She's a fountain of wisdom, that one. Just don't tell her anything you want to keep to yourself.'

Lucie chuckled. 'Right, thanks for the advice.'

'What have you got on for the rest of the week?' George asked with an inquisitive look written across his face.

Lucie pretended to contemplate. 'My life is not that exciting if I am completely honest with you, George. At the moment, it's about all I can do to make it through a day of DIY.'

George smiled. 'I feel the same sometimes. My life is pretty boring, too.'

A few minutes later, the tram was pulling down to the end at the ferry stop. Lucie naturally fell into step beside George as they started to walk home. When they got to the Coastguard's House, Lucie put her hand on the gate. 'Rightio, nice chatting. I'm sure I'll bump into you again at some point.'

'Yep. You'll be bumping into everyone all the time now you're working in Darlings.'

'I guess so,' Lucie said and pulled up the latch on the gate.

George spoke as she closed the gate. 'What are you up to Friday night?'

Lucie had to stop herself from whipping her head around and then jumping up and down. She frowned. 'Friday night? Sorry, what do you mean?'

George looked embarrassed. 'Oh, I err, wondered whether you fancied going for a drink. Have you been to the pub yet? Loads of locals down there on a Friday night now the weather's warming up.'

Lucie was now the one embarrassed. She felt a deep tremble, followed by a weird hot flush starting on her chest, rising up her neck and landing on her cheeks. She stumbled over her words. 'Err, oh, right.'

George waved his hand. 'No worries. Sorry, I shouldn't have asked. I wasn't meaning a date or anything.'

*That's a shame. I was very much wanting a date. Perhaps, indeed, there would be the option of skipping the whole dating part and moving onto the next base. Take me there now.*

This time it was Lucie who batted her hand. 'Oh, goodness no! I wouldn't have thought you would be asking me out on a date. Ha! How completely preposterous! As if you would ask me that! Thanks, though, for mentioning the pub.'

'Do you fancy a stroll to the pub then? Just shoot me a text if you do.'

*Do I fancy a not-a-date stroll to the pub with the hottest man I've seen since I was in sixth form? Just a little bit on the hard side to answer. Or not.*

Lucie had to laugh to herself. She could barely get the words out to accept quickly enough. So what if it wasn't a date?

## 28

---

If there was one thing Lucie Peachtree was inexperienced in, it was dating. Maybe she should rephrase that; she was actually very experienced in her inexperience of dates. She had zero familiarity with dating or any kind of relationship other than the one she'd had with Rob since school.

There had been one boy before Rob who had taken her to the pictures on a sort of double date thing with Jane and another boy. It had not fulfilled any of her dating ideals. All her Grey and Swayze daydreams had been dashed forever whilst sitting in a grubby old cinema at the afternoon matinee on Cheap Student Tuesday. The skinny, on the sweaty side, teenage boy had bought himself a giant bucket of popcorn, a family bag of Revels, and an oversized cup of American soft drink with a horrible plastic straw in the top. He'd slurped and chomped his way through the whole thing, staring at the screen and wiping his mouth with the back of his hand more times than she'd believed was possible. She could still remember him shoving big handfuls of popcorn into his mouth and letting stray bits fall down his chin and spill into the bucket on his lap. At the end he'd put his sweaty, food covered hand on her leg.

After that there had been Rob, and even in the few 'breaks' Rob had called before their fate together was sealed, Lucie had never been out with anyone else. Not that she was going out with anyone else now, of course. It was just a stroll to the pub. A stroll to the pub, whereby she needed some assistance.

Opening WhatsApp, she looked down at her groups. There was the main Hold Your Nerve friendship group, her chats with Tally, one for her mum in Spain, one with a few girls she used to work with but hadn't had a message from in a long time. And then there was the Crisis Talk group. Tapping on the button, she scrolled down. The last crisis had been her in the cottage with the wine, coconut and lime candle, and the Maltesers. The one before that, Libby, and before that loads more; an Anais crisis with family problems, one with Libby and her boss at work, and of course, Tally. Tally had called one not long after the twins were born, announcing her problems and in a complete state about what she was going to do. That crisis was still ongoing.

Nearly all the events involved in crisis meetings were serious, but some had been more on the jovial side; what Jane was going to wear to the wedding of an ex, how Libby was going to cope on holiday with the heat, how Anais was in a conundrum about whether or not to buy another house, and if Tally had time to expand her training. She smiled to herself again, reminded how lucky she was to have the support of their funny little group, typed out a message and hit go.

*Attention: Calling a Wednesday night CT. 7pm GMT. All required.*
*Lucie x*

Immediately there were a couple of messages. One from Anais saying she'd be there and one from Jane asking if everything was okay. Anticipating that everyone might worry considering her previous state in the cottage, Lucie added another message saying that everything was fine.

Pulling her leggings on, she tied up her trainers, put her phone in her pocket, and tapped on a walking meditation. Five minutes later, she was travelling along Hennie's road, gazing at all the cottages, and making her way to the path meandering along the side of the sea. A deep, low, male voice filled her ears, instructing her to relax her shoulders, straighten her back, and to become aware of the sensations in her body, especially those in her feet.

'Bring yourself into the present moment. Express loving kindness to the air. Allow stress to melt away into the earth.'

Taking deep breaths in, Lucie didn't need a man in Woking to tell her how much she enjoyed the sea air. And she wasn't quite sure how to express loving kindness to it, but she continued to listen.

'Do not allow yourself to have walking goals. Allow your body to seep down through the heels into the very centre of the earth. Let good things happen.'

Lucie raised her eyebrows and carried on ambling without any goals until she'd walked along the coastal path, past the sailing club, past people sitting on the narrow stretch of beach and then made her way across the road and headed through the back roads towards Darling Street. She could just see the trams in the distance and make out the large green domed top of the town hall. Walking through the back roads, she gawped at a row of beautiful old Victorian houses. Each one showcased narrow iron balconies with slate bullnose roofs on the first floor. A whole line of them painted white, an odd one in the middle, pale blue. Old-fashioned coach lights lined the street and funny little parking bays were edged with beds full of flowers.

Peering down at her map, she made her way to the other side and stopped as her eyes followed along an old pier. She stood and read the plaque on the wall informing her that the Darling Palace Pier Co. built the pier in 1898 and it was still family-owned to this day.

Eventually arriving on Darling Street, she turned to start to make her way home and peered into the window of a double-fronted shop with a tessellated tile entrance. She read a small sign propped in the door about the new bakery opening soon. It promised freshly baked on the premises bread, the best cinnamon buns, and genuine sourdough, whatever that was.

Lucie watched as a tram trundled past, tempted to get on and rest, but the feel of her fat wobbling put paid to the temptation, and she pounded on taking in the sights of Darling Street until she was at the bottom and passing the floating bridge.

Arriving home a while later, she saw Leo walking up the road on his way home. Bursting into a big smile, Leo stopped as he got outside her house. Lucie took in his burnished skin, mop of hair, signet ring on his little finger, and what was undoubtedly one very honed Australian physique.

'How you going?' Leo asked.

'I'm good, thanks. How are you?'

'Keeping out of trouble.'

'Time for a cup of tea?'

Leo nodded. 'Indeed, I do. I have the next few days off and it's much needed.'

Lucie held the gate open for him. 'Sounds like you've got a heavy workload there at the hospital.'

'Yeah, I have. No rest for the wicked.' Leo laughed. 'It's not for the work-shy. She'll be right.'

Lucie led Leo past the Three Wise Men into the kitchen. 'Crikey! You've done a bit of work in the place,' he said, peering up at the open shelving above the spot with the kettle and the teapot. Kilner jars with ceramic tops were lined up from left to right, cream jugs in a selection of sizes adorned the next shelf up, and a huge bunch of flowers graced the now scrubbed, cleaned, and lime-washed Butcher's block worktop on the opposite side.

'I have. I've been working all hours,' Lucie said as she put the kettle on and opened the door to the pantry. 'Can I tempt you in a Darlings lemon and shortbread biscuit to go with your tea?'

'You can. Not a bad bonus for working there. How are you getting on?'

'So far, so good. Evie's lovely, not sure I'd want to cross her though.'

'I'm with you there. It's busy in there, isn't it? I don't think I have ever been in there when it's not at least three quarters full. It's a nightmare trying to get a table on the weekends.'

'You're not wrong. There is a long and steady trade coming through all the time,' Lucie replied as she pulled two mugs from hooks and poured in milk.

'Not a bad commute for you either,' Leo acknowledged.

'Nup. It's the best commute I've ever had. What about you? How do you get to the hospital?'

Leo leant on the worktops. 'Depends on what I've got on and what time I'm finishing. I either drive if I'm on a late or I walk to the ferry and then get the bus on the other side.'

'How long does that take?' Lucie said, pouring the tea into the mugs.

'Depends on the time of day. They put on these new subsidised shuttles for Darling residents to link up with the fast train, which really changed everything. They call it an "All Route" network. That's when Darling changed a bit. Now you can work here and get to the new train without too much faff.'

'I see, yes, I haven't really been off the island too much to try it out.'

'It's captured you already. Woah, be careful. They don't call us insular for nothing. Once you're on Darling Island, you don't get out much.' Leo laughed.

Lucie stirred the tea, passed over the shortbread, and smiled. 'I've noticed.' She unlocked the back door. 'We'll sit outside, shall we? I'll show you my spa.'

Chuckling, Leo followed her through the garden and they stepped over the fallen down fence. Leo sucked air in through his teeth and shook his head. 'Look at that water.'

'I know, right?'

'I still can't get my head around the hazy blue of this place. There's nothing like it.'

'I know. It sort of envelops you when you sit down here. I thought I was going a bit doolally at first.'

'Yep. Totally get you.'

Lucie pulled the two chairs from the water so they were just sitting at the edge and Leo sat down and bit into the shortbread. 'Best spa I've ever been to.'

Lucie laughed. 'My friend Tally loved it down here too, and she's been to some spas in her time.'

There was no doubt about the spark in Leo's eyes at the mention of Tally. 'She had a nice time when she was here, did she?' Leo asked.

'She did. She needed it.'

Leo sounded casual, but Lucie could tell by the minute change in his body language that it was more than an off-the-cuff question. 'Why's that?'

Lucie straight away regretted what she'd said. There was no way she was going to broadcast Tally's marital problems to anyone, let alone to Leo. She batted her hand in front of her face. 'Oh, you know, the usual; work stuff and looking after twins is no walk in the park.'

'No, I bet it isn't. So, how long have you two been friends?'

There it was, another question about Tally. 'Since the year dot!' Lucie laughed. 'About thirty-something years. There are five of us.'

'Wow. That's nice.'

'It is, actually. We've been through thick and thin together,' Lucie replied and gestured back to the house. 'And this is one of my "thins" in life.'

Leo frowned. 'Where did you think life was taking you then? Before you found yourself on Darling, I mean.'

'Not to an old house on an island where I know not a soul! Put it that way. Oh and being made redundant, that wasn't on my life plan!'

'Same here.' Leo laughed. 'I came for the watersport and haven't left.'

'Oh, I see. How did you arrive?' Lucie enquired as she dunked a piece of the shortbread in her tea.

'Now there's a story. An old mate of mine came for the sailing club. He posted some pics on social media and I showed my girlfriend at the time. She wanted a change of scene and got a job over here, and I sort of followed. Trouble was, she met someone who took her fancy a bit more than me. An English bloke. That was the end of that, and I came over here to surf one day.'

'Oh, dear.' Lucie screwed up her face. 'Doesn't sound good.'

'Nah.' Leo smiled and stretched his long, muscular legs out in front of him. 'It would never have worked out in the long run, but at the time I wasn't best pleased. She was as boring as the day is long, if I'm honest, as I look back now.'

'Hmm. Same.'

'You got shafted, did you? Your friend Tally was telling me it all got a bit messy.'

Lucie rolled her eyes. 'Not messy for him. He traded me in for a younger model and now he's going to be a dad. I was the one left in the mess.'

'Nasty. You live and learn.'

'Yeah.' Lucie looked out at the water. 'Funny thing is, I'm sort of okay with it now. Dare I say it, I'm relieved, in a way. We were trying for a baby for so long and we'd been together since we were kids, really. I think that may have slowly killed the love that was there, if it was there in the beginning.'

'Ahh, well. You'll have to try out other avenues.' Leo laughed.

'I think I'll give myself some breathing space first. Plus, I don't have that many avenues on offer at my stage of the game.'

'You never know what's around the corner, Lucie. Especially not when you move here. Darling is full of surprises. It well and truly does its own thing. Just you wait and see.'

Lucie finished vacuuming the room at the back, which she now referred to as her 'sewing room' and then sprayed and wiped down the door, the windows and skirting boards. There was one thing that was non-negotiable in her life, whether or not it involved an old house by the sea or a tiny cottage in the country, and that was that her sewing room was spotless. It was a habit she'd started when she'd first made things in the spare room at her mum's house. She'd hoover, wipe everything down, then make a cup of tea and start to plot and dream things to make in her head. She'd learnt that having her supplies organised, a spotless worktable and tidy surroundings made everything flow.

She pushed up the old sash window and as fresh air breezed through, she stood almost dreamlike, looking out to sea. A few minutes later, she was pulling fabric from boxes. Cutting out three different materials in circular shapes, she used coordinating fabric for frills and got to work on a cushion. Sitting at the sewing machine, she whizzed back and forth, up and down and as she popped on a button, she sat back and smiled. Another thing for her website completed. She hadn't had a visitor yet and the social media accounts were more than slow, but she was working to the premise that slow and steady won the race. Flicking on the iron, she pressed the cushion cover and then stuffed in a feather inner. It had turned out much better than she'd hoped.

Pulling her laptop over, she opened her website and clicked on 'web traffic.' Still no visitors, but it was beginning to come together nicely. She now had a little gathering of lovely things; beautiful ruffled edged quilts in Liberty fabrics, dress cushions with frills, a range of book bags, picnic blankets, and gorgeous pillowcases in an array of pretty ditsy prints.

Her Etsy shop was yet to make a sale but that was building too. It was peppered with little hearts where people had liked her things and she'd had a couple of questions about her baby bloomers.

With the cushion in hand, she made her way to the old shutters in the sitting room, propped it in the window seat, added a vase of flowers and started to snap away. Five minutes later, she had the pictures loaded into a photography app and not long after, they had joined her other things for sale online.

Opening Instagram, Lucie posted one of the images, did a video for the stories that no one yet watched, and sat down. On a whim, she started to scroll through her feed. All the beautiful people doing all the things. Living their best lives right there on the Gram.

Frowning on an image in her feed, Lucie tapped on a square. Why was her phone showing her a picture of Matilda Huntington-Jones? Clearly her phone was listening to her. There could be no other explanation.

She scrolled down through the images of Underwear Model; Matilda in the fedora with the red band sitting with her legs astride on the steps of a Brownstone in New York, Matilda on the side of a fashion runway in leather jeans and an oversized white shirt with the collar up, Matilda on a beach in a tiny white bikini and very nice white bits. Lucie fell down a deep and varied well of Matilda's fabulous life. Modelling underwear in Bali, working out with a celebrity trainer in Dubai. Matilda Huntington-Jones was most certainly not making ruffled cushions on a tiny little sewing machine with Three Wise Men in the hallway for company.

Everything was curated, including the one photo about halfway down where George appeared. Deeply tanned, in sunglasses and boardies, and a distinct lack of shirt, Lucie almost wanted to cry. She felt a mixture of humiliation and stupidity wash over her. She'd daydreamed about this man! She'd called a Crisis Talk over going to the pub with him when he'd clearly asked her there because he felt sorry for the tubby little pudding with the injured arm working in the local coffee shop.

*You are worthy of having good things happen in your life,* went through her mind. Lucie shook her head, not believing for one second that this was true.

By the end of the day, as the Crisis Talk meeting approached, Lucie felt more and more morose. She'd gone down another Insta rabbit hole, this time with Serena's Facebook account, spoken to her mum in Spain via video call who had said that yes she could see that Lucie was looking a bit 'chubbier,' and the foghorn had sounded and weather had turned. The afternoon had not been one of her best.

She'd spent most of it going from one bad thing to eat to the next, there had definitely not been any fenugreek seeds in sight, and the tears that had been so at the fore in the cottage were threatening to flood again. All because of blimming Matilda whatshername-whatshername and her perfect Insta feed.

Just like the night in the cottage, she found herself gathering supplies for the video call; she rescued an emergency box of Malteser Truffles she'd hidden in the back of the pantry, a bottle of wine which had been holding a similar position in the fridge, and a vanilla three wick scented candle. Patting one of the

Three Wise Men as she walked past with her arms full of the supplies, she pushed the sitting room door open with her foot, set up her laptop on the coffee table, and plonked herself down. A few minutes later, her four friends came one by one onto the screen.

Anais spoke first. 'What's up, Luce? Has something happened to the house?'

Jane was next. 'Oh, no. Don't tell me the baby has arrived. You poor thing. It must be so awful for you. It's bad enough from this end.'

Lucie held her hand up in a stop sign. 'I'm fine.' Then she let out a huge, dramatic sigh.

Tally shook her head. 'You don't sound at all fine. You sound like you've regressed about six months.'

Lucie held up the box of Malteser Truffles. 'You guessed that in one.'

'What's happened?' Jane asked.

'Okay. So. I called the meeting because George asked me if I wanted to go to the pub with him.'

'What the actual?' Tally yelled. 'I told you! I absolutely knew it. Yesssssss!'

'At that point, the meeting was going to be about the fact that I haven't had a date since school, and what I was going to do. And what the actual heck did I wear?'

'So, what's this now about? Oooh, this is so exciting!' exclaimed Libby.

'It's not exciting, Lib, because I'm not going,' Lucie stated sadly.

Libby frowned. 'What? Why not?'

'Yes, why not?' Anais asked.

'I've changed my mind. I must be actually crazy to have even said yes in the first place. I had a look at Underwear Model's Instagram. My goodness, there is no way I am even close to this world.'

'What world? I don't understand,' Jane asked.

Lucie sighed and sent them all a link to Matilda's socials. 'Just have a look. You'll know what I mean. This is the woman he was seeing, I think, and this is the world he moves in.'

Anais was the one to respond first, after they'd looked on Instagram. She swore. 'Oh dear. The one on the beach advertising the earrings. Where she stares into the camera and moves her hair away from her face. How up herself is she? Yowzas. It's painful to watch such vanity.'

Jane tutted. 'The one of her admiring herself in the sports car and the wing mirror. Gah!'

'The one where she's taking a video of herself in the bath. In. Full. Makeup,' Libby shouted. 'Who even does that? Every perv on the planet will be downloading it.'

Lucie took a massive gulp of wine and once it had gone down, popped a whole truffle in her mouth at once.

'Sitting on the bonnet of the car in a g-string,' Jane said, shaking her head.

'Thing is, Luce, Shelly said "she wishes" about George, right?' Tally added.

Lucie nodded. 'I know, but come on. There are a few pictures of them together.'

Jane interrupted. 'Hang on. Who's Shelly?'

Tally answered. 'Shelly is the conductor on the tram who was at the barbecue and knows everything about everything in Darling.'

Anais nodded. 'Yeah, she does from what I remember, and so yes, I'd make her right whatever these pictures say.'

Lucie nodded. 'It doesn't really matter because I'm not going now. I must have been crazy to even think about it after what I've been through. And my mum said I was chubby this afternoon to top it all off. Hello, meet Lucie, chubby and dumped from Darling.'

'Nooooooo!'

'Yep. Classic Mum.'

'You cannot let this Underwear Model stop you from going to the pub with a very, I repeat, *very*, hot man who has asked you,' Tally said. 'I am here to tell everyone that he is divine, and he has the hots for you. Defo. I'm a GP, I know these things.'

Jane giggled. 'She does, Luce.'

Tally joked, 'We learnt things in anatomy that I've expanded on with my studies of human psychology. He was all over you in the off-licence.'

Libby chuckled. 'I'm still agog that you ever got through the training, Tal.'

'Cheek. No, come on, Luce. We, your life wives, are here to tell you you can do it.'

'I've already decided I'm not going,' Lucie replied flatly. 'Me and my chubbiness are staying at home.'

'You are going!' Jane said.

Libby agreed. 'You need to believe in yourself.'

Lucie rolled her eyes. 'Goodness, you sound like that app.'

'It's true.'

'I can't go. I have nothing to wear.'

Jane took a sip of her wine. 'Jeans, nice top, ballet flats, job done.'

'You see, that's exactly my point. Underwear Model's jeans skim and elongate her already impossibly long legs. I have to tuck my roll of post-Rob-and-his-baby fat in the top of mine.'

'I think you're blowing this way out of proportion,' Libby stated solemnly. 'Just do it, or you'll never know.'

'Go, have fun, and if it goes wrong, so what?'

'So what? I'm stuck here on this island in the fog and everyone will know about it, that's what.'

'You'll be fine.'

Lucie raised her eyebrows at the same time as gulping another mouthful of wine. 'Well, if I do go, I'm going to need assistance.'

'I'm on makeup,' Jane said instantly.

'I'll do clothes,' Anais added.

'I'll research snippets of current affairs so that you sound interesting,' laughed Tally.

'Right. Let's meet back here tomorrow night,' Libby replied.

Jane said it first, 'Ladies, what do we say? Hold. Your. Nerve.'

## 29

Lucie spent the next day at Darlings feeling as if someone had smiled on her from above when it poured with rain, meaning that the café wasn't quite as busy as usual. She therefore, spent most of her shift in the back kitchen preparing and cleaning. She wasn't wanting to bump into anyone at all and quite happy to be lost in the monotony of the dishwashers, ironing the linens, and preparing the baskets.

Thank goodness for her friends and their rallying. Jane had already sent her a link to Lash Paradise, a mascara available to purchase at the Darling chemist that was going to add voluptuous volume and length and turn her eyes into those of does. Tally had forwarded her a pdf of the top things going on in the world and a short but sweet layman's synopsis on each. Anais had messaged asking for pictures of a shortlist of things she was prepared to wear and come back with a selection of outfit choices.

Now at home with a glass of wine beside her laptop and a basket of leftover shortbread, Lucie put the pile of clothes on the sofa, refreshed herself on Tally's pdf and opened the mascara. Leaning forward to look into a compact mirror, she pulled a funny face by stretching her top lip and began to pile the mascara onto her right eye. Sitting back and examining it, she had to admit that while not quite doe-like, it wasn't bad.

The girls began, one by one, to pop onto her screen.

'Right, I have one eye with this Paradise mascara on. What's the verdict?'

'Put your eye closer,' Anais instructed.

Lucie did so, and Jane nodded. 'See, yes, I told you. What about that blusher I told you to buy from the airport last year?'

Lucie frowned. 'What? I dunno. It's probably still in the packaging in the bottom of my handbag.'

'Hope so,' Jane replied as Lucie grabbed her bag and rooted around. 'Nope. Oh, hang on. I have that toiletry bag with all the fancy creams I never use. It's probably in there.'

Two minutes later, she was back with a Nars blusher in a little box. Waving it in front of the camera, she laughed. 'Still got the plastic on.' She fluffed her blusher brush over it and dabbed it on her cheeks and then squinted into the camera. 'Oh, right, actually yes, that doesn't look too bad.'

Twenty minutes later, after a lot of changes and toing and froing and voting by all of them, they had settled on black jeans, which they'd all said would mean she was comfortable, with a boho high-neck top she'd made herself from vintage fabric, after copying it from a girl at work. The girl had paid five hundred pounds for a top from a designer in Paris whose clothes were made in Cambodia. Lucie's had cost her nothing.

Lucie was standing on a plastic chair so that the girls could see her legs and the bottom of the outfit. Anais nodded. 'Yes, classy, but you.'

'Not sure what you mean by that. The "but you" bit.' Lucie chuckled, leaning down towards the screen.

'Nice with a little dash of weird,' Jane stated.

'Yeah, ha, that's so it,' replied Libby.

'I'm not sure whether or not I should take that as a compliment or not.'

Tally laughed. 'You are the woman who strokes strange statues of men in gold cloaks in her hallway. Say no more.'

The whole group burst into laughter. 'What about when she wore that horse outfit to that fancy dress party in Majorca and dropped the hoof on that girl in the all-white pants suit?' Libby could barely get her words out for laughing.

'I die,' Anais said, creasing up. 'That was a Lucie Moment.'

'No, no. When that horrible woman at work, what was her name? Something to do with Elvis, told her she couldn't have the day off and so she phoned in sick and then saw her in the M & S food department and threw those strawberries on the floor to cause a commotion so she wouldn't see her. Then she slipped over on one of them and slid right in front of her. Gold, absolute Lucie gold.'

Lucie plonked herself back down and stared into the circle at the top of her laptop. 'Sorry. I know you find me amusing, but this is serious for me. I am going on a date, something I haven't done since I was a teenager.'

'Of course. Sorry. Can't wait to see what happens. You've already saluted the sun in baggy joggers, got stuck in a drain, and hit his car. I mean what else can happen?' Tally asked.

'Thanks for the support, ladies. I'm now nervous about being weird.'

Libby laughed. 'Don't be stupid. That's why he likes you of course! Who wants to be with someone who takes themselves so seriously that they post two hundred and seventy-five pictures of different angles of themself in a crop top and glass of champagne on a balcony in the South of France?'

Jane nodded. 'So true. Underwear Model looks like she'd bore anyone to tears.'

Lucie sighed. 'I suppose I'll just have to suck it and see, and hope for the best.'

'And?' Libby questioned.

All of them chorused together, 'Hold. Your. Nerve.'

# 30

On the day of the date, as her Darlings shift came nearer to its end, Lucie sighed out. She'd not stopped since the moment she'd walked in the door and rather than being the new girl, she'd felt as if she'd been there forever as it had all become familiar. Piper and Evie had both been lovely and the Darling residents were friendly and welcoming. She'd spent the early morning setting up the made-to-order lunch baskets, including Leo's which consisted of double Darling Cacciatore and Shelly's, which included both a croissant and a baguette.

As customers began to tail off mid-afternoon, Lucie had started the task of setting up for the next day. Each week in Darlings was a slightly different version of the well-oiled Darlings brand, whereby table linens were changed, flowers sorted and coordinated, café au lait bowls integrated, and menus planned.

Lucie had spent a few hours with the industrial iron in the tiny room off the back kitchen with Radio 4 playing away happily beside her, pressing pale-blue linen tablecloths and napkins until they were coming out of her ears. Evie had told her that ironing linens was usually farmed out to the laundry, but they were away on holiday and she didn't trust anyone else. Lucie had thought to herself that she was quite happy to be standing being paid to iron and listen to the radio, put her head down and got on with it.

By the time the little place had cleared out as the day had worn on, she'd pulled off most of the tablecloths, shoved what she could in the washing machine, and had moved onto smoothing the clean and pressed pale-blue ones onto the tables. Piper had shown her the correct bowls to collect from the tops of the shelves and she'd set to work.

When she'd first entered Darlings as a customer and sat looking up at the piles and piles of vintage bowls and fluted cake tins, she'd thought it was all a delightful jumble of pretti-ness. Now, after a detailed explanation from Evie, she could see it was so far from a jumble it was untrue. Every shelf was organised to colour and size. With the pale-blue tablecloths, the bowls with the navy-blue pattern would come into play. Filling the shelf where they lived would be the previous week's rota-tion, meaning everything ran like clockwork. The one blip in the process was the climbing of the ladder to reach the bowls at the top. It was fiddly and had to be done when there were no customers below.

Lucie climbed up the ladder and started passing the bowls down to Piper. She went up and down until the blue contingent were down and the gingham ones in their place. Piper put her pile down as the back doorbell went and headed out towards the gate. Just as Lucie was standing by the front counter stacking the bowls ready for the next day, the door opened and the bell tinkled. Lucie turned around to see Matilda Hunting-ton-Jones strolling towards her.

'Oh, you're the one in the little Audi, aren't you?' Matilda said as she fiddled with the belt on her jeans making sure the double 'G' logo was firmly facing forward for the world to see.

Lucie would probably get the sack for not following Evie's

happy smile and quick personal service procedure, but Power Lucie was out in force. She frowned, pretending she had no idea what Matilda meant. 'Sorry?' She added a bemused look, as if she genuinely didn't understand.

Matilda could barely control her impatience and flicked her hand out towards the door. 'The accident along the road here. I was the passenger in the other car.'

'Oh, sorry, were you?'

A look of confusion crossed Matilda's face, as if being easily forgotten wasn't something that usually happened to her. 'Yes.'

'Sorry, I don't recall.'

Matilda's tut and subsequent eye roll indicated that she thought Lucie stupid. 'I'll have a coffee,' she commanded.

Lucie continued to load the bowls onto the counter. 'We've just shut down the machine.'

'What?'

'No can do on the coffee at this time.'

'Grrr! Seriously? How much does it take for places on this island to get with the times?'

Lucie was quite taken aback by the venom in Matilda's voice. Just as she was about to reply, Piper came bouncing in with a wooden crate full of vegetables in her arms. Clocking the situation right away, Piper raised her eyebrows and looked pointedly at Matilda.

'So sorry, we've just closed down for the day.'

'I heard.'

'Many apologies. Perhaps if you get here a bit earlier next time.' Piper beamed the Darlings Smile.

Matilda ran her eyes up and down Piper. The jealousy at Piper's pert youth and prettiness tangible in the sour look on her face.

'Don't bother. I'll put an order in for a basket for tomorrow, though,' Matilda stated.

'Oh dear. We've sold out of slots already. Would you like me to put you on the waiting list?' Piper asked and again smiled sweetly.

'You have to be kidding me!'

'Apologies. The baskets are so popular. Hopefully, you'll get one next time.'

'I won't be here for a next time. I'm on set in Monte Carlo for the rest of the week.'

Piper looked suitably unimpressed and didn't miss a beat. 'See you next week, then.'

Matilda huffed and pointed to the last few customers sitting in the window and a table of four outside. 'What, they were here before the machine closed down or something?'

Piper beamed again. 'Yes, they were.'

With that, Matilda stalked out and slammed the door behind her. Piper rolled her eyes and Lucie laughed. 'I didn't realise we are sold out of baskets? I thought apart from orders, it was first come, first served.'

'It is, apart from her and a few others. Has Evie not shown you the list?'

'Nope.'

'The Smile and Nod List.'

'Ooh, sounds heavyweight.'

'We smile and nod profusely and do not encourage them to come back. That one got on it on the first day she came in.'

'Ahh, I see. Why was that then?'

'Basically, she was rude. She told Evie the coffee wasn't great. We were in stitches behind the counter here. You must have picked up by now what Evie's like about coffee.'

'Umm, just a bit. She's borderline scary about it.'

'Yup. She also heard Matilda say something about Darling being a backwater and that she's travelled all over the world modelling blah, blah, blah.'

Lucie was dying to ask about George but resisted. 'So, why is she here, then?'

Piper put her head to one side. 'Well, George, obviously. I mean who wouldn't? If I was ten years older, maybe fifteen...' She giggled.

'I see.'

'She inherited a cottage on the other side. My nana lives down the same road. Matilda left it to rot more or less and then arrived last year. She did some hideous modern renovation on it. She had a fit when the council wouldn't pass her plans for a black double-glazed conservatory with bi-fold doors. It was the talk of the road.'

'She sounds awful,' Lucie replied as she pushed the tall ladder along the shelving back into the corner.

'Yeah.' Piper nodded. 'Don't worry, she won't last long. Give her 'til Christmas and she'll be toast.'

As Lucie walked home, the late afternoon air came in off the sea and she could feel a lovely but cool evening on the horizon. Strolling past the tram station, she waved back to Shelly who scooted by on a tram and made her way to the ferry slipway. Fresh sea air blustered off the water and in the middle of the estuary, little waves broke spraying water into the air. She stood and watched for a bit, letting the seaspray mist onto her face and taking big gulps of air to decompress her day in Darlings.

She recalled what she had read in Mr Cooke's pdf that humans are drawn to water: it was, according to Mr Cooke, well known that being by water gives brains a break from stimuli and calms the body. Lucie thought about how it was definitely working for her.

Continuing meandering home, she thought about going to the pub with George. Why had she said yes to this man she didn't even know? This time last year she was hoping that by now she would be about to give birth. How things had changed. There was now someone else giving birth, and she was going to the pub with a man for the first time since she'd left school. It felt all kinds of weird.

As she walked along, she cast her mind back to the dreadful date with the spotty boy eating popcorn in the cinema and couldn't recall a single other time when she had been out with anyone else. It shocked her now with hindsight at how sheltered and mundane her life had been. So very everyday. Maybe Rob had felt the same? She had been so laser focused on what she had thought her life was supposed to be, she realised that for most of it, she'd actually not had, or been, that much fun.

Maybe strolling to the pub with a more or less complete, and very, very good-looking stranger, would change all that. Maybe this was the chapter in her life where she learnt loads of new things. Maybe being on her own, living on this little island and making a whole new existence for herself, was where her life had been going all along.

The flag on top of the house flapped in the wind as she arrived at the gate. Opening the front door, she tapped each of the Three Wise Men on the head, slipped off her shoes, wiggled her toes, and put the kettle on. Five minutes later, with a cardigan wrapped around her and her jeans rolled up, she was sitting in the old plastic chair with her feet in the water.

Mr Cooke's email had informed her that he believed that standing on the shore and looking out to sea was a holiday for the body. It was a rest from the hectic and incessant deluge of information received as part of the daily load of modern life. Lucie let the water wash around her feet and certainly felt as if Mr Cooke and his pdf had a point. The lapping waves advancing and receding around her felt as if they were also inside her skull. The waves and the gulps of salty oxygen enabled her mind to drift. A quiet stasis seeped up from her feet as she looked out to sea and sipped on her tea. The sea gave her a calmness and a sense that whatever would be, would be.

~

L ucie stood in the shower, letting the water wash away the coffee smell that clung to her and gush over the remnants of the yellow-brown bruise on her upper arm. After scrubbing and double-conditioning her hair, defuzzing every possible orifice of her body, and buffing herself in instructed-by-Libby activated charcoal, she wrapped herself in a towel and sat on the toilet looking at her phone. There was a message from George that hadn't been there when she'd got into the shower.

*Hi Lucie. I'll walk by at about 6pm if that suits? G.*

Lucie swallowed. Anything suited. She sat there for ages, trying to think of something to respond. She had not a clue what the protocol was. She suddenly realised that the only male she had really ever texted was Rob, and before he had passed away, her dad. She thought about putting her conundrum in the group and seeing what the other four had to say about it. As she was about to do so, she told herself to get a grip. She did not need a meeting on sending a text.

*Lovely. Thanks. See you then.*

Putting her phone down and reading the back of the shimmering body lotion also bought along with the mascara, she rolled her eyes. This stuff was, according to the blurb, miracle performing. She slapped it on anyway and five minutes later, in her underwear, she shuddered as she squinted into the mirror. Whilst she'd most definitely dropped a few pounds, and the walking had somehow lifted everything, the extra weight piled on whilst holed up in a cottage in the country was still there. The body lotion with the 'all around white sand beach glow' had possibly reduced the appearance of the cellulite if she squeezed her eyes really tight, but overall, what looked back at her was all a bit pudgy.

Walking into the bedroom, she moved directly to the outfit she'd hung on the back of the door after the deliberation with the girls. There was no way she was even contemplating opening her wardrobe and going down the rabbit hole of trying on outfits. She knew from experience she'd get twenty minutes in, the bed would be covered, the rug a floordrobe, and she'd end up going out in the first one she'd tried on anyway.

A few minutes later, she was easing the rotating hot air brush through her hair. By the time her hair was dry, she was satisfied with the bouncy salon style result, said a silent thank you for its technology, added curls in the ends with the tongs and sprayed. She nodded as her reflection looked back at her. She might be 'chubby,' traded in for a younger model, and technically jobless, but the one thing she'd always had was beautiful hair. Its shiny golden natural highlights caught the light amongst the caramel-y hues of warm browns. Every hairdresser she'd ever been to had always commented and taken pictures of how it looked. She might not have Rob or what she thought her life was going to turn out like, but she did have a brain, options, and bloody good hair. Rock on.

Laughing to herself, she swished her hair as she ran down the stairs.

*Your life is waiting for you to happen. It's full of opportunities at every corner.*

Maybe this was an opportunity just as the meditation app had been talking about all along. She was about to fulfil her best life right here right now. She sat on the little chair beside the Three Wise Men and spoke to them as she did up the laces on her espadrilles.

'What do you think, guys? Is my life waiting to happen? Are opportunities around every corner?'

She paused as if the three statues were considering and then answered herself. 'Oh. You think I should go for my life, right, okay then. You consider George is the best thing since sliced bread. Right. I see. Hmm.'

She jumped at a sharp rap on the door.

'Hello,' a voice called out. Opening the door, she smiled.

'Hi, George,' she heard herself singsong.

'Hi. Sorry. Were you talking to someone?'

'No, no. I was just putting my shoes on.'

George's eyes looked around the room and landed on the statues. He didn't say anything about them. Lucie felt the colour rise in her cheeks and bristled around picking up her jacket and her bag. *I've totally just been talking to three waist high statues usually gracing the nativity scene in a church.*

'Okay. I'm ready to go.'

He smiled and stood back on the path and her eyes looked him up and down. She was suddenly taken by surprise by a funny feeling of being completely out of her depth. She had no idea what to do about whatever it was. She hadn't been out with anyone apart from Rob and popcorn boy ever. She tried to just think of it as if he was just a friend, just like Tally or Anais. This was very different though, at least for her. This was a friend whom she would like to wrap up and never let go. Or get lost in. Or dream about. Definitely dream about.

'Rightio. Where are we off to?' she asked, interjecting as much casual into her voice as she possibly could.

George smiled warmly and kissed her on the cheek as she stepped out of the house. 'The Darling Inn.'

'Lovely. I could do with a nice drink.'

'Long week?' George asked. 'I bet you were kept on your toes in there! A bit of a learning curve I would imagine.'

'Yes. It's good though. I've enjoyed it a lot. What about you? How's your week been?'

'Yes, busy too.'

Lucie heard herself do a strange out of character giggle. 'I don't even know what you do?'

A weird look passed over George's face. 'You haven't heard?'

'Heard? Why would I have heard?'

George shook his head and waved his hand. 'Nothing. I'm a manager, more or less.'

'Right.'

George quickly changed the subject. 'Have you been to The Darling Inn yet?'

'No. I haven't,' Lucie replied as she fell into step beside him and they walked along the road.

'You're in for a treat. The Darling Inn has its own microbrewery.' He frowned. 'Oh, I don't suppose you like beer, though. Wine, is it?'

Lucie smiled. 'I love beer, actually.' She went to say that Rob loved beer and then stopped herself just in time. 'One of my friends used to be quite into beer and breweries, so I've been to a few. I'm surprised I haven't heard about The Darling Inn, actually.'

'There you are, then. Well, you're going to love it. I know I said a stroll to the pub but if you're tired, we can hop on the tram.'

Lucie looked up at him. 'Sounds like a very good option to me, if you don't mind. I'm pretty shattered. I've done a million steps this week, or at least that's what it feels like according to my hips and feet.'

'Suits me,' George said as he squinted down towards the tramline. 'Here we go, there's a Bay tram in a few minutes.'

Following behind George's rather pert and definitely gorgeous bottom onto the tram, Lucie looked up as Shelly popped out from the front cabin and her eyes nearly fell out of her head.

'Evening!' Shelly said with a beam.

George replied, 'Good evening, Shelly.'

'How are you, Lucie?' Shelly asked, emphasising the 'are' and widening her eyes even further.

Lucie sat down on one of the highly-polished seats and held the rail in front of her. 'Good, thanks. You?'

'I'm very well. Sorry, I haven't had the microwave to you yet. I've been really busy.'

Lucie waved her hand around. 'Seems like we all have.'

'Where are you off to?' Shelly asked.

Lucie's mind suddenly went blank and she couldn't remember the name of the pub. She frowned and George answered for her. 'It's Friday night, Shelly. There's only one option on the table.'

Shelly giggled. 'I know where you're going really, Lucie. Just messing with you.'

George chuckled. 'As if we would be going anywhere else.'

Lucie frowned. 'Sorry, am I missing something?'

George turned to her. 'Not at all. The whole island, more or less, is in the pub on Friday nights. Goes back to the fishing days. If you don't make an appearance in there at some point, people start to worry.'

'I see.'

'Don't forget the specials,' Shelly added.

'The Friday Night Specials at The Darling.' George laughed. 'A whole new world.'

Shelly kissed her fingers. 'Have you heard what's on this evening?' she asked George.

'Nope, but I assume it's going to be packed in there.'

'I thought you would have heard this morning in the surf,' Shelly replied.

'I wasn't out there this morning. I had to go into the city.'

'Ahh, right you are,' Shelly said and then moved away to ring the bell and help someone who was asking a question.

George turned to Lucie. 'Have you eaten?'

'No and I could eat a horse.'

'Not sure I can help you out with a horse, but the seafood on a Friday is lovely if it's not too busy.'

'Works for me.'

George turned to her. 'You eat potatoes and fish and the like?' There was a little bit of surprise or possibly caution in his tone.

'Err, yeah. Why wouldn't I?'

'Nothing. You're not this pallo or plant thing?'

'You mean Paleo?' Lucie giggled.

'Yeah, that's it.'

'Goodness no! I can't be doing with all that,' Lucie replied, reminded of the fenugreek seeds and psyllium husk on the diet sheet. 'I love a good fish and chips any day of the week.' Lucie felt the wobble on her stomach and thought that perhaps in the cottage, there had possibly been too many days of the week which had included fish and chips.

'You found the right pub then.' George laughed.

Ten minutes later, they were standing outside The Darling Inn. The whole of the front was subway tiled in the pale aqua Darling blue. Old coach lights graced either side of the door and hung over the windows. Hanging baskets with blue and white flowers were propped on hooks all the way along the front. An anchor shape was cut out of the door just like the ones Lucie had seen in Hennie's garden, and a thick navy-blue doormat inscribed with 'Darling Inn' welcomed people in.

'It's busy,' George said. 'We might have to stand at the bar.'

Lucie followed him in as people turned around and nodded and said hello. A group of lads in the window table high fived him as they made their way to the bar. Walking through the pub, she was hit by the cosy smell and the amount of people. Most of the tables were taken, and a queue of customers were lined up waiting to be served. George turned and touched her arm. 'Follow me around to the back. It'll be a bit quieter around there.'

Lucie nodded, barely able to speak as she followed behind him and wondered what on earth she was doing. What the heck was she going to talk about? She remembered the pdf of current affairs and couldn't recall a single thing on it. She thought about Rob. What did she talk to him about? How hard could it be? She shuddered as she realised that having a baby, making a family, and IVF were what they had talked about nearly all the time. Not the most casual of topics.

'What can I get you?' George asked as they finally arrived at the bar.

'I'll have whatever you're having,' Lucie replied.

George nodded and leant on the bar, waiting. He ordered and then passed her over a half glass of dark brown beer. He smiled. 'Chocolate porter. It's strong.'

'Oh, my goodness. Delicious. Thank you,' Lucie said, taking a sip.

They moved away from the bar and started to chat. With the beer softening her edges, Lucie began to relax. Flashes of the pdf kept coming into her mind and she tried desperately to think of one of them and add something interesting to the mix. It didn't work. She could barely concentrate on forming coherent words. He must think she was a complete idiot.

'What's it like for you living by the sea?' George asked with an interested look on his face and kindness in his eyes.

'I'm loving it. It's much better than I thought on that first night in the storm. Mr Cooke has informed me of its benefits too.' Lucie chuckled. 'All in all I'm pleased to be here.'

'You want to be careful. Mr Cook will be trying to recruit you for his society.'

George continued with interest in asking about all things Lucie and she found herself telling him all sorts; about how she had been made redundant, about the little village with the cottage, her mum living in Spain, and the ins and outs of her new venture with her fabrics and sewing.

With another chocolate porter going down nicely, Lucie forgot about trying to *be* anything and the heading topics on the current affair pdf were a blur. With George, there was no need for all that; everything just clicked. The conversation moved and flowed to its own beat and before she knew it, a couple of hours had slipped past in a flash. Standing by the fireplace, she looked around the old pub, feeling quite pleased with herself at how the evening had turned out. She may not have had any experience of going out with anyone, but she'd been more than capable of holding her own. George had not appeared uninterested in the least. If he was bored senseless by her chat, he was doing a very good job of hiding it. She heard herself asking him what he did for a living. He paused.

'I work for Darlingdown Investments.'

Lucie frowned and lifted her chin a little bit in question. She was clearly supposed to know what that meant. She hadn't the foggiest. 'What's that, then?'

'Darlingdown. As in the island.'

She still didn't really understand and shook her head. 'Sorry, not with you.'

George shook his head and laughed. 'You really don't know, do you? It's a miracle!'

'Really don't know what?'

'My surname is Darlingdown. My family owns a lot of Darling.'

The penny dropped, and Lucie slowly put her drink down on the mantelpiece and felt her head moving in tiny little shakes. 'Sorry, run that past me again.'

George was now laughing a bit harder. 'I thought you were pretending when you said you didn't know. There was no way I thought Shelly hadn't told you or Evie in the café.'

'I see.' Lucie giggled and waved her hands around a bit. 'Very funny, George. I didn't have you down as a comedian. You own

Darling, do you? Course you do! Yeah, pull the other one. And I'm the Queen of Sheba!'

George raised his eyebrows. 'Lucie Peachtree, you're quite the joker yourself.'

Lucie frowned. How did he know her surname? The strong beer had loosened Lucie's nerves and putting her head on the side, she gestured towards the window. 'Rightio, for instance, you own, like what? Some property on Darling, don't tell me this pub, the sailing club? I know, I bet you own some property in the mews and down here on the bay.'

George's face was a mixture of humour and kindness. He acted as if he was joking and screwed up his lips and frowned. 'Hmm, let me see. The tram, the ferry, many of the shops on Darling Street, a large property portfolio, and my family built the town hall, the library, the community halls, and the bank.'

Lucie swallowed and blinked slowly. 'I'm not that daft, you know.'

George touched her on the hand. 'I'm not joking.'

'Sorry, can I clarify? You own the floating bridge and the tram? They're not like part of the government?'

George nodded. 'I do. Obviously not personally.'

'Right.' Lucie picked up her drink, put it down again, and suddenly wanted to run. He was clearly doing his civic duty by taking her for a drink! Of course. She felt herself go cold. What could this man with his eyelashes and shoulders and all-around gorgeousness be doing standing in a pub with a chocolate porter and her? He usually hung out with the likes of Matilda whatshername-whatshername. There was no way he was willingly standing with her in her little handmade boho top and eagerness out of choice.

George frowned. 'Lucie, are you okay?'

Lucie ran her hand across the top of her eyebrow. 'Yes, yes, I'm fine.'

He drained his drink and took a quick look at the bar and

went to the loo. As Lucie stood there taking everything he'd told her in, she wasn't quite sure what to think. But it did all make sense; the huge white house, the comment when she'd been saluting the sun about his land, the easy, confident manner. She felt like an idiot and completely gullible at the same time.

Squeezing her fingers between her eyes, she tried to talk herself up. *I expand my horizons. I push myself from comfortable zones to pastures new.*

As she stood staring into space with the packed buzzy pub noise around her, she came to as someone waved their hand in front of her face.

'Yoohoo, anyone in there?'

Lucie snapped back to reality and smiled at Evie. 'Oh, hi.'

'You didn't mention you were coming in here tonight.' Evie smiled. 'It's really busy!'

'Oh, didn't I?'

'Nope.' Evie looked Lucie up and down. 'Wow, you look amazing! Love your hair, you lucky duck.'

'Thank you.' Lucie smiled in response.

'How are you feeling after work?'

'Good, thanks. My feet know about it.'

'Yeah.' Evie chuckled. 'I don't need to go to the gym working in there.'

'No, I bet you don't.'

'You're still good to help out?'

'Yes, of course.'

'Excellent. As I said, we can keep it on a rolling basis if you like. I know you said you had your little business to think about.' She smiled. 'Anyway, we'll talk about that next week.' She looked over towards the bar. 'Have you tried the food yet? It's so busy tonight I'm not sure I'm going to bother.'

Just as Lucie was about to answer, George came back from the loos. Evie did a double-take as he joined them. 'Oh, hi, George,' she said with a confused look on her face.

'Hey, Evie. How are you? I've heard you've had a busy week,' George said, nodding towards Lucie.

Evie looked from one to the other. 'Yes, I have.'

'Right.' He looked at Lucie and jerked his thumb towards the door. 'I think it might be time to head off.'

Lucie nodded. So that was the end of that then. Clearly, this was just a neighbourly drink that had now come to an end.

Evie went to move around George. 'Yes, I was on my way to the loo. Have a nice evening. See you.'

George spoke as she walked away. 'I think it's time to blow this joint. I haven't seen it this busy for a long time. You must be starving by now. I know I am.'

Lucie smiled up at him, pathetically happy that he was interested in how hungry she was. 'I am, too.'

George flicked his eyes towards the bar. 'It'll be ages for food. I was thinking we abort the mission and head for the Chinese. We might be lucky with a table. I should have thought about this earlier and called ahead.'

Lucie nodded, thinking that anywhere sounded good to her. 'I'm easy.'

'Okay, let's go then, follow me for the easiest route out of here.'

Lucie ambled along beside George after they'd walked out of the pub, around the bay and made their way to Darling Street. She felt all kinds of strange. Here she was on a little island, with a man who was most definitely not Rob, with her hair done and makeup on and wondering where the night was going to take her. Ten minutes ago she'd felt sorry for herself, now they were on their way to a restaurant. Life worked in mysterious ways. Part of her kept wondering if she was, in fact, in a dream.

They strolled along past the Darling deli, looked in the window at the progress of the new bakery and finally made it to the Chinese. George pushed the door and held it open for Lucie to walk inside. As she stepped in, she felt as if she had been whisked to another land. Soft tinkly music played, tiny gold and white lights were woven through a multitude of upside-down umbrellas hanging from the ceiling, a water fountain trickled from behind the desk. A woman in a white silk high-collared jacket with blue embroidery and immaculate hair broke into a huge smile when she saw George. The woman zipped around the desk, took George's hand and held it in both of hers. Her eyes looked concerned. 'How are you?' she asked.

'Very well, Mey. Very well.' He turned to Lucie. 'This is my friend, Lucie. Lucie, this is Mey.'

Mey's eyes lit up, and she smiled at Lucie and then laughed. 'You forgot the other bit, George.'

George chuckled. 'Ahh, yes, sorry. Mey likes everyone to know that Mey means pretty.'

Lucie laughed. The name was not wrong about the woman or the restaurant. She felt as if she had been dropped into an ancient Chinese folk story and it was divine. Tiny little gold clips sparkled on the side of Mey's glorious updo of hair. 'Lovely to meet you, Lucie.' Mey then looked up at George. 'You should have called, we're fully booked.'

George smiled. 'Right, sorry, we've been to the pub.'

'I didn't think I'd see you in here on a Friday night, well, not at least until later.' Mey looked over towards a waitress and then to the back. 'Hold on. We can add an extra table at the back there.' She looked at George in question. 'It might be a bit of a squeeze.'

George turned his head to Lucie. 'Would that be okay with you?'

By the smell of the food, the look of the place, and the calibre of the company, Lucie wouldn't have minded sitting on the floor or outside on the pavement. 'Of course. I'll sit anywhere.'

George and Lucie stood and watched as a flurry of activity took place. As if by magic, a small table and chairs were placed in a space tucked into a tiny alcove. Mey waved them down through the restaurant and they passed under umbrellas towards the table. Blue silk flower lanterns with thick tassels hung throughout the room, and Lucie felt every last piece of tension whisk away as she sat down. The ambience was nothing short of mind-blowing.

An hour or so later, after a never-ending supply of food in little bowls that just kept on coming, Lucie sat back in her chair stuffed to the brim and unable to eat another thing.

'Had enough?' George asked. 'How good was that? I could live in here.'

'I don't think I'll need to eat for a week. That was so nice, I've never had Chinese like it,' Lucie replied, thinking that in her old life with Rob she would have totally undone the top button of her jeans as she leaned back in the chair. She couldn't stop a yawn from escaping, covering her hand over her mouth.

'Keeping you up?' George joked.

'Gosh, sorry! That food has pushed me over some imaginary edge I didn't know I was on the precipice of.'

'We'll make a move, shall we?' George asked. Lucie loved how he was making it about the two of them. She'd wondered earlier how she would be getting home, but he was speaking as if they were leaving together.

'Might be a good idea,' Lucie said. 'Before I conk out, can't make it home, and have to sleep on the floor.'

As they left the table and went out, Lucie noticed how there was no mention of payment. Mey walked them to the door and stood outside with them as the foghorn sounded in the distance and a tram went past not far from where they were standing.

'Fog's coming in,' Mey said. 'Yep, it's getting low already.'

Lucie followed Mey's gaze. 'Oh, wow, I haven't seen it from up here before. It really does come in.'

Mey smiled. 'Yep, it does. No storm for us tonight though,

thankfully.' She held out her hand to Lucie. 'Nice to meet you, Lucie.'

'Likewise. Thank you for a lovely meal. I don't think I've ever tasted food like that.'

Mey chuckled. 'We do our best. Cheerio,' she said and waved as she headed back in the door.

George looked along the tramline. 'What do you want to do? We can stroll or wait for the next one.'

Lucie wished she could be transported to her bed. The week, the food, and the strong beers had finally caught up with her. She suddenly felt exhausted by the whole thing. Tired by being in a new place, all the chatting and meeting new people. Tired being on a date where she wasn't wholly sure what to do. She couldn't stifle another yawn. George put his hand on the small of her back. 'I think we'll wait. I don't think you'll make the walk.'

'Thanks for taking me home.'

George frowned. 'What else would I do?'

'Sorry, yes, I just wanted to say it.'

'Not a problem, Ms Peachtree. Besides, I'm not sure I'd trust you to make it in one piece from what I've seen of you so far.'

Lucie laughed. 'You've really got the wrong impression of me.'

'Just joking with you.'

'Thanks for tonight. It's been really nice. I've enjoyed myself.'

'Yeah, me too. I've really had a good time,' George replied and patted his hand on her back.

Lucie sat in the tram shelter and could barely keep her eyes open. An easy silence descended as a tram arrived and as they got on, they heard the foghorn go again in the distance. It soon arrived at the last stop adjacent to the ferry and before she knew it, even though Lucie's feet felt like lead, the walk from the station to the Coastguard's House had not taken long.

Thick, dense fog swirled in off the sea. 'It's really come

down. I can't even see the flagpole up there,' Lucie said, looking up at the roof.

'You'll get used to it,' George replied, following her gaze to the top of the house.

'Coffee?' she heard herself ask as she stood at the gate.

'Love one,' George replied quickly.

As Lucie opened the front door, George took off his jacket, she took it and hung it on the end of the bannister. George looked at the Three Wise Men. 'I like your, umm, what are we calling these things? Decor, is it?'

Lucie giggled. 'I've grown attached to them. They were in the sitting room when I arrived, keeping guard of the fireplace, or did I tell you that already?' She didn't mention that she'd started talking to them on her way past and had more than once asked them for their advice. She opened the door to the sitting room and George sat down.

Five minutes later, she was back with coffee. Fifteen minutes later, they were in her bed.

## 31

A shrill beep sounded in Lucie's ears. She wondered why Rob wasn't turning off the alarm. Then she remembered there was no Rob. Then she remembered the night before. She opened her left eye a tiny little bit and looked out through her eyelashes. Straining her ears, she couldn't hear anything but the waves outside. She turned her head a smidgeon to the left. There was no one in the bed. She sat bolt upright and clutched the duvet to her chest. She definitely had no clothes on. She had spent the night with a man she didn't really know. Her, him, and her chubs, in the nude, in her bed.

She closed her eyes, not quite able to believe what she had done. Oh, how fabulous it had been! Wild, even. Whatever George had done differently to what had gone on in the bed in her old life, it had worked for her. It had worked for her more than once. He'd seemed to quite enjoy it too.

Letting her eyes settle on the rumpled sheets on the other side of the bed, she wasn't sure what to think, and she absolutely wasn't sure what to do. The girls would know. Her eyes took in the room and she could hear the soft patter of rain on the window. She remembered his clothes dropping on the floor.

Her resolute boldness. His exquisiteness. Her complete abandon. Who even was she? It had been all sorts of glorious. She hadn't even realised places like that existed. She'd enjoyed making their acquaintance.

Pulling her dressing gown on, she noted that his clothes were nowhere to be seen. Padding down the stairs, she went up the two little steps in the hall and then down again and into the kitchen. Making herself a cup of tea, she sat with her dressing gown pulled tightly around her and couldn't stop herself from smiling. A message came in from Tally.

*Blimey! Come on, Luce! No message in the group last night and nothing this morning. I am starting to worry a little bit. Are you alive?*

Lucie sent back a kissing emoticon.

*What happened????*

*It was a nice night.*

*Pleased you went now?*

Lucie chuckled. That was the understatement of the year. She was ecstatic she went. The end bit was much more than pleasing. She knew that as clear as day.

*Yep.*

*Yep??? What does that mean? I'm calling you.*

Lucie waited for the video call to come through and propped her phone up against a candle. Tally, with one of her twins on her lap, came onto the screen.

'Hi, beautiful,' Lucie said and Tally's daughter smiled shyly.

Tally's eyebrows widened as she looked into the screen. Shuffling in her seat, she held up a hand. 'Hold on. I'll be back' Two minutes later, she was back on her own. She put her face nearer the screen. 'Oh. My! Did you? Did he?'

Lucie burst out laughing. 'I don't know what you are talking about.'

Tally swore. 'I can't believe it!'

'I didn't say anything.'

'I can tell. It's written all over your face. You wouldn't make a very good spy.'

'What can you tell?'

'You had more than a few drinks down the pub. Oh my!'

'I'm saying nothing.' Lucie giggled and took a sip of her tea.

'What happened then? I want every single detail.'

Lucie smiled and shook her head. 'We just went to the pub and then for something to eat and that was it.'

'Wait!' Tally almost shrieked. 'Back up. Right from the beginning. The outfit, the hair, the doe eyes courtesy of Jane.'

Lucie giggled again. 'It was a night full of educated conversation.'

'Pah! Yeah, right. Of course it was. By the look on your face and the flush on your cheeks, it was a lot more than that. Come on, my life is so boring, and you know the state of my marriage, I need involvement here.'

'I did my hair, have to say it looked winning. The outfit was just right; I didn't feel too much like a pudding, not that that mattered in the end because it was all just so simple, and I dunno, friendly. I didn't care about anything, Tal, nothing. Not my chubby status, the thing that happened with Rob, the failures, the rainbow babies. None of it. It was so weird. It was like he just got me.'

'Friendly with a side of something else?'

'Maybe.'

'Oooooh! This is fabulous.'

'Yeah, so…' Lucie trailed off.

'Luce, what's happened to you? You sound dreamy!'

'It was more than dreamy. It was an out of body experience. What have I been missing all these years?'

'This is unreal! Woohoo! So you went to the pub and then what?'

'To the Chinese restaurant, then we got the tram home, and then he came in for a coffee.'

'And then?'

'Put it this way. The coffee lasted about ten minutes.'

'I can't believe it!'

'You can't? I'm in shock. I have never done anything like this in my life. Like ever.'

'I don't know what to say. I'm speechless. For someone who didn't know what they were doing, you certainly didn't hang around.'

'Tally, my sex life involved charts and temperatures and hormones and cycles. I just went for it. I don't know where it came from!'

Tally sighed. 'Yep, I know it did.'

'This… this was just wild and abandoned and so, so, so, good. My god, so good.'

'Ahh.'

'I can't believe it went where it did. I didn't even see it coming and then bang, he was carrying me up the stairs. Carrying old pudding basin me through the hallway, past the Three Wise Men, and into bed.'

Tally sighed. 'This is Lucie gold. Wait until the girls hear about this.'

'I went to heaven and I don't think I've come back down to earth yet. I'm floating, Tal.'

'I'm so happy for you, Luce. Rob McKintock. You ain't seen nothing yet.'

## 32

Later that day, Lucie took a whole tub of lemon shortbreads out of the pantry, made a coffee, and walked down to the end of the garden and onto the beach. The initial furore of the morning after had slowly, but surely, begun to seep away as the day had worn on. It was all very well acting with reckless abandon, but now what did she do? She had zero prior experience to work from. Horrible regret was rearing its ugly head in the pit of her stomach. What was George thinking about it all? More importantly, why hadn't he left a note or sent a text, or done something? There had been radio silence from his end and she was perplexed as to what to do.

She went cold as she dipped the third piece of shortbread into her tea. Had she been played like a fiddle? The new girl on the island and the lord who ran the place. Was that what it was? She sighed as an imaginary penny dropped. Of course, that was it!

'Stupid. Stupid. Chubby. Stupid,' Lucie said out loud to the water.

All sorts of things went through her mind. Standing up

against the back of her bedroom door! What the? Going in for seconds in the middle of the night! Wrapping her legs around. Who even was that person? That had never happened in all the time she'd been with Rob.

Sloshing her feet around in the water, she forced herself to think about Power Lucie. What would Power Lucie do? She went through a few scenarios in her head. Opening the app, she navigated through until she came to a meditation named, '20 positive affirmations for mind-blowing female desire,' and clicked play.

'I radiate sensuality. I deserve to fulfil every core of my being with pleasure. I am a sexual goddess.'

Yes, yes, that was it! She deserved last night. Of course she did. That was going to be her stance on it. She, Lucie Peachtree, former partner in life to Rob, previous occupant of grey office cubicle, and owner of very boring life was, in actual fact, a sexual goddess.

A little voice somewhere inside was trying to mimic the woman on the app. The voice was having a bit of a hard time being heard. It squeaked, more mouse than goddess, 'Bring it on.'

Later on, Lucie felt much more positive about it all. She'd spent a lot of time perched on top of a pink cloud floating around the Coastguard's House, listening to affirmations and a radio drama on the BBC. It was very nice on top of the cloud as she gazed down happily at her fabrics and sewing around her. As she'd cracked on with her day, the silence from George had been short-lived and she'd sighed a huge woosh of relief when she'd read his text.

*Now that was what I call a Friday night. G x*

As she'd read his message, she'd nearly dropped her phone into a bucket of water she was standing beside whilst she was cleaning the sitting room windows. After considering what to do in response to the text, asking the opinion of the Three Wise Men, and deciding against sending screenshots to the girls and calling a meeting, she decided to keep it all simple.

*Same here. Most enjoyable. xx*

*Sorry I had to leave. I've got my daughter. Spk soon.*

Lucie had tried her utmost not to analyse what "spk soon" meant and instead continued to bolster her self-esteem by way of the app and by the end of it, she was so much the goddess, it was borderline concerning. One thing she did know; Friday night had been one of the best nights of her life.

The rest of the weekend went by in a flash, with Lucie spending most of it in her sewing room making up things for the order with Monica, taking pictures for her shop, and slowly turning the room into a productive working space.

On Monday morning, she'd left the house, gone past the ferry waving at one of the customers from Darlings, and as she watched a ferry drop down into the water, a blue car in the queue rolled its window down. Mey from the China Darling smiled and waved and as Lucie strolled along, she said a silent thank you for this new place she was calling home.

As she stood in the queue for the tram, as much as she tried, she couldn't stop thinking about the night with George. The most astonishing thing about it was that it had occurred at all. Sitting just above that astonishment was bemusement about how much she'd enjoyed it. Deep down inside, she'd always wondered what other people were talking about when they spoke about their fabulous sex lives, and she'd often frowned at scenes on the screen and wondered if they were based on fantasy.

There had been no fantasy on Friday night. Far, far, from it. It had been passionate, wild, and she realised now, most of all, freeing. Free from worry about babies, free from cycles and ovaries and free from hoping she would get pregnant. Pure, unadulterated, delicious freedom, and boy did it feel good.

She sat on the tram as it trundled along Darling Street in the sunshine. The ding-ding of the bell accompanied her thoughts, and the bright Monday morning suited her mood perfectly. As she hopped off the tram with a spring in her step, she passed the deli and China Darling and took a left away from the main street towards the bay.

Five minutes or so later, she was crossing the road and approaching the beach. Sitting in the Victorian weather shelter, she took off her trainers and socks and then, just as she was taking the steps down to the beach and peering down carefully at the mossy surface, she heard someone coming from the water. Looking up, she saw George standing in the shallows, his right hand over his head unzipping his wetsuit. He hadn't seen Lucie yet, and she gulped as he shrugged the top of the wetsuit off so it dangled around his waist.

Stepping onto the sand, he looked up, smiling as he saw her. Lucie felt her pulse racing, her mind catapulting straight to the back of her bedroom door on Friday night.

'Morning.' Lucie smiled, stopping just before she got to him.

George pulled his goggles over his head and ran his hand through his wet hair. 'Morning. How are you? I was going to come in and see you today in the café.' He put his hand on her right arm and kissed her on the cheek.

'Oh right,' Lucie replied and suddenly felt embarrassed. It was all very well thinking about him from dawn to dusk in the comfort of home, but now she was standing in front of him in the cold light of day, she felt clumsy and awkward. She sucked in her stomach and fiddled with her earring. 'How was the rest of your weekend?'

'Yes, good. Busy. I had my daughter.'

'I remember you mentioning it. Lovely weather this morning.'

'Yeah, the water's nice,' George agreed.

'Not too cold in there?'

'Nope, not at all.'

Lucie shuffled her feet in the sand and wondered if this was how it went. A few days before, she had been naked in her bedroom, standing up against her bedroom door with this man. Now they were discussing the weather.

'Did you spend the weekend working on your business?' George asked.

'I did, yes.' Lucie nodded and stepped out of the way as a group of runners splashed along the shoreline. She looked along the beach and then back at George. 'Right, well, I'd better get on with my walk. I wanted to get some sea air before the onslaught today.'

George took a step closer to her. 'I'll be in later.'

Lucie felt as if something inside her had died. Clearly, what they had done was part of his normal. He wasn't even going to mention it! He was just going to carry on as before. It was so very far from her normal, she wanted to cringe and the ground to open her up, take a big swallow, and bring her up again on a remote part of Scotland or perhaps the Himalayas. She made to continue her walk but George put his hand on hers and looked her straight in the eye. 'I had an amazing time. I wanted to say thanks in person. I didn't want to text.'

Lucie felt her cheeks burning. 'Mmm, yep, me too.' She wanted to yell that it was completely out of character for her. That before, there had only been Rob.

'Right. Good. That makes two of us then.'

'Might see you later,' Lucie said and turned.

'Yep. Oh and Lucie. I was, umm, wondering if you wanted to, you know...' He let the sentence dangle and ran his hand through his wet hair again.

She raised her eyebrows and felt somersaults going over and over in her stomach. 'Yes?'

'Well, it was very nice. I was wondering if you wanted to go out at all? You know. I, umm, well, I don't make a habit of doing things like that, if you know what I mean. No worries if not.'

Lucie looked down at her feet and then up again. She wasn't sure if he was asking her to go on a date or what he was asking. Suddenly, she couldn't be bothered with the wondering. She felt too past it and too battle scarred from Rob and Serena to play games. Power Lucie arrived on the beach and turned her head to the side and screwed up her lips. 'Yeah, I would like to go out, but before we go anywhere with this, a couple of things. So, you know, we're completely clear. Firstly, I've never done anything like that before in my life, and secondly, well, secondly, I'm not interested in mucking around. You know?' Lucie stated and shook her head in tiny little movements back and forth. 'I've sort of had enough of that. So, if you are kind of into dicking around, then no, just no. No, I wouldn't be interested at all. Oh, and while we're at it, there's a thirdly; if this is just a bit of fun for you, then I'm *so* not interested, to be honest.' She waved her hands around in front of her. 'If this is all a bit of a giggle with the silly new girl on the island then, really, I'd rather not.' She looked up at him questioningly.

George nodded slowly and didn't say anything. Little droplets of water hung on his eyelashes and dripped from the goggles hanging on his wrist. He remained silent for a second contemplating what she'd said.

Lucie nodded, acknowledging that on her terms he wasn't interested. She felt waves of disappointment wash in and out with the sea. As she went to turn, he put his hand on her arm, pulled her to him and kissed her on the lips. Lucie then stood back and blinked.

George smiled and replied, 'Well, thanks for that and in response to your question: no it's not a giggle and yes, I rather would.'

## 33

The pink cloud Lucie had been sat atop was now a freight train. She hung on for dear life as it hurtled up and down, and she tried to concentrate on running around Darlings taking orders whilst simultaneously running the dishwashers, and filling baskets. All she could think about was what had happened on the beach. Where had her speech come from? It had been nothing short of Churchill-like in its delivery. There had been no doubt that she had been clear on her intentions, at least there was that. She couldn't believe she'd said the thing about being the new girl. She couldn't believe he hadn't told her to take a running jump.

As the morning turned into the afternoon, and Darlings got busier and busier, she didn't have too much time to dwell on it further or pontificate on the arrival of Power Lucie. With the sun shining and the people of Darling out and about, there had not been a spare seat in the shop all day and the queue at the counter for takeaway coffees and baskets had been continuous. Lucie, Piper, and Evie worked seamlessly together, and the afternoon had flown by. Lucie had just slotted in as if she had always been there, and by the end of the afternoon, as customers tailed off and things slowed down, Lucie began to breathe again.

Clearing, cleaning and laying tables, she smiled as the door went and Mey from China Darling came in. Evie looked up from behind the counter and scooted towards the door and hugged Mey. Mey handed Evie two large blue cool bags and spices filled the air. Evie put the bags on the counter and then turned to Lucie.

'Lucie, this is Mey. I would kill for her food.'

Lucie smiled. 'Yes, we've met. Hi, Mey.'

'Hi.' Evie started to make Mey a coffee and Mey smiled at Lucie. 'How was the rest of your evening?' she asked with a twinkle in her eye. Lucie raised her eyebrows and nodded. She chuckled inside at what would be said if she let on what had really happened that night. No doubt their jaws would drop. She wondered what they would say if she let them in on the knowledge that George had ended up in her bedroom and that what had taken place had never happened to her before.

Evie handed Mey a bowl of coffee and then looked at Lucie. 'Do you fancy one too? We could do with a bit of a sit down. I know my feet are killing me.'

Lucie nodded and sat down beside Mey with Evie shortly joining them, putting two more bowls of coffee on the table, and a basket with lemon shortbread in the middle.

Evie laughed. 'So, please do tell us, because we, all of us, are all absolutely dying to know what occurred on Friday night. You were the talk of the Pride of Darling on Saturday morning.'

Lucie blushed, and Evie continued. 'How in the name of goodness did you manage it?'

'Manage what?'

'To end up in the pub with the elusive George.'

Batting her hand in front of her face, Lucie tried to make light of it. She attempted a casual, tinkly little laugh. 'Ahh, it was nothing. Just a neighbourly drink. Nothing more, nothing less.'

Mey twiddled the stack of gold bracelets on her arm and let out a little chuckle. 'George doesn't do neighbourly. At least, not since the accident. My goodness, it was good to see him looking so relaxed.'

Lucie didn't know what to say. Mey was clearly referring to the accident with George's daughter Shelly had told her about at the barbecue.

Evie made a little tutting sound. 'Awful. That was a dark day on Darling.'

Mey nodded in response. 'Thank goodness she pulled through.'

Lucie swallowed and picked up her bowl and sipped her coffee. 'Shelly told me it was a fancy dress costume that caught fire.'

'It was indeed. Up like a light in a matter of seconds. Leo literally saved her life,' Mey added gravely.

'Juliana, the partner, took it very, very badly,' Evie added.

'It was a terrible situation. She was in hospital for months.'

Evie pushed her chair back. 'Sorry, Lucie, for sounding all doom and gloom on you. That conversation took a turn!'

'No, no, all good. I'm glad you're telling me, thanks.'

Mey broke a piece of shortbread off. 'So you went to the pub and then came to the restaurant for the evening?'

'Yep, that's pretty much it,' Lucie replied. *And then I got carried upstairs to bed.*

Mey looked at her intently. 'Will you, umm, be seeing him again?'

Lucie gulped some coffee and looked up. 'Yes, yes, I most definitely will.'

## 34

A month or so later, with a bowl of café au lait in front of her and a warm croissant from a batch just out of the oven, Lucie sat with her phone in the little courtyard behind Darlings.

It had been another full-on day. In addition to the hectic pace that was Darlings, Matilda, in high-waisted white crepe trousers, a tucked-in shirt, and tied just-so silk scarf around her neck, had flounced in and sat down in a flurry of self-importance. With a grandiose flick of her hand in Lucie's direction, she'd summoned Lucie, telling her to hurry up and take her order.

It had taken all Lucie's resolve not to tell Matilda to run and jump off the nearest cliff without a life jacket. Instead, Lucie found herself taking Piper's lead and smiling and nodding. The smile was small and tight and more on the side of grimace than beam, but it was there.

She'd also wanted to let Matilda in on a few things; mostly her fledgling relationship with George. In the time since the pub date, they'd been all over the place. Some days it had ended in the same way the evening in the pub had. It had been mind-boggling to not only Lucie but the Hold Your Nerve girls too, but everyone had been on the same page to make hay while the sun shined. Lucie took much pleasure in doing just that.

Now, with Matilda long gone and on her break, Lucie was sitting with her feet up and sipping her coffee mindlessly scrolling through Matilda's social media; Matilda in a satin dress with her back to the camera peeking over her shoulder, Matilda with a wrap tied to her head and "statement" lip, Matilda in her underwear and heavy overcoat in the middle of a deserted street.

Biting into her croissant, Lucie rolled her eyes as she read that Matilda's style was "Young French Bardot," whatever that was. Lucie chuckled, wondering what her style was and decided it was Late Thirties English after too many pies.

Lucie pressed on one of the many little dashes along the top of Matilda's stories and watched as the reel played from one to the next. Matilda certainly loved to document her day. The stories moved from one scene of Matilda's fabulous life to the next. Lucie watched as the camera pointed across what looked like a Parisian road. Matilda then appeared in the scene from afar in jeans, stilettos, and a bobble hat and sauntered over the road. Lucie burst out laughing as trying to be cool Matilda is narrowly missed by a passing scooter. Getting closer and closer towards the camera, she picked up her drink, sipped, and then eyed the camera moodily.

On and on the stories went. Just watching them made Lucie exhausted; Matilda standing by a train door with a bum bag, complete with designer branding on the front, strapped to her chest, her arms hanging uncomfortably to the side. Lucie winced. The stories kept on coming and then Lucie stopped, put her bowl on the table, and held the screen down. Frowning, she took a screenshot. She recognised the kitchen. Matilda was admiring herself in a selfie in George's kitchen, and according to the timestamp up the top, it had been a few hours before.

Lucie didn't know what to think. There was a possibility that it wasn't time-sensitive, but if it was, Matilda had clearly spent time that day with George. It irked her enormously. She forwarded the screenshot to Tally and then pressed the button to call her.

'Hey, I just got your message. Who is that? Is that Underwear Model?'

'Yes. It's Underwear Model in George's kitchen and unless she's uploaded an old video, it was taken today.'

'Oh, I see.'

'Yeah, not happy. Not happy at all.'

'I'm just looking at her social media now. Me oh my. She's surrounded completely and utterly by an aura of smugness. If there is such a word for her, it's "smuggery." My goodness, she is so in love with herself.'

'I know.'

Tally made a funny sound. 'Oh dear. I'm embarrassed for her. The one where she sort of moodily crosses the road in that ridiculous hat pulled down to her eyes.'

'I thought it was me being mean. Who even does that at our age?'

'She must have totally got someone to film her from inside the bistro. She gets closer and closer and then looks meaning-fully into the camera.'

Lucie started chuckling. 'Yeah, but then she's clearly in George's kitchen. The timing is right. She was in here earlier.'

'Oh, no, was she?'

'Yep. She summoned me.' Lucie laughed. 'Such an idiot. She doesn't realise the place actually has her on a list of awful customers. Piper, the young girl who works here, said that she told her she didn't have time for niceties with people who work in the service industry.'

'Ouch. No way! How does she think that the world goes round then?'

'I know. She had that attitude with me too.'

'She sounds beyond awful.'

'Yes, she is.'

'I wonder what she was doing there?' Tally asked.

'I don't know, but I'm definitely going to find out.'

'Go Luce.'

A pitter-pattering of warm weather rain tapped against the open window as Lucie stood in the kitchen with her arms crossed and face screwed up in contemplation. Taking a bottle of chilled Pinot Grigio out of the fridge, she undid the top and tried to kid herself that she was only going to have half a glass.

Gulping, she felt the cold liquid slide down to her stomach and then closing her eyes, she inhaled the Darling smell filtering in through the window and attempted to let her shoulders drop. It was all very well launching herself headfirst into a relationship, but she was loath to admit how much she cared. The image of Matilda in George's kitchen had knocked her for six and she didn't like how it felt at all.

Taking deep breaths as she'd learnt via the meditation app and letting the wine fizz along through her veins, after a couple of minutes she started to feel a bit better. With her phone on the worktop, she clicked to the app and scrolled through to the section on relationships, found a track and pressed play. A high-pitched, slightly whiny American voice emitted from her phone.

'I deserve to have a relationship where I am loved.'

Nodding in agreement, she lugged another mouthful of wine, trying to stay positive and not let the Matilda thing play out in her head.

'It is in my power to feel secure.'

She wasn't really sure about agreeing to that one. When

she'd read the note from Rob, she'd been stripped of everything she felt she'd known, and secure had been the last thing she'd felt. The power thing was quite apt though in light of the new Power Lucie who had appeared on the scene. Putting her wine down, she stopped the app, opened the back door, stood looking out at the soft haze of warm rain and called George.

He answered and seemed pleased to hear from her. 'Hey, gorgeous, how are you? I was just about to call you. I'm on my way home and wondered what you were up to?'

'Oh, right. Were you? I thought you were at home.'

She could hear the confusion in George's voice. 'No, why would I be at home? I told you when I left that I was over here at work all day.'

Lucie thought to herself that in light of her experience with Rob, it didn't actually matter what he told her he was doing. 'You haven't been home, then?'

'No. You don't sound yourself. Is something wrong?'

Lucie stalled for time to think about what she was going to say. 'I'm fine. How's your day been?'

'Apart from the fact that Matilda made an appearance, it's been productive.'

Lucie tried to stop her voice from wobbling. 'Matilda? What, she's been at your office?'

George assumed Lucie hadn't remembered their conversation about Matilda. He clearly had no idea that Lucie knew not only precisely who Matilda was, but that because of Matilda's incessant broadcasting of her stories all over the internet, she also knew the ins and outs of not only her day, but a large part of her life. 'Yeah, that one I told you about. Anyway, she left something in my car when I did her a favour months ago. She suddenly arrived out of the blue and said she was near the office and could she pick it up.'

'I see. What, so you went for lunch or something?'

George laughed out loud. 'No way! I bumped into her on the

ferry a while ago and couldn't get rid of her, and you probably won't remember but the day of the accident I was giving her a lift home and she hung around then too. No way I'd go for lunch!'

Lucie made a little sound and George continued, 'She'd left a jacket or something in my car supposedly, but it wasn't there and I said it might be at the house. I told her to just go round and get it. I'll have to move the spare key now, though.'

Lucie rested her head on the architrave of the back door and sighed. 'You let her go to your house while you weren't there?'

She heard the tone in George's voice change. 'Hmm. Maybe that wasn't such a good idea. Too late now. I just didn't want to have to deal with it, you know? I have to at least attempt to be civil to her because of the business. She's so irritating. Grinds my gears, to be quite honest.'

Lucie stepped back into the kitchen and picked up her wine. She smiled and nodded. She couldn't have said it better herself.

## 35

Quickening her step, Lucie could see the Pride of Darling halfway across the estuary. She watched amazed as in its blue and white livery it seemed to glide through the water. Approaching the slipway, she stood in the foot passenger queue next to a glittering sea. Water churned down beside her, hazy sunshine fell onto her bare arms, and a gentle, briny sea breeze whispered in her ears.

Along with all the other foot passengers, after watching and waiting patiently, she stepped onto the ferry. Making her way to the middle, she leant over the railing and looked across the water. Rummaging around in her bag for her glasses, she put them on and could just make out the Coastguard's House, or rather, her house down on the left, its blue and white striped flag flapping back and forth in the wind coming off the sea.

As she stared at the house, she felt a strange feeling of comfort that Darling Island was where she had always been meant to be. Watching the cars slowly load onto the ferry, their bumpers nearly touching, the gate then closed behind them, and the ferry lowered down into the estuary. With the slipway slowly moving further and further away, Lucie's phone buzzed in her pocket. Fishing it out, she saw Libby's name flashing across the top with a video call. Moving right to the end of the passenger section so as not to disturb anyone, she held her phone out in front of her and pressed the button.

'Ooh, blimey, look at you all dolled up!' Libby exclaimed. 'I thought you might be at work but thought I'd chance it. Clearly not, where are you going?'

'I'm going to meet George,' Lucie replied.

'Ahh, sounding all coupled up.'

Lucie nodded. 'I know. Weird, eh?'

'Hmm, yes and no. I'm not surprised you got snatched up.'

'I'm surprised! It wasn't on my radar, as you know. I was even talking about sperm donors,' Lucie joked.

'Thank goodness for your old joggers and saluting the sun, that's all I can say.'

'I know.'

'And nights that end up like that first night did.'

Lucie laughed. 'I feel like my relationship is keeping everyone in the group entertained, at the very least.'

Libby nodded enthusiastically and swigged on a bottle of water. 'Tell me about it. You've been on more dates than any of us for a long time. We haven't had this much fun since Tally had the twins. How many times have you been out with him now? It's gone so quickly!'

Lucie tilted her head slightly and screwed up her lips. 'Hmm. I've lost count.'

'You might have, but we're all keeping tabs. It looks amazing there today. Look at the sunshine on the water. All the sparkles,' Libby acknowledged.

'I know, right?' Lucie sighed. 'I love it here, Libs. I really do. I was just thinking that as you phoned.'

'Yeah, it shows. You look better than you have in years. Are you sure you haven't been tweaked?' Libby asked, squinting into the camera.

'What? Been tweaked?'

'Yeah, you know, had a little bit of help?'

'Laughable. Do you mean Botox or something? Nup. Even if I could afford it, I think I'd be too scared.'

'You're doing something right, that's all I can say. It must be the coastal air.'

'I'm just happy,' Lucie replied simply.

'It's so good to hear that.'

'I didn't realise that I wasn't happy before all this,' Lucie said, gesturing out to the sea and ferry behind her.

'Yeah, it's a funny old world. How come he's not with you now?'

'He's been working and seeing his daughter. I'm on my way to meet him.'

'Have you met his daughter yet?'

'Gosh, no! Bit early days for that. He's told me about her now.'

'She had that terrible accident, that's right, isn't it?'

'Yep. It sounded awful, but he didn't want to talk about it too much. I guess you don't when something like that happens.'

'No. I get it. You really like him, don't you? I can tell.'

Lucie made a funny face. 'I really do. We just clicked after that initial few hiccups. It's not just the, ahem, you know what, we just chat and stuff. I love just listening to him. Cripes, Libs, I've got this bad. For goodness' sake, he could read me a shopping list and I'd be hanging on his every word.'

'Just as it should be at the beginning, and what's more, you deserve it after all the crap you've been through in the last few years.'

'I guess so.'

'Anyway, where are you off to today? The weather looks lovely for a day out.'

'Pretty Beach down on the coast there.'

'Ahh, I haven't been there for years! Years and years.'

'I know.'

'Well, have fun then. Put some pics of you two lovebirds in the group.'

'Yeah, I need to go, we're just getting to the other side. Speak later.'

'Bye, Luce. Have a fabulous time.'

Lucie watched out the window as the fast train slowed and the fields of saturated green that had whizzed past slowly began to fade. Glimpses of the coast appeared and the backs of the lovely old houses of Pretty Beach trundled by. George's long legs were stretched out in front of him, his hand on her leg. She turned to him and smiled. 'What's the plan?'

'Lunch, a walk up to the lighthouse, and see how we feel. How does that sound?'

Lucie wasn't going to say that she really couldn't care less as long as she was with him. 'Just right. Where are we having lunch? Did you book something?'

George tapped her leg. 'I certainly did. The Old Sugar Wharf.'

'Sounds lovely,' Lucie replied as the train slowed down and the 'Pretty Beach' station signs came into view.

Fifteen minutes or so later, they'd walked down the main street in Pretty Beach and were slowly ambling along hand in hand, looking into shop windows. Lucie had ducked into a little bookshop with a pale-yellow cruiser bike outside and came out with a delightful scented candle, a coffee table book, and a recommendation from the woman inside about a Facebook page with secret dinner events.

'Ahh, it's lovely here. They could do with a tram.' Lucie laughed.

'It is,' George replied, pointing along a line of shops to a bakery. 'There we are. The people who own that are doing up the shop on Darling Street. The one we talked about the other day.'

'Ahh, yes. Right.'

'Apparently, the bread is outstanding and the cinnamon buns are the best.'

'Yeah. Evie's all over it already.'

'Blimey, she didn't waste much time!'

'I thought the same. She's put in an order for mini-cinnamon buns for the morning baskets and vanilla ones for the afternoon.'

'Sounds right up my street.'

As they got to the bakery, they stood outside and observed the comings and goings. A tall, very tanned man in board shorts and flip-flops winked and said hello as he walked out and a tiny woman with identical twins smiled as she left with her arms full of French sticks.

'Mmm. It smells good enough,' Lucie noted. 'Roll on the Darling branch of Pretty Beach bakery.'

'Yeah, I make you right,' George agreed.

By lunchtime, they had meandered around, taking in the sights and sounds of Pretty Beach. Arriving at the Old Sugar Wharf, Lucie blinked as she took in the gorgeous weathered wharf, the hut at the front, and the huge plant pots full of palms. As they entered, she didn't know where to look first. It certainly gave Darlings a run for its money; an old-fashioned counter on the right was piled with glass cloches holding homemade cakes, a huge vintage coffee machine was tucked in by the wall, and to the side a little display area held candles and bunches of flowers. As they waited, Lucie stepped over towards the flowers and touched the paper on a hand-tied bouquet. 'Ooh, look at these! They're fabulous!'

George nodded. 'Nice.'

'Ha, they're more than nice,' Lucie replied as she touched

scrap ties of vintage fabric on the posies and read a chalkboard pinned to the wall. The information on Pretty Beach Posies told her how the scented flowers were grown in a little garden by the sea without any chemicals. Poking her nose into a tea rose, she inhaled. 'Ahh, gosh, yes, the scent is out of this world.'

She looked around as they were shown to their table. 'This whole place is divine,' Lucie whispered as they were led out onto the deck. 'So much eye candy and inspiration for my house. The granny flat out the back has a deck like this. I just need an army of people to help me achieve something like this.'

George nodded, and she felt shudders of pleasure go through her as he replied, 'We'll get there with it. One step at a time.'

A couple of hours later, Lucie and George strolled away from the Old Sugar Wharf after a delicious lunch, one too many glasses of wine, and more than a few slices of cake. Lucie felt as if she didn't have a care in the world as they strolled along towards the Old Town walking off the lunch. George suddenly turned to her as they stopped outside a delightful looking hotel.

'Let's book a room.'

Lucie widened her eyes. 'What, now? Really?'

'Yeah. Why not? What's to stop us?'

Her eyebrows shot up. 'Hmm.' She'd never done anything like it before in her life. For so long she'd spent a lot of her time either thinking about cycles, or plotting the inner workings of her ovaries, that spontaneous nights away in hotels had not been on her radar.

'Do you have anything to be back on Darling for tonight?'

'Nup, not a thing, apart from painting the hallway with three funny old men for company.'

'Up for it?' George asked with a twinkle in his eye.

Lucie couldn't stop herself from giggling as she looked up into his eyes. Was she up for it? Hmm. Tough one. She felt like a different person with George. The old Lucie would have made all sorts of excuses as to why it wasn't a good idea; that she didn't have her toothbrush or clean underwear, that she couldn't just do something impulsive like that. She heard herself replying, 'All the way to the bank.'

George squeezed her hand and kissed her as they walked up the steps to the foyer and whispered into her ear, 'This is going to be one very good night.'

## 36

Lucie was surprised she'd been invited to the Darling Dinner at all. Even though she was slowly but surely finding her feet on the little island, she still felt more newcomer, less native, and being new surrounded her at every turn. She didn't know her way around yet, didn't know the little nuances of island life, and was still getting used to the way everyone either knew each other or was related.

She opened the multi-cooker and checked it for about the millionth time. The mashed potato was nothing short of delicious, but she was more than concerned about how it was going to hold up. She'd spent a long time poring over mashed potato recipes and the miraculous little pot apparently held the key to the best mash in the world. She just hoped it was true. She spooned it, as instructed by Shelly, into a tub clearly labelled with her name and decided that she would no longer dwell on whether or not her potato cooking skills were going to effectively mean she was either in with the good folk of Darling, or out.

Putting the tub in a frill-lined basket, she hooked the basket over her arm and started the stroll to Hennie's house, Hennie being the drop-off point for various items of food for the dinner. From what Lucie could work out from the email and the community page, some of the event was a potluck affair. Each participant was given something to donate or cook. Alongside that, the butcher on Darling made once-a-year secret recipe Darling sausages. The event took place around Darling Bay with an inclement weather backup plan of the town hall.

Lucie made her way down Hennie's road and paused to peer skywards when she got to the gate. The weather was definitely looking dicey to her, but she'd begun to learn that the fog, the position of the island, and the way the wind was going was all very unique to Darling, and the weather changeable by the hour. So, in actual fact, she had no clue about what would happen with the weather at all.

Walking up the path, the front door was open. Lucie rang the bell, and a few seconds later, Hennie, in ankle-length jeans and an oversized linen shirt, came to the door.

'Ahh, I was just thinking about you! How are you?'

'Really well, thanks.'

'That's good to hear. Come in,' Hennie said, holding the door open wide and gesturing for Lucie to go through.

Lucie followed Hennie into the back of the house and put her basket down on an enormous kitchen table. Hennie leant over and touched the frill on the basket. 'I love these.'

'Thanks,' Lucie replied and took out her container of mash. 'I hope this is going to be okay.'

Hennie took it, opened the fridge and popped it inside. 'Of course it will be. Cup of tea while you're here?'

Lucie nodded. 'I'd love one.' As she sat down and watched as Hennie made the tea, she asked, 'How does the Dinner on Darling work?'

Hennie rolled her eyes. 'There's way too much food usually and definitely too much alcohol. The brewery makes a special lot each year. Let's just say it's potent. Honestly, here's a tip, don't drink too much. You'll think it's nothing and then bam, it'll hit you like a tonne of bricks.'

Lucie widened her eyes. 'Good to know. I wouldn't want to make an idiot of myself at my first Darling social event.'

'Don't worry about it. You wouldn't be the first. We've had all sorts over the years. You never know what's going to happen at the Dinner on Darling.'

'And what's your role in it?'

Hennie passed over a cup of tea. 'I'm chief co-ordinator and I'm involved in the making of sausages. I've been in the butcher's all week, more or less.'

'Right, meaning that you know the secret ingredients, do you? I'll have to kidnap you,' Lucie joked.

'Meaning that I don't know that. It's a DJ Meats family recipe. It's kept from all the helpers too.'

Lucie sighed. 'It's all so quaint and sweet here on the island. I really am loving it.'

Hennie took a sip of her tea. 'I never really thought about it like that, but I suppose you're right. There are loads of funny little Darling things. When you stop and think about them, they are quite quaint, I suppose. I couldn't imagine a year without a Dinner on Darling.'

'Well, I'm so glad that I've been invited to be part of it.'

'Yes and we're very happy to have you.'

Lucie had deliberated about a lot of things about the dinner. Very shallow things like what she was going to wear, who she was going to talk to, and things like what was going to happen at the end of the night. She, of course, hadn't spent hours lying in bed imagining a certain man's bed. Not at all. She was much more interested in the conversation she and George would have.

As she stood in the hallway looking in the mirror, she nodded at her hair. It had gone just right. Just the right amount of pouffe, super shiny on top, and the ends were curled to perfection. She spoke to the statues.

'Right guys, I'm off. I am in possession of seriously good hair. Long may it last. You may see me later. You may not.' Giggling as she closed the door, she saw Leo walking out of his house further down the road. He had a beer in his hand and a smile on his face.

'Oi, oi, neighbour. How are ya?' He held up his beer. 'Can I interest you in a roadie?'

Lucie's eyes widened. 'I hear the alcohol offering this evening will be strong enough as it is and you're getting in on it early.'

Leo laughed as he turned around and went back in his front door. Two minutes later, he was holding up a bottle. Lucie took it and frowned at the label. 'What's this? Is it safe to drink?'

'Good question. Like the sausages, it's a secret Darling recipe. All I can say is that it's good stuff. Very good stuff indeed.'

'Where'd you get it from?' Lucie giggled.

'Contraband, my friend. Only open to the male Australian contingent on the island.

'Are you being sexist, Leo? I didn't realise there was such a thing as an Australian contingent on the island,' Lucie bantered. 'How many of you are there then, just out of interest?'

Leo paused. 'That would be one. Nah, my mate works there. I get loads of stuff from him. Mostly unlabelled cans where you don't have a clue what's inside. Stuff they can't use because of legislation.'

'Sounds dangerous to me,' Lucie replied, taking a swig. She then looked in the top of the bottle. 'Ooh goodness. This is delicious. Delicious and dangerous.'

'Yup. That's why it's lethal. Trust me, my first year I ended up in a bush on the way home from this event. Never again. It took me days to recover. Days and days.'

Lucie laughed. 'Oh, gosh, there's no hope for me then.'

Leo clinked her bottle. 'Cheers, Lucie. Welcome to Darling.'

'Cheers.'

'So, how's it going with you know who?' Leo asked as they strolled along.

Lucie frowned and pretended she didn't know what he was talking about. 'Who?'

'You know who. Mr D himself.'

'Really good.'

Leo frowned. 'Where is he this evening, then?'

'He's getting the ferry later, he had something with his daughter that went until early evening.'

'I see. So, are you official, as it were?'

'Hmm, I guess so. Yes and no.'

'That makes total sense. Not.' Leo laughed.

'It's officially a yes.' Lucie smiled.

'Excellent.'

'Yeah, we've been out loads and, well, it's kind of morphed into a relationship, I suppose.'

'Lucky George,' Leo joked.

Lucie chuckled. 'It's just a bit of a surprise for me after everything that happened and how I actually ended up on Darling.'

'Did I, or did I not, tell you that things happen on this island that you don't expect?' Leo asked.

'You did,' Lucie replied, smiling. 'I thought it was another one of those many strange things that took place in the first few weeks. I really should have listened.'

'You won't go wrong there. He's a good bloke.'

'Thanks. Yes, I really think he is.'

Stopping in the road, Lucie's eyes widened as they approached Darling Bay. She hadn't been quite sure what to expect, but as she stood next to Leo and looked at the curve of the bay, it was definitely not what she was presented with. A long line of beautiful canvas awnings with domed roofs snaked around the bay. Pretty flickering gold lights hugged their tops and blue and white paper lanterns hung from each one, fluttering in the breeze coming in off the sea.

'It's gorgeous!' Lucie exclaimed. 'I was not expecting this.'

Leo chuckled. 'What were you expecting then?'

'Something a bit more, I don't know, low key. When it said tents, I thought it meant plastic gazebos. It looks like something from a travel brochure.' Lucie smiled. 'A very nice, very expensive travel brochure at that.'

'One thing with the residents of Darling; they don't do things by halves.'

'This is the poshest sausage and mash event I've ever seen in my life,' Lucie joked.

'Gourmet sausages, don't you forget it,' Leo added. 'And whatever you do, don't ask anyone for the secret recipe. You'll be frogmarched off to the floating bridge.'

'I'll remember that.'

Lucie left Leo chatting to someone from the sailing club and made her way to the drinks tent, where a bar with beer barrels was set up on vintage trestle tables. As she stood by the door, she looked over at the bay and the darkening sky. Darling residents appeared to be unperturbed by the clouds, but to her it looked as if the heavens were going to open. The weather forecast for Darling Island and the estuary had indicated rain, fog, sun, and wind in different patterns throughout the day, so Lucie had given up attempting to ascertain what it was actually going to do. As the day had gone on, though, it had felt more and more as if rain was imminent, but so far it had held off.

She stood lost in a world of her own, gazing out at the water and the little glints of lights on the top. She came back to reality and smiled as Shelly approached.

'Hi. How are you? You look lovely. I love your hair.'

'Thank you. I'm good, thanks. Do you need any help with anything?'

Shelly screwed up her lips and peered up at the sky. 'Are you any good at controlling the weather?'

'Ahh! I was just thinking it looked as if it was going to rain and then I thought, what do I know about the intricacies of the changeable Darling weather?'

'I can feel it in my bones. I think we're going to see rain and then a thick Darling fog is going to descend in the night.'

'How do you know that?'

'You get a feel for it. It's in my blood.' Shelly chuckled. 'Or at least that's what my mum used to say.'

'What happens if it rains and all of this?'

Shelly laughed. 'We all get wet. No, these awnings are pretty good. We've only had to abandon ship once in my memory and that was due more to the gale than rain. You'll be fine in here. It's just that you'll probably get soaked getting home.'

'It won't be the first time.'

'I'm sure. Okay, well, have a lovely evening. I'd better get on.'

'You're sure you don't need any extra help?'

Shelly shook her head. 'Nope, we'll save that for you for next year. You get yourself a Darling beer and have fun. Did you get the seating plan?'

Lucie nodded. In the Dinner on Darling email, there had been rather a lot of instructions. It was a tightly organised event including a comprehensive seating plan with numbered tables and allocated seats.

'Yes, yes, I did. Thank you for that.'

'You're welcome. You're right where you should be, obviously, next to our gorgeous George. Rightio, see you later. Enjoy.'

Lucie looked at the queue for the bar and decided to head to the table to put her coat and bag underneath. Weaving in and out of the linen-covered tables, she made her way to one about halfway down. Fairy lights ran under the awning and huge vintage bottles held bunches of gypsophila. Pale blue and white tassel garlands were strung above, and each table setting held a bunch of bay tied with blue and white bows.

Standing by the table and scrolling through her phone, Lucie found the allocation email, checked the table number and her seat next to the one marked for George. Lifting up the table-cloth, she crouched on the floor, rolled up her coat, tucked it in the centre near the foot of the table, and wedged her bag underneath.

Just as she was about to crawl back out, she saw Matilda prance past the table in a shimmering dress. Matilda was talking to a woman with red hair piled up on top of her head with huge sparkly earrings. Just looking at Matilda's outfit made Lucie shudder with cold. The temperature, however, seemed of no concern to Matilda, who looked as if she had been poured into the shiny red dress. A small fishtail billowed out behind her and the fabric fell away to a cowl scoop at the back. Lucie, still crouching, swallowed and looked down at her own dress. She'd thought she'd done well, but looking at Matilda, she felt more like a pudding than she ever had in her life. With the tablecloth draping over her shoulders, Lucie stayed where she was and pricked up her ears.

'I know, I know. I had such a fabulous time,' Matilda enthused to the friend whose dress reminded Lucie of a peacock.

The friend gushed. 'You looked amazing in your stories. You always do. Ahh, Matilda, you really do have the most lovely life.'

'Thanks, yes. I really do.'

'How come you left so quickly? I'm surprised you came back for this.' The woman flicked her hand around at the tables.

Matilda quipped, 'There are some interesting things on Darling, you know.'

The woman smirked. 'I thought that was just a simple case of friends with benefits. Has that changed?'

From Lucie's precarious stance underneath the tablecloth, Matilda's face was hard to read. 'I never wanted to commit, and I certainly didn't want to end up here, but it is what it is. Maybe I'm mellowing a bit and you know, the old biological clock is ticking.'

'My goodness, I've never ever heard you say anything like that!' the friend exclaimed.

Matilda flapped her hand in front of her. 'Well, I know, but I don't want to be too old and doing the school run, not that I actually intend to be doing a school run too often. There'll be a nanny for that.'

'So, let me get this straight, are you telling me that you're back here for George?'

Matilda rolled her eyes. 'I'm not telling you anything. Maybe it's time though that I settle down, and there are a lot worse places to end up.'

'I wouldn't want to settle down here, but if there's a catch out there, George is certainly up there.'

Matilda rolled her eyes. 'Err, yeah. Why do you think I've been coming here? I know.'

Lucie froze as something must have caught Matilda's eye. A puzzled look crossed Matilda's face, and she took a step towards the table and looked down at Lucie. 'Err, what are you doing?' she asked with an incredulous tone to her voice to accompany the look.

Lifting the tablecloth completely over her head, Lucie wriggled and crawled out from under the table. Pulling herself to stand up straight, Matilda looked her up and down and curled her top lip. 'Are you cleaning or something? What are you doing?'

Before Lucie could think of something sassy to retort, she heard herself stuttering, 'Just putting my coat under the table.'

Matilda frowned and dangled a red sparkly evening bag from her wrist. 'Coat?'

'For later, the weather forecast is for a downpour.'

Matilda looked at her as if she was mad and then nodded. The same smug look that accompanied her Instagram photos was written all over her face. 'Is there not a place for the waitresses to put their stuff?' She turned back to her friend. 'You'd think they'd have things like that sorted.'

With that, she turned her back on Lucie and made her way to the end of the tables and headed towards the bar. Lucie peered down at her phone with a frown and pressed on the list of names. Running her eyes down, she smiled and let out a sigh of relief. Matilda and her friend were four tables away. Good old Shelly. She relaxed, gave Matilda a wide berth, and made her way to the bar.

After getting a drink, chatting to Piper and her boyfriend, and generally enjoying taking the Darling event in, Lucie stood by the drinks tent observing all that was going on. She could see Shelly instructing people, Mey from China Darling was scuttling around putting things on tables, and then in the corner of her eye, she saw George talking to someone on the far side. Her heart felt as if it was melting as she watched him. Staying where she was, she relished in the fact that they were a thing as he slowly made his way through people chatting here and there.

As he was passing the table where her bag was, Matilda and her friend appeared. Matilda kissed him on the cheek, arched her back, threw her head back, and laughed. Lucie did not laugh. Matilda gesticulated towards her friend who nodded and joined in with the jovial scene. Lucie watched as George took a step back, appearing to try and distance himself from Matilda. His eyes flicked around the room and then he turned the other way and looked back towards the rest of the tables. He put his hand on Matilda's elbow and stepped to the side and started to walk towards the tent. Clutching her drink, Lucie moved so that he would be able to see her. As he did so, his face broke out into a broad smile. He approached, put his hand on her waist, and kissed her.

'Evening. I couldn't see you anywhere. How are you? Looking good to me. Very good.'

Lucie felt a warmth flood through her whole body. 'I'm well. Pacing myself with this, though,' she said with a giggle, holding up a glass of Darling beer.

'Yeah, be careful.' George laughed. 'It's lethal.' He then frowned. 'I messaged you as I was getting off the ferry. Did you get it?'

Lucie shook her head. 'Oh, sorry, I didn't get a text notification,' she said, and pulled her phone out of her pocket. Navigating to her messages, she held up her phone. 'So you did. Sorry, I didn't see it. How did your afternoon go?'

'Very well. I'm looking forward to tonight though.'

Lucie thought to herself, *not half as much as I am.* 'Yes, I've heard the sausages are amazing.'

George winked. 'I wasn't actually thinking about the sausages myself, but there you are. Right, I'll get us some drinks.'

After a drink, standing and chatting to George, he'd gone to the loo and Lucie was behind Leo, making their way to the table. As they got there, they could see Matilda and her friend sitting down at what Lucie thought were her and George's seats.

Lucie frowned and addressed Matilda. 'I think you've got something wrong.'

Matilda's face didn't break out of its supercilious resting mode. 'Sorry. What do you mean?'

'You're in my seat,' Lucie stated.

Matilda rolled her eyes. 'Are you serious?'

Lucie didn't move. 'I am.'

Matilda waved her hand in front of her face as Leo took his seat next to her friend. 'Oh! You're a guest! Whatever, no one sticks to the table planning. We are hardly at a state banquet.' She sneered.

Lucie was wrong-footed. She rested her hand on the back of a chair for a second, wondering what to do. Matilda flicked her hand to the other side of the table. 'Anyway, I thought you were waitressing. You can sit there or something.'

Not wanting to make a scene, Lucie was just about to pull the back of the chair out when George arrived at the table. He stopped on seeing Matilda. He didn't smile. 'I thought you said you were down there near the front?'

Matilda smiled. 'I was, but I moved.'

George frowned and whipped out his phone. 'I see. What, you've done a swap, have you?'

Matilda nodded. 'Yes. That old couple you know, can't remember their names, they moved. They said they'd rather be nearer the front anyway for the raffle.'

George peered down at his phone and then looked up. 'Yeah, right, but that's Lucie's seat. They were over this side of the table.'

Matilda flicked her eyes upwards. 'Lucie? Oh, you mean the waitress. I thought she was working. She's sitting over there now.'

Lucie still hadn't said anything as George looked back down at his phone and then back up at Matilda. 'Lucie is with me,' he said and pulled the chair next to him out. He turned to Lucie and flicked his eyes skyward without Matilda seeing. 'There you go. You sit here and I'll go here. Is that okay with you? If not, I'll find us somewhere else to sit.' As she sat down, he kissed her sweetly on the head.

Lucie could have punched the air as daggers shot across the table. She sat down and answered George at the same time, just loud enough so that Matilda could hear, 'Absolutely fine by me. I don't mind where I sit. All the same to me. It's hardly a state banquet.'

As she picked up her glass and sat back in her seat, she smiled. It felt ever-so-nice to gloat.

By the end of the evening, through the courses of amazing food and the best sausages she'd ever tasted, Lucie was on the end of some very black looks from the other side of the table. She felt warmth filter through her body as George put his hand on hers as the music came on and the main lights went down.

Leo leaned over. 'Well, the rain's held off. What a turn up for the books.' He looked out towards the bay. 'Not for too much longer though, by the looks of it. I might push off home. It's been a long week and it's hit me all of a sudden. I'm shattered.'

Lucie agreed. 'Yes, I feel the same, whatever's in that beer is working for me.'

Leo pushed his chair out. 'I'll see you guys later, unless you're going to head off now, too.'

George looked at Lucie. 'Up to you.'

Lucie felt all sorts of pleased. She wasn't quite used to it but George was naturally speaking as if they were a couple. It felt strange to be part of something new. For as long as she could remember since she'd been a teenager, it had always been Lucie and Rob, and now not only was it not, but there was someone else in the equation. 'I don't mind.'

George looked back at Leo. 'I think we'll stay. I could do with the coffee before the walk home.'

Leo smiled. 'See you, chaps. I might bump into you over the weekend.'

Lucie stood up and kissed Leo on the cheek. He whispered in her ear. 'Be good.'

Lucie giggled and batted him away with her hand and as she turned to sit back down, Matilda was staring right at her with a look on her face, as if she wanted Lucie dead. Sitting beside George, Lucie smiled in thanks as flasks of coffee were put into the middle of the table.

Shelly stopped with a plate piled high with squares of home-made Turkish Delight. Lucie smiled, popped a piece into her mouth, and sat under the fairy lights lost in a world of her own. Since the night when she'd been carried up to her bedroom, she'd not come down from the cloud. The cloud had involved a trip on the ferry to the mainland for a very nice dinner, a romantic breakfast on the other side of Darling, George had stayed over more than once on a midweek night, and they'd been to The Darling Inn loads of times. She'd been over to his house for dinner, and he'd met her by the old pier for a take-away coffee and ended up pulling her into his arms.

Clearly, Matilda knew nothing of it. Galavanting around Europe in big coats and her underwear, she'd probably not been in the slightest bit interested as to what had been happening on Darling.

Lucie let out a little, barely audible sigh of pleasure. Despite thinking it was all going way too fast, and that she had not been anywhere near looking for a relationship, she was enjoying the ride on the cloud. And to her pleasure, what had happened after the first night had been far from a one-night stand. What it had been was exciting and passionate and so very, very different from her long-term relationship with Rob. She felt almost guilty looking back at the Lucie in the Lucie and Rob scenario now. That Lucie was someone she no longer recognised at all. It was as if her whole outlook on life had shifted.

Part of her mind had kept on going back to the idea that what was happening to her life had always been meant to be. Not just the nice things but all of it; the hurt and pain at the news of Rob's baby, the grief for the loss of what she thought had been the trajectory of her life, and the sheer panic she'd felt when she'd found herself in the Coastguard's House in the storm. Now she was sitting surrounded by a dark foggy night and twinkling fairy lights with George's hand resting so naturally on her leg that she had to keep reminding herself that she hadn't known him all her life.

Tally had been adamant from the moment in the off-licence that the whole thing was being coordinated by a higher being. Lucie had chuckled and responded that she didn't think Tally believed in that sort of thing. Tally had replied that this had changed her mind and from now on she was willing to embrace anything and everything in life.

The funniest thing about the whole thing for Lucie, though, wasn't the moving to Darling, or the meeting George, the accident, the dropping of her phone, or the first Darling Inn date. No, the funniest thing about it all was that on Lucie's side, there was no holding back. The old Lucie would have been much more cautious and taken things very slowly. But Power Lucie was different; from the time in the sitting room when she'd put her coffee down on the table and fallen into George's arms, she dived right on in. She'd flung herself headfirst into something very delicious and so far she wasn't looking anywhere near back.

# 37

There had been a lot of laughing and giggling as Lucie and George had made their way home in the rain. By the time they'd got back to George's house, Lucie was soaked through to her underwear. They'd sat in George's kitchen having a cup of tea with wet hair and wrapped in towels. After finishing the tea, they had moved onto much more interesting things. The daydreaming about the Dinner on Darling ending up in George's bed had turned into a very nice reality.

Now, the next morning waking up on her side, Lucie opened her eyes and looked around the room. The curtains blew gently in the breeze and she could hear the birds chirping away outside. The distant sound of the waves from the sea filled the room, and she smiled at the memory of the night before. As quietly and as carefully as she could, she slipped out of bed, padded over to the other side of the room, silently removed George's dressing gown from the back of the door, and crept down the stairs. Putting on the kettle, she opened a few cupboards looking for something for breakfast, and made a pot of tea.

Deciding she'd take a tray back upstairs and see if George

was awake, she set out a couple of mugs and some plates and popped crumpets into the toaster. With her back leaning up against the worktop waiting for the toaster, she scrolled through her phone and tapped on the green WhatsApp square to read her messages. Smiling at a picture of her and George at the dinner, she smiled at the responses.

*You look so happy. Have a wonderful evening.* Jane had written.

Underneath Jane's message, Anais had sent a load of heart eye emoticons.

*Not jealous at all.* Was the message from Libby.

Tally added. *See, I told you. The best looking and loveliest couple ever.*

As Lucie scrolled through, she realised that she felt happier than she had for a very long time. She realised now that everything had not been right with Rob under the surface for a while. It felt weird with the clarity of her feelings now that, at the time, she'd not only not addressed her unhappiness, but hadn't actually known it. With the benefit of hindsight, she could now see that Rob had probably felt the same.

She flicked her head to get rid of any thoughts of him and scrolled through some more pictures of the dinner, picked one of her and George in a funny selfie pose at the table, and added it to the group.

*I had a wonderful time. I can't believe all this. Me sending you a picture where I feel so happy. I wanted to say thank you all for looking out for me.*

*You deserve it.* Tally typed back and Lucie watched as she could see the little dots indicating that Anais was typing.

*Love you. So pleased to see you like this.*

Lucie smiled as she put the teapot onto the tray, put the crumpets on the plates and read her phone before heading back up to the bedroom.

*I'm so happy for you, Luce.* Libby had added. *You deserve this.*

*Darling Island suits you.* Came back from Jane.

Walking up the stairs and into the bedroom, Lucie could hear George was in the ensuite shower. She took the pot off the tray and put the mugs and tea by the sides of the bed as George walked out with wet hair and a white towel around his waist.

'Morning,' he said, kissing her on the cheek and looking her up and down. 'Nice dressing gown.'

'Crumpets in bed?' Lucie asked with a giggle. 'It was all I could muster up.'

'I don't think I've ever had a better offer,' George said, and whipping off the towel, hopped back in the bed. He took the tea from the side. 'I could get used to this.'

'Used to what?' Lucie laughed.

George waved his hand around. 'Someone getting up before me and serving me breakfast in bed.'

'Don't get too cosy.' Lucie laughed. 'It's the first and last time. From now on, it's the other way around.'

George chuckled and picked up his phone. 'What's going on in the world then?'

Lucie did the same and looked down at her phone while she drank her tea. 'Same old sensational headlines. There never seems to be anything good in the world these days. There's always something awful going on somewhere. A terrible flood here, a crisis there.'

'Hmm. You're not wrong. It does seem like that sometimes.'

Lucie flicked up with her thumb and clicked on Instagram. As she scrolled her feed, she came across Serena's profile. She stopped, closed her eyes and dropped her phone into her lap. Feeling tears prick the edge of her eyes, she put her head back on the headboard.

'Everything okay?' George asked, turning to look at her.

Shaking her head, Lucie picked up her phone and held it out so that George could see the picture of Serena, Rob, and a tiny little baby wrapped tightly in a blue blanket. George got who it was right away and put his hand on her leg.

'Sorry, that must make you feel pretty awful from what you've told me.'

Lucie nodded as she looked down at Serena's loving smile and Rob gazing down at the baby. She gulped, willing herself not to cry. 'It's so weird. I wanted or thought I wanted, that moment for such a long time, and now I look at him and feel as if I don't even know him at all. It's all so alien and strange.'

George patted her leg and waited for her to say something else. She continued, 'The thing is...'

'Yep.' George nodded. 'What?'

'I realise now that I never really loved Rob at all. Not really. Not like...' She let her voice trail off.

'Not like what?' George frowned.

Lucie closed her eyes, pondering what she was going to say. 'Quite simply, not like, I don't know, George. It's just that, I love you. There you are, I've said it. As I said when you asked me to go out with you, I'm not really interested in mucking around.'

George picked up her hand and looked into her eyes. 'Well, that's a stroke of luck then because, Lucie Peachtree, I am most definitely not mucking around either.'

Lucie looked into his eyes. 'You're not?'

'No, I'm not.'

'Okay. Good.'

George turned. 'And, I love you too.'

～

Find the next part at Amazon.

# SUMMER ON DARLING ISLAND

For Lucie Peachtree, things are definitely on the up, and island life is giving her all the things. After a horrible break up, she found herself catapulted to coastal living in the form of the Old Coastguard's House, sitting right by the sea. Then, when she was least expecting it, she met ever-so dashing George, and the life ticks just kept on coming.

We catch up in Summer on Darling Island with the next part of the story, as Lucie settles into life on Darling, navigates her new small business, gets stuck into her part-time job, and snuggles up with her man.

The old Lucie seems nothing but a distant memory as she starts to fall deeply in love with not only George, but also herself. However, things on Darling aren't always rose-tinted and when a little blot on the landscape masks the famous island blue, Lucie has to take a long hard look at how she wants her life to pan out.

*'Polly's writing is like being wrapped up in a hug. There's nothing better than getting cosy with a Babbington book.'* S Quinn.

*Summer on Darling Island available ON AMAZON.*

# READ MORE BY POLLY BABBINGTON

# AUTHOR

*Polly Babbington*

*In a little white Summer House at the back of the garden, under the shade of a huge old tree, Polly Babbington creates romantic feel-good stories including The PRETTY BEACH series.*

*Polly went to college in the Garden of England and her writing career began by creating articles for magazines and publishing books online.*

*Polly loves to read in the cool of lazing in a hammock under an old fruit tree on a summertime morning or cozying up in the Winter under a quilt by the fire.*

*She lives in delightful countryside near the sea, in a sweet little village complete with a gorgeous old cricket pitch, village green with a few lovely old pubs and writes cosy romance books about women whose life you sometimes wished was yours.*

*Follow Polly on Instagram, Facebook and TikTok*
*@PollyBabbingtonWrites*

*PollyBabbington.com*

*Want more on Polly's world? Subscribe to Babbington Letters on my website.*

Printed in Great Britain
by Amazon